GHOSTED

SARAH READY

CROWN

PRAISE FOR SARAH READY

PRAISE FOR FRENCH HOLIDAY

"Ready (The Fall in Love Checklist) whisks readers to the South of France for a saucy enemies-to-lovers romance...This is a winner."

— *Publishers Weekly* starred review on *French Holiday*

"Ready has written a tale that deliciously taps into its French trappings...A charming dramedy featuring a promising sleuthing duo."

— *Kirkus Reviews* on *French Holiday*

PRAISE FOR JOSH AND GEMMA MAKE A BABY

"Romance author Ready gives Gemma rich and complex motivations for wanting a baby...An unusual and winning read about a little-discussed topic."

— *Kirkus Reviews*

"A lively, entertaining, romantic comedy by an author and novelist with a genuine flair for originality, humor, and narrative driven storytelling..."

— *MIDWEST BOOK REVIEW*

PRAISE FOR JOSH AND GEMMA THE SECOND TIME AROUND

"In this sequel—which stands well enough on its own—the happily-ever-after moment is merely the starting point...Ready effectively leads readers to wonder if she isn't going to upend every single one of the genre's expectations. It's a testament to her exceptional writing skill that even the most romantic-minded readers won't be sure which outcome they prefer. A charming and disarmingly tough story of the many ways that love can adapt to crises."

— *KIRKUS REVIEWS*

PRAISE FOR CHASING ROMEO

"A fun and sweet love story..."

— *KIRKUS REVIEWS*

PRAISE FOR THE SPACE BETWEEN

"...emotional roller-coaster, but in the end true love prevails. For hopeless romantics, this one's got the goods."

— *PUBLISHERS WEEKLY*

"A touching tale of adult reckonings and reunions with some heart-tugging reversals."

— *KIRKUS REVIEWS*

ALSO BY SARAH READY

Stand Alone Romances:

The Fall in Love Checklist

Hero Ever After

Once Upon an Island

French Holiday

The Space Between

Josh and Gemma:

Josh and Gemma Make a Baby

Josh and Gemma the Second Time Around

Soul Mates in Romeo Romance Series:

Chasing Romeo

Love Not at First Sight

Romance by the Book

Love, Artifacts, and You

Married by Sunday

My Better Life

Scrooging Christmas

Stand Alone Novella:

Love Letters

Find these books and more by Sarah Ready at:

www.sarahready.com/romance-books

ROMANCE IS DEAD...

Jillian Nejat is the only dating and relationship expert on the planet who is incapable of speaking to men. If they're living, if they're breathing, it's game over.

With her bank account at zero, her career a dumpster fire, and her dating life in a ten-year slump, she moves into a tiny, dirt-cheap NYC apartment.

Unfortunately, the apartment is already occupied.

Daniel (no-last-name) is a sexy, shirtless, six-pack wielding heartthrob who is also...dead.

He isn't living. He isn't breathing. He's a ghost. He's also the only man on the planet who Jillian can talk to.

Soon, Daniel's convinced that it's his afterlife mission to resurrect Jillian's love life. He knows, if he helps her fall in love then he can move on. Jillian agrees. The last thing she needs is a Lothario ghost haunting her living room.

But then, one practice date leads to another, one confession leads to more, and suddenly Jillian fears she's falling for the one man she can never have.

Ghosted

SARAH READY

CROWN

W.W. CROWN BOOKS
An imprint of Swift & Lewis Publishing LLC
www.wwcrown.com

This book is a work of fiction. All the characters and situations in this book are fictitious. Any resemblance to situations or persons living or dead is purely coincidental. Any reference to historical events, real people, or real locations are used fictitiously.

Published by W.W. Crown Books an Imprint of Swift & Lewis
Publishing, LLC, Lowell, MI USA
Cover Illustration & Design: Elizabeth Turner Stokes

Library of Congress Control Number: 2023903272
ISBN: 978-1-954007-60-4 (eBook)
ISBN: 978-1-954007-61-1 (pbk)
ISBN: 978-1-954007-62-8 (large print)
ISBN: 978-1-954007-63-5 (hbk)
ISBN: 978-1-954007-64-2 (audiobook)

Ghosted

1

IF I'D KNOWN MY NEW APARTMENT WAS A SEX MANIAC'S love den, I would never have invited my parents along.

In my defense, it's not as if the real estate listing explicitly said, "Warning: studio apartment moonlights as center for titillating orgies and acrobatic loving."

No. It said, "Affordable, quiet studio apartment in Murray Hill, wood floors, street view, unique décor."

I stare out the apartment's single, narrow, grime-coated window at the bustling, crowded Lexington Avenue, and watch a city bus chug past. I can almost make out a patch of blue sky between the buildings, muddy and weak, filtering light through the apartment.

Through the open window, the familiar music of buses rumbling, sirens fading in and out, and horns honking swirls to me, carried on the cool spring breeze.

I'm airing out the apartment. When we first walked in it smelled like sensual spicy massage oil, sandalwood, and sex. Now it smells like bus exhaust, city dirt, and stale coffee—courtesy of the coffee cart parked on the sidewalk below.

Which is...better.

For the moment, I avoid looking at the rest of the apartment, at my parents, and at Fran.

I need a minute to regroup.

The key here is to look on the bright side. To look beyond the apartment's exterior and find the good. You should always look beneath the surface to find the good inside.

So. What's good?

First, I like quiet. I'm a quiet person. Excessively quiet, some might say. A quiet person and a quiet apartment? What could be better? Nothing, not even erasable pens.

Second, wood floors are lovely. Even the ones that creak, collect dirt between the planks, and are ice cold on your toes—they are *lovely*.

Third, Murray Hill is close to my office on East 44th Street, which means I'll save money, because I can walk instead of slogging to work on the subway or the bus.

Finally, it's affordable. Sensationally affordable. So affordable I don't have the option to walk away. I just can't.

The low monthly rent, the location, this apartment is the holy grail of Manhattan real estate.

Which is why I signed the lease agreement and collected the keys from the harassed, jittery real-estate agent, *sight unseen*.

I mentally run through the amount of money I have in my savings account, my checking, and on that gift card Fran gave me last Christmas, and, yup, I can't afford to walk away.

So, looking on the bright side, this apartment isn't an orgasmic abomination, it's a godsend.

There. See? A godsend.

Pasting a bright smile on my face and smoothing my hands over my baggy gray sweatshirt and jeans, I confidently turn to my mom and Fran.

My mom has a deep wrinkle where her eyebrows are pulled together and she's frowning, slowly spinning in a circle, as she takes in my new home. The old wood floors squeak and moan as she turns.

I don't look like my mom, she's willowy, with wispy blonde hair, green eyes, and a gentle expression. She prefers flowy dresses in pastels and quilted vests. Some people think she's pretty in an airy, delicate way, but most people agree it's my dad who's really good-looking.

I don't take after him either.

He's robust, rough and charismatic, with dark olive skin, black curly hair, and an energy that sucks you in like an F-5 tornado.

I guess, from my dad, I inherited thick, black curly hair, and from my mom I inherited green eyes the color of spring leaves in the rain. Other than that, I'm just me.

Five foot three, happily curvy, with a heart-shaped face, a nose that's almost too long, and with, well, I suppose my best feature is my mouth. It's wide, full, and always looks like I've just been kissed. Passionately.

My mom always said, "Jilly, with your beauty and your personality, you'll have to beat off the boys." But she's my mom, and she has maternal blindness to all my flaws.

Fran, our neighbor of thirty years, doesn't suffer from that affliction. She sees me pretty accurately. A decent-looking twenty-seven-year-old with a terminal inability to speak to men.

Scratch that. Not all men, just men who are interested in sex. Or dating. Or kissing.

Or...breathing.

Fine. All men. Except my dad, my cousin Ari, Michael, and my Grandpa Joe.

But anyway, Fran's here, in her leopard print and diamonds, and she's smirking at me with a knowing expression. I know that look. She's imagining all the fun someone could get up to here.

I casually look around the apartment, keeping my expression placid, neutral.

"It's bigger than I thought it'd be. Really nice," I say, nodding at the wide, long room. "I hadn't expected it to be so big...and the location..."

Fran restrains a smile and nods as I list off the attributes.

"And lights. It has lights." I walk over to the wall and quickly click on and off the single overhead light, a massive, gaudy, Liberace-inspired golden candelabra hanging from the ceiling.

Fran keeps nodding, her leopard print diamanté-encrusted turtleneck sparkling in the blinking lights.

My mom keeps turning, inspecting the one-room studio apartment, the line between her brows deepening.

"And there's a kitchen. With a counter. And a sink. And...floors." I gesture at the wooden floors, and all my cardboard moving boxes stacked in a neat row on those lovely wooden floors. "This apartment has floors."

Oh jeez.

"Jillian?" My mom finally stops and gives me a confused look.

"Hmm?" I bite my tongue and uncomfortably tug at the neck of my sweatshirt.

"Why are there so many mirrors?" my mom asks.

Okay. Right.

There's no avoiding it, is there? No matter where you look, there's a mirror.

The walls, they aren't painted, or papered, or paneled. No, they're mirrored.

The ceiling? Mirrored.

The two stairs, leading up to the small elevated platform where your bed goes? Mirrored.

The kitchen cabinets? Yes, indeed, they are mirrored.

The kitchen countertop? It's not mirrored, but it is stainless steel buffed to such a high shine that it's like a mirror.

The bathroom? It's my worst nightmare. Because when I wake up in the morning and stumble to the shower, my hair sticking straight up, my eyes bloodshot, and my face full of pillow wrinkles, the last thing I want is a three-hundred-and-sixty-degree mirrored view of *everything*.

Fran snorts, then says delightedly, "Can't you tell, Geeta? It's for eff-you-see-kay-ing."

I sigh and rub the back of my neck. "You don't have to spell it, Fran. We're all adults—"

"Fucucking?" my mom asks, frowning. "Jilly, are you into fucucking?" She glares at the mirrors, "What is that? A cult?"

"The u comes before the c," Fran sings, but my mom ignores her, frowning worriedly at me.

I shake my head, "No. No, Mom. Not at all. No cults."

She shrugs and turns back to inspect the apartment —twenty-two feet by eighteen feet of mirrored splendor, chock full of boxes, my brass bed frame and mattress, my white faux-leather couch, my white desk and swivel chair, and my two wooden bookshelves.

From the mess, it looks like it won't all fit, but it will. My last place was fifty-square-feet smaller.

Fran primps her frizzy blonde hair, the black roots showing, and winks at me in the mirror.

The breeze blows through the window, carrying up the impatient honk of a car horn. I can hear my dad down below, arguing with the moving truck driver. It's one of those "we drive, you unload" companies. We're all finished except for my box of *Star Trek* collectibles which my dad promised to be extra careful with.

"It's not anything like that. It's unique décor," I say, reassuring my mom by taking a cue from the real estate listing. "I like it a lot. All these mirrors really brighten up the space, reflect the light. It's going to be great for my creativity."

My mom makes a wincing, disbelieving face, but I don't blame her. She's lived in the same Long Island red brick rowhouse for thirty years and the height of her decorating risk-taking is a new lace doily for the TV dinner tray.

"I don't know..." she says.

"It's not what's on the outside, it's what's on the inside. Try this," I say. "Listen to those city sounds, the rush of traffic, the people, even the birds. Smell that coffee and... is that bagels? Mmm. Now, close your eyes."

Both Mom and Fran close their eyes, so I say, "What do you see?"

My mom sighs. "Nothing, Jilly. You told us to *close* our eyes."

Okay. Yes.

"But what do you imagine? Can't you imagine what it could look like?"

"No," my mom says.

"I think it'd look incredible if you put mirrors on the floors," Fran says, rocking back on her heels and humming happily.

"Never mind, you can open your eyes," I say.

My mom digs in her purse and pulls out a pack of sanitizing wipes, thrusting them toward me. "Here, honey. I noticed the bathroom is dirty. You should wipe it down before you use it."

I nod. "Thanks, Mom."

She pats my cheek and I take the wipes and tuck them in my pocket.

"Are you sure you like it?" she asks worriedly.

If I don't veer her off course, she'll worry for weeks about me, and call every other hour asking if I wouldn't be happier in Long Island, living in my childhood bedroom, working as a columnist at The Bargain Shopper's Mailer for my cousin Ari.

I give her a quick squeeze, enveloped in her lavender scent. "I love it, Mom. What more could I ask for? It's close to my work, which I love. It's near coffee, which I need. And it's quiet, which is perfect."

She pats my back, momentarily reassured. "Okay, honey. If you say so."

My dad stomps into the apartment then, his footsteps booming over the wood floor, a large taped cardboard box filling his arms.

"That's everything!" he shouts, not because he's angry, but because shouting is his normal volume.

He drops the box on top of three other boxes, stacking them high. He's in his usual get-up, which I call

8

safari-man. Khaki buttoned shirt, olive pants, leather boots, leather belt, and a military-style watch, which he's looking at now.

"We have thirty-seven minutes and fourteen seconds to board the train," he says.

"Oh my." My mom looks at my dad with a startled expression. "That soon?"

My dad frowns at the mirrors, the gold candelabra, the gold fixtures, and the deep, boudoir red of the platform's shag carpet. Then he turns and scowls at me. "The plumbing works. I checked the toilet. The sink. The hot water will scald. For goodness sake, be careful. I noticed the circuit breaker will blow if you use your microwave and computer at the same time. The window has a lock for a reason, use it. Don't let any perverts in here." He scowls at the mirrors. "I left an aluminum bat by the door—"

"Dad, I've lived on my own for five years. I know how to take care of myself. It's fine—"

"And for goodness sake, Jilly, get some paper and cover up these mirrors. It looks like a fun house in here."

Before I can argue, or object, my dad folds me in a bear hug that squeezes my breath out. "Love you too, Dad," I say when he steps away and I can suck in some air.

"It's not a fun house," my mom says, frowning at my dad, "it's more like a haunted house."

I shake my head. "There's no such thing as ghosts."

Besides, this apartment was decorated for love not fright.

"If there aren't ghosts then why do doors sometimes slam behind you?" my mom asks in a long-suffering voice. "And why do you sometimes feel a cold breeze, like a chill?"

"Wind," I say.

My mom clearly doesn't agree. "I don't think so."

Fran laughs, a happy cackle, and then pulls me in for a goodbye hug. "Don't forget your date tonight. He's an orthopedic surgeon, very charismatic. He's the one, I'm certain of it. You could bring him here after dinner." Fran waggles her penciled eyebrows at me.

"No perverts!" my dad shouts, stomping toward the door and giving the aluminum bat a meaningful look.

"He's not a pervert, he's a surgeon," Fran argues. "He'd be a pervert if he cut people open for the fun of it, but this is his job. It's different when you get paid to do it."

My dad scoffs and my mom looks at me worriedly.

"Don't worry, I'm not inviting any men into my apartment," I reassure my parents.

They're conservative when it comes to that sort of thing, and since we avoided the mirror fiasco, I don't want to kindle another fire.

My parents' relationship is family lore and the map for how dating and marriage should proceed: introduced by their parents when they were both twenty-two, first kiss on the *sixth* date (*after* Dad asked Mom to marry him), then a wedding, a wedding night, and a kid. Inviting men back to your apartment, pre-engagement kissing, and pre-marital sex are *not* part of the equation.

Fran gives me a disappointed scowl.

Fran watched me grow up. I spent so many afternoons and weekends at her house as a kid, that I can transport my mind back to her turquoise kitchen, sit at her round wooden kitchen table, and smell the turmeric and mustard seeds frying with onions as she cooked homemade curries on the weekends.

Unlike my parents, she's determined to find me a "lifelong companion."

To that end she badgers me, nudges me, and blatantly pushes me into blind dates that she arranges using her vast network of friends, acquaintances, and even strangers she meets at the doctor's office, on the bus, or standing next to her in line at the grocery store.

Every few weeks, sometimes even once a week, I'm shuttled into another date arranged by Fran. Some people might wonder why I let Fran do this, or why I keep trying after years of failure. Because. She's Fran. I owe her this much. More.

And I'm me. And I keep hoping, that even if a man might have more fun on a date with a rock, that someday, someone will see me, and not see what I am on the outside, but who I am on the inside. That man, when he comes, I want to spend my life with him.

I know that someday—even though I find it impossible to speak coherently when a living, breathing man looks at me—that someday, I'll find the man I'm supposed to love.

There's a flurry of kisses then, goodbyes, and thank yous, and then my apartment is empty and silent. There's only me, a few dozen cardboard boxes, and enough mirror innuendo to wallpaper the Chrysler building.

I have a few hours until my date, so I may as well start unpacking. I head for my box of *Star Trek* collectibles, arguably the most important box here, and tug at the clear packing tape sealing the box shut. The tape sticks to my fingers and the cardboard smell surrounds me as I rip the tape free.

I smile, a bite of pleasure filling me as I lift from the crinkled packing paper my rare Franklin Mint USS Enterprise NX-01, the cold pewter of the heavy model smooth in my hands.

"This apartment is kind of like the holodeck, isn't it?" I ask the Enterprise.

"Now that is one big spaceship," a man says, his voice deep, rich, and *in my apartment.*

2

THERE'S A *MAN* IN MY APARTMENT.

Did he climb in from the fire escape, slithering through my open window? Was he hiding behind the shower curtain in the bathroom? Was he lurking in the closet by the front door, just waiting for my parents to leave so he could disembowel me and play with my organs?

Or is he the owner of the apartment—the sex-crazed, kinky mirror maniac? Does he lie in wait, hiding under the bed platform, expecting to perform depraved acts under the watchful gaze of three dozen mirrors?

I don't know. I only know that he's here. I'm here. And the door is *locked*.

It's my dad's worst fear. There's a pervert in my apartment and I'm nowhere near the aluminum bat.

I whirl around, my heart leaping into my throat, the hair on the back of my neck standing on end. Cold sweat springs onto my brow and the chilly spring air from the open window hits me. I stagger when I see him and clutch the sharp edge of the Enterprise's impulse engines.

Because...what in the ever-loving...

Not five feet away, just past the row of stacked cardboard boxes, a man—a shirtless, ab rippling, underwear model, heart-stoppingly good-looking man—lifts his eyebrows and smirks at me.

"Hello," he says simply, sending a questing look over my messy hair, my baggy gray sweatshirt, and my jeans.

His face is rugged, chiseled, and so masculine, that anyone with a nickel of sense would immediately buy a padlock for their jeans so his smile doesn't make their zipper automatically fly open.

My gosh. He's a top-tier pervert.

He has this down. His face, his playfully full lips, his sandy brown tousled hair, his cobalt blue eyes shining as they settle on my mouth and light happily.

This is bad. Supremely, urgently bad.

This man sneaks into women's apartments half-naked and ready to rock.

He has to be six-three, his bare (naked) skin is golden, his chest solid, and his abdomen is so muscled that I could easily shatter a ceramic plate on it.

His wide shoulders are bulky, his torso tapers down and narrows until it meets his jeans, which, thank goodness, are still zipped and buttoned. But there's so much man-flesh that I can't, I can't...he takes a step toward me.

My heart assaults my ribcage, banging frantically and the acrid taste of fear curls around my tongue. A police siren from Lexington Avenue tears through the apartment, rising then fading.

He takes another step toward me and then says in his rich, honeyed voice, "Do you know—"

I scream and hurl my Franklin Mint Pewter USS Enterprise NX-01 at his head.

He dodges, diving to the side. I don't wait to see what happens to my Enterprise. I whirl around and sprint toward the door and the aluminum bat. There's a loud crash, the heavy pewter hitting the wood floor. I flinch. I loved that model.

"Stop," he calls. "Wait."

Yeah. Right.

I grab the aluminum bat, wrapping my fingers around the cold, solid metal, and spin around, swinging the bat wildly.

He's close. Closer than I realized. He's only a step away, his hand reaching out. When he sees the bat violently crashing toward his head his eyes widen in stunned disbelief. I hold my breath and flinch, waiting for the impact of metal bat against flesh and bone.

And then, the strangest, wildest, most unbelievable thing happens.

The bat doesn't hit him. The aluminum doesn't connect with head, neck, shoulder, or naked rippling abs. It doesn't even clip him.

And that's because the pervert, the shirtless sex maniac, the apartment trawler, flashes me a startled, comical look of stunned disbelief, and then he winks out of existence.

The man in my apartment *disappears*.

3

THE POWDER BLUE SKY LOOKS LIKE THE FADED EDGES OF A centuries old painting found in a dusty attic. It weakly shines its late morning sunshine through my single dirty window, smearing faded light across the apartment.

The mirrors reflect the weak light, and the barren room reflects the noise from outside—honking, growling engines, the rat-a-tatting of the jackhammer two blocks down at 36th and Lexington—all the noises jumble into a bouncing, jarring cacophony. They battle with the banging of my heart, thudding around my chest.

What just happened?

What was that?

What?

I drop the cold aluminum bat, letting the smooth metal slide from my grip. The bat clatters as it hits the floor and then rolls a few feet to settle next to the stack of cardboard boxes.

I drag in a breath, filling my lungs with the coffee-exhaust-scented air and then let it out again. I stare at the mirrors, and in each of them I see only the single room, empty expect for the long stack of boxes, my furniture, the aluminum bat, my poor abused Enterprise, and me.

There are about a gazillion reflections of me, staring back at myself. The breeze from the window has ruffled my hair, and I'd say it almost looks like it's standing on end in fright.

My face has lost color, my usually bee-stung kissable lips are thin and drawn. My hands shake as I lift them and pat my cold, clammy cheeks.

I'm waiting, I realize. I'm waiting for the shirtless man to pop back into existence and say, "Boo!"

I'm stretched tight, my muscles tense, my eyes wide open, so that I won't blink and miss him. But after fifteen seconds, then thirty, then a full three minutes of nothing happening, I let my muscles relax, my shoulders fall, and I give a slow, shaky exhale.

Then I walk across the groaning wood floor and pick up my model. I expect scratches, perhaps a dent, maybe even a broken engine, but the pewter model looks like new. Not mint condition, obviously, but like new. Unboxed like new.

I don't know what I was thinking throwing something so valuable at...

Okay. Fine. Obviously I have to address what just happened.

"Hello?" I call tentatively. I look around the quiet apartment. Key word—quiet. "Anyone here?"

Then when no one answers, I feel ridiculous. Like a kid fearfully searching under their twin bed for monsters and only finding a stuffed animal and a dust bunny.

But still, I slowly tiptoe around the apartment, peeking behind the boxes and the bed, and then even poking in the kitchen cupboards, and finally, looking in the bathroom.

No one is here but me.

The door is still locked.

The window is still only open six inches.

There's no one here.

No one.

I slam the window shut and turn the lock firmly in place.

Then I pull my phone from my pocket, toss the sanitizing wipes my mom gave me on my desk, and pace the creaky floor as the phone rings.

It's late morning here, which means it's early evening in Switzerland, and Serena should be home from work. She picks up on the fourth ring.

"Ms. Otaki, master of the universe, goddess of science, what's up?"

And that, in a nutshell, is my best friend, Serena. She's a particle physicist, works at CERN, the largest particle physics lab in the world, and enjoys playing with the fate of the universe.

Once, Stephen Hawking said that the scientists at CERN could destroy the universe and we wouldn't even see it coming.

Done. Boom. End of.

I mean, they have fun theorizing about creating mini black holes right here on Earth, so, why not?

But what Steven Hawking said about CERN destroying the universe was after they discovered the Higgs boson particle, also called the God particle. Serena and I were at a *Star Trek* convention together when we heard his warning. We were still teenagers, but Serena's eyes lit up and she said with die-hard conviction, "I'm going to work there."

I didn't doubt her for a second.

She's the kind of person that decides what she wants and then gets it. For instance, we met at a trekker convention in New Jersey when we were twelve.

I really, really wanted Wil Wheaton's autograph. I would've stood on my head and sucked orange soda through my nose for that autograph. Unfortunately, the autograph session time ended before I made it to the front of the line and he had to go give a talk. I watched Wil walk away with the tears of youthful disillusionment.

Then the girl behind me in line, a short girl with pigtails and thick horn-rimmed glasses, dressed in the blue science officer uniform said, "I'm getting his autograph. Are you in?"

I didn't know how she was going to get it, but I knew she would. I was definitely in.

From that day on, we were best girl friends. She lived in California. I lived in New York. She loved Spock. I loved Kirk. She was sciencey. I was artsy. She was boy crazy. I couldn't even talk to boys. None of that mattered. We learned to speak Klingon together. We traveled to conventions together. We were friends from the moment we met. We still are.

Which is why she's the first person I call.

"Serena. I need your brain," I tell her, my voice a little too high and a little too breathless.

"That's what they all say," she says, laughing. Through the phone, I hear an announcement in French, then Serena says, "Hang on, I'm getting off at my stop."

There's shuffling, then wind in the phone. Serena

must be walking home. She lives in Geneva, and commutes to Meyrin.

"Okay, what's up?" she asks, "How was the move?"

I glance around the apartment again and squint at the mirrors, blurring my reflection. "I have a problem. There was a half-naked man in here."

"Really?" Serena says, sounding incredibly interested. "That does not sound like a problem. Which half of him was naked?"

"His top half—"

"Shame."

"No. I mean he was here and then he wasn't."

"Then you should've asked him to stay."

"No. I mean my parents and Fran helped me move. They left. The door was locked. The window was only open six inches. And then I'm holding my pewter USS Enterprise NX-01—"

"Of course—"

"And then, out of nowhere, this bare-chested barbarian says, 'Now that's a big ship,' with all this sexual innuendo—"

"Is this guy into *Star Trek*? Did you *speak* to him? I knew it. I knew this day would come! You found the one man you can talk to and he's a trekker. Yes! The universe is benevolent."

"Serena!"

"What's his name?"

"Serena."

"What does he look like?"

"Serena!"

"What?"

"I'm trying to tell you, he came into the apartment when the door was locked. He stalked toward me, all shirtless sexy man stride, and I freaked out and threw my model at him."

"But that's a Franklin Mint—"

"I know! But he dodged it, so I ran for the aluminum bat my dad gave me to smash intruders with, and I swung it at him—"

"Did you kill him? Jillian! Unbelievable. Okay, hang on. I never told you this, but I have this friend from Sicily, and he can help dispose—"

"Serena! No! I didn't kill him."

"What?"

"I didn't kill him, because he doesn't exist!"

I stop pacing and stare at my flushed face in the mirror. My hair is frizzing in the stagnant humidity growing in my closed-up apartment.

On Serena's end, there's silence except for the wind passing over the phone's microphone.

"Sorry," she finally says, "I'm not sure I'm following. You just made this whole story up? So you didn't throw your USS Enterprise—"

"No, I did," I admit sadly. "What I meant was, this man can't exist because when I swung the bat at him, he looked all startled and surprised, and then, he just...disappeared."

I pace over to the bed platform and perch on the mirrored steps. Then I prop my elbows on the red shag carpeting and lean back.

"What do mean *exactly* when you say 'disappeared'?" Serena asks.

I hear her key jangling in her door, then I hear her cat, a former fuzzy black stray named James Tiberius Purrk meowing loudly.

"I mean, he was there, and then poof, he was gone.

No blur, no sparkles, no vapor, fade, or smoke screen, or anything like that, he was just...gone. Like a blink. Gone."

"Okay," says Serena, "I can see why you called. Let me feed Purrk. Give me your hypothesis."

Purrk meows excitedly at the grinding noise of the can opener. I tick off all the explanations I've thought of.

"One, I've had a mental breakdown from the stress of moving and my job and the shirtless man was a hallucination."

"Possible, not probable," Serena says.

I nod, even though Serena can't see me.

"I agree. Then there's number two. This apartment is pretty crazy. Every surface is covered in mirrors. The walls, the ceiling, the cupboards—"

Serena covers her laugh with a snort.

"And the man could've been an optical illusion. And what he said, it could've been someone on the sidewalk." I shrug. That explanation is pretty lame.

"No," Serena says.

"Yeah. I didn't think so either." I tilt my head back and stare at the ceiling mirrors. The stairs aren't very comfortable, and the carpet is scratchy on my elbows, but it's interesting staring at myself in the ceiling mirror. It's a whole new perspective. Upside down.

"What else?" Serena asks.

"The only other explanation I can come up with is..." I pause, but this is Serena, so she won't laugh. "I think... maybe...possibly...he was an alien. A humanoid alien. Yeah. I just made first contact."

Okay, I was wrong. Serena laughs. She laughs long and hard and I scowl at myself in the ceiling mirror and shove off the steps to stand.

"What? It's not funny! You believe in alien lifeforms. Why can't one be in my apartment?"

I stomp over to the boxes and tear open one marked *books*. Then I carry a handful of sci-fi novels to my bookshelf.

"You are in friend time-out," I tell Serena, scowling at her continued laughter.

"Sorry," she finally gasps, "sorry. That was just too good. Only you would immediately jump to sexy alien in my bedroom."

"No. I went for mental breakdown and optical illusion too."

"Valid point. But you realize, there is another explanation that ninety-nine point nine percent of the population would think of first."

No. I don't realize that.

"What?" I ask, narrowing my eyes.

"Ghost," Serena says. "Your apartment is haunted by a sexy, shirtless ghost."

A cold breeze blows across my neck, ruffling my hair, and I spin around, my heart pounding.

"Ghosts aren't real," I say, as I press my hand against my pounding heart. The window isn't open. Where'd that breeze come from?

The door to the bathroom slams and I jump and let out a shriek.

"Jillian?" Serena says, sounding concerned for the first time in the call.

I hurry to the bathroom, fling open the door, flip on the lights and peer around. There's no one. Just my frightened face staring back at me in the mirrors.

"Nothing," I say, "I'm just jumpy." Then I add stubbornly, "I don't believe in ghosts."

"But you believe in aliens."

"Alien lifeforms are logical. They've already discovered a meteorite from Mars with fossilized bacteria. But ghosts? That's not science, that's make-believe."

"Hmmm," Serena says.

"It's inconceivable," I argue. "Science says so."

Serena snorts. "Let's try this," she says. "And while I'm at it, get out of your apartment and grab a coffee. You're always calmer after caffeine."

That's true. I'm one of the only people on the planet who grows calm after large doses of caffeine. I grab my purse and hurry (without running or retreating) out of my apartment and down the stairs.

"Okay, tell me," I say, the brisk spring breeze tugging at my sweatshirt and kissing my cheeks. I head toward the stainless steel coffee cart parked out in front of the neighborhood nail salon/laundromat.

"Think about the *Enterprise*—"

"Which one?"

"I don't know. The D. It doesn't matter. The point I'm making is, to fly, you don't need to see out the window, right? You can fly it entirely by instruments."

I nod. "Sure. Of course."

I stop at the coffee cart. Behind the counter is a thirty-something man. He has a lumberjack beard, long hair and he's wearing a black beanie. He has that world-weary, cynical expression, and when I see that he's reading Plato's Allegory of the Cave, I know why he does. Everyone who reads the allegory is depressed for at least a week after.

The bearded barista is a sad philosopher.

Unfortunately, he's also a man, which means my

tongue is stuck to the roof of my mouth and all my words have shriveled up and died a quick death in my throat.

"So," continues Serena, "you can navigate, fly, and survive using only the instrument panel. The captain doesn't need to see out the window. They can fly using only the controls."

"Sure. Got it."

I hold up a finger for the bearded barista and then point to a large blue coffee cup and then point at the black coffee listing on the menu taped to the counter. He grunts at me, not much for talking either, and gets busy making me a cup.

I turn away from the coffee cart and take a step toward the curb and the rushing whiz and noise of the traffic.

"What does this have to do with ghosts?" I ask.

"People are like the *Enterprise*. Our five senses—sight, sound, taste, hearing, touch—they are our instrument panel. We navigate our world through them. But we make a massive mistake if we believe that what we see on our instrument panel *is* the world. That would be like a Starfleet captain thinking the readout on the controls *is* the universe. It's not."

"Of course it's not," I say.

"Hey, your coffee's ready," the barista says, leaning over the cart's metal counter to get my attention.

"Hang on," I tell Serena.

I step back to the stand and smile at him.

"You want cream and sugar?" he asks.

I nod.

"How much?"

I smile.

He expects me to answer him. Pin pricks of sweat line

my forehead, my skin goes cold, and it feels as if I'm sucking in air through a narrow half-blocked plastic straw.

But then the barista grunts and pours in a load of cream, three heaping tablespoons of sugar, and then stirs it all together.

He doesn't ask me anymore questions, and with that comes the trickling of relief and an easing in my chest.

When he slides the coffee toward me I put five dollars on the counter and give a smile of thanks.

As I walk away, he says under his breath, "Stuck-up snot. Too good to talk, isn't she?"

My shoulders barely tighten and I don't even miss a step.

It's not the worst thing anyone's ever said. Not by far. My mom and dad always worried how I'd get by. They sent me to child therapist after child therapist, convinced I would be irreparably hindered by my case of extreme "shyness."

Nothing worked. Nothing fixed it. But I learned to cope. I smile. I nod. I use email and texting as much as possible. And sometimes, if I look at the floor, or my watch, or anything but the cute guy actually talking to me, I can have a conversation. But that's not easy. It feels a bit like trying to paddle against the current of a raging river in a rickety wooden boat that's full of holes. Regardless, I get by. It's fine.

I shove back into my apartment building and say to Serena, "Okay. Got my coffee. Where were we?"

"I'm sciencing you," she says, not bothered by the wait. "You've got your five senses. You don't have windows. And your control panel *only* includes those five senses. Do not make the mistake of thinking those five senses are the universe. Do not make the mistake of thinking what you perceive is the entire universe."

"Got it," I say, taking a sip of the coffee. Wow that's sweet. I think I just swallowed a sugar cane field. I take another sip, because, well, I like sugar cane fields.

Serena continues, "Those senses only tell us what we need to know to reproduce and survive. In that order. Everything else out there, everything else in the universe, we don't know about it, because it's not displayed on our control panel."

I take another sip of my coffee, then turn my key and slip into my apartment. The mirrors and the unpacked boxes are there to greet me.

"So you're saying there's an entire universe of things that we can't perceive?" I ask.

"That's right," Serena says, a gleeful note to her voice, "We can't perceive it, therefore we can't even conceive it. There is an infinity of things surrounding us that we can't perceive, and because we can't perceive them, we can't even conceive of them."

Okay. That's sort of terrifying. However...

"I perceived this guy. I saw him. Ghosts are perceivable. If they existed. Which they don't. Because...science."

"Uh huh," Serena says, then I hear another meow from Purrk. Apparently he's finished his dinner. "Jillian, you know how there are scientists out there? The loud ones? The outspoken ones? You know how they say"— she puts on a deep, pompous voice—"'we have it all figured out. We know the answer. Absolutely. Irrevocably. We know because of *science*.'"

"Yesss?" I say, taking a sip of my sugar coffee.

"Remember Lord Kelvin said they had the universe

figured out and nothing more could be discovered in physics, right before Einstein blew everyone's minds open?"

"Yeah." I take another sip of coffee and start unpacking my warp jump mugs. They make a satisfying clink as I set them on the stainless steel counter.

"If a scientist ever tells you they have everything figured out, they're stupid."

I snort into my coffee. I love that my double doctorate best friend just used the word stupid.

"So says the scientist," I tease.

"Trust me," Serena says, "History cautions against hubris. Every age has stories—its science—to explain the nature of the universe. But our science is continuously changing. What is the chance that the science of this age holds up in the next age?"

I wrinkle my nose, "Slim?"

"Nil," Serena says. "Virtually zero. And all of us, scientists and laypeople, should be more aware of the limitations of our own stories. Our science."

"Wow. You're a real revolutionary, Serena. I never knew," I joke, thinking of her as a twelve-year-old in her blue *Star Trek* science officer uniform.

"No, I'm not revolutionary. I'm a scientist, which means I accept that the only absolute of science is that it is not absolute. That the only thing we know is that we cannot know and do not know. That the joy of science is the joy of questioning, searching, and continuously challenging. If you don't question science then you're not a scientist. If you accept science as absolute then it is no longer science, but a dogmatic religion of thrallish fanatics."

I frown, and pause in digging through my box of

collectibles. Serena's fired up, which can only mean... "Is everything okay at work?"

Serena sighs. "It's fine. I'm butting heads with my supervisor. He's uptight and despises anyone who questions him. Especially a five-foot-four, deliciously adorable woman, who is only twenty-eight and has an IQ higher than he weighs. He acts like he hates me. Which means he loves me."

She's probably right. Serena is freakishly appealing to men. They love her. She says it's because seeing a woman as smart as her is a challenge, and their testosterone brain makes them want to subdue the threat of her intelligence through sex. She claims lots of sex is her burden to bear.

"If it gets unbearable, you could come work in New York. You can live with me in my magic mirror pad." I offer this, even though I know Serena won't. She'd never leave CERN.

"No, thank you," she says, a smile in her voice. "I'll handle it. In the meantime, you likely have a ghost."

I scowl at the apartment. Of course this sex maniac's den would be the home of a shirtless, sex-crazed ghost. He probably died while having a threesome, no foursome, or...sixteensome, on the shag carpet platform.

"I'd rather I didn't," I say. "I'd rather the optical illusion, or the alien." Saying this makes me feel like a curmudgeonly, unsciencey skeptic. Which is ridiculous, because we're talking about a smirky ghost.

"You'll test our hypothesis next time he appears."

Jeez, I hope he doesn't appear again.

"Alright," I say, then I ask, "How will I do that?"

"You'll experiment," Serena says, like it's obvious.

"So he's either a hallucination, an alien, or a ghost, and I'm going to find out. By experimenting."

"That's right."

I think about this, then say, "Better yet, he'll never come back, never, ever again, and I'll live quietly and happily in my new uniquely decorated apartment."

Serena laughs, and then we hang up, because her uptight boss texts a question from the office and her mood plummets because she has to call him and walk him through her latest report.

When she's gone, I unpack my boxes, organize my furniture, set all of my *Star Trek* models, collectibles, and memorabilia on my bookshelf, and then hang Wil Wheaton's framed autograph on my wall next to a picture of Serena and me in our uniforms—blue for Serena, red for me.

Three hours pass without a hint of any ghostly happenings. My coffee is gone. I'm calm and relaxed. And in another few hours I'll be on my date. It's just another normal Saturday.

I'm confident, one hundred percent certain, absolutely positive that the man I saw earlier today won't be back.

He won't.

I push away the voice that reminds me that Serena warned that history cautions against hubris.

It doesn't matter. I know it for a fact. He won't be back.

It was a one-off, and that is that.

4

The clatter of my keyboard, the satisfying clack of the keys, and the warm glow of my monitor soothe away the last of any stress.

I parked my desk and computer opposite the bed platform, near the window and the tiny kitchen.

Outside, the sliver of sky turns dusky blue, promising a cool spring night. My date is in an hour, but I promised Bernardo, my boss, I'd have my column to him by six, which is in five minutes.

So here I am, typing at lightning speed. I work at *The Daily Exposé*, an online news site that is entirely funded by our (very) small readership. I write a weekly advice column called "Just Jillian" where I answer questions about love, dating, sex, and marriage.

Readers write in questions and I give eloquent, thoughtful, insightful answers.

Or that's the idea at least.

In regard to the man you admire, I type, *my answer is no, you don't need to dress differently, or act differently, or pretend to be someone you're not to attract him. If you like sweatpants, wear sweatpants. If you like anchovies, eat anchovies. If you like competitive duck herding, keep doing that. The only thing you need to do is be yourself. If he's the one, he'll see you, and he'll love you just as you are.*

I smile as I write this advice.

"You're kidding. This is a joke, not advice, right?"

It's him. His voice is low, rich, melodious, and it plucks at my insides and makes my whole body vibrate.

I shove back from my desk, the wheels of my chair screeching over the wood floor.

I'm facing the mirrors, and in them, I see myself, my desk and computer, my bed, everything. That is, everything except the man that just spoke. There's no one behind me.

I kick my chair back and stand, turning to face where his voice came from.

And yes, there he is. He's here, but he doesn't have a reflection.

He's still shirtless, muscled, unbelievably good looking, but he's also *not* a man. I mean, not a human. Not anymore at least.

He's scowling at my computer monitor, his eyes quickly scanning my column. He shakes his head in disgust. "Unbelievable."

Then he turns to me, a slight frown on his face, "People actually write to you for advice? And then they take it?"

Gosh. He doesn't have to sound so surprised.

I glare at him and take a step back, bumping into the edge of my desk.

He's only a few feet away from me. If he were truly here I'd be able to smell him, feel the heat of him, touch him. But the only thing I smell is the garlicky spinach from the saag paneer I had for lunch. The only thing I feel is a cold chill, as if I just opened the refrigerator. And touching?

Touch him?

He's still glaring at my computer, as if it mortally offends him.

He turns to me. "Your advice is criminal. *Be yourself?* No one *actually* wants you to be yourself. Don't bother looking good? Wrong. Don't bother flirting? Really? Flirting is foreplay. Don't bother sending out signals? Good lord. If she follows your advice, she'll be single until she's dead. And then..."

"Then?" I ask, my voice emerging in a stunned squeak.

He scoffs and levels a hard blue gaze on me, "Then she'll be dead. Single and dead."

A hysterical laugh works its way up my throat, escaping in a tight short laugh.

He smiles at me in quick approval.

And then it hits me. I *spoke.*

I spoke to an insanely good-looking, half-naked man, who is obviously interested in dating, kissing, and sex. I spoke.

Which can mean only one thing.

He isn't breathing.

He isn't living.

He's dead.

"You're a ghost," I say, my voice shaking. I take another step back, dragging my hand over the cold metal of my desk.

"What?" He scowls at me, then shakes his head, as if I've lost my mind.

"You're not a ghost?"

Don't panic, Jillian. Do not panic. Except, where did I put that aluminum bat?

"No, I'm not a ghost. Ghosts aren't real."

"Yes they are. Science," I say, throwing the word out as proof.

He chuckles. It's warm and amused, and a shiver runs over my arms, so I wrap my hands around myself and rub quickly, trying to get rid of the goosebumps.

"They're not real. Sorry," he says again.

Where is that bat?

He catches me then, frantically scanning the apartment, trying to find the bat. He looks around then too, his eyebrows lifting when he sees all the mirrors, the red shag carpeting, and the golden Liberace light.

Which makes me wonder, "Have you been here before?"

"What? In your apartment? The first time was when you tried to knock me out with your Louisville Slugger." He shakes his head, as if me swinging that bat at his head was the height of rudeness.

"But..." Okay, there's no getting around this. "Are you visiting Earth from another planet?"

He flashes me a wide smile and then he laughs, his eyes lighting up with delight. He's laughing even more than Serena did, which means he's definitely not an alien.

But if he's not a ghost, and he's not an alien, that means...I'm seeing things.

"You're a hallucination then. Awesome. Super." I sigh and my shoulders slump. I wave my hand. "Do whatever you want, I have to get ready for my date."

His laughter cuts off and he gives me an interested look, his eyebrows rising. I notice then that the light falling through the window slices right through him to land on the wood floor where it meets shadow. That's it, neither shadow nor light touches him. He's not real.

"What do you mean, a date?" he asks.

"Go away," I say. "This is my apartment. This is my life. Go away."

I stalk to my dresser, ignoring him, and pull out the first clean outfit I see, a knee-length jean skirt, a gray Starfleet Academy t-shirt, and a navy blue cardigan.

"Jillian?" he says, his voice uncertain.

I spin around, the clothes clutched to my chest, and shake my head. My mouth fills with the choking taste of panic.

"How do you know my name?"

That's it. I've lost my mind.

He takes a step forward, moving toward me. And when he's so close that he could grab me, in fact, he tries to, he reaches for me, I drop my clothes and I shove him.

Or...I try to. But instead of shoving him, my hands go right through him.

I don't feel anything.

No ectoplasm, no goo, no cold chill, no shivers. Nothing. It's as if he isn't even there.

I stumble forward. He holds out his hands to steady me, but when he reaches for me, his hands go right through me.

When they do, he lets out a stunned curse and looks at me as if he can't believe what just happened.

5

"You're either a hallucination, or you're a ghost," I tell him matter-of-factly.

After that initial moment of stunned, shell-shocked surprise that flickered across his face, he's been implacably, unmovably calm. His face is as unreadable as a stone, and just as expressive.

He crosses his arms over his chest. "I'm not a hallucination. I'm a person. And I'm not a ghost."

He casually leans against the mirrored wall, not actually resting on the mirror, but close. Which makes me think of something. I point at the mirror.

"Look. No reflection."

He turns, looks at the mirror, and when he does his eyes narrow and his mouth tightens imperceptibly. I'm the only person reflected in the surface. His reflection isn't there.

He swallows, his Adam's apple bobbing, and then he turns back to me, a look on his face that tells me he's going to ignore the mirror evidence. Stubborn man.

"Jillian," he says.

I hold up my hand for him to stop. "If you aren't a hallucination, then how do you know my name?"

He shakes his head, his jaw tightening. "Because we know each other."

"No, we don't," I say quickly.

We definitely, really don't.

I can guarantee that I have never, ever been on first-name basis with anyone like this guy.

"Yes we do," he says.

I shake my head. "Where'd we meet then?"

He frowns, stares at me like it's my fault he doesn't immediately have an answer.

"I don't know," he says grudgingly.

"Uh huh. And what did we do together? That time we met that you can't remember."

He paces across the room then, toward my shelf full of collectibles. I follow him. He reaches out and traces his fingers over my model of the Klingon Bird of Prey.

"I don't know," he finally admits.

"I imagine you probably heard my parents talking to me. That's how you learned my name. Right?"

He shakes his head no. But really, that's the only logical explanation.

"Anyway. What's your name?" I ask.

He shifts his gaze over to me, and gives me an amused look. The edges of his mouth lifting. "Don't you know?"

"No," I say, shaking my head. "Remember. I've never met you."

"Daniel," he says, pulling his hand away from the model.

He turns and stalks to the window. I walk after him. My footsteps make the floors creak, his don't.

I wonder if I should point that out. I don't really know the etiquette for convincing someone that they're dead. Because I'm going with that one. I'm not having a mental breakdown. He's not an alien. Which leaves...ghost.

Dead, shirtless ghost.

"Daniel what?" I ask.

We both watch a yellow taxi weave through the line of Saturday evening traffic flowing down Lexington.

"I don't know," he finally admits, and this more than anything else seems to bother him.

My hope at an easy obituary discovery to prove his death crashes to the sidewalk below, hope dashed.

"Did you live in New York?" I ask, sitting down in my desk chair.

He thinks for a second, then gives a small nod. "Maybe. I think so."

"You don't know?" I ask.

He scowls at me. "New York's familiar. But I also vaguely remember yachts, women in bikinis, a mountain lake, gambling in Monaco, clubs in Paris—"

"Okay," I hold up my hand and type into the search engine *Daniel, wealthy, New York, obituary*.

"I'm not dead," he says, when he sees the word obituary.

I get about two hundred pages of wealthy Daniels that have died in New York in the past few years.

"When did you die?" I ask him, looking up at the expanse of his bare golden chest, the line of his shoulders, and the tautness of his abdomen.

"I didn't," he says. "I'm not dead."

"How come I can put my hand through you then?" I ask, poking my finger through his bicep.

He steps back and scowls at me. "Don't do that."

"Where did you go when you disappeared this morning?"

He shakes his head. "I don't know. I was with you. Then I wasn't. Then I was again."

Okay. That's a bit disconcerting. He's only aware when he's with me.

"What did you do before you showed up this morning?" I ask. "Have you haunted other people?"

He gives me a frustrated look. "I'm not a ghost."

I stand and head back toward my dresser and the clothes I dropped earlier.

I say over my shoulder, "I'm sorry, but you are, and you really, really need to accept it. Then you can move on. Go find the light. You know. Beam me up, Scotty. Which, fun fact, no one ever actually said, that's a misquote."

I bend and pick up my skirt, t-shirt, and cardigan. I'll go change in the bathroom. There's no way I'm undressing in front of my ghostly companion. But when I look over my shoulder, about to tell him to go away, I realize, he's already gone.

6

_____

IF I THOUGHT FOR EVEN A SINGLE SECOND THAT TALKING with Daniel meant I could easily talk with all men, then I would've been extremely disappointed.

But I didn't think it, so I'm not disappointed. I'm a realist.

I give my date, Ronald, aka the orthopedic surgeon, a wide, happy smile from across our candlelit table. Fran was right, he's extremely charismatic. I can see why she had high hopes for me inviting him back to my place.

The flickering candlelight glows over us, bathing our small round table in an intimate warmth.

We're at the back of a small Moroccan restaurant in the East Village. The walls are washed with porcelain blue and dandelion yellow, with geometric designs etched into the borders.

The seductive scents of cinnamon and saffron curl around me and pull me toward the round clay pot that holds my tagine, the steam rising as I pull the coned lid free.

The tagine is beautiful, with subtle orange broth cradling perfectly browned chicken, bright yellow preserved lemon rinds, green olives, and a cinnamon stick for flavor.

The restaurant has eight tables, spaced tightly, and the sounds of the kitchen ride through the space, echoing off the beige ceramic tile floors and the high ceiling, melding with the hushed murmurs of the other diners.

The bright colors, the fragrant teasing spices, and the taste of mint tea lingering on my tongue, make me feel as if I've been transported to a land of hot desert winds, fragrant spices, and cool white buildings baking in the sun.

It's the perfect date.

"This is a painful date," Daniel says, frowning at me from where he's standing beside our table. "Why aren't you talking? And why won't he *stop* talking?"

I glare at Daniel, sending him *I will kill you* vibes with my eyes.

He scoffs and waves his hand in front of Ronald's face. Ronald, of course, doesn't notice Daniel's hand, or for that matter Daniel. Because as I found out when Daniel popped into existence next to my chair, no one can see him but me.

"I'm interested," Ronald says, sawing at his lamb and quince tagine, "in the management of thumb metacarpophalangeal hyperextension, that's the MCP I mentioned before—" He stops sawing and flicks a glance at me to make sure I'm paying attention.

I nod. I remember the MCP.

Ronald, or Dr. Metcalf to his patients, is beefy, thick chested, has a square jaw, wide forehead, and thinning brown hair. He also, per one of Fran's requirements, doesn't mind doing all the talking.

Unlike Daniel—who's pacing behind Ronald, looking incredibly out of place, bare chested and annoyed—I think the date is going okay.

It's definitely not the worst I've ever had. At least Ronald is polite.

"I'm investigating volar plate capsulodesis, tenodesis, arthrodesis, and sesamoidesis, and the established sequela of non-invasive and invasive—"

"How's the chicken?" Daniel asks, eyeing my tagine. He leans close and sniffs my dish. Obviously he can't smell anything. At least, I don't think he can. "Is that saffron? Did you know saffron is an aphrodisiac?"

Ronald's still listing multi-syllable medical treatments, but I can't hear him over Daniel.

"Go away," I hiss.

"Excuse me?" Ronald asks, stopping mid-sentence. "Did you say something?"

He sounds surprised, probably because I haven't spoken more than a few mono-syllabic words since we shook hands and awkwardly half-hugged outside the restaurant thirty minutes ago.

Ronald studies me intently, waiting for my answer.

Daniel also watches me with interest, since he's clearly noticed I've been communicating strictly in smiles, shrugs, and nods.

I shake my head no and then give Ronald an apologetic smile. He reaches across the table then, and pats my hand, his skin cold and dry. He rests his hand on top of mine.

"You don't need to worry," he says in a quiet,

reassuring voice, "It doesn't matter to me that you don't talk much."

"What's he on about?" Daniel says, swinging his narrowed gaze between me and Ronald.

"I can talk enough for the both of us. And the most important things...they don't need words." At that, Ronald squeezes my hand and looks meaningfully into my eyes.

"Oh. Ah ha," I say, which pretty much sums it up. Then the heat of a flush rushes over my cheeks and throat.

"Okay. Time to go," Daniel says, scowling at my blush. "This guy's no good. Let's go." He gestures at the exit.

I pull my hand back from Ronald and then pick up my fork and take a bite of my chicken.

Ronald dips his head and then spears his lamb.

"Where was I?" Ronald asks.

"About to get your ass kicked," Daniel answers.

I snort then cover it with a cough. I grab my mint tea and listen as Ronald jumps into another story.

"I was at M&M yesterday, that's morbidity and mortality, the department meeting where us physicians run through recent clinical cases, and Dr. Hirschberg gave an inspiring talk on countersinking the lag screw during cephalomedullary nailing—"

"Jillian. This guy doesn't like you. He doesn't care about you. The only reason he's here is because he wants to get laid."

Ugh. I glare at Daniel. He's so annoying. What is he? My ghostly chastity belt?

"Sorry," Ronald says, "I'm getting paged." He glances at his phone, then says, "I have to take this. I'll be back."

He doesn't bother to wait to see if I respond, instead

he shoves back from the table and hurries out the front door of the restaurant.

Daniel doesn't even wait a second after he's left to start the inquisition.

"What is this?" he asks, gesturing at the table, laid out with colorful pottery, steaming tagines, and flickering candlelight.

"A date," I whisper, glancing around the restaurant to make sure no one notices the crazy woman talking to herself.

Daniel doesn't buy my response. "Why aren't you talking to him? Why does he think you can't talk?"

"Because I can't."

Daniel lifts an eyebrow and gestures between us. "Clearly, you can."

I scowl at his rippling chest muscles and the candlelight shining through him. "I can't talk to men who are *real*."

"I'm real," he says, giving me a disappointed look.

Okay. Now is the time to settle this. I point at the cash register near the back of the restaurant, where our waiter is printing out a bill.

"Later, I want you to go and see what our bill will be. If you can tell me the exact number before I see it, then I'll agree that you're real."

I don't say what will happen if he gets it wrong.

"Fine. But you need to cut this date short. He's planning a smash and dash."

"A what?" Is that when you leave a restaurant without paying?

Daniel looks toward the windows at Ronald, his jaw hardening. "A pump and dump."

I have no idea what he's talking about. "Daniel, I'm a doctor, not a linguist."

Daniel grins at my reference. It makes me wonder if he really is a trekker. Maybe Serena was right.

"A nail and bail, Jillian. He wants to ejaculate and evacuate."

Okay. That's gross.

"How do you know?" I ask, glancing out the front windows, pretending to be casual. Ronald's still on the phone, standing on the sidewalk near the yellow lights of the front door.

"Because I'm a man and I like sex too. It's clear, he's not interested in you as a person."

"How do you know?" I ask again, actually curious.

"Because I'm a man," he reiterates, "I know these things. He wants sex, that's it."

He shakes his head and runs his hand through his hair. Funny enough, when he does, his hair brushes through his fingers and falls messily over his forehead. I wonder how that works. I didn't think a ghost could adjust their appearance.

"Are you really this naïve about men?" he asks, peering at me curiously.

I straighten in my chair and sit stiffly, raising my chin. "I am not naïve. I give people the benefit of the doubt. I don't judge based on outward appearances or first impressions. And someday I'm going to meet someone who feels just the same as I do. They'll see past whatever preconceived notions they may have about me. They'll see past my exterior and they'll see me. Me. That's how love works, you look past the exterior right into a person's heart."

"Not this again," Daniel says, crossing his arms.

"Yes, this again. And maybe Ronald is the one."

"Not a chance." Daniel looks toward Ronald and gives him a dismissive glance. "I guarantee, when he comes back in he'll brush his hand over your back and linger a second too long. Then he'll compliment your appearance. Probably your hair, it's pretty, not as knock-out stunning as your lips, but a safer compliment. Plus it's not cliché, like complimenting your eyes would be."

I flush, because Daniel just said, in a backward sort of way that he thinks I'm pretty.

"You wouldn't compliment my eyes?" I ask.

"No. I would," he says, shrugging.

"What would you say?" I ask. Then I clarify, "As a man who likes sex."

"You really want to know?" He focuses on me with a single-minded intensity that makes me wonder who he was and what he did when he was alive. He must have been a force to reckon with.

He's waiting for my response, so I give a small nod. "Let's hear it."

Daniel smiles, and leans close, the flickering candlelight passing through him, "I'd say," he says in a low, cinnamon and saffron tinted voice, that makes me shiver, "the first thing I thought when I saw your eyes was that I'll die a happy man as long as I can die looking into them."

He stares into my eyes, the deep blue of his irises like a dark flame. I lean forward, my breath held. Then suddenly he winks, and I shake out of his spell.

"And that's how it's done if you want to have sex."

I'm stunned. "My gosh, you're...you're..."

Daniel nods. "Yeah. I know."

"You've had a lot of sex," I say, recognizing a master at work.

He lifts a shoulder. "I think so."

"I'm not surprised, you're a half-naked ghost—"

"I'm not a ghost."

"What's the last thing you remember?"

He frowns and sends his hand through his sandy brown hair again. "I only remember impressions. Bits and pieces. Nothing clear. There's the impression of a woman—"

"Of course."

"She was lying down—"

"No doubt."

Daniel lifts an eyebrow and gives me a quelling look. "And my heart was racing—"

"As it does when you have sex," I say.

"And then I pulled off my shirt—"

"Yeah. Luckily you didn't make it to your pants or this would be awkward."

He shrugs, then says, "And then, I remember pain. Lots of pain. And that's it."

I tap my finger against my chin. "Maybe she murdered you."

"I'm not dead," Daniel argues, although he doesn't sound as sure as he did earlier today.

"Or her husband murdered you," I offer.

He shakes his head.

"Or you had a heart attack, because the anticipation of sex was too much to bear."

"No. Sorry. I'm certain I've gone entire nights. Weekend marathons. I'm sure of it."

"Gah. Be quiet."

Daniel shrugs. Then the bell over the door jingles and

he narrows his eyes. "Ronald's back. I forgot. After the bill, he'll ask you if you want to swing by his place for coffee. Say no."

I start to roll my eyes, but as I do, I feel Ronald's hand casually settling on my back.

Daniel nods, as if he's saying, "what did I tell you?"

"Apologies for the interruption," Ronald says, his hand brushing over my shoulder, lingering for a second too long. Slowly he lifts his hand and then sits in his chair, setting his napkin in his lap.

When he looks at me he says, "Did I mention? Your hair is quite beautiful."

Ronald looks at me expectantly. A wide smile freezes on my face.

"He's moving fast," Daniel mutters.

I lift my hand for the waiter and when he starts toward the table I signal for the check.

"Oh, already?" Ronald asks, "I was thinking we could swing by my place after, have a coffee. I could show you my latest peer reviewed journal article on total joint arthroplasty."

I cough into my hand.

Daniel sighs and shakes his head, then he saunters over to the cash register and peers over our waiter's shoulder at the receipt printing out.

"Well? What do you say?" Ronald asks.

The waiter strides to our table, Daniel follows.

I hold out my hand.

"Sixty eight dollars and fifty-seven cents," Daniel says, a confident smile on his face.

"I can get that," Ronald says, holding out his hand.

I ignore him and take the bill, scanning the printed numbers. They blur and then come into sharp focus.

$68.57.

Holy crap.

I only half believed it before. There was still a part of me that worried this was all in my head.

But it's not.

It's really not.

Daniel's real, and whether he wants to admit it or not, he's a ghost, and he's haunting me.

I slap down enough money to pay for my half of the meal.

"Now will you admit I'm real?" Daniel asks, with a happy smirk.

I nod, unable to say a word through my slowly ebbing shock.

"Is that a yes to coffee?" Ronald asks, in a pleased tenor.

Coffee is apparently today's euphemism for sex.

"No thank you," I manage, shaking my head.

After paying, I leave the seductive spices of the restaurant and hurry onto the sidewalk, Daniel following close behind.

7

THE CHILL BREEZE GRABS MY CARDIGAN AND TUGS, SENDING cold fingers down my arms.

I glance over at Daniel, who doesn't have a shirt on. I imagine that if he could feel the cold, he'd be shivering right now. But he's impervious to the cold April night.

The flickering glow of a streetlight falls through him, illuminating the dark sidewalk and stretching toward the long row of cars parked for the night.

I hurry toward the warmth and shelter of the subway. It's only a few blocks away, past brick apartments with lights on and TVs flashing, and businesses that are dark —a butcher, a candy shop, a tailor, a salon.

Daniel keeps pace with me easily, stepping around the people we pass. They don't see him, and they'd walk through him if he didn't dodge them.

"So," he finally says, glancing at me from the side of his eyes.

I don't respond, because I have a good idea of what he's about to say.

And I'm right.

"Why didn't you talk on your date?"

I shake my head, stepping around the steam rising from a manhole. "I already told you. I find it difficult to talk to guys."

"Why?" he asks, sounding curious but not judgmental.

"Why not?" I lift an eyebrow and then stop at the crosswalk. Daniel doesn't see the flashing Don't Walk sign light up. He steps out into the street.

A yellow taxi races at him.

"Watch out—" I shout, holding out my hand.

Daniel turns back to me, his eyes wide and surprised, and then the taxi rushes through him.

He flinches. Then he shudders, like someone just stepped on his grave.

That taxi went right through him like he was a hologram.

He glares after the bright taillights of the speeding taxi.

"I will never get used to that," he says.

Then he steps back on the curb and looks down at me expectantly, shrugging off what just happened. "You were saying?"

I shake my head. It's hard to brush away the sudden flash of fear that I experienced when I forgot he was already dead. The taxi shouldn't have scared me. I tug on my cardigan sleeves and pretend I'm fine.

He frowns, "You were telling me why you weren't talking on your date."

No. I wasn't.

Obviously he isn't going to let this go. He's annoyingly single-minded and persistent for a ghost.

"Can we just say that this is the way I am and leave it at that?"

The light turns at the crosswalk and we walk across the street, passing through the bright headlights of the cars stopped at the red light. In the intersection buses and cars whoosh past, their tires crackling over the pavement.

When we're back on the sidewalk, Daniel says, "That's what you want? To leave it at that?"

"Yes."

He studies me for a moment, then nods. "Alright."

My shoulders sag with relief.

I think he's going to disappear, because he fades a bit, but then he says, "Jillian?"

"What?"

"Let's talk about sex."

I start to cough, then hit my chest with my fist. "Sex? You want to talk about sex? With me?"

A craggy-faced man in a beige trench coat and a black suit stops on the sidewalk in front of me.

"Hell yeah," he says with a toothy smile.

"She isn't talking to you," Daniel says, stepping between us.

I shake my head no and hurry around the trench coat man.

"Hey, come back!" the man shouts after me with a loud laugh.

"I meant," Daniel says, catching up to me, "let's talk about why you live in a porn set from the nineteen seventies and why you're dating nail and bail douchebags. If you want sex, you don't need to go to such extreme lengths." He holds out his hands and gestures at himself, "For instance, you and I—"

"Ugh. Go away." I hurry down the sidewalk, the sound

of laughter erupting as a couple pushes open the door of a brightly lit vodka bar.

"We could get up to some interesting—"

"Go away! Why are you here?"

"Activities, for instance—"

"Ugh. No. Why are you following me? Why can't you take a hint? I don't want a horny, annoying, Lothario ghost!"

"Lothario?" He stops and I stop too, stepping out of the flow of bustling people. I back into the dim entry of a laundromat closed for the night.

The woman who was walking behind me shoots me a suspicious glance, probably because it looks like I've been arguing heatedly with myself, accusing the air of following me.

Once she's past, I say to Daniel in a quieter voice, "Yes, Lothario."

Daniel's shoulders stiffen. Apparently he takes offense at that.

"I'm not a Lothario."

I hold up my hand. "You died while getting it on. And per your own recollection, while you were alive all you did was sun on yachts, stare at bikinied ladies, and have lots of marathon sex. You know all about flirting, smashing and bashing, and getting women into bed. You are the *epitome* of a Lothario. Which is why as a ghost, you're shirtless and muscled and sexy. So, go away." I wave my hands at him.

"Sexy?" he asks, smirking at me, his earlier pique forgotten. In fact, I think he really likes it that I called him sexy.

I wave my hands in a shoo gesture. "Go. Scram. Leave."

He runs his hands through his hair and looks adorably disconcerted. "Jillian, we're friends. I can't leave."

I shake my head and push away from the laundromat entry.

"We're not friends. We don't even know each other." I hurry down the sidewalk. The subway's in sight.

"Yes we do," he argues, following after me.

Then I smile, because on the corner of the street, I see exactly what I need. It's what I should've thought of when Daniel first appeared. It's the perfect solution.

"Why are you smiling like that?" Daniel asks suspiciously.

I point at the business. It's in the lower level of a five-story yellow brick building, down a short flight of stairs. There's a spice shop upstairs, and apartments above that. But the business I'm pointing at? It's lit up with neon blue Christmas lights and has hot pink plastic beads hanging in long curtains over the windows. And glowing brightly in fluorescent blue letters is one wonderful word.

Psychic.

8

GOLDEN BELLS TINKLE MUSICALLY AS I THRUST OPEN THE door. I've never been to a psychic before. I don't believe in them. But I don't believe in ghosts either, so here I am.

The heat hits me first, it's dry and crackling hot. The temperature must be at least eight-five degrees, which is nearly forty degrees warmer than outside.

My skin prickles, little needles dancing over my cold skin as I adjust to the warmth. I take a shallow breath. The air is thick with incense—a stick lets off curling strands of smoke, burning in a bronze bowl near the front door. I take shallow breaths. I loathe incense.

On the wall near the front door, there's a small sign. It says in thin blue cursive, *Zelda Vertruse, Psychic.*

I step further inside. The small square room is dark, lit only by a glowing pink Himalayan sea salt lamp, and a gold table lamp, its shade draped with a red silk scarf. At the back of the room there's another door, which is closed.

The whole place has an otherworldly pink glow infused with blue from the Christmas lights.

The ceiling is low—we're in the basement after all—and the floor is covered with a threadbare blue and gold oriental rug.

There's only one table, a small folding card table, with two metal chairs. Other than that, the only decoration is the rose-colored bead curtain hanging over the window.

"What are we doing here?" Daniel asks, stepping through the front door and casting a skeptical look around the empty room.

"*We* are asking the psychic to help you move on," I tell him, refusing to feel bad about this. That's what ghosts are supposed to do. They're supposed to *move on*.

"You don't want me to move on," he says, walking over to the incense and frowning at the smoke rising from the burning orange tip.

"I really do," I say.

He turns back and grins at me, and I notice for the first time that he has a dimple in his left cheek. I guess it only appears when he's really smiling, like he is now.

He catches me staring at his dimple and his grin widens even more. "No you don't. Besides, psychics are fake, they don't know anything."

At that, a woman slams open the door to the back, banging it against the wall.

"What?" she asks, glaring at me. "What do you want?"

The woman, Zelda I think, is about six feet tall, bone thin, with skin so pale that it glows pink in the light. She's wearing black leather biker pants and a leather jacket with metal spikes on the shoulders. Her face is wrinkled and looks like a dried up mud puddle baking in the sun.

She has a glistening orange drumstick in her hand, and as she glares at me she takes a bite, fiery-orange sauce staining her thin lips. She's not happy I'm here, that much is obvious.

"Um...I was looking for...the psychic? Zelda Vertruse?" I say, not quite sure how to respond to the woman tapping her foot impatiently and taking quick, forceful bites of her chicken.

Daniel, for once, doesn't have anything to say. He's just looking between me and the leather-clad, metal-spiked woman.

"What's with you? I have to eat, don't I? You people always come when I'm eating. Or peeing. Or sleeping. You come at the worst time. What's wrong with you? Don't you have any decency?" she asks.

She's finished with the drumstick. She glares at the chicken bone and then flicks it to the table. It rattles over the vinyl top, leaving a trail of sticky orange sauce. Then she spears me with a disgruntled look, as if I should apologize. But that's ridiculous. The sign on the door said *Open*.

I open my mouth to say something, then close it again.

"What do you want?" Zelda asks, flinging a hand toward me. "Love life? Career? Neither looks good right now." She frowns, her lips drawing down in a thin orange line.

I'm speechless.

"I was wrong," Daniel says, shooting me a teasing smile, "Maybe psychics do know some things. I bet she saw Ronald. Maybe your terrible advice column. Love... career..." He shakes his head sadly.

I lift my chin and say under my breath, "You. Be quiet."

Daniel laughs.

Zelda grunts. "No, I bet you want to talk about that freak ball of energy hanging around you."

It's like an electric wire zaps me. I stiffen and swing toward Daniel.

"She can see me?" he asks, stunned. He stares at her intently, then waves his hand, checking her reaction.

"You can see him?" I ask, goosebumps rising on my arms.

Her mouth twists and she shakes her head. "No. It's a him? Figures. His energy is loud. Annoying. He's right"—she points a long, thin finger at Daniel—"there."

"Hey," Daniel says. "I'm not annoying."

"You kind of are," I tell him.

"I'm not. I'm endearing."

I snort. Yeah right.

"He talks?" the psychic asks.

"Yes, I talk," Daniel says, looking more put out than I've seen him all day.

"He's been following me around," I explain. "I moved into a new apartment today, and he was there, and now he won't leave me alone. He won't admit he's dead—"

Daniel stiffens at that and walks to the window, pretending to ignore us. The muscles on his back are bunched, and his shoulders are tight. His head cocks to the side, so I know he's listening.

"He won't admit he's a ghost," I say, "So I thought, maybe you can help him move on."

Zelda rubs her hands on her leather pants, wiping the last of the orange chicken sauce off. Then she purses her lips and frowns up at the ceiling, tilting her head as if she's listening to something only she can hear.

I wait in silence for nearly a minute, not wanting to disturb her.

Then she abruptly turns toward the window where Daniel's standing, the light glinting off the metal spikes on her coat.

"He's dead," she says, then more loudly, "hey you. Jerkhole. You're dead. Got it? Dead. D-E-A-D. Dead." At that she wipes her hands together and turns back to me. "That'll be a hundred bucks."

"What?" I shake my head. "That's not—"

I cut off. At the window, Daniel lets out a broken sigh, then his shoulders slump and he bows his head. I stare at the line of his back, the blue Christmas lights shine through him, nothing touches him, not the light, not the heat, not the cold.

By the forlorn slope of his shoulders, and the slow movement of his hand as he reaches out to touch the window where his reflection should be, but isn't, I think he's finally admitting to himself that he's gone.

Dead.

His fingers pass through the window, and when they do, he slowly drops his hand and turns away from the glass.

Suddenly, I have the strongest urge to walk over to him and pull him into my arms, tell him I'm sorry.

I didn't realize until now that he truly hadn't known that he was gone. I thought he knew it but was stubbornly denying it. But now? He knows it. And by the look of him, it hurts.

But you can't hug a ghost. I can't even rest a reassuring hand on his arm.

So instead, I say to the psychic, "Why hasn't he moved on?"

When I ask, Daniel turns away and paces the length of the room.

Zelda sucks a breath through her teeth, then shrugs, "Unfinished business. It's always unfinished business."

I frown, then I ask Daniel, "Do you have unfinished business?"

"No," he says, then he stops pacing and gives me a considering look. His shoulders come up and the forlorn, heavy air that had momentarily cloaked him falls away.

"What?" I ask, suspicious of the sparkling light in his blue eyes.

"Maybe you're my unfinished business, Jillian. Maybe you and I—"

"He says I'm his unfinished business."

"Did you know him?" Zelda asks, then she turns a glare in Daniel's direction and says, "Hey, lover boy, tone down the horny vibrations."

Daniel scoffs, then turns to me, "I'm not vibrating."

I hide a smile. "No. I never met him before today."

"At your new apartment," Zelda says, reiterating what I already told her.

"That's right. It's a...like a...sex den," I hold up my hands when her eyebrows go high, deepening her wrinkles. "I didn't know it was a sex den when I rented it. But it is, and he was there, and he's..." I flush.

"Sexy," she says, but she says "sexy" the same way you'd say phlegm or seepage.

I nod. "Yeah. And he's weirdly obsessed with my dating life."

She snorts. "Your dating life is a disaster."

"Hey," I say. I mean, it's true, but she doesn't have to

point it out. I didn't come here for her to tell me things I already know.

"Your career too," she adds. "It's a trash fire."

I mean, there isn't really any arguing with that.

"If you don't want him around, you should move out of that apartment," she says. "He could be tied to it. It's probably where he died."

"Did you die there?" I ask Daniel, trying not to think about the fact that in a few hours I have to sleep in the apartment where he apparently died.

"I don't know," he says, shoving his hands into his pockets, his expression not giving anything away. "I can't remember."

I consider this, then ask him, "If I move out, will you still be able to find me? Will you still come around?"

"I could find you anywhere," he says dismissively. "You're like a flame. I'm drawn to you. Everyone else is muted, but you burn bright."

I stare at him for a moment, gauging the truth of this, and he stares back, his gaze steady, as if I'm the only bright thing in his universe.

I nod. He dips his chin. That's it.

I turn back to the psychic. "He says he'll follow me, even if I move out."

She grunts, walks to the door, flips the sign to *Closed* and then says, "You got yourself a ghost. Congratulations. My advice?" She pauses and I nod. I want her advice. "He's zoned in on you for a reason. Either he's here to help you or you're here to help him. Or he's a psycho and you'll wake up with blood oozing from the walls and metal chains floating in the kitchen."

My eyebrows go sky high when I picture the love den with floating chains.

I shoot a quick glance at Daniel.

He shakes his head. "I'm into kink, but not that kind of kink."

I repress a smile.

"He's not a psycho," I say.

Zelda shrugs, like it doesn't matter to her either way. "Then finish the unfinished business. He'll move on when it's done. That'll be one fifty."

I blink.

Daniel laughs. "She's unbelievable."

"But you said it was one hundred dollars," I say.

"That was before you annoyed me and made me miss the first half of my TV show." She holds out her hand, tapping her foot impatiently.

I let out a long sigh. "Do you take credit cards?"

"Yes. But you pay the three percent vendor fee. That makes it one fifty four fifty."

I tug my credit card out of my wallet and hand it over. While she runs it through the machine, I ask, "What about holy water, or burning sage, or sprinkling herbs, would any of that work? To help him move on?"

Daniel gives me a hurt look, as if he can't believe I'm even suggesting this. "Really, Jillian? Really?"

"No," Zelda says, "he's a ghost, not a ham. Why do you people always want to throw water and herbs on everything? Idiots."

She shoves my card back in my hand and then says, "Now go away." Then she turns and looks right through Daniel, "And you too. Get lost."

Daniel shakes his head and walks toward the door, but I pause, feeling like I'm missing something.

"We're supposed to help each other?" I ask, just to be sure.

Zelda scowls, the lines on her face deepening, then she gives a long-suffering sigh.

"What did I tell you? Yes. His energy is loud. Yours is quiet. His is hard. Yours is soft. He's open, you're all closed up. He's pulsing with love, you...not so much." My shoulders slump at that. Zelda glares at me. "Everyone has vibrational energy. You two are like the opposite poles on a magnet. You're magnetically drawn. You stick." She slams her hands together and clasps them tight. "Like this." Then she says, "Deal with it."

With that, she stalks from the room, banging the back door shut after her.

The door shudders, vibrating noisily, then falls quiet.

"I liked her," Daniel finally says, smiling down at me.

I scoff. "You liked her because she said I'm stuck with you."

He grins, his dimple winking at me. "I told you we were friends. I knew we were."

I shake my head and push out of the heat and the cloud of incense, the golden bells tinkling as I open the door. The spring chill blasts me as I climb the steps to the busy sidewalk.

"Maybe," I say, then at Daniel's raised eyebrows I say, "Fine. We'll be friends."

Kindred spirits.

Emphasis on spirit.

9

WHAT DOES IT MEAN TO HAVE A GHOST AS A FRIEND?

From what I can tell, it's like being an actor on stage and the ghost is that annoying guy in the peanut gallery who is loudly cracking jokes, inserting fake dialogue, and tossing popcorn at the stage. Just like the theatre actors have to ignore the heckler, the people in the real world ignore (can't see/hear/feel) Daniel.

Only I can.

On the subway home last night, Daniel tried to get this beefy macho guy spreading his legs so wide he took up three seats to move over so that both I and the pregnant woman with swollen ankles could sit down.

He patiently explained to the guy that he wasn't winning any awards by being a dick. The guy kept his legs wide, his headphones on, and his eyes on his phone the entire time, even though Daniel gave a strangely convincing argument in which he equated giving up your seat for a lady to ushering in respect, harmony, and world peace.

I held onto the metal pole, standing next to a weary man in a wrinkled off-the-rack business suit, his scuffed briefcase bumping my leg with each turn, pretending to ignore Daniel's lecture.

Besides the macho guy, Daniel called after a tourist couple that they were walking the wrong way to get to Grand Central, told me to trip a man that was sprinting past us (I didn't, but I should have because it turns out he'd stolen a woman's purse), and finally, he pointed out all the little things he didn't want me to miss—how a streetlight streamed over a street puddle in a yellow glow so that it looked just like van Gogh's swirling stars, or how the deep purple and red spring tulips in the sidewalk gardens had closed for the night, their petals shut tight, or how two plump gray and white pigeons were huddled close on top of a window air conditioner, cooing a quiet evening song, barely heard above the hum of the traffic.

He delighted in delighting me.

Every time I smiled, or more likely, repressed a smile, he grinned, his dimple flashing.

When we finally made it back to the mirrored sex den it was night-dark, quiet, and I was so tired that I changed into my fleece pajamas, washed my face, brushed my teeth, and collapsed into bed.

When I turned out the light, I asked Daniel, *are you going to be here in the morning?*

And from the darkness, he said, *where else would I be?*

I don't know. But when I woke up, he was gone.

10

THE HOT WATER TRICKLES OVER ME IN A FLAGGING, HALF-hearted stream, as if the shower gave up on pretending to have any water pressure years ago.

I tilt my face into the water and let the steam curl around me, closed in by the white shower curtain.

The steam has fogged up the surfaces of all the mirrors, so that my reflection is an indistinct blob. Soap suds from my peppermint soap slip down the drain of the old enamel iron bathtub, and I breathe in the smell, letting it wake me up and invigorate me.

Daniel isn't here.

It's nine o'clock and he isn't here.

Maybe I dreamed it all? Maybe I imagined it? Maybe...

I tilt my head back, close my eyes, and rinse the apple and mint conditioner from my hair, working it through my thick curls.

I didn't imagine it.

He disappears, he reappears. He pops out of existence, he pops back into existence.

He...

I open my eyes, swiping the water away, and he's here.

Here, here.

In the shower.

With me.

He stands a foot away, his chest bare, his jeans on, the shower water streaming through him and hitting the mirrored wall behind him.

He stares at me with an expression of stunned disbelief, as if he's frozen in place from shock. As if he stepped outside one day, expecting to see a blue sky and instead the sky was green.

His eyes are wide, his mouth falls open into a stunned O, and his eyebrows fly high.

He's stunned? How does he think I feel? He popped into existence while I'm naked, covered in soap suds.

"Get out!" I shriek, wrapping an arm over my breasts, and dropping my hand to cover my bits. A full body flush races over me, prickling every bit of skin.

Daniel blinks, coming out of his sudsy shower moment stupor, his eyes flying to mine. But he's still not *leaving*.

I take a millisecond to decide between keeping my bits covered or chucking something at him.

I grab the shampoo bottle and fling it at his head. "Get out of my shower! You...deviant!"

Daniel flinches when the shampoo bottle soars through him. I grab the bar of soap next and hurl it at him. But before the soap reaches him, he disappears, winking out of existence.

The soap smacks against the mirror with a thwap, then thunks to the iron tub, washing toward the drain.

I take in a gulping breath, my heart drumming in my ears, my skin burning from embarrassment, but the only evidence that Daniel was ever here is the shampoo bottle and soap circling the drain, and the white streak of soap left on the mirror.

But he was here. He definitely was here, in my shower.

Gah.

I shake my head and try unsuccessfully to banish the memory of Daniel's stunned expression while I finish rinsing off.

I've never been naked in front of a man before. When would I have been?

Call me crazy, but I've always wanted to be able to converse with a man before stripping down with him. So Daniel, my ghost friend, is the first man to ever see me naked.

I step out of the shower and wrap a bath towel around myself, letting a puddle form around my feet on the cool tile floor.

The bathroom is filled with steamy fog, and it looks especially ghostly. The only sound is the dripping of the final waterdrops falling from the showerhead to the enamel tub.

Drip. Drip.

"Are you still here?" I ask.

Drip.

"Daniel?"

Drip.

No answer. No ghostly cold breeze, no door

slamming. I scowl at the steam and then decide I'd better get dressed while I'm still alone.

Which is a good idea, because the minute I've pulled my hair into a bun, and popped on a pair of jeans and a bright yellow cashmere sweater, Daniel appears in front of me.

"Go away." I fight the urge to throw something else at him.

He takes a step back and holds up his hands. "Now hang on. I didn't know you'd be in the shower."

I cross my arms over my chest, but it reminds me of how I covered my breasts in the shower so I quickly drop my hands. "But when you came, you didn't immediately leave. A gentleman would've left, or at least averted his eyes!"

He thrusts his hand through his hair in exasperation. "I'm dead, not blind! I was shocked stupid."

I pause and consider him. "Shocked stupid?"

I've never heard that phrase before, but it pretty accurately describes what happened.

He looks away, and if I didn't know better, I'd think he's embarrassed. If ghosts could blush, his face would be bright red.

"How could you be shocked stupid?" I ask, walking closer to get a better look at his averted face. He shifts uncomfortably, and I narrow my eyes on him. "Wait. You were shocked stupid for ten seconds?"

His eyes fly to mine. "I was in there for two, max."

"Five."

He shakes his head. "Three, tops."

Okay. He's right. It was more like three seconds, but still, it was a long three seconds.

"Shocked stupid for three seconds," I say, musing.

Then, I decide that's not possible. "Nope. I don't believe you. You've had countless sex marathons, night-long orgies, and you spent your life on yachts full of bikini-clad ladies. How could seeing me in a steamy shower shock you stupid?"

His eyebrows lift, as if he's wondering how I could possibly ask such a question.

"What?" I ask.

He leans close, his gaze dragging over my face like a physical touch. His eyes snag on my lips and I resist the urge to bite my bottom lip. Finally he looks up from my mouth, his eyes as warm as a blue sky summer day.

"Don't you know?" he asks, his voice low and intimate.

I'm taken aback by how close he is, by the questioning light in his eyes, and the way the sunlight from the window falls through him.

"Know what?" I ask, wanting the answer but also afraid to hear it.

"You're beautiful, Jillian," he says, then when I don't respond, he says again, more firmly, "You're beautiful."

Then he lifts a shoulder, gives me a small smile, and steps back, like he didn't just drop a bomb into the middle of my life.

For a moment I'm too stunned to say anything. But when I do, I shake my head in denial.

"No, I'm not. No one has ever said I'm beautiful. Well, except my mom, but she doesn't count. I could be considered cute, if you go for the virgin-geek look—"

Daniel raises his eyebrows and stands straighter when I say the words "virgin-geek." He's like a dog that just heard the word "biscuit." I scoff and wave my hand, brushing off his interest.

"What I'm saying is, I'm not buying it, I'm not—"

He holds up a hand. "The hell with that. You see that bar for beauty, the one you're measuring yourself against?"

He waits for me to respond, so I give a short nod. I know the bar, it's the one that's told me since I was a kid what beauty looks like and it's never been me.

When I nod, Daniel smiles and says, "Good. Here's what you do with that bar. You take it. You break it. You throw it in the trash. Got it?"

I don't say anything. I can't really. I don't mean that I've lost the ability to talk to Daniel because he's a man who is clearly interested in sex. No. I don't say anything because that's one of the nicest things anyone has ever said to me.

He's watching me, waiting for me to agree.

Finally, I nod. "Okay. I've tossed it in the trash."

"Good," he says, then he rolls his shoulders, his abs contracting, and he gives me a smirky grin. "So...virgin-geek?"

I walk to the kitchen, the wood floors creaking, grab an apple off the counter, and throw it at him. He laughs as he dodges it.

"Am I forgiven?" he asks.

"For what?" I mutter, nearly forgetting the steamy shower fiasco. "Oh right. Yeah. Next time, close your eyes when you pop in. What if you show up when I'm changing, or peeing, or"—I think through the options —"having sex."

Daniel gives me a considering look. "You wouldn't want me to watch? Give the guy pointers?"

I throw another apple. It passes through him and rolls across the floor, hitting the mirrored stairs.

"You're wasting your apples," he laughs.

"You're wasting your breath."

"I don't have breath."

We grin at each other.

"You're forgiven," I tell him. "Now be quiet, I have a bunch of articles to write before tomorrow."

"Will they be as bad as the last one?" he asks curiously as I wander toward my desk.

"Definitely," I say over my shoulder. "You can count on it."

His eyes light with mirth. He likes my answer, I can tell.

For the next few hours he reads over my shoulder, gives content suggestions (which I ignore), corrects my typos (which I don't ignore), and makes me laugh with ridiculous relationship advice.

When the afternoon glow shines through the window and my stomach starts to growl, I stretch back in my chair and raise my arms over my head, working out the kinks.

I'm about to say that I'm going to make a peanut butter and jelly sandwich and take a coffee break when my door buzzer rings.

"Who is that?" Daniel asks, looking out the window at the stoop four stories below. I stand next to him and stare down at the street.

Standing on the steps of my apartment building, wearing a leopard print windbreaker and pearls, is Fran.

There's only one reason she'd take the train in on a Sunday. She's here to set me up on another date.

11

Fran waltzes into my apartment, her arms wide for a hug, enveloping me in her warmth, smelling of roasted onions, toasted fennel, and lazy weekends from my childhood. She presses a kiss against my cheek and then backs up, giving me a thorough once-over.

I catch a reflection of myself in the mirrors. There's nothing unusual, my cheeks are pink, there's an erasable pen sticking out of my bun, and I'm smiling.

I look like I normally do, but I take a moment to look a little longer, because Daniel said...I'm beautiful.

I wonder what *specifically* he finds beautiful? My eyes? My mouth? My breasts?

My cheeks blend from pink to red.

Fran claps her hands together. "Your date went off like fireworks," she says finishing her inspection. "You're glowing like a woman who fucucked all night long. I knew it. These mirrors are magic."

Daniel chokes on a laugh and then coughs, saying, "Fucucked? What is fucucked?"

I shoot a glare at him, quickly though, so Fran doesn't notice.

He smothers his laughter. "I know for a fact you didn't fucuck, I was here. But I wonder why she thinks you're glowing? Maybe because you and I—"

I turn my back on him and say to Fran, "No. I left early. There wasn't a connection."

"But..." She pauses and studies me, her dyed blonde hair sticking straight up from the spring gusts.

She purses her lips and shakes her head, her pearls clicking against the zipper on her leopard print windbreaker.

"I don't believe it. You look like a woman who's had some action. I swear, I thought he was going to be the one."

"He was *not* the one," Daniel says firmly.

I shake my head, ignoring Daniel. "Sorry, Fran. Ronald was a fine doctor, I'm sure, but we didn't hit it off."

"Is she the one who set you up?" Daniel asks, turning his gaze on Fran and inspecting her, from her bright red shoes, to her leopard print coat, to the black roots of her blonde hair. "Is this your mom?"

I look at him and give a subtle head shake. First a yes, then a no.

He frowns at me, "What does yes-no mean?"

Fran waves her hand, sweeping my failed date with Ronald away. "It doesn't matter. I met another man this morning...this one...whew...he is raw sexual magnetism. I met him at Bergdorf's. I dropped my watch, my little Tag that Michael gave me, remember?"

I nod. Fran loves going to Bergdorf's, it's her favorite store in Manhattan. She goes at least once a month. Judging by the shimmery mauve lipstick and the perfect cat eye she's sporting, she paid a visit to the make-up counter.

"What is this? What's she talking about?" Daniel asks, crossing his arms over his chest and looking like he disapproves of this entire conversation.

"Well this man, wow, he bent over to pick up my watch and about fifty women stopped shopping just to stare at his firm, hard—"

Daniel considers me. "Jillian, if you want firm and hard, then—"

I cough, and Fran stops.

"Are you alright?" she asks. "Do you need a cough drop? I have eucalyptus."

I wave her offer away. "I'm okay."

Daniel smirks.

"Anyway, he picked up my watch and then noticed that the second hand's movement had stopped, so he fixed it for me. Right there! Now he was a man that was good with his hands."

"He's a cliché," Daniel says.

"He was with three stunningly gorgeous women. I think they were models," she tells me, her eyes widening. "The ladies at the make-up counter said he's worth millions."

"He sounds like a douche," Daniel says.

And just to goad him, I say, "I think he sounds nice."

Fran gives me a surprised look. "You don't typically like the international playboy type."

"Scratch that, he is a douche," Daniel says.

"Is that what he is?" I ask.

"Yes," Daniel says.

Fran nods. "Yes."

"But if you know I don't go for that type, then why do you want me to go out with him?" I ask Fran.

"I don't," Daniel says.

"Well," she says, "I wouldn't usually, but I'm casting a wider net, and when I told him about you…"

"What did she say about you?" Daniel asks, frowning at Fran.

I'm curious too. "What did you say about me?"

Fran smiles and holds her arms open wide. "I gushed about you. Cleverly of course. I told him my goddaughter was near his age. He was maybe thirty-two or thirty-three—"

"Too old for you," Daniel says.

I shake my head at him, I bet he's early thirties. Or at least, he was when he died.

"—and I said that you are a brilliant writer." I glance at Daniel to see if he denies this, but he's watching Fran intently. "And I told him you're funny, and intelligent, and gorgeous—"

"Excellent. This guy's probably a philandering serial killer and she's serving you up to him on a platter with lettuce garnish," Daniel shakes his head in disgust.

I frown at him. Is he…jealous?

Fran continues. "Because clearly he likes gorgeous women. The ladies at the make-up counter said he dates actresses, models. He has a yacht where he takes his lady friends—"

Daniel steps in front of me, blocking my view of Fran. "Please do not go out with this douche. Any guy that dates actresses and models and takes them on his yacht is desperately crying out for attention. He's compensating. This is "how to spot a douche one-oh-one." Just say no."

I grin at him, then say, "When the ladies are on his yacht, are they wearing bikinis?"

Because Daniel had a yacht full of bikini-clad women. Does that mean he's a douche too?

"I would think so," Fran says.

Daniel gives me an exasperated look. "That's different."

I raise my eyebrows. Is it?

"I wonder if he goes clubbing."

"He does," Fran say gleefully.

Daniel scowls at me. "I'm not a douche, this guy clearly is."

I step to the side, so I can see Fran again.

She waves her hands happily. "He's rich, he looks like Adonis, and after I told him about you—well, I told you were writing an article on owning a yacht—he gave me his card and told me that you can call and set up an interview anytime." Fran looks at me expectantly. "You never know, he could be the one. Maybe he even likes sci-fi as much as you."

I bite my bottom lip to keep from laughing and try not to look at Daniel.

He scoffs, shaking his head.

"Even if he doesn't like sci-fi," Fran says, "he'd be a good one to pop your cherry. He wasn't shy. I bet he's popped a lot of cherries."

My cheeks burn, and I hold very still and try very hard not to acknowledge Daniel's stare.

I'm not sure what he'd do if he tagged along for another pump and dump date. For a certified Lothario, he's oddly straight-laced and starchy sometimes.

"I think...I think I'm going to pass on the

international playboy," I say, darting a quick glance at Daniel.

He nods in approval.

"No matter," Fran says, pulling her purse from her shoulder and unzipping it. "I brought you a few things."

She tugs a wrinkled paper bag free. "Rose water for your complexion, a loaf of cinnamon raisin bread." She pulls them from the bag and hands them to me. "And a prayer candle blessed by a bishop. Your mom says she felt a ghostly draft in here and she asked me to pick one up for you. Just in case."

She waves the candle high, "It should work."

Daniel walks close and stares down at the candle. It's a thick white beeswax candle in a glass votive jar, with a cross etched on the glass. Daniel pokes his finger through it.

"Yes indeed, it'll work," Fran says, handing the candle to me.

"I doubt it," I say under my breath.

Daniel throws a grin my way, his eyes lit with humor.

I take the rose water, the bread and the candle and set them on the kitchen counter.

"Well, I'll be going," Fran says, "I only wanted to stop by to see how you settled in."

"Thank you, Fran. I'm good. I'm doing great."

She reaches up and pats my cheek. "Your parents might believe that, but I don't. Which is why I already made you a date for tomorrow night."

"With the playboy?" I ask, appalled. I'm not interested in the playboy.

Daniel shakes his head. "No. Nope."

"No, of course not," Fran says, zipping her purse and

putting it back on her shoulder. "With my new dentist. It's at seven tomorrow night, at Grange Tavern. His name is Tyson Greer, he's forty, divorced, and I think you'll hit it off."

With that, she folds me into another hug, and I wrap my arms around her, giving her a tight squeeze.

"One of these days, you'll meet the one," she says. "Conversation will flow. You'll click. It'll be as easy as breathing. You'll find your Kirk."

I smile at her reference. She knows me too well.

"I know," I tell her, reluctantly letting her go.

I'm reluctant because I know that when she leaves here, she'll take the train home, and even though my parents live next door, she'll still go home to an empty house, and have dinner alone, and go to sleep alone, and wake up alone.

"Thank you for coming by, and for the gifts," I say.

She pats my back, and then in a swirl of leopard print and pearls, she's gone.

After the door clicks shut I stand still in my small one-room apartment, avoiding looking at the mirrors and the man next to me.

Outside, the gusty spring wind rattles the window and speeds through the street faster than the traffic. Inside, the subtle scent of cinnamon raisin bread fills the room. Finally Daniel breaks the silence.

"Jillian?"

I swallow. "Yes?"

"Are you going to tell me why you let that woman set you up on dates you don't want to go on?"

I swing to him. "What? I want—"

He shakes his head no.

"I like—"

He shakes his head again.

"Her name's Fran," I say.

"How many dates has she set up?"

I scrape my toe over the wood floor, looking down at the crack between the planks, decades of dirt lodged there. "Maybe fifty," I mumble.

He makes a stunned noise.

"Or one hundred..." I shrug.

His makes another noise that sounds like someone punched him in the gut.

"Or one hundred and...fifty."

I look back up at him, but instead of an expression of derision or mocking laughter, he just seems upset. For me.

"Were they all as bad as the one last night?" he asks.

"No," I say quickly.

"Good."

"Some were worse," I give him a quick smile.

He's not buying my cavalier attitude. "One hundred and fifty times?"

I bite my bottom lip and calculate all the dates in the past five years. "Maybe a few more."

Definitely a few more.

"And you didn't talk during any of them?"

I shake my head. I know how bad it sounds.

"Why?" he asks. "You need to tell her to stop."

I shake my head no.

"Why?" he asks again.

"I already told you, I try because I believe that one of these days, on one of these dates, I'm going to find someone who can love me. Who sees me for who I am, who can see past my appearance—"

"You're beautiful," he growls.

"—and look past my lack of conversation—"

"You converse just fine," he argues.

"—and not care that I'm obsessed with a sci-fi show from the sixties."

"The hell with that. Live long and prosper."

I grin at him. "Are you a trekker?"

Daniel blinks at me. "No? I don't know." He shakes his head. "It doesn't matter. I like your obsession."

I smile at that. "Yes. But you're a ghost. We can't kiss, or fall in love, or have sex. If you were alive, I wouldn't be able to talk to you and you wouldn't give me a second look."

He disagrees. "You would. I would."

I shake my head. "You wouldn't. I know guys like you. You don't go for girls like me."

He steps forward then, stalking toward me across the floor. My heart jumps and I take a startled step back, the floor creaking under my feet.

"What?" I say, my hand coming up to cover the thudding in my chest.

Daniel reaches me then. I stop, hold my ground, lift my chin. He stares down at me, his eyes lit by the sunlight streaming in from the window. "Tell her to stop fixing you up."

"No," I say.

He narrows his eyes. "Why?"

"Because I don't want her to stop."

We stare at each other. Him willing me to stop, me willing him to...kiss me?

Then he lifts his hand, presses his fingers to my lips, except not, because he isn't really there.

His fingers drag across my mouth, his eyes flare, and I can't feel him, I can't feel his touch, but my heart is racing, my lips are tingling, and my mouth falls open, yielding to him.

"Dammit," he breathes.

And then, he's gone.

Disappeared.

He doesn't come back for the rest of the night.

And lying in bed, tossing in the sheets, feeling achy and hollow, I promise myself that I really, really don't care.

12

THE GRAY CHILL OF THE MORNING SHUDDERS IN, DARK clouds looming heavily, spitting cold raindrops against my umbrella.

The thwap, thwap of the rain splattering against my umbrella and the concrete matches my mood perfectly. I didn't sleep well. Not at all.

Usually on those paranormal TV shows, the hassled and haggard homeowners want the "ghosts" banished so they can get a decent night's sleep. They don't want the things that go bump in the night.

Well, I'd like a bump in the night. Although, I might be the only person alive who wants to be haunted so I can get a good night's sleep.

I shiver. The gusty April shower blows a sheet of cold misty rain over my face and down my neck. I flip up the collar of my trench coat and pull it tight, dodging around a man with an oversized umbrella. When it rains, the sidewalks become nearly impossible to navigate.

I'm on 44th Street, near my office. The sidewalk is

crowded with morning commuters shouldering past each other, umbrellas lifted up and down, high and low as we pass.

The busy morning traffic casts hissing and whooshing noises as taxis and buses run through puddles and over wet pavement. I dodge the dirty asphalt water that splashes as a garbage truck passes, and duck toward my building entrance.

My hands are cold, my nose is numb, but the strong coffee smell pumping out of the coffee shop next to my office building makes me hesitate.

I take a deep breath, ignore the smell of wet asphalt and instead concentrate on the scent of brewing dark roast.

But it's five 'til nine. If I get coffee I'll be late for the morning meeting.

"What are we doing?"

I swing my umbrella around, water drops arching out. Daniel ducks just in time, narrowly avoiding my bright red umbrella passing through his head.

I sweep my eyes over him. He doesn't look any different. His burnished golden hair is still tousled and slightly wavy. He still isn't wearing a shirt, and he still has a six-pack. And he still has that confident, happy, teasing light in his blue eyes.

The wind, the sleety rain, the cold, none of it touches him. In fact, the rain darts through him, and the wind doesn't ruffle his hair. He looks as if he's standing in his bedroom, about to tug down his low-slung jeans and make love.

Which, I'm sure, is what was happening when he died.

I smile at him. My first smile of the day.

He stands straighter when he sees my smile and tilts his head.

"Morning," he smiles back.

"Good morning," I say, rushing toward the entrance of my building. I've chosen to forgo coffee. I don't want to be late. Bernardo hates it when anyone is late.

"You missed me," Daniel says, hurrying after me.

"You think so?" I ask.

I close my umbrella, flick the water off, and then shove open the door to my building. I'm greeted by a warm draft of air and blessed dryness.

"I missed you too," Daniel says, thrusting his hands in his pockets and looking around curiously.

"Hmm," I say. I give him a skeptical look and his eyes crinkle at the corners as he gives me a slight smile.

Then he returns his attention to the lobby. It's nothing fancy. The building is only eighteen stories. It's beige brick with little square windows spaced uniformly and is the epitome of uninspired city design.

The lobby is small. It has a black runner at the door, and I stomp my feet on it and wipe off the raindrops from my coat.

Besides the runner, there's a small gray metal desk where the security guard Mike sits, checking in visitors. There's a gray plastic pot with a fake lemon tree, and another with a fake viney, wide-leafed philodendron. The lighting is dim fluorescent, the walls are beige, and the floor tile was once beige, but is now greige, from all the city dirt and grime scuffed in from years of people treading over it.

I stopped noticing the lobby years ago, but I'm seeing it again now that Daniel's here. It's nothing special. One might say it hides the genius above.

That is, if you like *The Daily Exposé*, you'd say that.

Bernardo rents the thirteenth floor for our offices. There aren't many thirteenth floors in the world. Most buildings skip from twelve to fourteen. But Bernardo scoured the city for one, because, as he says, superstition makes people stupid, and he negotiated the rent down because no one else wanted to move in.

Bernardo has one religion, and that one religion is cheapskatery. He bows down to the god of tightfistedness. It's his only flaw.

I wave to Mike at the security desk. He's known me for years, although we've never spoken. He looks up from his newspaper (not *The Exposé*), waves me on, and goes back to reading.

"Do you work here?" Daniel asks, following me to the elevator.

"Mhmm," I say quietly.

No one else is near, but still, I don't want my colleagues to think I've started talking to myself.

The elevator doors whoosh open. Daniel waits until I step inside, the door dinging, then steps on after me. I hit the button for thirteen, and when I do he lifts his eyebrows.

"So what are we going to do today?" he asks, standing casually against the paneled walls.

The elevator climbs slowly, groaning as it goes. It's one of the many tight, creaky, shaky, ancient elevators that populate the old buildings of the city. They can be terrifying at first, but you get used to them.

"I'm going to work," I tell him, casting a glance over him. "I have a meeting first thing. But I can't talk to you there. I can't answer you. It'll look crazy. So don't ask me questions."

The lights flicker and the elevator jerks. We've passed the seventh floor. The warm, closed air of the elevator is heating my skin, bringing a flush back to my cheeks.

Daniel considers my statement. "No go. You could pretend to talk on your phone. Or you could write your answers down."

We stare at each other as the elevator climbs. Debating—yes, no, yes, no.

His gaze snags on my mouth. Heat rushes over me, extinguishing the rest of the cold from the chill. He's the first to look away. A tight fist squeezes my chest.

"Alright," I agree. Then before the elevator reaches the thirteenth floor I say, "But I still don't understand why you're actually here."

"We'll figure it out," he says, full of confidence.

The elevator lurches to a stop then, jostling me toward the doors. They slide open with a squeak and I step out into the perpetual chaos of *The Daily Exposé*.

The noise and the hustle rush over us like a crashing wave.

"What is this?" Daniel asks, his expression stunned.

I grin. "Welcome to the madhouse," I say from behind my hand.

Daniel looks around, and then he laughs.

13

WHEN YOU FIRST STEP INSIDE THE OFFICES OF *THE DAILY Exposé*, you're confronted with The Wall.

The Wall is exactly what it sounds like, it's the entire back wall of our open concept office covered in flat screen TVs. It's thirty screens across and twelve screens high of non-stop-twenty-four-seven around-the-world news coverage.

That's three hundred and sixty different news stations, from every continent, from dozens of different countries, all pushing the latest, greatest news.

The volume is turned off, obviously. The noise of the office is loud enough as it is.

There's the constant clacking of keyboards, the shouting of story ideas, arguments over story angles, phone calls to sources, and the usual office banter.

As soon as you step onto the floor, you're invigorated. The only thing better for waking up in the morning is a strong cup of coffee.

The office is huge, open, and brightly lit by overhead

lights. The ceiling is high, the floors are covered in blue industrial carpet, and the walls are white. The space is furnished with randomly placed laminate conference tables for collaborating, cheap metal desks topped with laptops and desktops, and mountains of paper and stacks of old newspapers heaped on the floors, mounded under desks, and pinned to the walls.

There isn't any order, people move their desks around the office almost daily. It's almost like the room is an ocean and the desks randomly floating icebergs. My desk, a small white metal piece that Bernardo found online for five dollars, was near the back wall last week, but now it's placed closer to the elevator.

"This is an office?" Daniel asks, staring at the ping pong table covered in a pile of old newspapers.

Bernardo didn't buy it for playing ping pong, he got it because he found it free online, and he thought it'd make a good conference table.

I glance around the space. The clock over Bernardo's office (he's the only one with a private room) reads 8:58. I head toward our morning meeting spot, a large wooden table at the far end of the office, near the office kitchen.

I smell donuts and coffee. Thank goodness.

"Can't you tell?" I ask, trying to talk like a ventriloquist, without actually moving my mouth.

I'm guessing it looks either ridiculous or frightening, because Daniel flashes me a grin.

The office is bustling. Bernardo is already at the conference table. So are Hayley, Buck, and Ned. Which means I'm the last to arrive.

The four of us are the only employees on payroll, and we've all been here since either the beginning or since the first year of operation.

The techies, billing, human resources, they're all contract or freelance. That aligns with Bernardo's belief of keeping costs down.

There are a dozen interns already here, scurrying around the office, shuffling papers or making phone calls. I'm sorry to say, it's almost impossible to keep track of their names because they rotate in out and out every few weeks. Bernardo keeps the place running on interns because they are plentiful, desperate for experience, and follow his number one tenet—free.

"What's on the agenda?" Daniel asks, studying the group at the long conference table.

"Morning meeting," I say.

"Who is everyone?" he asks.

I give the quickest introduction possible, because we're nearly to the table, and Buck is watching me like he's waiting to pounce on my leg and chew it off like the feral wolverine that he is.

I glance down at a pile of newspaper stacked next to a metal filing cabinet. I pretend the top paper catches my attention, pick it up, and hold it in front of my face, blocking me from view.

"The bald guy on the right with the thick eyebrows," I say, meaning Buck, "he's in charge of local interest and business. His name's Buck Bronson, also known as Jerk Bronson. You'll see why." I peek around the paper at the table, and talking quickly say, "The blonde in the pink silk pantsuit with all the gold jewelry and the faux Chanel purse." I wait for Daniel to nod, then say, "That's Hayley Bancroft, former Miss Ohio, currently in charge of entertainment and sports."

"Alright," Daniel says, and I'm glad to see that he isn't

checking out Hayley's assets like every other man that has ever seen her for the first time.

"Last is Ned, the short, wispy-haired, jittery guy with the shaking hands. He just went through his third divorce, he's neurotic, bitter, and a die-hard conspiracy theorist. He's in charge of crime and horoscope."

Daniel lifts his eyebrows. "Really? You gave the neurotic jumpy guy the crime beat?"

I shrug, "That was Bernardo's choice." I nod toward the head of the table, still hiding behind my newspaper. "The man in charge. Bernardo Martin. Thirty-three, black hair, thin, a visionary and a collector of strays, leans toward robotic, and an utter cheapskate."

I check to see if Daniel's followed my rapid-fire introduction.

He nods, "And then there's you…"

"Short, curly-haired, perpetually single, socially awkward and in charge of the on the town feature, dating, and relationship advice," I say, wondering what Daniel thinks of us all. I smile at him. "I'm aware of the irony."

"Jillian. Let's go," Buck shouts across the room. "We need your eloquent addition to the conversation."

I drop the paper to the pile and glance at the table. Buck's the only one looking my way. Hayley's putting on lipstick. Ned's standing again, pacing back and forth nervously, probably playing out the last argument he had with his most recent ex. Bernardo's focused on his phone, probably scrolling through our numbers.

"You're right," Daniel says, watching Buck. "He is a jerk."

I nod and stride over to the long conference table.

I slip off my wet coat, hang it on the back of the chair

next to Buck, and then pull a notebook out of my purse to take notes.

"Good morning," Buck growls, baring his teeth in what he considers a smile.

I nod and smile back. I've known everyone at this table for nine years. I started working here on *The Exposé's* first issue, my freshman year of college, and then I went full-time after graduation. Everyone at this table is as much family as co-workers, which means we all know each other's quirks, and even if we don't always get along, we all have a common purpose, making *The Daily Exposé* a success. That keeps us together more tightly than the strongest glue.

Ned stops pacing when he realizes that I'm sitting down. He gives me a nervous look, then sinks down to his chair, the one on the other side of Buck.

"Don't sit," Daniel says, but it's too late. Not that Ned can hear him or heed the warning, but still, I don't have the time to stop him either.

Buck subtly kicks his foot against Ned's chair, and it scoots out from under him, just at the right moment. Instead of sitting down, Ned falls to the floor.

He hits the carpet with a hard thud. Ned blinks up at Buck, his eyes darting between the chair and Buck.

Buck though isn't looking at Ned. He's concentrating on writing the date on his legal pad. "Are we starting this meeting or what?" he asks.

Ned scrambles up and tugs his chair to the table, crashing down into it.

"I got you a coffee," Buck says, nudging a steaming white mug of cream-colored coffee toward me.

I smile a thanks at Buck and he smirks back at me. He has an identical mug of coffee closer to his legal pad.

Daniel stands close and peers down at the mug Buck gave me.

"When he looks away, switch the mugs." He moves his fingers in a loop, conveying that I do a switcheroo.

I lift an eyebrow.

"Trust me," he says, "you don't want that coffee."

I lift my shoulder in a half-shrug. But when Bernardo clears his throat to get everyone's attention, and Buck focuses on him, I quickly and discreetly switch the mugs.

Daniel grins at me. "Now we'll see. Nobody picks on my Jillian."

I grow warm, because he called me his. I drop my head and write in cursive, *thanks*.

Bernardo sets down his phone with a hard click against the table. "Ned, let's start with you. Your numbers are good. Your conversion rate is above average, your bounce rate dropped, and your read-through is the highest it's been all year. I need three long pieces this week and two short, and I need next week's horoscope. Tell me what you have."

Ned glances around the table, never settling on anyone, his eyelids twitching, his leg shaking. Hayley spins her tube of lipstick between her fingers and looks bored.

Buck smirks at Ned.

"I think..." Ned starts, then he clears his throat, shakes his leg again, the change in his pocket jingling, and then he says, "there have been fifty-two missing person cases originating in the city parks this year alone, I have evidence of...organ harvesting—"

"What?" Daniel asks, leaning toward Ned, "What does he mean organ harvesting?" He looks horrified, but also interested, albeit against his will.

I shake my head. Just wait.

"—where the reptilians are harvesting uteruses and testes to create hybrids—"

"Who? What?" Daniel asks.

I take my pen and write in my notebook *aliens*.

Daniel doesn't see it, he's too busy focusing on Ned.

"—I also have a lead that this could be a case of the military-industrial complex…" Ned looks around at us and says in a reedy voice, "Abducting humans for illegal weapons testing."

"What the…" Daniel trails off, then he narrows his eyes and looks at me, "Wait. He's the conspiracy theorist, isn't he?"

I nod and tap my pen against my notebook and the word *aliens*.

He reads it and shakes his head.

Hayley clicks her tongue. "Ned. Why would the military abduct humans when they can use animals? Animal testing is a tried and true method of experimentation. Nobody likes it, but everybody does it. It's like the tapeworm diet." Hayley says, fiddling with her tube of lipstick, which was probably tested on animals.

When there's silence, Hayley looks at each of us then says in a prim voice, "Are you objecting to animal experimentation or tapeworms?"

"Both," Daniel says.

I hide a smile.

Bernardo shakes his head. "No on the organs, no on the military Ned. What else do you have?"

Ned clears his throat and casts a nervous look at the mugs of coffee, "Last week, three people died in coffee shops around the city. I think there's a coffee…killer… targeting coffee lovers—"

"Right," Buck interrupts. "I bet. And if I drink my coffee am I going to die too?"

Buck grabs the white mug next to his legal pad and raises it for a drink, lifting it up to Ned in a swaggering toast. "Bottoms up."

Daniel leans forward an anticipatory gleam in his eyes.

Buck tips back his head and takes a large gulp, but instead of swallowing, he suddenly gags, coughs, turns to the side and sprays the coffee across the carpet.

Then he slams the coffee mug back to the table, coughs loudly, and wipes his mouth. His face is red, his eyes are watering, and beads of sweat line his forehead.

"Hot sauce," Daniel says happily.

"Buck...are you...are you..." Ned asks, his face pale, his hands shaking. But then his eyes light up. "I knew it! I knew there was a coffee killer. Vindicated! Take that, Shareen!"

Shareen is Ned's second ex-wife. She hated his conspiracy theories.

Buck shakes his head and clears his throat, wiping his watering eyes. "No. I swallowed it wrong. There's nothing wrong with my coffee."

Daniel laughs.

Bernardo taps his phone, his expression flat. His mouth hasn't twitched, he hasn't blinked, just like always, he isn't fazed by anything. "No on the coffee shop deaths. What else?"

"Telepathic—"

"No," Bernardo says.

"Subliminal subway messages that—"

"No."

"The mayor has been replaced by a lookalike from—"

"No."

Ned sighs and then shrugs, "Mugging in Riverside Park...arson fire in...Harlem...grocery robbery on twenty-fifth."

"Good. Go." Bernardo says. "Did you finish the horoscope?"

Ned tugs a crinkled paper napkin out of his pocket and squints at the scrawled words written on it. "Yeah, it says...Venus is in retrograde, your love life is dead, and your ex-wife will haunt your nightmares because she couldn't keep her hands off the delivery man's package."

"Maybe a little too specific for a horoscope," Daniel says, "but I like where he's going with it."

"No," Bernardo says.

Ned nods, "Venus is in retrograde, your love life will experience ups and downs. Wait for Mercury to rule for better communication."

"Good. Hayley, what do you have?"

Bernardo turns to Hayley, and she sits straight, brushing off an imaginary speck of lint from her pink silk sleeve.

"She likes him," Daniel says, watching Hayley.

I lift an eyebrow in question.

"Look how she's fixing her jacket and touching her hair. Look how she's positioning her body toward him and smiling. She likes him."

I write on my notepad *not a chance*.

"I'll be attending the opening of *Nights in the Hills*," Hayley says, naming the most anticipated Broadway show of the year. "I have an interview with the cast, since of course I'm invited to the after party."

I watch Bernardo, but he's as straight-faced as ever, not even flickering an eyelash. But I study Hayley too, and Daniel's right, she's leaning toward him, rubbing her blonde hair between her fingers, smiling with her eyes.

When did this happen?

"What about sports?" Bernardo asks, interrupting Hayley's rendition of all the cast members' hobbies. "The sports section brings in the most subscribers. Your conversion rate is highest there. What do you have?"

She sits back, her gaze cooling. "The same as ever. It's always the same. Basketball is scoring, swishing, and sweating. Baseball is scoring, sliding, and sweating. Football is scoring, sacking, and sweating. I'm covering it all." She waves her hand, rolling her eyes.

"Good," Bernardo says. "Buck, your numbers are average. But you aren't pulling in enough subscribers. You need to find solid stories with unique angles. I need six short articles this week, two local interest feel-good stories—"

Daniel gives me a comic look. "He does your feel-good stories?"

I hide a smile. Buck's nodding, mainly because once Bernardo starts talking, he agrees with whatever he says.

When Buck started here, he thought he was going to get the sports slot. He's a former college defensive lineman, but Hayley already had the sports position. He's been gunning (unsuccessfully) for it ever since.

Buck throws out ideas for his section, mostly consisting of gotcha pieces that make business leaders and local politicians look bad. It's his specialty. While he's talking I watch Daniel. He's walking around the room, studying the newspaper clippings on the walls and the framed awards we've received.

There's even a picture of all of us, toasting champagne for our one year anniversary. Back then, Buck wasn't such a jerk, Ned wasn't such a nervous wreck, and Hayley, well, she was the same.

"How long ago was this taken?" Daniel asks, running his hand over the photo.

I shrug, then discreetly hold up eight fingers.

"You look sad in it," he says.

I turn away from him, then realize everyone is staring at me.

I open my eyes wide and then look at Hayley.

"What?" I ask, my voice scratchy.

She tilts her chin toward Bernardo.

Slowly I turn in my chair and face Bernardo, opening my eyes wide, feigning ignorance. Apparently I tuned out an important bit of the conversation. And by the look on Bernardo's face I'm pretty sure I know what it was.

"It's bad, Jillian," he says.

Daniel walks over, stands next to me, his brow furrowed. "What's bad? What's he talking about?"

"You have a ten percent unsubscribe rate per every article read. Last week we received thirty-seven email complaints about your article on speed dating. Here's a quote." He holds up his phone and reads in a flat, factual voice, "Ms. Nejat lives in a delusional fantasy world where pigs fly and everyone wears rose-colored glasses. Get rid of her." And another," Bernardo says, "this is from a woman who unsubscribed, 'I married my husband based on your advice, and he turned out to be a cheating prick. How can you call yourself a relationship expert? Unsubscribed.' As of last month, we are losing money every time you write an article. Your conversion rate is abysmal. Your negative comment rate is high. You..." Bernardo finally looks up from his phone and glances at me, his jaw softens when he sees my face. "You..." He sighs then and shakes his head.

Bernardo was there nine years ago when everything went to hell. He was there and he picked me up and gave me a purpose and a place to belong.

Just like he helped Ned after his first divorce when he was a wreck. And how he took Buck in even though he'd been through anger management courses four times and couldn't find a job anywhere else.

And he hired Hayley, even though she had no experience, and they met because she was trying to sell him a fake Rolex one night on the subway.

My shoulders drop. I know what he wants to say, and I know he's not going to say it.

"Is he going to fire you?" Daniel asks, looking between Bernardo and me. "Are your articles really that bad? Do people hate them that much?"

I shrug, my throat tight. The office feels cold suddenly, the dry chill air running over my still rain-damp skin. I run my finger over the wooden edge of the table then clasp my hands in my lap.

Bernardo is quiet, waiting for me to say something, even though he knows I won't.

"Jillian," Bernardo finally says, "you need to stop writing articles and advice columns telling people that they'll find their 'one true love' if they just keep being themselves. They hate it. You may believe it, it may sound good on paper, but I have the statistics here, and people hate it."

"Because it isn't true," Ned says, jostling his leg nervously. "Ask my ex-wives. They all hated me when I was myself."

"I don't know, people love me," Buck says, leaning back in his chair and folding his arms behind his head.

"We could trade," Hayley says, perking up.

I shake my head no. I may be in a slump, but I love what I do. It's important, it's necessary, it's...

"If Hayley gets relationships, I get sports. Are you canning Jillian?" Buck asks, eyeing the mug of coffee he gave me suspiciously. "If you want my opinion, I always thought it was moronic to have the awkward geek who can't talk to men write relationship advice. No offense, Jillian."

I ignore him and watch Bernardo. It's his decision. I've known for a few months now that my job has been on the line. Nobody wants to hear that they should be their authentic selves and love will find them. They want to know what they need to change, who they need to become, or what they need to do. And sometimes I agree with them, but then I remind myself what's at stake.

Daniel snaps his fingers, "I've got it," he says. I look over at him and he nods, "I've got it. This is why I'm here. I'm supposed to help you. You're no good on dates, I'll help you. Your articles are failing, I'll help you. Once you find the man you're supposed to be with and your job is secure, then my job will be done and I'll..."

He stops, not saying *move on*.

His mouth tightens and a distant look enters his eyes, but then he says, "We'll fix everything. We'll do it together."

I nod then look back to Bernardo. He's watching me, his expression flat, but I know there's concern there, hidden behind the façade. "Can you do it, Jillian?" he asks. "Can you turn this around? I can give you a month. I can't afford any more than that though."

Everyone turns to look at me.

Can I do it? Can I give relationship advice that people will love? Can I write dating articles they will want to read? Can I fix my own life?

"You can," Daniel says firmly, "We can. This is why I'm here. I know it. Say yes, Jillian."

I look at Ned, Hayley, Buck, and Bernardo.

Then I look at Daniel, standing at the end of the table, urging me to say yes.

So I do.

"Yes."

Yes.

Daniel grins at me, a happy light in his eyes. I'm saying yes to Daniel and me.

"Good. We're counting on you," Bernardo says.

By which he means, if I don't turn things around in a month, I'm out of a job.

"We've got this," Daniel says. "Don't worry."

At his words a niggle starts in the pit of my stomach. And I realize I'm not worried about whether or not we've got this, I'm worried about the fact that if this really is why Daniel's here, then when we succeed, he'll be gone.

Forever gone.

14

GRANGE TAVERN LIES NESTLED IN THE SHADOW OF THE Brooklyn Bridge, a squat, brick building brimming with the smells of fried fish and frothy beer, the sounds of raucous conversation, and the heat of ovens and fryers working overtime in a tight space.

It's a wood, brass, and mirror kind of tavern, with black and white photos of famous patrons pinned to the mirror behind the bar, and a ragged ambience of tattered pride. The main draw to the tavern is the fact that sitting presidents sometimes eat here, the view of the water and the Manhattan skyline is unsurpassed, and they host live music every night.

It's the perfect setting for a casual blind date. At least, that's what Fran must've thought when she arranged for me to meet her new dentist.

I rub my hands down my thighs, smoothing out my navy blue knee-length dress. The fabric hugs my curves, the neckline dips low enough for a hint of cleavage to show, and the silver belt adds sophistication.

I wouldn't have worn it, but Daniel pointed it out in my closet and said, "This one's nice."

And then, when I came out of the bathroom, with my hair curled, lipstick on, and my hands nervously smoothing down the fabric of the dress, Daniel gave me that shocked stupid look again. So instead of changing into my usual date outfit (trekkie t-shirt, cardigan and jeans or a skirt) I kept the dress on and added a silver charm bracelet and a pair of black high heels.

But looking at the scuffed wood, the beer foam sloshed on the floor of the tavern, and breathing in the fried grease, I'm not so sure about the dress anymore. I'm a lot overdressed.

"Alright," Daniel says, rubbing his hands together and glancing around the tavern.

There's the bar, with shelves of liquor, a dozen beers on tap, and two dozen square wooden tables scrunched together.

A gangly teenager plucks at his guitar, standing near the windows overlooking the water. Every table is full and I run my eyes over the diners, trying to find Tyson Greer the dentist.

Near the windows, a tall man with closely shaved brown hair and eyes that droop like a sad hound dog's stands and holds his hand up to me in a brisk wave.

"That's him," Daniel says. He frowns at Tyson then looks over at me. "We're good, right? You're ready?"

I nod, taking a deep breath, and fighting to calm the rolling in my stomach. Daniel and I worked out a strategy earlier today. Since I haven't had any luck going about dating my way, then I'm going to date Daniel's way.

Which means I'll be taking cues from Daniel, and if I

can, I'll be answering Tyson's questions by answering Daniel when he asks me the same question.

"I'm ready," I say, swallowing down my nerves. I smile and wave at Tyson, then say under my breath to Daniel, "I'm still going to be myself though. I won't change or pretend to be someone I'm not."

Daniel gives me a surprised look. "I wouldn't want you to be anyone else."

"Good," I say, then I stride forward, weaving through the tightly spaced tables, avoiding people's elbows, pushed out chairs, and waiters carrying trays full of beer and baskets of fried fish and French fries.

When I reach Tyson, he steps forward and holds out his hand, "Jillian?"

He's nearly as tall as Daniel, but instead of having the lounging grace that Daniel has, he stands as if he's balancing a book on top of his head, and moves with controlled precision. By the navy blue blazer, the Phi Beta Kappa key pinned discreetly to his blazer pocket, and his striped red and gray tie, I'd say that Tyson doesn't let loose very often.

I nod and clasp his hand in mine. He has a firm grip.

"Nice to meet you," he says in a deep baritone. "I've heard a lot about you."

"I've heard a lot about you," Daniel says, repeating Tyson's words so I can respond, but then he continues with laughter in his eyes, "I've heard you like cinnamon raisin bread and coffee with ten teaspoons of sugar, feather dusting your trekkie collectibles obsessively, and writing award-winning articles. It's a pleasure to meet you."

I widen my eyes at Daniel and repress a smile. He's standing just to the left of Tyson, closer to the windows.

"Thank you," I say, ducking my head. "It's nice to meet you too."

Tyson lets go of my hand and then strides around the table to pull out my chair. I smile at him and he helps me take off my coat, then gestures to my chair. I drop into the old wooden café style seat and then Tyson scoots it in.

I dart a quick glance at Daniel. He's watching Tyson, his head tilted to the side, as if he's working on cataloguing everything that Tyson does and says. He's taking his role seriously.

Tyson sits down across from me and then clears his throat and leans forward. "This is my first blind date. I don't know how much Fran told you about me?"

I lift a shoulder, biting my lip.

"What did Fran say?" Daniel asks.

"Just that you're a dentist," I say to Daniel.

He smiles. "I don't think I am."

Tyson nods. "I am. I divorced last year. I'm not interested in a fling—"

"Are you?" Daniel asks me, and he seems genuinely curious.

"No. Neither am I," I say.

Daniel smiles warmly. "I didn't think so."

"I'm looking for a partner I respect," Tyson says over the guitar music, a cover of a pop song.

I nod at him. I'm looking for a partner I respect too.

Tyson continues, "Fran said you're shy and you don't talk much. That doesn't matter to me. I'm a dentist. Half my life is spent with the people I interact with not talking because my tools are in their mouth. I suppose you could say, I like it that way."

Tyson pauses, and I think he's waiting for my response so I nod.

Daniel flashes me a disbelieving look. "His tool is not going anywhere near your mouth."

I cough and then cover my mouth with my hand.

"Stop nodding," Daniel says, crossing his arms over his chest.

I smother another laugh.

Tyson leans forward, his mouth turning down. "Are you alright?"

I nod, and cough again.

"Jillian," Daniel says, narrowing his eyes. "It's a no. We're done with Fran's fix-ups. Let's go."

I discreetly roll my eyes at Daniel. He's overreacting. Tyson wasn't actually making an innuendo, I don't think he'd recognize an innuendo if it clobbered him on the head.

Besides, how am I supposed to succeed at my job and my love life if I don't *try*?

Daniel scowls when he realizes that I'm not going to get up and leave. "We could go back to your place and watch *The Voyage Home*," he says.

"I'm fine," I say to Daniel, but also to Tyson.

Although going home is tempting because *The Voyage Home* is one of my favorites, and somehow Daniel knows it. Probably because I have the framed movie poster leaning against my bookshelf.

Tyson sits back in his seat and then grabs the plastic menu leaning against the napkin holder. "Let's order a fish platter to share, a side of mushy peas, and two pilsners. Sound good?"

He barely looks at me to make sure I nod, before motioning over the waitress to place our order.

"Is that what you wanted to eat? Mushy peas?" Daniel asks, reading the menu over Tyson's shoulder. "Jillian, they have a bacon burger with chipotle aioli"—his eyes roll up toward the ceiling as if he's having some sort of food ecstasy moment—"and parmesan bacon fries. Why are you getting mushy peas when you can have bacon?"

Daniel looks at me as if he's actually pained by the prospect of me choosing mashed green goop over crispy bacon.

"I can't smell, I can't taste, I'm not hungry, but I have to be honest, it would make my night to watch you eat that bacon burger. Vicarious eating. It would be so good. I loved bacon..." He pauses and thinks about this, his forehead wrinkling. "At least, I think I loved bacon."

Tyson is finishing up our order, and the waitress is writing it down on her pad, but at the wistful look on Daniel's face I say to the waitress, "I'm sorry, actually, can I also get the bacon burger with bacon fries?"

Daniel grins at me. "You are the greatest person alive."

"You want two entrees?" Tyson asks, cocking his head and casting a censorious look my way.

"Is that it?" the waitress asks, her pen held high, waiting.

"The chocolate brownie and the triple chocolate shake," Daniel says, looking up from the menu, and then when he sees my expression of near denial he says, "Please?"

I hide my smile. I suppose if this date goes south, at least the food will be good, and Daniel will get to eat vicariously through me.

The waitress taps her pen against her menu pad, so I quickly say, "And the chocolate brownie and the triple chocolate shake."

Tyson frowns, shaking his finger at me. "I wouldn't advise sugar. The deleterious effect on tooth enamel far outweighs any pleasure you may receive." He says the word "pleasure" as if he doubts I'll get very much.

"Don't listen to him, Jillian. You deserve chocolate. You deserve pleasure. You like chocolate, don't you?" Daniel sounds so much like a devil sitting on my shoulder tempting me and coaxing me toward vice that I almost laugh.

"I love chocolate," I agree.

"It's not a good idea," Tyson says. "You shouldn't exceed more than six teaspoons of sugar per day. I'm quite passionate about this actually. Tooth decay is a critical health risk."

The waitress shrugs and scratches my order on her pad and drops the paper into her apron.

"Fifteen minutes," she says over her shoulder as she hurries back toward the kitchen.

Tyson stares after the waitress, then tugs on his tie, the knot tight around his neck.

"I suppose," he says dryly, letting go of his tie, and turning to me, "if you get a cavity, I could give you a discount on the drilling and filling."

I let out a startled laugh and Tyson cracks a smile.

"I'm going to be honest," he says, tugging on his tie again, "I'm nervous. This is my first date since my ex-wife and I divorced. It takes a lot of courage to get out there again, but Fran convinced me that you're worth it."

Tyson holds my gaze for a moment, his expression searching. I drop my eyes to the scratched and scuffed wooden table, my throat tight and my chest clenching.

This is where I'm supposed to say something, anything.

But I can't, and the only noise is the teenager on the

guitar plucking out a pop song, and the conversations swirling around us.

Tyson's waiting for my response.

But instead of answering, I shove my chair back and stand abruptly, desperate to flee. I look at Daniel, he's alert, concerned.

"What is it?" he asks.

"I have to go the bathroom." I nod toward the back of the tavern.

Tyson stands, "Take your time."

I rush through the crowded tavern, avoiding tripping over a purse on the floor, and then push into the single stall bathroom and lock the door. The noise from the restaurant grows muted, the only sound is the slow drip of the leaky faucet and the hum of the overhead fan.

My breath is tight in my chest, and the chemical floral bathroom deodorizer is suffocating.

I take in heaving breaths and stare at my pale face in the mirror, my bright red, lush lips stark against my skin.

I'm shaky, and the white walls, the cracked tile floor, and the flickering fluorescent light, don't calm me. I flip on the faucet and run my hands under the ice-cold water, then splash it over the back of my neck.

"Jillian?" It's Daniel, he's come in through the door, his eyes closed. "You wanted to talk?"

"You can open your eyes," I say.

The bathroom is tiny, maybe four feet by four feet, and most of the space is taken up by the toilet and the ceramic pedestal sink. Daniel and I are so close we could be dancing.

Daniel takes a close look at my face, pale from nerves, and the shaking of my hands.

"What happened?" he asks quietly.

"I can't do it," I say, shaking my head and staring down at the cracked tiles. "Even with you here. I can't do it."

I know I've done it more than a hundred times before, over and over again, but this time, it's different. Harder.

Daniel is quiet for so long that I finally look back up again. The expression in his eyes makes me take a quick step back and I bump into the cold ceramic sink. His gaze holds understanding, compassion, empathy.

"You don't have to stay," he says quietly. "You don't have to." He shrugs, "I won't mind missing my bacon burger and chocolate shake, if you don't mind it." He gives me a regretful smile. "If you stay, I'll stay. If you go, I'll go. It's your choice."

"Thank you," I say.

He puts his hand over mine, resting it there, and suddenly I feel stronger and steadier. I look down at his hand, and even though I can't feel him, my heart beats faster.

"I want to stay," I finally say. "I just need a minute."

"Do you really think he's the one for you?" Daniel asks, staring at his hand resting on mine.

I shake my head. "I don't know. I always want someone to look beyond their first impression of me, to look beneath the surface. I'll do the same for him."

Daniel pulls his hand away and grins at me. "Why didn't you ever give me that chance? You thought I was a Lothario from the first and nothing will change your mind."

"Aren't you one?" I ask, lifting an eyebrow.

Daniel shrugs. "Probably. Who knows?"

"I don't mind if you are," I tell him. "I like you. I like you a lot."

He smiles at me, his eyes warm. "Thanks. I like you too." Then he nods at the door to the bathroom, "Alright. Let's go. And when you eat that bacon burger, really enjoy it, okay?"

I wink at him. "I will. For you."

And that's why the date with Tyson isn't half bad. I relish the burger, the bun is freshly baked and soft, the burger is juicy and charred, the bacon is crispy and smoky, and the aioli has the perfect hint of spice.

It's so good that I close my eyes with each bite, and then I lick the juice from my fingers.

Daniel stands in front of the window, backlit by the setting sun shining over the golden hued river and reflecting off the silver skyscrapers.

He watches me, at first with laughter in his eyes sparking every time I make a sound of enjoyment, but then his humor fades and is replaced by a look of deep hunger.

I flush when I catch the needy, hungry look in his eyes. He may be dreaming about eating a bacon burger and fries, or he may be remembering that moment he reached out and traced his fingers over my lips.

Because he looks the same as he did then.

I look away from him and take a long drink of the triple chocolate shake.

Tyson stops talking and sets the piece of fried cod he was eating down on his plate. He's been telling me about the new innovations in dental implants and how he recently went to a conference in Lisbon.

"Do you enjoy travel?" he asks, scraping his fork across the mushy peas, which honestly look like a mound of gray-green slime.

At the question, Daniel wakes up from his erotic food

dream, he shakes himself off and comes to my rescue. "I wonder, where would you go, if you could go anywhere in the world?"

I send him a grateful smile and say, looking down at my nearly finished burger and golden crisp fries, "I'd love to go to Riverside, Iowa."

"The future birthplace of Captain Kirk," Daniel says nodding, and I do all I can to hide my shock. He's a trekker, there's no doubt about it.

"What would you do there?" Daniel asks.

I smile, thinking about it, "I'd just want to sit there and soak it all in. I've never been. I guess I've been waiting for a special reason to go." Or a special person to go with.

I imagine sitting in the grass near Captain Kirk's plaque, the sun shining down on me, warming my face, the grass soft, a bee buzzing past to settle on the hostas planted beneath the plaque stating the birthdate of Captain Kirk—March 22.

I can feel the soft breeze, clouds flitting by trailing shadows over me, and then I look to my right, so I can see the person who came with me.

Always before, I thought Serena and I would go together. But this time, when I see the person next to me, it's Daniel. He's lounging in the grass, the wind ruffles his hair, the sun lights on his skin, and when I reach over to take his hand, he's solid and warm.

"You'd go to Iowa?" Tyson asks, his voice tight and disbelieving. "Not Lisbon, or Tokyo, or Rome? *Iowa*?"

I glance quickly at him, shaking out of my imaginings.

I nod. Yes. Iowa.

Tyson frowns.

"I'll go with you," Daniel says. Then he thinks about

it, "If I can. I don't know if I can leave New York. Huh." He looks disturbed by that thought.

To be honest, I'm disturbed by it too. The dream of holding his hand in Riverside, Iowa completely vanishes, as if it never was.

I take a long drink of my triple chocolate shake, the sweet, cold ice cream numbing my mouth.

"What do you like to do in your spare time? Any hobbies?" Tyson asks, moving on from the travel topic.

I look over at Daniel. "What do you want to do tonight?" he asks, "We can do whatever you want."

"Watch old sci-fi," I say, "I love them."

"Why? What do you love about them?" Daniel asks, tilting his head.

"Really," Tyson says, he dips a torn piece of fried fish into the mushy peas and scrapes it back and forth.

I think about the reason I fell in love with science fiction, all the way back in junior high.

"I like it because it has so much hope for humanity," I tell Daniel, although I look at my shake and fiddle with the straw. "There isn't another genre that has so much hope. I mean, there's the morality tales, and dire warnings of course, but there's also hope. For instance, when we were in the depths of the Cold War, when peace seemed a million light years away, the creators of *Star Trek* brought in a Russian main character, which perfectly illustrated the unending, irrepressible belief that humanity would have peace. That peace would prevail. The belief in the strength of the human spirit is inspiring. I really love it."

I look up then and catch the expression on Daniel's face.

"You're incredible," he says, looking into my eyes as if he can see me, and he likes what he sees.

I flush and shift under the weight of his gaze.

"I don't care for sci-fi," Tyson says, frowning at my milkshake, "I don't see the appeal. To me, it's just a load of tin foil hats, lasers, and silly outfits. It seems like the people that like sci-fi refuse to grow up and enter the real world." He takes his napkin out of his lap and lays it over his plate. "I prefer living my own life, traveling to places myself, rather than watching someone else do it. Vicarious living isn't really living, is it? It's not living at all."

I stare at Tyson, unable to look at Daniel. A hot, prickly blush creeps up my cheeks. *Vicarious living isn't living.*

"I mean," Daniel says in a slow drawl, "I have to say, *vicariously*, that was the best damn burger I've ever not eaten."

I bite my bottom lip and repress the laugh bubbling up in my chest.

"And the shake, it was the Sistine Chapel of chocolate shakes. You can't touch or lick the chapel, but you can look, you can imagine, and when you do, it's pure heaven."

I make a small noise, half-choke, half-laugh, and say, "I know what you mean."

Tyson nods, assessing me. "I suppose you do."

"Thanks, Jillian," Daniel says, "if I didn't mention it, thank you for dinner."

I give a small nod and smile, looking at Daniel from the corner of my eyes.

Tyson flags down the waitress, motioning for our bill. Then he gives me a tight smile and says over the music and the conversations rumbling around us, "I like being direct, so I'm going to tell you, I don't think we have much in common. I'm physically attracted to you, but I don't think that's enough for a relationship. We could drag this out for a few more dates, see where it goes, but..."

He waits for my response.

"Jillian," Daniel says, his voice low, "do you want to drag this out?"

"No thank you," I say. "I don't think it'll work out."

"Agreed," Daniel says.

"I agree," Tyson says, mirroring Daniel's statement. Then he takes the bill from our waitress. When he glances at it he hands it back to her with a shake of his head. "We need the bill split, make sure to include half the fish and chips on her bill. Thanks." He looks back at me, "Philosophically, I'm a feminist. I never pay for dates." He adjusts the sleeves of his blazer. "It's one thing my ex and I always agreed on. At the end we didn't agree on anything else, but we agreed on that. Fifty-fifty."

I nod. Okay. Fair enough.

"Sorry, Jillian," Daniel says. "If I had money, I'd pay for my burger you ate. And the shake."

"It's okay," I tell him.

"I thought so," Tyson says.

And that is the end of the date.

As we're walking back to the subway, the sun down and the lights of the buildings shining down on us, I tell Daniel, "I feel bad about that date."

"Why?" he asks. "Which part?"

I think about the odd feeling that came and went during the date, and then put it into words. "It felt wrong, the fact that you were there and Tyson didn't know it. It felt sort of Cyrano de Bergerac, and you know, that never works out the way it's supposed to..." I trail off, avoiding looking over at Daniel.

The headlights of a taxi slash through him and light up the night. Across the street a group of rowdy men pour out of a brightly lit bar, laughing boisterously.

"Anyway, it felt untruthful. I don't ever want to be dishonest. That's not a great way to start a relationship. Although, what am I supposed to say? Hey, there's a ghost here with us and I'm talking to him too." I look away, walking more quickly.

Daniel keeps pace, stepping onto the crosswalk with me, heading toward the glowing lights of the subway entrance. The wind tugs at my curls and yanks at the collar of my coat. I pull my collar tight against the cold, buttoning it tight.

"It wasn't dishonest," Daniel says, his voice quiet.

"I don't know," I say.

"Jillian, it wasn't. I'm only helping you express who you are. And when you come across the right guy, you won't need me anymore. This isn't *Cyrano* because in *Cyrano*, he always gets the girl, and you ending up with me, that's impossible. It's a tragedy not a romance. I don't have a future. I just have this moment, helping you. That's not dishonest. You need my help now, but you won't always. You won't always need me. There's nothing untruthful about that."

He stops, and I grab the railing of the stairs and take the steps leading down to the subway, the warmth of the tunnel circling me.

I look back up at him, standing in the dark, fading a bit around the edges. A couple walks past him, the man stepping through him, not even realizing he's there.

Daniel flinches as the man passes through him.

The couple walks around me.

Down below, the windy, whooshing noise of an approaching train fills the tunnel. The cold metal railing vibrates in my hand.

The feeling I had at the tavern dissipates, Daniel's right. I'm still me, Daniel's just helping other people see me too. That's honesty.

I lift my fingers to Daniel and say, "Alright. I see what you mean. Are you coming then? You promised we'd watch *The Voyage Home*."

He smiles at me then, wide enough that his dimple winks at me. He walks down the stairs, and I notice for the first time that his feet don't quite touch the steps.

"I can't remember," he says. "Is it good?"

Is my favorite movie good?

"Better than good," I promise.

He takes this in and then says with a wide smile, "That's what I like to hear."

15

I'M SLIDING MY KEY INTO MY FRONT DOOR WHEN MY PHONE rings.

"Hi Fran," I say, cradling the phone between my ear and my shoulder and pushing my door open.

"How was it?" she asks, loudly enough for Daniel to hear.

She's always been a loud phone talker. I remember playing video games in her floral and chintz living room when I was a kid, her talking on her kitchen phone so loudly it was like I was standing next to her.

I flip on the lights in my apartment, the Liberace candelabra casting a golden glow over the mirrors.

Daniel steps into the apartment after me and gives me a questioning look. Apparently he's waiting to hear what I tell Fran.

"It went...okay," I say, glancing at Daniel.

He gives me a sardonic look, then walks toward my bookshelf full of memorabilia, collectibles, and autographed swag.

Fran clicks her tongue. "I thought he was virile. Wasn't he virile?"

Daniel swings back around halfway to the bookshelf, his shoulders stiffening, the muscles on his abdomen tightening.

He raises his eyebrows. "Virile?"

Virile, meaning strength, energy, and a strong sex drive.

I remember the psychic, Zelda, calling Daniel lover boy and telling him to tone down his horny vibrations. I think about the way Daniel watched me tonight with needy hunger. I remember how he dragged his fingers over my lips after he called me beautiful.

I look Daniel in the eye and say, "No. I didn't think so. He wasn't my type."

The corner of Daniel's lips lift into a smile. Then he turns and heads to the bookshelf, his shoulders relaxed and his stride loose.

I stare after him as he bends down and studies the models on the lower shelves, his head tilted and his hair falling over his brow and dusting his chin.

I never thought I'd like the look of a man with sun-kissed hair that's wavy and long enough to brush his collar if he wore a shirt. But I've revised my opinion. I like it a lot.

It's *virile*.

I wonder what his hair feels like. Is it soft? When I rub it between my fingers, would it feel like warm silk sheets, or soft sea water whispering over my hands.

I shake my head. He's a ghost, Jillian. Ghosts aren't virile. Ghosts can't be felt.

Fran gives a long, considering sigh and mulls over my response.

"I think," she says finally, "medical professionals are not for you. You never liked Bones," she says, mentioning the doctor from the original *Star Trek*. "Scientists are okay. Teachers, maybe? Or hmmm, I met a trash artist today rummaging through the dumpster outside the grocery store. He was fascinating. He makes sculptures from trash. His last piece made from plastic milk jugs sold for ten thousand dollars. It was a cow, with working udders."

Daniel looks over his shoulder. "We'll find your next date."

Fran's still talking, "I think the problem is I've been looking in the wrong place. This trash to treasure idea is appealing. Ever since this year began I've had a feeling, Jillian. A feeling that something marvelous is coming. That wonderful things are on their way. Have you ever felt this way? That good things are coming?"

"Maybe," I say, watching Daniel.

"I have this anticipation that any day now you'll meet the right man, you'll marry, and I'll be able to spoil your little ones. I can almost touch it, that's how real it feels. I'm doubling down, Jilly. Even if your parents would be fine with you remaining single until you're seventy, I'm not. I have the trash artist's number. I'll set up a date for this weekend. He's very artistic, very broody, very manly. His beard is thick, that means he has a lot of testosterone."

Daniel shakes his head no.

But is that a no on the testosterone or a no on the date?

"No on the date," he says, apparently reading my mind.

"Just a minute, Fran," I say, then I mute the phone. "Why?" I ask Daniel. "You're being picky."

"I'm not being picky, I'm being practical. We'll pick your dates from now on. Fran is zero for one hundred and fifty-something."

He's right. I know he's right. Although I don't think it's actually Fran's fault that I never make it to a second date. The fault has always been with me.

I unmute the phone. "Fran? I'm going to pass on the date."

"What?" she says, her voice high with surprise. I've never turned down one of her dates. "But Jilly, didn't you hear what I said? Something momentous is coming, I just know it. One of these dates, someday soon..." She pauses, and then says more slowly and in a quiet trembling voice, "Is this...are you giving up again? Are you considering—"

"No," I say quickly. "No. Never. No, Fran."

She sighs. "I see. You're okay?"

"I'm okay," I promise.

Daniel's watching me with a strange look on his face as if he's trying to decipher the subtext of my conversation, but he can't, and it's frustrating him.

"So you don't want the trash artist, but what about a photographer?" she asks, perking up again.

I shake my head. "No, actually, I'm planning on finding my own dates for a bit. I think it's time I"—I shrug and reach for a cliché—"spread my wings."

"Spread your wings?" Fran repeats, sounding intrigued. "You mean talk to men? You're talking to men? Who? When?"

Daniel studies me, waiting for my response.

I bite my bottom lip and look around my apartment,

at my bed on the red shag carpeting, my white couch, and the walls of mirrors, reflecting me and no one else.

"You talk to me," Daniel says finally, shoving his hands into his pockets.

"I am talking to a man," I admit.

Fran gasps, and then I hear a crack and the shattering of glass.

"Sorry," she gushes, "Sorry. That excited me so much I dropped my cup of ice coffee on the kitchen floor. Darn. What a mess. Never mind that, you're talking to a man? A real man? An actual man? A *man* man? Who is it? You haven't spoken to a man in years. Marry him. Make babies with him. Bring him back to your mirrored sex apartment and eff-you-see-kay his brains out. Don't let him get away."

I flush at Fran's response. It's embarrassing for Daniel to witness it.

With great effort, I slowly lift my eyes from the floor and meet Daniel's gaze. My cheeks burn and I mouth, "Sorry."

He lifts a shoulder. "I'd marry you, but I don't think the state recognizes unions between the living and the dead. Plus, there wouldn't be any fucucking."

He has to be joking, not about the sex obviously, but about the marrying.

"He's not a real man," I tell Fran.

"Thanks, Jillian," Daniel says dryly. "My ego is crushed."

"What does that mean?" Fran asks, "If he has a pulse and is over eighteen and below eighty, then I'd say he'd do the job."

"Well, that does disqualify me," Daniel says. "Shame, I was looking forward to a spoooooky wedding."

I snort at the humor in his voice. "He doesn't meet those requirements," I tell Fran, and then quickly say, to avoid any further questions, "the point is, I'm gaining confidence and I don't need you to set me up anymore." I can almost feel Fran's confusion through the phone, so I add, "If it doesn't work, I'll tell you."

"It'll work," Daniel says, all confidence.

After that, Fran hangs up to clean up the broken glass in the kitchen, and I pull off my coat and change into a long t-shirt for pajamas, making Daniel turn his back and close his eyes while I do.

Then I settle on my faux-leather white couch and pull my gray fuzzy blanket over my legs. I lean against the couch pillows and then turn on the TV, pulling up *The Voyage Home*.

"Are you sure you're comfortable like that for the whole movie?" I ask Daniel, glancing up at where he's casually standing next to the couch. I've dimmed the lights, and the soft glow of the TV screen shines through him.

"I don't get tired," he says.

The opening scene begins, filling the dark room with the shifting stars of the universe and the sound of trumpets rolling over an orchestra.

"Are you sure?" I ask, "You don't sleep, you don't eat, you don't rest. You could try sitting?"

"Jillian?" Daniel says.

"Yes," I ask, looking at him with concern.

He smirks at me, "Be quiet. I'm trying to watch your favorite movie."

So I hug my knees to myself, wrap my blanket around me, and stay warm and cozy as the familiar credits play over the screen.

"If you don't like it, lie to me and say you do," I tell him.

He laughs. "I never lie. If I don't like it, I'll tell you."

Before the movie begins, I ask one more question, "So when I asked where you went when you aren't with me, you really don't know?"

He shakes his head, then points to the black of the screen, filled with tiny pinpoints of starlight. "It's a lot like that. There's nothing, or there's you. There's darkness and a single point of light. All I have to do to come back to you is think about you, and I'm here."

"But what about the first time?" I ask. "You didn't know me."

Daniel frowns at me, thoughts racing behind his eyes.

"I did though," he says with quiet conviction.

I think that's something we'll always disagree on. I never met Daniel until the second he popped into existence in this very apartment.

The opening scene begins, and we settle into a warm silence, but instead of falling into the action, I remain tense and aware of the man standing next to me, feeling his every move and his every sound.

But finally, fatigue cradles me, and I fall asleep, tucked under my blanket, the light of the TV flickering over me, the sound of Kirk's and Daniel's laughter merging, pulling me under into a deep, dark sleep, filled with a single bright light, far, far away.

16

THE FLICKERING OF THE WALL AND ITS CONSTANT NEWS coverage pulses across the office, infusing the early afternoon with bright colorful light.

I rub my forehead and try to ignore the rumbling of my stomach. The carton of peach yogurt and cup of coffee from this morning are a distant memory, the only lingering trace is the subtle hint of coffee and sugar left in my empty mug.

Daniel casually faux-leans against my small metal desk, now positioned near the ping pong table. Someone must've moved it overnight, probably Hayley, since her desk is now where mine was, and is buried under a mountain of fake Coach purses. She receives shipments here all the time, and there's a constant rotation of knock-off products she's turning a profit on.

Her business sense is so acute, her ability to bargain so fine-tuned, that I once watched in awe as she convinced a stodgy CEO to buy a ratty old lamp she found on the sidewalk for a thousand dollars—because the lamp was "vintage found-art."

Years ago, Hayley legend goes, that when Bernardo turned down the fake Rolex she was peddling, she bargained a job offer out of him instead.

"It's genuine leather," Hayley says, trying to sell Ned one of the purses.

She holds the black leather bag out to him, running her manicured hand over the surface like a model in an infomercial.

"Then why is genuine spelled with a j?" Ned asks, his eyes darting nervously between Hayley and the purses. "Did you scan the shipment for bugs? All frequencies?"

Hayley drops the purse on top of her desk. "Why would there be roaches in my purses. I only buy quality, genuine, top-of-the-line, one-of-a-kind, limited-supply—"

"Bugs," Ned whispers, eyes wide. "They're tracking you through your purchases."

"Roaches aren't that intelligent," Hayley says disdainfully. "If you're not going to buy one, just say so. I'm on a deadline."

Daniel grins down at me. After only a half day at the office, he's decided that he loves it here. I already bought one of Hayley's purses. I haggled her down to twelve dollars, which only succeeded because when I threw the number out, Bernardo walked out of the elevator and Hayley was so flustered that she agreed.

"Is it always like this?" Daniel asks, his amusement growing over the argument that Ned and Hayley are now having about the bugs in her purses.

I glance at them and then at two interns tossing a ping pong ball back and forth, Bernardo on the phone in his office, and at our IT people frantically pounding on their keyboards because Buck clicked on a link in an email this morning and now a virus is on our server, redirecting all of our outbound links to a video of two dolphins having sex. They promise it'll be fixed by five. Anyway, it's mayhem. But is it always mayhem?

"Yeah," I tell Daniel. "Pretty much."

The elevator doors squeak open and Buck stomps out carrying a bulging take-out bag from Fratelli's Pizza that smells like garlic knots and heaven. The scent wafts to me as he storms past, his bald head red, his brown off-the-rack-suit wrinkled, and his wide shoulders bunched.

I have no idea how someone can look so angry when they have a bag full of happiness. Buck sees me staring and pauses on his way past my desk.

He lifts up the take-out bag. "I got these garlic knots because I know you love 'em."

Daniel narrows his eyes, leaning forward in a way that if Buck could see him, would make him stop talking.

"You eaten lunch yet?" Buck asks, shaking the bag and letting it emit garlicky wonderfulness.

I shake my head no and my stomach gives a rumble.

Buck chuckles, "Good. Then it'll be that much better when I eat them all in front of you."

"This guy," Daniel says.

I shrug a shoulder.

Daniel turns back to Buck and waves his hand in front of him. "Hey. Listen up. First, you need to treat people better. Everything you give out comes back to you tenfold. Act right. Second, no one is watching you eat. No one is eating vicariously through you. No one. Alright? Clear?"

I bite my tongue and restrain a smile. Buck has no

idea that he's receiving a lecture from a morally outraged ghost. Apparently Daniel is very protective of me, and also of who gets to eat vicariously with me.

"I'll miss you when you're fired. You're more fun than the rest of these fools," Buck says, glaring at Ned and Hayley who have moved on to haggling over the price of the purses.

"She's not fired yet," Daniel says, then he turns to me and says determinedly, "You aren't getting fired."

"I know," I say. We've got this. At least, Daniel thinks we've got this.

Buck grunts in surprise. "Don't let it go to your head."

Then he stomps off to his desk, leaving the scent of garlic butter and toasted bread in his wake.

"I'm hungry," I tell Daniel, rubbing my head again and glancing at my computer screen full of story notes and interview questions.

I've spent the last five hours sending emails and making phone calls for Daniel's Big Story Idea. The capital letters are his. He had me pitch it this morning to Bernardo, and Bernardo told me to chase it.

When I woke up this morning, snuggled deep in the couch cushions, my fuzzy blanket pulled up to my chin, Daniel had been standing next to the window, looking over the tips of green-leafed trees to the street below.

When I yawned and stretched, he looked over his bare shoulder at me, smiled, and said, "The answer to all your problems is sex."

I threw a sparkly couch pillow at him. But after that, he explained that I needed to write a series of articles on sex.

"Everyone loves sex. Everyone loves reading about sex," he claimed.

"No," I said, cranky and still waking up.

"If you write a series on sex, you will keep your job. I promise."

That was a very convincing argument. So here I am, five hours later, knee-deep in researching sex and phoning sex therapists for interviews.

"What do you want for lunch?" Daniel asks, looking toward the elevator. "We can grab something on your way to your two o'clock interview."

I lock my computer, grab my bag from under my desk, and stand. "I don't know. What do you want?" I ask Daniel, making sure my head is down and my hair fans around my face so that no one sees me talking to myself.

He makes a humming noise and glances up at the ceiling, thinking it through. "If I were eating, I'd want a fresh mozzarella, tomato, and basil panini from that hole-in-the-wall deli down the block." He thinks for a moment, then adds, "With prosciutto."

My stomach growls, agreeing with his plan. "Sounds good."

Daniel gives me a happy smile, his eyes warming.

"You're easy to please," I say, walking toward the elevator.

Hayley waves after me. "Are you heading to lunch, Jillian?"

I nod. "And I have an interview at two." I already put it on the shared calendar so everyone will know where I am.

"Good luck," she calls, waving me off, her peach-toned silk suit shining in the light of the news screens. "Go get your story."

I give her a sharp salute.

17

Dr. Leticia Brown, relationship coach and sex advisor, has an office the size of a cardboard box in an old stone building on Park Avenue.

There's only enough room for her desk and two purple beanbag chairs, and even those are squeezed in tight. The walls are lilac and a small diffuser pumps out a cloud of steam full of floral jasmine scents. Her credentials and awards are framed and hung on the wall behind her solid pink resin desk, which I'm fairly certain...

"Is her desk a vagina?" Daniel asks, blinking at the flowing rounded resin. He tilts his head and moves across the tiny office to view it from another angle.

"It's a rose petal," Dr. Brown says, and I jump, because...did she hear Daniel?

He throws me a stunned look. "Can she hear me?"

Dr. Brown clearly doesn't, because she gestures at me from behind her desk with a casual flick of her wrist and says, "You were staring at my desk. It's a rose petal. Most people think it's an elephant, but it's not, it's a petal. Although, I think what people see in the flowing lines gives insight into their psychology."

"It's a vagina," Daniel says, crossing his arms over his naked chest while he studies the pink flesh-toned desk. He seems affronted that anyone could think anything else.

I press my lips together, trying not to laugh.

"What do you see?" Dr. Brown gives me a questioning look.

I clear my throat and shift in my beanbag chair, the fabric crunching beneath my thighs. "Ah, right, I see an elephant."

If I cross my eyes, squint, and stand on my head.

Daniel throws me a disbelieving look and snorts.

Dr. Brown sagely nods. "That indicates sexual repression. Also, there's an elephant in the room. Metaphorically, there's something in the room with you that you can't or don't want to talk about."

Daniel laughs delightedly and grins at me. "Really?"

Goodness. He thinks he's my metaphor. Or my elephant.

I refuse to look at him, but he's standing next to Dr. Brown's vagina/petal/elephant desk, grinning down at me.

Dr. Brown, a petite woman, who barely reaches five feet, is wearing a voluminous lilac-colored sack-like gown that threatens to swallow her, and sits behind her desk, regarding me with a patient smile. She's probably in her late sixties, has curly gray hair, gold wire-framed glasses, and a soft but energetic presence, sort of like a quickly flowing woodland stream.

"Makes total sense," I say, and Daniel laughs again.

Then I take out my phone, pull up my interview notes, and ask for permission to record the interview. After that, we're ready.

"Thank you again for agreeing to see me, Dr. Brown. I have a few questions."

Dr. Brown folds her hands and places them on her desk, "Yes. Proceed."

Okay.

"As I mentioned, the series of articles I'm writing have to do with sex..." I pause and then glance nervously at Daniel.

He smiles encouragingly, and my heart, stupidly, gives a little flip.

And then, because of that irrational flip, I ask a question that wasn't on our list.

"Many couples don't go straight to sex, what do you propose for couples who want intimacy but can't have sex?" My face and the back of my neck grow hot, and I know if I was fairer-skinned I'd be bright red right now.

Daniel tilts his head, focusing his gaze on me. He helped me come up with the questions. He knows this one isn't on the interview list.

Dr. Brown's eyes crinkle at the corners as she smiles at me. "You hit on my passion," she says, leaning forward, her desk chair squeaking under her. "When people arrive at my doorstep, they believe everything revolves around the sex act, the penetration, the orgasm, what have you." She waves her hands in front of her, emphasizing her point. "But in reality, that moment comprises only a thousandth of a percent of what you can experience during sexual intimacy. And why would you limit yourself to a lifetime of vanilla when you can experience all the flavors?"

"What are the other flavors?" I ask, and Daniel sends me an unreadable look. I wrinkle my brow at him then turn back to Dr. Brown.

"That is months' worth of sessions, a lifetime of exploration. But when a couple comes to me, I have them start with a simple exercise."

I nod and try to swallow down the lump in my throat. I avoid looking at Daniel, at the line of his back, his shoulders, at the questioning look in his eyes.

"It's a touching exercise. Touch is intimate. Touch is love. You take turns touching each other, but you are only allowed to touch the arms and hands, the neck and shoulders, and from the feet to the knees. No erogenous zones. While touching, your partner tells you what sort of touch feels good on a scale from 1-10. You each get ten minutes to explore. No sex. No kissing. None of that. Not after either. This is an intimacy exercise, not a sex exercise."

She stops and looks at me expectantly.

"That's it?" I ask, feeling deflated.

Daniel paces across the room, then back again, his gaze on me, "What do you mean is that it? You're touching."

When he says "touching" his voice deepens, although I don't think he knows it. I want to ask him if he ever did something like this, if during his sex marathons he spent hours caressing and stroking.

"How often do you have your couples do this?" I ask.

Dr. Brown takes her glasses off and clears the steam off using a bit of her voluminous dress to wipe them. "Until they understand that not all pleasure and intimacy derives from activities leading to the sexual act or from engaging in the act."

I frown at Daniel. He's still pacing, and he looks like a tiger caged in a cardboard box.

Dr. Brown slides her glasses back onto her nose. "I see you're frowning. Let me ask you this, have you ever orgasmed while dreaming?"

Daniel turns toward me, faster than I've ever seen him move. My cheeks burn with heat. I refuse to answer that with him looking at me that way.

Have you, his expression asks.

I want to say *none of your business.* But to be perfectly honest, the night I thought he'd left for good? That night I tossed and turned, and when I finally fell asleep I dreamt about Daniel. And then I woke up gripping the sheets, arching my back, and orgasming. So. Yeah.

"No," I say. "I haven't."

Dr. Brown nods, and then taps her desk meaningfully. "That's why you saw an elephant. Usually people who see elephants don't experience nocturnal emissions."

"I think you have," Daniel says, eyeing the flush on my cheeks. They grow even hotter, like I've been lying too long in the summer sun and I've been sunburned. He smiles. "If we'd met when I was alive, I would've had one—"

I kick him, but my foot goes through his shin and hits the vagina desk.

"Sorry," I gasp, my toe throbbing with pain.

"About you," Daniel finishes, his eyes dancing with laughter.

Dr. Brown waves it away. "It's only natural to feel frustration. My point is though, when people orgasm in their sleep, they are orgasming purely through the power of the mind. Sex is mental. Sex is spiritual. It doesn't have to be physical. You can have intimacy, and pleasure, and even orgasm purely through the use of your mind. People don't have to be physical together to have intimacy together."

At that Daniel goes still. Incredibly, unbelievably still. I know this because I was watching him from the corner of my eye while Dr. Brown was speaking. And when she says her last sentence, he goes so still that he doesn't look real. He's not moving, not breathing (obviously), he's not anything.

He shifts from laughter to profound stillness in the blink of an eye.

The hair on my arms rises, as if a breeze has passed over me and caressed my skin. My whole body lights up, like a firefly at dark, and I lean forward, closer to Daniel.

"Are you saying that two people can make love without making love? Without even touching?" I ask, my chest tight.

Dr. Brown smiles at me, the smile a teacher gives a student that has finally caught on, "Indeed I am. The spirit is more powerful than the body."

I glance at Daniel, but he isn't looking at me, he's staring down at his hands, his jaw clenched, his shoulders tight. He shakes his head firmly, as if he's engaging in an argument with himself.

I sigh, breathing out the jasmine-scented air, and then lean back, scrunching the bean bag chair, and say, "Interesting. I have a few more questions."

Then I ask all the questions on the list that Daniel and I came up with this morning—how to prolong orgasm, five ways to please your lover, how to communicate during sex—standard, boring questions. Safe questions.

And after a few minutes Daniel looks up again,

loosens his shoulders, and shrugs off his internal debate. He gives me a casual, nonchalant smile and spends the rest of the interview making irreverent, self-deprecating comments about sexathons and sexcapades.

But I can't help but wonder, when I asked about making love without making love, was he thinking the same thing I was?

And if so, is that bad or is that good?

18

WHATEVER DANIEL FELT AT THE INTERVIEW, WHATEVER conclusion he came to after his internal debate, I never imagined it'd be this.

The chill of the evening stings my nose and bites my cheeks, buffeting me with its cold winds. I pull my trench coat tighter and wish that I'd worn pants instead of a dress. Even my toes, pinched in an old pair of high heels, are complaining about the lingering cold.

But I dressed up because when we left Dr. Brown's office, Daniel said that tonight we were going out. I thought he meant he and I, but he actually meant me and another man. One that I had to find myself.

"All you have to do," Daniel says, pointing like a general directing his troops to the interior of the coffee shop, "is go in, order a coffee, sit down on the couch, and smile at the guy."

I peer through the large window at the interior of the cozy coffee shop. It's one of those indie, we-take-coffee-more-seriously-than-life, comfy-couch, thick-wood, dim-lighting places that has open mic nights and weekly poetry readings.

On the couch there's a man in his early thirties, with spiky black hair, sun-browned skin, and a trace of stubble. He's wearing a black t-shirt, jeans, and motorcycle boots, and has that effortlessly cool vibe. He's reading a thick hardcover book, leisurely thumbing through the pages.

"That's all?" I ask, skeptical.

"Trust me," Daniel says, giving me a distracted look. "That's all it'll take."

"A smile?" No offense, but I've smiled at plenty of people and I've never been asked out because of it. Thank goodness. That'd get awkward really fast.

"A smile," Daniel confirms.

I don't believe him, and he realizes it. He waves his hand in a give-it-a-try gesture. "Try it on me."

I stretch my mouth and give him a bright, big smile.

Daniel blinks. Rubs his hand over his mouth as if he's hiding a grin. Clears his throat.

I drop the smile. "See?"

He brushes his hand through his hair, his chest flexing, and nods. "I get your point. I didn't mean smile like you're a ninety-year-old lady showing off your new dentures, I meant, smile like..." He pauses, and then his lips curl at the edges, hinting at secrets and connection and pleasure and vice, and holy crap my heart flips, my stomach bottoms out, and a glowing fiery warmth pools inside me and spreads like wanton heat licking over my limbs. I sink into the warmth of his smile and take an involuntary step toward him. His eyes darken to a burning flame blue and drag me under, singeing me from the inside out. I take a shuddering, aching breath, and the air burns my lungs. He's right...that's a smile.

But then Daniel blinks, wipes the smile from his face, like a fire doused, and takes a careful step back.

"Like that," he says, clearing his throat. "That's how you smile."

No way. If I smiled like that at someone, I'd be on my back with my legs thrown over my head in a millisecond. The only person I'll ever give a smile like that to is the man I love.

"Do you smile at everyone that way?" I ask, curling my cold hands into my coat pockets.

Daniel shrugs, his shoulders lifting. "The only person who can see me is you."

He sounds matter-of-fact, but my chest pinches at his words all the same.

"I'm sorry," I say, regretful I asked him and reminded him that he's in this ghostly limbo.

"Don't be," Daniel says, avoiding my eyes, looking out towards the street, where scaffolding and graffitied plywood wrap a building under construction, and taxis and buses sweep noisily past.

I nod, then put my hand to the concrete window ledge of the coffee shop. I fiddle with my ring for a second. It's a large amethyst held in place with silver prongs.

"You're sure about this?" I finally ask.

Daniel looks back to me, the overhead streetlight glowing through him, the outline of his golden skin fading like an old photograph.

"It's why I'm here, right? I'm supposed to help you. Which means—" he gestures at the man he decided I should hit on after fading in and out of half a dozen coffee shops looking for a decent guy.

"And if he asks me a question? If he wants to engage in conversation?" I ask, frustrated because it makes me cranky that Daniel's so determined to foist me off on another man.

"Conversations are what I'm here for," Daniel says, waving my concern away. "It'll be good."

Then, without waiting to see if I'm following, he confidently strides through the front door.

"What's the hurry?" I ask the streetlamp, which obviously doesn't answer.

However, a bearded homeless man I hadn't noticed sitting on the stoop of the apartment building next door lifts his coffee cup to me and says, "Who're you talking to? The grays?" He squints, his eyes furtively darting around the dark block.

I smile to myself. Serena was wrong. There's at least one other person on the planet who thinks aliens before ghosts.

I shake my head apologetically. "No. I'm talking to myself."

Then I hurry after Daniel, tuning out the homeless man's laughter.

19

I WRAP MY HANDS AROUND THE PAPER CUP, LETTING THE heat sink in, and breathe in the bolstering scent of strong, dark coffee and copious amounts of sugar.

The coffee shop has that freshly ground espresso smell, that low hum of voices over soft acoustic guitar, and the dim yellow-tinted lighting that blends morning seamlessly into night so that you don't notice the time passing while sipping your drink for hours.

I smile thanks to the barista, drop cash into the tip jar and then turn to pretend a casual study of the interior— as if I don't know exactly where I'm going to sit.

Daniel finishes his rapid-fire monologue on the essential steps to letting someone know you are both attracted and available. He spoke in a quick voice over the whine of the grinder and the hissing of steaming milk, trying to impart a lifetime of wisdom in ninety seconds.

"Got it?" he asks, his brows drawing down in concern, as if he can tell I'm not quite clear on his theory of attraction. "Jillian?"

"Mhmm," I say, nodding and walking across the reclaimed wood floors toward the thickly cushioned, gray upholstered couch near the back wall, where Daniel's choice of a "decent-seeming guy" sits reading his book.

My heels tap against the floor as I hesitantly wend around dozens of coffee-lovers chatting, reading, and tapping on their phones while parked at cute little wooden tables.

"You don't, do you?" he asks worriedly, keeping pace with me by walking through backpacks and empty chairs.

I shake my head no and clutch my cup more tightly. The closer I get to the guy the cuter he looks. He has a confident aura, a way of reading and smiling at his book that makes you know *big thoughts* are happening.

I stop and think about turning around and rushing back into the cold spring night.

"Nope," Daniel says, catching my expression and reading it correctly. I swear, it's ridiculous how well he can read me. "It's fine. It's easy," he says reassuringly, dropping his hand to my arm. I look down at his curved palm resting over me and sigh.

"Repeat after me," he says firmly.

I look up into his eyes and widen my own in protest. How am I supposed to repeat after him when I'm standing in the middle of a coffee shop surrounded by dozens of people?

"Say it into your cup. Now repeat after me—I'm a beautiful woman."

I take a sip of my coffee and raise my eyebrows over the rim.

"Go on," he says, his blue eyes implacable and demanding.

"I'm a beautiful woman," I say into my cup, the coffee scent fanning around me.

Daniel smiles in approval. "I'm passionate and kind."

"I'm passionate and kind," I whisper, the coffee heating my cheeks. I let the liquid singe my lips.

Daniel nods. "The man who loves me will be the luckiest man alive."

I swallow the coffee, the sweetness overwhelmed with bitterness. But I hide my reaction behind the cup and say in a scratchy, thick voice, "The man who loves me will be the luckiest man alive."

Daniel considers my response, his sandy-brown hair falling across his forehead, my fingers itching to brush it back, and then he nods. "You'll do great."

At that we walk to the couch together, and once I'm there, I casually sit on the opposite end from the black-haired man and set my cup on the wooden coffee table.

"Okay," Daniel says, stationing himself next to the arm of the couch, like a coach on the sidelines.

The acoustic guitar plays overhead, stretching out the silence as Daniel takes in the scene, probably going through his playbook of moves.

What were the essential steps he mentioned before?

I can't remember. I've forgotten them already. Prolonged eye contact? Was that one? Or does that just make you look like a psychopath?

I shift on the couch, sinking into the cushions, take off my trench coat, and cross one leg over the other. My red dress, one patterned after Uhura's from the original *Star Trek*, slides up my thigh, revealing a good amount of skin.

I glance at Daniel, waiting for his coaching, but instead find him hungry-eyed, staring at the hem of my dress. Warmth flows through me at the heat in his gaze, but as soon as my fingers trace over the hem of my dress, he blinks and shakes his head.

"Right," he says, all business. "All you need now is to attract some attention. He knows you sat down, he glanced up momentarily, so now...attract him more."

The coffee shop is warm, I didn't notice how warm before, but it's *warm* warm. Slowly, I put my fingers to the hem of my dress and push it up an inch, another inch, and one more.

Daniel's eyelashes flutter, as if he can't quite believe what he's seeing, and he lets out a puff of air.

"That's..." He swallows, his throat bobbing, "You can ask him the time, and when he looks up, hit him with your smile."

Daniel moves around the coffee table to stand behind the black-haired man. I bite my bottom lip and focus on Daniel. The line of his long chest, his strong arms, his wide shoulders, the steadiness of his gaze.

"Do you know what time it is?" Daniel asks me, his mouth curved into a smile.

I shake my head no. "Do you know what time it is?" I ask back.

At that, the man who had been absorbed in his nonfiction tome, completely ignoring me, glances at his watch, then says without looking up, "Quarter to nine."

Then he goes back to reading, chuckling at something funny on the pages. I give Daniel a surprised look, and Daniel scowls at the man.

"When a lady asks you the time," he explains patiently, "You look at her when you respond."

I hide a smile. I wonder what Daniel did when he was

alive. Maybe he worked for Emily Post, writing treatises on etiquette.

He glances back to me, shaking his head, "That didn't work. Round two. Drop a pen near his foot and then twist your hair seductively as you ask him to retrieve it for you."

I hold back a snort. Seductively twist my hair? Who does he think I am?

I give him a sardonic look, and he grins at me.

"Like this." He takes his hand and twists a finger through his hair, letting the ends brush against his chin. I stare at the way his finger glides through his waves, and when Daniel sees that I'm watching, he drops his hand and says, "Try it."

I root through my purse, pull out my favorite erasable pen, a turquoise one with a hot pink eraser, and then casually toss it to the ground. It plinks against the wood and then rolls and skitters, coming to a stop against the man's black motorcycle boots.

Of course, he doesn't notice. But, "Good shot," Daniel says approvingly.

I grin at him, and he gives a triumphant smile.

"Now, twirl your hair and put on a smile."

I thread my fingers through my curls, spinning them around and around, and try to smile like Daniel did.

He shakes his head. "You look like someone just told you Picard never actually escaped the Borg. Smile, Jillian. Smile."

A laugh fills my chest and I give Daniel a blindingly brilliant smile. He may not remember being a trekker, but he is one, even in death. No one else would care whether Captain Picard was assimilated to the Borg or not.

"Now *that* is a smile," Daniel says, leaning toward me, drinking in my expression. "Ask him," he says. "What do you need?"

What do I need?

I need Daniel to not be dead.

I need him to be the one to love me.

I need him to never leave, to never move on.

His eyes widen as if he can hear my thoughts, then he says. "Ask him for your pen."

My smile dims a bit, but I say, "Excuse me, I dropped my pen. Could you please..."

And wouldn't it be wonderful if Daniel could pick it up? Instead of his hand passing through it.

The black-haired man finally looks up from his book, he glances at me, his forehead wrinkling. He gives me a sharp stare and shakes his head. "What?"

I twist my hair more furiously, flutter my eyelashes, and smile the most I'm-attracted-and-available smile I can muster.

The man frowns, clearly not understanding, so I nod meaningfully at my pen resting next to his foot. He looks down, sees my pen, and grunts. Then he gives my favorite, my most wonderful erasable pen a quick kick, sending it skittering back toward me.

"There you go," he says gruffly.

I suck in a stunned breath, the smile dropping from my face, and bend forward trying to execute a quick grab. But I don't reach down because my right hand, formerly *seductively* twisting my hair, has become tethered, no knotted, to my curls.

My hair is snarled in the prongs of my ring. So instead of reaching for my pen, I jerk my head down, yank out multiple strands of hair, and let out a sharp, pained yelp.

The pen smacks against my heel, ricochets away, and spins to a stop under the coffee table. When it finally stills, I look at the man in helpless outrage. He's paying me no attention because he's back to being impossibly cool and completely absorbed in his book.

I tug at my hand in frustration, but my fingers are still stuck in my hair, attached via prongy ring.

"What..." Daniel pauses, his eyes moving from me tugging at my captured hand, to the man lounging on the couch and reading his book on the history of free jazz.

"How can he ignore your smile? How can he ignore your..." Daniel scowls, then says determinedly, "Round three."

Gosh, maybe he wasn't an etiquette arbiter, maybe he was a boxing or a jiu-jitsu coach. That would explain his physique at least.

"All you need to do is crawl under the table and retrieve your pen. It's game over after that."

I give Daniel a skeptical look. If smiles and seductive hair twisting didn't work, then crawling under the table won't work either. However, this is my favorite pen, it's out of reach, and the only way I'll get it back is by crawling. So, here goes.

I hobble down to the wood floor, one hand still stuck in my hair, and drop to my knees. Out of the corner of my eyes, I notice that the black-haired man is finally paying attention. But instead of being wowed by my beauty, he looks as if he thinks I'm some crazed lunatic.

My cheeks flush, and I scooch forward, one hand still in my hair, the other reaching forward under the long coffee table. I look like a trussed up turkey being shoved into the oven. It's humiliating.

But my pen!

I fall forward, my elbow cracking on the wood, and then grasp my pen in my fingers. But my position, my stretching, and my tiny 1960s sci-fi mini dress, all conspire against me. There's a tearing, the sharp whine of fabric that you *never* want to hear when you're bent over, and then there's the cold breeze hitting my butt, covered, mortifyingly in white Starfleet granny panties.

"Jillian," Daniel says, as I freeze. My mind screams, *"Drop and roll! drop and roll!"* but my body refuses to move.

"You're...you..." Daniel cuts off.

The black-haired man coughs and that finally manages to pull me out of my paralysis. I drop to the wood floor and then roll over, grabbing my dress with my one free hand, and pulling the torn fabric together.

I scoot out from under the table, like an injured crab scuttling back to the ocean. My poor pen is still under the coffee table. The black-haired man has his book raised to hide his entire face.

I slink up to the couch and drop onto my coat, pulling it around my lap.

"Jillian," Daniel says.

I shake my head, my cheeks burning, refusing to look at him. The black-haired man is thankfully ignoring me, just as he's done since I sat down.

"That was..." Daniel stops, and something in his voice makes me look up.

When I do, I level him with a hard look.

He's trying so hard not to laugh that he's practically crying.

"It wasn't funny," I say under my breath.

"I really like your underwear," Daniel says, his mouth quivering. Then he salutes me. "Captain."

I tug at the ring in my hair, trying to loosen my hand. "If you laugh, I will kill you. I will redshirt you. I will murder you in your sleep."

"Can't," Daniel says, as he barely holds back, his chest shaking. "Too late. It's too late for me."

Then he laughs, a rich, loud, happy sound, his eyes brimming with mirth.

And when he laughs I grin at him, unable to repress my answering smile.

It's that moment that the black-haired man slams closed his book, levels me and my gleeful smile with a glare and says, "You are dangerously unhinged."

Then he stands, grabs his coffee, and stalks away.

I look at Daniel with wide eyes, he looks back at me, and then with a smile I say, "You can't win them all, but you can at least flash 'em while you're losing."

Daniel gives me a delighted look. "It was a good try. He clearly wasn't ready for your stunning, starry appeal."

I nod. "I wouldn't really redshirt you, you know," I say, referring to the red-shirt-wearing characters in *Star Trek* who were commonly introduced into the plot only to die a quick death seconds later.

"I know," Daniel says confidently. "Because I'm not wearing a shirt."

"Exactly."

I finally free my finger from my amethyst ring, leaving the ring dangling in the tangled snarl of my hair. I'll brush it out at home.

Speaking of... "Can we go home now?" I ask. "I'll drink my coffee slowly for you and moan with pleasure as

I do. And then we can play a board game together. I'll make all the moves."

Daniel gives me a lopsided smile as I stand. "I like your spirit."

We walk toward the exit and as we do he puts his hand over mine, and it almost feels as if he's holding onto me.

20

WE DECIDE TO WALK HOME. IT'S ONLY A DOZEN BLOCKS meandering along the river, and watching the headlights from the cars whizzing by, reflecting off the black inky water, I feel as if I could reach down, trail my hand in the water and touch the lush night sky and all the shimmering stars.

A sunset sail tour boat cruises the swiftly flowing river, its lights a beacon in the darkness as it passes under the towering metal bridge spanning the water. Across the river, Roosevelt Island is a hazy, dusty shadow blurring into the darkness, the suspended cable car sweeping down over the water toward its graceful landing.

The night air is cool and crisp like the first bite of a bright red apple. My fingers are shoved in my pockets, protecting them from the cold, my toes are pinched and my feet are achy, but it's worth it.

I smile over at Daniel. He's pointing out the little things again, just to delight me. The bits of life that no one notices. How the red and green lights shining on the boats sailing past, look for all the world like Christmas in April. How the whooshing of the cars on the FDR sound like the whisper of a heartbeat on a baby's first ultrasound. How the river, and the path along it, grow quiet and slumberous as night falls.

"The city is more alive when I'm with you," I admit, glancing over at Daniel. "I don't want to say something cliché like the colors are more vibrant, but...the colors are more vibrant."

He peers down at me, his hand still resting near mine, then he gives me a searching look. "Jillian, about what happened. You know I'm not—"

By his tone, I know he's going to mention Dr. Brown's, how I asked about making love without making love, so I forestall him and say, "Do you like Monopoly or Catan? Real life or fantasy?"

I weigh the two with my hands, holding out the imaginary choices.

He's about to answer when he stiffens, his shoulders tightening, his jaw hardening. He stands almost like a wolf with his hackles raised. He swings around and scans the dark mouth of the street behind us.

We're on one of the cross-town numbered streets, close to the river, where buildings under construction are boarded up with plywood, and scaffolding rises above us like the spidery legs of a daddy longlegs.

During the day, the street is crowded, busy with construction workers and pedestrians. Now, the block is deserted. The only noise is the mechanical buzzing of the fluorescent light half a block away, weakly lighting the end of the scaffolding tunnel.

I wasn't thinking when I turned down this block. I never would've come this way if I'd been thinking. I was too engrossed in talking with Daniel. And I think, he was too engrossed in talking with me.

But he's not really here—no—I'm a woman, walking alone, down a dark, deserted block by the river.

My hands go cold and the hair on the back of my neck stands on end.

Daniel grabs at my hand. His passes through mine with a whisper of breeze.

"Daniel?" I ask, my voice shaking.

I peer into the darkness, trying to see through the murky light, past the piles of black trash bags heaped in man-high mounds, tossed out for the trash collectors.

My chest constricts, and my heart thunders as Daniel swings around, and says with desperate urgency, "Cross the street."

"What?"

"Jillian, cross the street. Walk as fast as you can. Now."

I glance behind me, but the only thing I see are moving shadows, and the only thing I hear is Daniel urging me to move faster.

"Go Jillian," he says, glancing behind him.

I hurry past the pile of trash, holding my breath at the rotting, fetid smell. My heels click against the pavement, a gunshot explosion of tat tat tat as I hurry to the opposite sidewalk. My breath grows tight as I move faster.

Daniel keeps looking back, then disappearing from my side and reappearing in short second-long bursts.

"What is it?" I ask him, and then before he can answer a man steps in front of me, two sidewalk lengths away.

"Dammit," Daniel swears furiously. "Dammit."

A threatening violence rolls off the man in spidery waves, sneaking toward me.

I take a step back.

"Dammit." Daniel sounds desperate, afraid, the fear in his voice thick, and I think it comes from the knowledge that whatever happens, he can't do anything to help me or to stop it.

His fear comes from his inability to save me, and I know *exactly* how he feels, because not being able to save the person you love is one of the worst feelings in the world.

The man winds his way from behind another mound of black-bagged trash. He's short, mean-eyed, and wearing a thick puffy black coat.

"You all alone?" he asks, his voice a rasp that draws over my spine.

"Lie," Daniel says, his eyes pleading. "Lie, Jillian."

I shake my head, my throat tight.

"No?" the man asks, stepping closer. I take another step back.

Daniel thrusts at the man, he rams his fist into the man's head, knocks him with such force that if Daniel were really here the man would be flat on his back.

"Shit," Daniel says, snapping his fist at the man again, his arm passing through his head.

The mean-eyed man, his mouth tight, his head shaved, doesn't notice the ghost attacking him, instead his cold eyes remain on me.

"You look all alone," he says with a twisted smile.

I glance behind me, desperate to see another person or even better a group of people walking down the block. But there's no one. It's just me, the short man, and the graffitied plywood boarding up the building looming over us.

"Jillian," Daniel says, his voice low. "Look at me."

"Your purse," the man growls, gesturing at my leather bag thrown over my shoulder.

I hold onto Daniel's gaze, my hands shaking.

"You have to run," he says. Daniel's calm now, cold, the desperation buried, "Throw your purse at him. Throw it as hard as you can, and then kick off your shoes and run."

He's right, there's no way I'll be able to outrun anyone in heels.

"Give me your purse," the man spits, taking a threatening step closer.

"Jillian," Daniel says, his voice breaking on my name. "I can't help you. Please."

At the sound of that "please," the fear, the helplessness, I take my purse and...look, I meant to throw it at the man, I really did, but something happened between the throwing part and the letting go part.

So instead of violently chucking my purse at the man, my hand catches on the strap, it loops around my forearm, and my purse (loaded with my laptop and two notebooks and a passel of pens) yanks me off-balance.

I stumble, then twist over my heels, and smack the man across the head with my bag, hitting him with all the force of a misguided missile.

I fall, ram into the man, try to catch myself and instead shove him into the mountain of trash.

The man shouts a curse as he slams into the black bags, they split open and the reek of sour spaghetti, rotten and old, hits my nose. I gag and then gag again as the man lunges for me and clips me in the stomach. I stagger back with a pained cry.

Daniel swears, hits the man, his fists flying through

him. Daniel tries to keep him down with hands that can't hold him.

The man grasps the rotten spaghetti and the slippery trash-filled bags with murder in his eyes.

I don't wait to see what he says or what he'll do next. No, I kick off my shoes and fly down the sidewalk, my purse banging against my back, my feet pounding against the cold, hard concrete.

I sprint down the dark blocks, broken glass and busted concrete stabbing at my bare feet, until I make it to the bright lights and the laughing people and the rushing cars.

I take in great gulping breaths, breathing in the pizza parlor scents and the exhaust and subway scents. And then when I make it to my building, I run up the stairs, thrust my key in the lock, bang into my apartment and slam the door.

The quiet darkness envelops me. The mirrors reflect my shadowed face.

Daniel steps through the door.

He's quiet.

I'm quiet.

We stare at each other. I look up at him, he looks down at me.

And then, he takes another step toward me, wraps his arms around me, holds himself over me, but never touching me, and whispers in a broken voice, "Jillian. Thank God."

When I look up into his deep blue eyes, show him everything that I felt and feared, he lets out a curse and then his mouth crashes over mine.

21

I'M SURROUNDED BY DANIEL, ENGULFED BY HIM, HIS NEED IS an ocean and I'm drowning in it. His kiss pulls me under, and the only life raft I can cling to is him.

His mouth settles on mine, and even though there isn't pressure or warmth, I can still feel him. My mouth burns from the look in his eyes, the hunger, the desperation, the unleashing of what's been denied. I make a noise, a tight cry, and my lips tingle and warm.

Daniel's arms wrap around me, and the breeze, the cold one that comes with ghosts, it passes over my skin, but this time, it's not cold, it's as warm as a summer breeze rustling through sunlit sheets hanging on a clothesline.

I luxuriate in the warmth stroking over me, tilt my chin up and offer my mouth for more. Daniel's eyes are open and as wide as the summer sky and as deep as the balmy ocean. I sink into them and fall deeper into him as he traces his lips across mine, brushing his mouth over me in tingling, whispering kisses.

He reaches out, strokes his fingers over my cheeks, my jaw, tenderly traces my lips. It doesn't matter that he isn't truly touching me, because this touch, this moment, I can feel it in my soul.

I take my fingers, shaking from the need to touch him, and rest them against his mouth. At my touch, Daniel closes his eyes and takes a shuddering breath.

"Jillian," he whispers.

I run my hands along his face, the beloved lines, I touch the spot where his dimple lives, and I stroke the ends of his sandy-brown hair. A quiet breeze whispers over me, and I swear, I can feel the soft warmth of him.

"I want you," I say, the darkness of the room, the quiet holding its breath with me.

Daniel stares down at me, depthless yearning written on his features. His hands feather over my mouth, my jaw, my collarbone, and everywhere his hands touch but don't, he leaves behind a glowing, aching need. It spreads, tempestuous and luminous, reaching through me.

"I need you," I say, and in the dark of my apartment, the light from the street is the only illumination so that the shadows in the mirrors don't show that I'm the only person visible in this room.

Daniel's gaze falls over me, heats me and cradles me, and then he presses his mouth to mine and whispers, "You're my light."

At that, I take my dress, and I pull the short red mini over my head and drop it to the floor so that it folds in on itself like a scattered rose petal.

Daniel pulls in a sharp breath, his eyes taking on that luminescent glow.

"I've not done this before," I remind him.

He swallows, nods. "I know. We can't have sex, you know."

I smile, unclasping my bra, freeing my breasts.

"But we can make love," I say.

I let my bra slide from my fingers, dropping it to the floor, where the fabric whispers against my dress.

Daniel watches me, blue fire in his gaze.

Then I step out of my underwear, the fabric scraping over my thighs, dragging down my calves until I kick them free and stand completely naked before him.

His eyes lick over me, trailing over every single inch, lovingly tracing each curve, my breasts, my lush thighs, my hair curling over my shoulders, and falling to brush over my puckering nipples.

Daniel steps forward. "Can I touch you?" he asks reverently.

And I know he isn't asking whether or not he can really touch me, instead, he's asking if he can worship me with his hands.

"Yes," I say, swaying toward him.

Then he's there, and I can feel him, because the emotions coming off him, the need, it's here, so that his insubstantial touch feels more real than anything I've felt in my entire life.

His hands trace my wrists, and I feel the wings of a butterfly, his fingers drag over my collarbone and kiss my pulse, and I feel an answering kiss rushing through my veins.

I throw my head back as his lips fan over my throat and then finally, thank goodness, he drops his head and brushes his lips over my breast. My nipples bead, aching from the tingling touch.

As his mouth trails over me like warm sunlight passing through a window, he travels lower, and I run my hands through his hair, over his broad shoulders, down his thickly muscled arms, to the taut line of his abdomen, tracing the outline of him.

I always wondered what he would feel like, and now I know, he feels like holding starlight in my hands.

"I want to kiss you here," Daniel says, looking up from the juncture between my open thighs. "Can you feel me?" he asks, then he says quietly, "I can feel you."

"Yes," I say. "I feel you here." I reach up and place my hand over my heart.

He smiles at me then, a happy, aching smile, and he drops his mouth to my clit, brushing a kiss over me. It feels like the breeze. Like the teasing wind that strokes you as you lounge next to the cool blue sea. He licks me, kisses me, wants me, and as he does, he whispers to me.

"If I could dream," he says, "I'd only dream about you."

There's a throbbing between my legs, a growing, aching pulse, like the slow, glowing birth of a star in the vacuum of space.

"If I could live," he says, "I'd live for you."

His hand curls over my hip, and I reach down and place my hand in his.

"Jillian," he says, and then whatever he does, I feel it, I feel it deep inside, where a bright, glowing ball of need pulls me under.

I arch my hips, offering myself to him.

"If I could give you anything," Daniel says, "I'd give you heaven."

At that, the glow, the light, the star, it explodes inside

me and I grip my hands, tilt my hips and scream as an orgasm tears through me, breaking me apart and realigning everything inside me, so that all of my insides, the magnet of my heart, points due north.

Toward Daniel.

I take shuddering breaths and wait for my body to come back to earth.

Daniel lingers over me, placing another kiss, trailing his hands over my thighs, my calves, my stomach, and breasts, until he comes back to my lips, where he presses a kiss against my mouth.

I reach up and put my hand to the outline of his jaw, draw my fingers down in a tender caress.

I love you, my heart says.

I love you, my mind says.

"Thank you for heaven," I say. "Thank you for making love with me."

Daniel stares at me, his eyes opaque, unreadable. He gives me a small, quiet smile.

I realize then that Daniel can't take off his jeans, maybe can't experience orgasm since he doesn't have a body, maybe can't even...

"Did you..." I ask quickly, my cheeks flushing.

Daniel traces a finger over my cheek. "Yes," he says, his voice deep. "I did."

I sit up on my elbows. "It felt like making love?"

He smiles, "It *was* making love. You were right."

With that, all my elation comes plummeting back to earth, like the space shuttle, on fire, hurtling toward the ocean.

We made love.

I made love with Daniel.

I'm in love with Daniel.

It's wonderful.

It's terrible.

Because when you're in love with a man who is already dead, there's no way to make a life together. There's no life at all.

22

THE DEEP SLUMBEROUS QUIET OF THE NIGHT BLANKETS THE apartment, wrapping it in the city's half-light, a perpetual gloaming that begs for the sharing of secrets.

You love him, the night whispers, you *love* him.

I turn my face into the cool cotton of my pillow, breathe in the fabric softener scent, and tug my worn quilt to my chin. The sheets scratch over my skin and my legs itch to stand and pace my apartment floor.

Daniel stands at the window, the glow of the streetlight passing through him, casting light and shadow around my mirrored apartment.

He's as still as a sentinel, his chin tilted toward the street and his face turned from me. He watches the midnight cars whooshing down Lexington, the lone strangers walking, and the moonlight flickering through the lacy leaves of the sidewalk pear trees.

"You're still awake," he says, turning to gaze at my bed, stuck high on the wine red carpeted pedestal.

You *love* him, the night insists.

I kick back my rumpled quilt and sheets, and sit, swinging my legs over the side of my mattress.

"I can't sleep." I stretch my toes, digging them into the thick shag carpeting, and say, "You're still here."

Daniel studies the thigh-length fandom T-shirt I'm wearing for pajamas, then says with a smile, "I don't sleep."

After I brushed my teeth, washed the makeup from my face and climbed into bed, Daniel asked if I minded if he stayed for a while. I didn't. I remembered how he said that every time he was away from me, there was only darkness, nothing more. He can stay with me as much and as long as he likes.

"We could play that board game," I suggest, stretching my arms over my head, feeling the taut sensitivity still coursing through me.

Daniel shakes his head, the light catching the pensive expression on his face.

I lean forward. "What?"

"I have a question," he says, silently striding from the window, his feet a half inch above the wood floor. He winds around the couch, passes the bookcase and then climbs the two steps up to my bed.

I grip the cool cotton sheets in my hand and drag in a shaky breath. "Okay?"

Daniel's gaze is steady, down on Lexington the rumble of the street sweeper sounds, whooshing and groaning as it sweeps away the dirt and dust.

I wonder if he's going to ask about making love or even about love. I shift on the bed, the mattress sinking beneath my weight.

If Daniel asks, will I be able to tell him that I'm falling in love with him?

"Today," he begins, his voice low, his expression one of a man who has thought long and hard about a question and hasn't been able to find the answer. "Dr. Brown said you have an elephant in the room."

I blink up at him. That's not the direction I was expecting him to go.

"I didn't really see an elephant," I say, shaking my head.

Daniel nods, the question still in his eyes. "But there's something there. Something Fran knows, something your coworkers know. Something everyone knows and no one's talking about."

I stand quickly, push away from the bed, and climb down the stairs, the floor creaking beneath me. I stride to the kitchen for a glass of water, because suddenly, my mouth is dry, my throat aches, and beads of sweat line my forehead.

The faucet moans as cold city water sprays out, I hold a glass under it and watch air bubbles rise to the top of the water and disappear, then I take a long, cold drink.

Daniel's there behind me, I know he is. He waits until I finish the water, the cold sliding down my throat, and then when I've set the glass down on the stainless steel counter he says, "Jillian, if I'm supposed to help you, I have to know what's wrong."

I turn around then, away from the sink, and look at Daniel. I don't expect him to have so much caring, or so much compassion written in the lines of his face.

Now the shoulders, the muscular wide shoulders that at first seemed like they were merely there to attract women, now seem like they were made to help carry burdens and worries.

"There's a reason you let Fran treat you like she does.

There's a reason you've let her set you up for years. There's a reason you work at the job you do. And there's a reason why the only man you can talk to isn't..."

He cuts off, stares into my eyes.

"Alive," I say into the charged silence.

Daniel nods. Then he takes a step forward, brushes his hand over mine leaving a warm breeze in his path.

Let me help you, the echo of his touch says.

My shoulders drop and I let out a shuddering sigh. "The reason I let Fran set me up and talk to me like she does," I say, and Daniel nods, his blue eyes lighting with relief that I'm finally sharing with him, "is because it makes her happy. And I'd do just about anything to see her happy."

Daniel's eyebrows lower. "Why?"

I lean back against the counter, the cold stainless steel digging into my low back. Daniel looks down at me pulling back and reaches out and wraps his hand over mine.

The tension I was holding inside softens. "Fran has lived in the duplex next to my parents since I was born."

Daniel nods, he knows Fran is my parents' neighbor, that I spent a lot of my childhood playing at her house and eating her deliciously spicy curries, and also that she thinks of me like a daughter.

"Fran had a son," I say, and my voice cracks, just a little, mirroring the cracks in my heart. "Michael."

When I say his name out loud, I realize it's been a long time since I've said it. I stare down at the lines of the wooden floor, the dirt settled in the cracks, and I wonder if that's what my heart looks like, the cracks so old that they've become a part of the whole.

I glance back up at Daniel. "Fran was always bright,

and fun, and loud. She was the best neighbor a kid could ask for. Always giving me cookies, finding me funny little toys, babysitting when my parents went out. I remember how happy she was. Whenever I got a good grade in school, she'd find out and she would hug me. I still remember how it felt, that happy warmth, the smell of cardamom and ginger surrounding me."

"She's like that now," Daniel says.

I nod, give a small smile. "She is. When Michael died she didn't go out, she didn't eat, she didn't speak. She caved in on herself and..."

I stare down at the floor again, remembering how I found her a week after the funeral, sitting on her kitchen floor, her arms around her legs, just staring at the open refrigerator, the light dead and all the food rotting.

"It lasted for four years. She wasn't there anymore. She buried herself with Michael. She never smiled, or laughed. When I saw her at the store, I'd wave, and she'd walk right by, as if she couldn't see me, or see the world anymore. It was as if there was only darkness. She was like..."

"A ghost," Daniel says.

I look into his eyes, at the light I see there, and nod. "Then one day, when I came home from classes, Fran was on her porch, and when she saw me...it was like a spark lit inside her, and she said, 'Jilly, I'm going to help you. I'm going to help you find your love. And then I can spoil your children and love them as much as I love you.' And after that she started smiling again, and laughing, and living. And no matter how hard it was, going on awkward, terrible, no-hope dates, the alternative was so much worse. I never want to lose Fran again."

I trace my hand over the cold edge of the counter,

glance at the rippling reflection barely discernible in the dark, and then take a breath, looking up at Daniel.

"You're a good person," he says. "You're a kind person."

I shake my head, denying it, and then the admission is torn from me, because the place I've locked it has finally cracked opened. "It was my fault."

"What?" Daniel asks, and I look down at his hand on top of mine, weightless and insubstantial, but comforting all the same.

"I feel like I'm the one who killed him," I whisper. "I always have. I wanted to ask forgiveness, but he's gone. And until you, I wasn't sure if he was there anymore to even hear me, to know how much I needed his forgiveness."

A hot, burning tear slides down my cheek, and Daniel reaches out, brushes his fingers over it. "He can hear you," he says. "I promise you. He can hear you. It's okay. You're okay."

The dark of the apartment blurs and my throat aches, and I have to remind myself to breathe. Breathe, Jillian, breathe.

I grip the counter, press my feet into the cold wood floor, and breathe in the dry, cool air tinged with the smell of plaster, wood, and dish soap. Normal, everyday smells.

I wipe my hand across my face, the salt from my tears pooling at the corner of my lips, tasting of old grief.

"We were the same age," I say, smiling as I remember the early years, running through sprinklers in the front yard, riding bikes down the sidewalk, sneaking cookies before dinner.

"I was always painfully shy. My parents even sent me

to child therapists trying to fix me. I realize years later, that one of those therapists should've told them, love your daughter for who she is, not for how outgoing you want her to be."

I shrug. "But they didn't. No one did. Instead they pushed me and pushed me. One summer day, when I was ten, I was at the city pool. I was hanging around the edges of the kid's playing, not interacting, just watching. I was so quiet no one really noticed me. I slipped, hit my head on the concrete, and fell into the deep end. My eyes were open the whole time. I could see all the kids, I could see the lifeguard helping a toddler put on floaties, and I couldn't cry out for help, I couldn't breathe, I couldn't even move my arms. I was deep underwater. I could see all the kids swimming in a group, I could hear them shouting and laughing, and I couldn't make them hear me, or see me, and I knew, even at ten, that I was drowning."

Daniel reaches out then, holds me, offers his gaze as a lifeline.

"When my lungs felt like they were going to seize up, and they were shrieking at me to breathe, a boy dove into the water, grabbed my hand, and yanked me to the surface. My head was spinning, my lungs were screaming, and then I looked at Michael, tugging me to the edge, and I knew he'd saved my life. He'd saved me."

"Thank God," Daniel says, running his hands over my cheeks, brushing through my tears.

I give Daniel a watery smile. "My parents sent me to CPR certification after that, and every year I go back, just in case someone needs me like I needed Michael." I shrug. "Anyway, after that, Michael and I were inseparable. I was painfully shy, but mostly kids just ignored me. Michael was my friend though, and with him, I could talk and talk and talk. He was different too though, just like I was. He was smart, sarcastic, he had the driest sense of humor, even as a little kid. But he didn't fit into the mold, and he knew it. And whenever kids at school said awful things, or teachers, or other adults told him he was bad, or wrong, or going nowhere, he didn't know how to let it go. He hung onto it all. He clothed himself in all the stupid things they said about him. I wish..."

I think about sixth grade, about walking home after school, and how the boys on the basketball team jumped him. I was too scared to help, I was too scared to do anything at all, and when they ran off and I dropped to my knees and reached for Michael, and there was blood dripping from his nose, he just shook me off.

"I wish I could go back in time. I wish I could change the past. I wish I could pull him into the future."

"What happened?" Daniel asks, his voice low, his gaze gentle.

I clench my hand. "We grew up." I hug my arms around myself. "I went to prom, back then I could still talk to boys"—I smile—"barely. Michael told me not to, he said the guy that invited me was setting me up. I didn't believe him, but he was right. It was one of those scenes out of a bad teen movie, where the awkward girl gets a huge bowl of bright red punch chucked on her fairytale prom dress by all the popular kids. And then, just like at the pool, Michael was there, in his ripped jeans and old t-shirt, and he pulled me, sopping wet, out of there, and he took me home, not even saying 'I told you so.' He always showed up for me, he always saved me, but he never saved himself. Not once. I want to go back. I want to go back so bad."

I turn toward the window. The night is still dark, the deep slate buildings across the street are silent and waiting. The rush of a car driving by breaks the silence, and then it falls back to quiet again.

"We went to college then. I was in Manhattan and Michael was in Queens, and even though we were only a train ride away, or a text away, I was so excited, so involved that I..." I look down, shame burning through me. "I didn't text him back when he texted. I didn't call him back when he called. I was dating. I was partying. I was attending eye-opening classes. I had an internship at a newspaper."

"*The Daily Exposé*?" Daniel asks.

I nod. "That's right. I was so enthralled with my new life that I didn't have time for Michael. And so when he was calling out to me, I ignored him. He was drowning, he was underwater, trying to reach me, and I didn't hear him, I didn't see him. I didn't know that unlike for me, college wasn't amazing, it was hell. He was breaking down, trying to reach me, and I didn't see it. The kids in his dorm, they said things about him, that he was worthless, ugly, that he should never have been born. And you know what? He believed them. He *believed* them. So while I was out making friends, going out with guys, having the time of my life, my best friend was drowning and alone. The weekend he died, he called me three times. *Three times*. And I never picked up. I was out at a party, kissing a guy whose name I don't even remember. The next time I answered my phone, it was my mom telling me Michael was dead."

I look at Daniel, let him see into me, at all the shame

I've carried, all the regret. "He saved my life, and me, I couldn't even answer the phone. I want...I want so badly to go back in time. I'd grab his hand, and I'd grab those pills, and I'd stop him. I'd stop it, and I'd say to him, don't listen to them, don't believe them, don't believe a word they say, they can't see your heart like I do, I see you, I see your heart, I see you and you are the best person I know. I see your heart, I see you."

Daniel slowly moves his hand to my heart and I look down at him, holding himself over me, offering me solace.

"He knows," Daniel says. "Whatever happens after, he heard you, and he knows."

I pray for that to be true. I want it so badly.

"After Michael," Daniel asks in a quiet voice, "you stopped talking to men?"

"I couldn't. It was hard before, it was impossible after."

He studies my expression, looking inside me. "You're punishing yourself."

I put my hand over his, feel my heart beating through him. My hand is warm, his isn't even there, but still, his touch feels necessary.

"I can't seem to stop," I admit, "I never got to ask him to forgive me and so I can't forgive myself."

"It wasn't your fault," he says, gentle and firm at the same time. "You know it wasn't your fault."

I drop my gaze, the words are easy to hear but hard to believe.

"How long has it been?" Daniel asks, the shadows sifting through him, a cold breeze tingling over my skin.

"Nine years," I say, then I drop my hand, let his fall

away from my heart. "I know. Anyone would tell me that it's been long enough."

That Michael would want me to be happy.

Daniel shakes his head, touches his fingers to my cheek where the salt from my tears has dried. "Only you can decide how long and in what way you'll punish yourself. Only you can decide when you're ready to be forgiven."

I lean into his hand, and the warmth of him fades into me.

And at his words I let free the flood I've been holding inside for all these years. The guilt that's clogged my throat, the regret that's stilled my words, the fear that I was wrong, that no one in the world can see you for who you are, that no one can truly see another's heart.

I sink to the floor, the cold wood pressing against me, and wrap my arms around my legs. "I went on all those dates, and wrote my column for years, because I wanted so badly to believe that the one you love can see your heart. That you don't have to change, or be someone different, that the one who is meant to love you will see your heart and love you just as you are. But a hundred dates have failed, and my column is on the verge of being cancelled, and I'm scared, I'm terrified, that all these years I've been wrong."

Daniel crouches next to me, resting his forearms on his knees, and when he does, the early morning dawn, golden and hopeful, sifts through the window and falls over us.

His gaze captures mine, as gentle as a kiss. When he touches my cheek, it feels as light as sunlight wisping over me.

"I see you," he says, his voice steady. "I see your heart."

And when I look up into his blue eyes, the morning light shining over him, I don't see how the light moves through him, or how the air from the HVAC doesn't rustle his hair, I don't see any of that, all I see is something in his eyes that looks a lot like love.

23

I GRAB MY PURSE, HEAVY WITH MY LAPTOP AND NOTEBOOKS, and take a quick bite of my toast slathered in butter and grape jelly.

After Daniel and I talked, I thought I'd try to sleep for an hour before leaving for work. Instead, I curled up under my quilt, closed my eyes and slept through my alarm, my *second* alarm, and three phone calls from Serena.

Daniel isn't here, so I don't know whether or not he tried to wake me, or even when he left or when he'll be back.

It's after nine now, the traffic outside the window is rush-hour loud with insistent honking, the roar of motorcycle engines, and the rumble of city buses.

But even though I'm late, and Bernardo hates it when people are late, I'm feeling lighter than I've felt in years. I feel rested, and peaceful, and...hopeful.

I straighten my wrap dress, slip on my sneakers, and

toss my heels in my purse. This morning calls for a half-walk/half-jog. With the traffic, it'll be faster than trying for a taxi or a bus.

I take the last bite of my toast and grab my keys, ready to run. My phone rings again, the fourth call from Serena in the last two hours. I know if I don't answer she's going to call my mom, then my dad, then Fran.

"Hey," I say, popping in my earbuds, "I'm late for work."

I bend down to knot my shoes when Serena says loudly, "What is wrong with you? I thought your ghost went on a psycho-killer haunting spree, took a kitchen knife to you, and wrote cryptic messages on the mirrors with your blood. Why haven't you called me?"

The shoelaces slip from my hands and I blink. "What?"

Then I remember, the last time Serena and I talked I hadn't actually had a conversation with Daniel. The only thing she knows was that he appeared, he tried to talk to me, and then he disappeared.

Plus Serena loves sci-fi, but she also loves horror, which means sometimes, her imagination takes her to wacky and dark places.

She continues, "I was envisioning the number one thirty seven, written over and over, all in blood. It was gruesome. And of course, I couldn't figure out the message's meaning."

I hold back a laugh, because the number one hundred and thirty seven is one of the great mysteries of the universe, at least to physicists like Serena. Relativity, quantum mechanics, and electromagnetism are all unified by one over one hundred and thirty seven, and it might hold the key to the Grand Unified Theory. I've had to sit through many of Serena's lectures on the mysteries of this number. The fact that my imaginary-murder-mystery-death-by-ghost involves this number is not at all shocking.

"Okay, so, I'm fine," I say, reassuring her. I pick up my laces and quickly tie my shoes. "Actually, I'm better than fine. Daniel came back—"

"He has a name?" she asks. "The sexy, shirtless ghost has a name?"

"You just assume you were right that he's a ghost. What if I confirmed he was an alien from—"

"Did you?"

"No. You were right," I say, smiling. "And I have to tell you, he's amazing, he's kind, he makes me laugh, he's—"

"Oh no," Serena interrupts. "No Jillian, no. In a universe of infinite variables for love, you have chosen the one variable that can never—"

"It's not like that," I say, standing and shoving open my door.

Serena scoffs, and in the background I hear the clang of a door closing, "I'm closeting myself in the breakroom so I can yell at you." She takes a breath and says sharply, "Jillian Nejat!"

"Yes?"

She sounds like my mom when I nabbed oatmeal raisin cookies before breakfast.

I close my front door and slide my key into the lock, turning it. If I hurry, I can make it to the office by 9:30, which won't make Bernardo too upset, especially if I deliver an article this morning.

Serena sighs. "I have known you for years, and I know

that tone. You are falling for the sexy, shirtless ghost. You are falling in love with a dead guy."

Sometimes, silence is the best defense.

"Oh no. Your silence tells me you've already fallen in love. What are you thinking?" Serena asks.

Okay, silence is the worst defense.

"It's not like that."

It's exactly like that.

"Ha," Serena says, then there's the creaking of a door, and Serena barks something in French. I'm guessing she's protecting the solitude of the breakroom for our phone tête-à-tête.

"We're friends," I say, "he's helping me, and I'm helping him. The psychic told us we have to work together so he can...move on."

I flinch, the fluorescent bulb of the hall light shining coldly down on me.

"You're too attached," Serena says. "This won't end well. You need him to move on pronto before you become even more emotionally involved."

Gosh, if she only knew.

"What do you know about him?" she asks. "When did he die? What did he do with his life? What kind of person was he? Where is he from? What was he like?"

"Ummmm," I say, starting for the stairs. I'm on the fourth floor, there's no elevator in the building. Instead we have wide, old stairs, with creaky wood and strips of black no-slip treads. I grab the wooden railing and start down the flight, but when I do, my neighbor thrusts open the door to her apartment.

"I heard you scream last night," she says caustically, and I swing back around and stare at her, wide-eyed.

My neighbor, who I've never met, or even seen before,

is a stout woman in her late-fifties. She's wearing a floral robe, a clear shower cap covering pink hair rollers, and has an unlit cigarette in her mouth that she's chewing on like a piece of grass. The smell of canned dog food wafts from her apartment.

"Who's that?" Serena asks, "Is someone talking to you?"

"Oh. Sorry," I say. I know exactly what I was doing last night when I screamed, and apparently, my neighbor knows what I was doing too. I flush, and say, "I saw a cockroach."

My neighbor scoffs. Her disbelief clear.

I jump when Daniel appears next to me, a smile on his face.

"Hey—" He cuts off and his smile fades as he looks between me and my neighbor.

She's still scowling.

"Good morning?" Daniel says, a question in his voice. "What's up?"

"Ask her if she knew Daniel," Serena says. "I bet he died in your apartment. Ghosts always haunt the places where they died. Maybe he was murdered."

Luckily my earbuds don't carry sound, so neither my neighbor or Daniel can hear Serena.

I clear my throat and give my neighbor a neutral smile. "I was wondering...do you know who lived in my apartment before I did?"

I quickly glance at Daniel then away again.

My neighbor narrows her eyes on me, then pulls the unlit cigarette from her mouth and drops it into her robe's pocket.

Daniel looks between the two of us, "Why are you

asking? It wasn't me," he says, "I guarantee, I never lived in the mirrored hall of sexual misadventure, I—"

"You mean Daniel?" the woman asks, her lips curling in distaste.

Daniel cuts off and gives her the most stunned, shocked stupid look I've ever seen.

I cough and hit my chest.

"But..." He gives me a wide-eyed stare.

"Aha," Serena says. "She said Daniel, didn't she? I knew the ghost died in your apartment. It's Occam's Razor. The simplest explanation. How did he die?"

"Do you know what happened to him?" I ask slowly, then at the woman's glare, I amend, "I mean..."

She snorts. "Are you one of his floozies? He was always bringing the women around, every night a new one, waking me and Daisy up at three in the morning, all that banging coming from next door. I was glad to see him gone, I finally got rest, until you went about it last night, waking me up just like old times." She glares to emphasize her point.

"Jeez," Daniel says, taking a stunned step back. "What..."

"What happened last night?" Serena asks.

A tiny, coarse-haired terrier with a potbelly and a sparkly pink shirt charges the doorway and lets out an irritated bark. Daisy, I suppose.

"It was a cockroach," I say to both Serena and my neighbor.

"It was not a cockroach," Daniel says, recovering from his shock. He shakes his head and studies the woman. "I don't believe her. I never lived here. I didn't..."

He trails off, because as we both know, he does remember lots of women, lots of sex, lots of...Lothario.

"Ask her how he died," Serena says again. "If you find out how he died, you can help him move on. Go to the light, sexy ghost!"

My neighbor, though, is finished with our conversation, she's already shushing Daisy and moving to close her door.

"Cockroach or cock," she says curtly, "I don't care. Just keep the noise down. Daisy needs his sleep."

"Wait," I say quickly.

She pauses, the door half-closed.

"What happened to him? To Daniel? Do you know?"

Daniel leans forward, his gaze intent, and it feels almost as if he's holding his breath.

My neighbor shrugs. "He's gone, thankfully. Good riddance."

Then she slams her door. Behind the wood I hear the hard click of a bolt sliding into place, the jangle of a door chain, and then the loud boom of a metal floor lock banging down.

Daniel looks as if he's just been kicked in the stomach. He flinches at each lock slamming into place. He stares at the closed door, as if he can't quite comprehend that he really did live in the mirror-sex-den, and he really did have random sex every night, and he really did have a neighbor who is *glad* that he's gone.

"I have to go," I tell Serena.

"What? Why? You have to talk to me. From the sounds of it, he was the king of sexy times, which isn't a bad thing, obviously, since I'm the queen of sexy times. However, Jilly, he's a ghost, and in life he was a one-night slam-bam-thank-you-ma'am kind of guy. He's not someone to devote your life to. Because he's a *ghost*. A sexy-times *ghost*."

"Yeah," I say, watching Daniel stare at our neighbor's door, his shoulders falling, and his blue eyes clouding. "I know. Trust me, I know. I have to go. Sorry, I'm late for work."

At that, I hang up and then take a step toward Daniel. The hallway is quiet now, the thick old plaster of the building, the brick walls, and the wood insulating the interior from the busy rush of the street outside.

On my floor, there are three apartments and the landing, covered in gray industrial carpet. The light bleeds over the hall and highlights the age of the space, calling attention to the cracks in the century-old plaster. I always loved the smell of old plaster, it reminds me of home, but right now, looking at Daniel, it just feels lonely.

"I didn't think I lived here. I didn't think..." He trails off and gives me a rueful smile, but even though his lips curl, his eyes are still clouded, "I wonder what kind of man I was? I wonder what kind of things I did? I don't sound very—"

"Stop," I say, holding up my hand. "Stop."

I take a step forward, reach out and touch the outline of his chest, resting my hand against his heart, just like he did for me last night. "No matter what you did or didn't do, no matter who you were or weren't, I see you and I like you just as you are."

He stares down at me, judges the truth of my statement by my expression, and then like the cool wind rushing across a field on a hot day, his smile is filled with relief and gratitude. "Thank you."

I nod, tightness in my chest, a lump in my throat. Serena's warning echoes in my head. *You can't fall in love with a ghost. It won't end well.*

"Are you coming?" I ask Daniel, giving him a bright smile. "I'm late for work."

He studies me, then nods, and with that, I rush down the creaking stairs and out the door, into the loud rush of city traffic, the cool spring wind, and the bright, blinding morning sun.

24

THE SUNLIGHT SIZZLES OVER THE GRAY CONCRETE OF THE steps and I grip the warm metal railing, sliding my hand over the painted handrail. The noise of Yankee Stadium —the loud music, the roaring crowd—vibrates through me, reaching deep inside.

The noon sun splays over me, toasting me, and the familiar smell of roasting hot dogs, salty popcorn, spilled beer, and grass and leather fill me with energy. Yankee Stadium is as large, energetic, and raucous as the colosseum must have been at the height of the Roman Empire.

The rows and rows of seats, rising to the sky like an unending escalator, are filled with baseball fans soaking in the pleasure of spending the day sweating, drinking beer, and lobbing insults at both bad and good umpire calls.

I'm more of a fly-into-the-sky-aboard-a-spaceship than fly-into-the-sky-on-a-baseball kind of woman, but my dad loves the Yankees, and I spent too many days and nights as a kid, perched on the stadium seat next to him, eating salty popcorn, and drinking cherry cola, to deny the pleasure of a baseball game.

"There's our seat," Daniel says, his eyes lighting happily when he spots our two empty seats in the nosebleeds.

It's been two weeks since Daniel and I teamed up to save my job and find my "lifelong partner." We've been pushing Daniel's Big Idea articles, a ten-part series on intimacy, sex, and relationships. I think it's going well; Daniel's convinced it's going great.

Two weeks ago, when I ran into the office thirty minutes late, Bernardo wasn't upset at all, because shortly after I delivered my first Big Idea article based on my interview with Dr. Brown.

I delivered five articles the first week and five the second week. Even my "Just Jillian" column veered from my usual content and addressed questions like how to keep the spark alive in long-distance relationships.

It's all looking up. Tomorrow's our Monday meeting, and I'm hoping my numbers have taken a turn for the better.

Daniel's convinced that my job is safe, especially because he's now my biggest fan. That probably has to do with the fact that he's there when I write the articles, cracking jokes, suggesting titles, and reminding me to keep it real, but keep it me as well.

So work is progressing, but my dating life? That's a different story.

After my fail in the coffee shop, the near mugging, and Daniel and I making love, I haven't tried to date or talk to men. I'm not interested.

Or at least, I'm not interested in anyone but Daniel.

Our first night after making love we went to *Nights in the Hills* on Broadway because Hayley gave it a rave review. She sold me two tickets that she'd scored, and I managed to haggle her down to a bargain basement price.

I bought the second seat for Daniel, and even though he couldn't sit, he stood next to me, and rested his hand on my arm, absentmindedly brushing his fingers over my skin the whole show.

I sank into the plush, red velvet seat, the gold trim and bright paint opulent, the lights falling to darkness, the large theater shifting from expansive to intimate, and I smiled the entire time, my face aching from the feeling.

The next night we went to The Hayden Planetarium and watched stars being born, then we played my favorite *Star Trek* trivia game, and for each wrong answer, Daniel pressed his mouth to mine in laughing defeat.

We took a long walk in Central Park, I nibbled on honeyed almonds bought from a street cart, and then dropped the petals from a red rose Daniel asked me to buy, so I could throw the silk-soft petals into the mirrored surface of the lake flowing under the gracefully curving Bow Bridge.

We watched the sun set from the Empire State Building, the sun's golden light reflecting off the silvery skyscrapers, Daniel's arms folded around me, his insubstantial warmth as gentle as the falling sun.

We played street chess in Union Square, me making moves for both of us, Daniel winning every time, his eyes laughing at each pawn captured and every rook stolen.

The symphony, an evening dinner cruise, a weekend watch-marathon of every notable original *Star Trek* episode and all the original movies, exploration of all the foods that Daniel loves (burgers, bacon, and chocolate were just the beginning), a night-time movie on a checkered picnic blanket under the Brooklyn Bridge— we've managed to fit a lifetime of experiences into two weeks.

If I thought I was in love before, now I *know* I'm in love.

Is Daniel in love with me? I don't know.

And I don't know what he'll do when he finds out I'm in love with him.

We haven't made love since the first night. But we also haven't pursued me finding another "decent-seeming" man to spend my life with.

Now we're here, at Yankee Stadium. I have a large bag of popcorn crushed in my arms, the salty, buttery scent teasing me, and a frothy beer, because when Daniel looked at one with longing, I bought it instead of a cherry cola.

I squeeze my way down my aisle, pressing close to the seats in front of me to avoid the knees of the people I pass, "Sorry, excuse me, sorry," I say, some of my popcorn spilling as I sidestep my way down the tight aisle.

Daniel doesn't bother avoiding knees. As soon as I pass, the people drop back into their seats, sprawling out, and Daniel walks through them. He still shudders, like he said, he's never gotten used to it, but sometimes there's no avoiding walking through objects or people.

At my seat, I pull down the dark plastic chair and drop into it.

Daniel stands casually next to me, studying the emerald and apple green stripes of the grassy outfield, the vibrant flashing of the jumbotron screens, and the players, so far away that they're the size of toy figures.

He doesn't remember if he's ever been to a baseball game. I smile up at him, and settle into my hard seat, the dark plastic hot from the sun.

We're late. It's already the third inning, the Yankees are up to bat.

A few rows down, there's a skinny, irate woman in shorts, a pink Yankee's jersey, and pink baseball hat, screaming insults in a ragged voice, which tells me she's been throwing insults the whole game.

"Are people always like that?" Daniel asks, staring in stunned awe at the petite woman.

Her blonde ponytail swings, and she's vibrating mad.

I nod, conscious that the sunburned man next to me, with the visor hat, and the pencil in his mouth, is paying careful attention to both the game, and me. If I start talking to the air, he's going to have something to say.

The woman jumps up from her seat again, and screams, fist raised, "Hey! I've had better calls from my ex! You suck! Why don't you apply for a job as a telemarketer? Bad calls are in your blood!"

"Who is she talking to?" Daniel asks, obviously finding her insults more interesting than the game.

I nod toward the umpire, his blue figure far across the field.

Daniel smiles at me, "What? Not talking to me?"

I roll my eyes, pull out my phone and press it to my ear. "Hi."

Daniel grins at me and loops his thumbs into his pockets, then casually drawls, "Well hello there."

I snort and the sunburned man next to me turns sharply and sends me a glare. I ignore him and soon enough he takes the pencil from his mouth and the sound of the pencil lead scratching on his notebook tells me he's invested big in the game.

"How's the popcorn?" Daniel asks, eyeing the bright yellow, fluffy, stadium-popped corn.

I grab a handful and shove it in my mouth, making a show of enjoying it. The warm butter and salt are delicious enough to make me lick the warm butter from my fingers in appreciation.

"That good?" Daniel asks, his voice rough, his eyelids lowering over his blue eyes in the heated look that I've come to think of as *Daniel's vicarious food orgasm*.

I lick my lips and then tip the beer, condensation running over my fingers, as I take a long, cool swallow.

"Jeez," Daniel breathes. Then as I wipe the back of my hand over my mouth he says, "I've decided I love baseball."

I laugh and say into my phone, "Really? Just like that?"

He nods, his eyes crinkling as he takes in my midriff t-shirt baring my abdomen and my short shorts hugging my hips. "Just like that," he confirms.

"Good. We'll come again. We have plenty of time," I say, the sun beating on the back of my neck, making my skin prickle.

Daniel's smile fades, and as a cloud passes over the sun, a shadow passes through him. He looks away from me, out toward home plate, and I can almost hear him thinking, "Do we?"

But then he looks back to me again, and he's giving me a rueful smile. "I was thinking, I wish we could go to some of the places I remember. I'd take you to Monaco, and Paris, and we'd sail the Mediterranean Sea. It'd be like the first time for me too, I can barely remember them."

My mouth goes dry, and I take a quick drink, then ask into my phone, "Can you? Can you leave New York?"

Daniel shakes his head and glances out over the circular curving expanse of the stadium. "No. I've tried. I can make it to the Bronx, Brooklyn, but Jersey, Long Island, Westchester, those are all out of reach. It's like I'm on a bungee and as soon as I travel too far I'm yanked back. I think something is keeping me here."

His eyebrows pull together, and his forehead wrinkles in a pensive frown.

Around us, people jump up and cheer, shouting exuberantly.

"That's normal, lots of New Yorkers don't ever leave the city," I joke, trying to lighten his mood. "They think crossing a bridge or driving through a tunnel is worse than a transatlantic flight."

Daniel gives me an amused smile. "I guess that's it."

The crowd roar subsides, and the people in front of us sit down. The sunburned man on my right plops into his seat and joyously scratches in his notebook.

Everyone has settled back into their seats except the blonde ponytail woman. She's still standing, shaking her fist in the air, giving the players a piece of her mind. "You call that running? My dog can run faster than you, and he's dead!"

The man next to me stiffens, then jerks his head toward the woman.

"Hey!" she shouts, her voice raw from yelling. "Slow-pants! Move it! Or we'll trade you to the Tigers! How would you like living in Detroit? I bet you'd run then!"

I take another handful of popcorn and enjoy the

show. The woman is cultivating reactions from the fans in our section, mostly boos and hisses, and "sit down!" shouted her way.

When it's strike two, she yells, "Hey! You couldn't hit a wall if you ran into one!"

The sunburned man throws his notebook down and stands. "Lady!" he yells angrily, "Would you shut up?"

His voice is so loud and booming that it echoes around our section. Half a dozen people turn around to stare. The heckler woman stiffens and then slowly turns around, searching for the sunburned man.

"Is that..." Daniel cuts off, his eyes wide.

My mouth falls open and I lean forward, blinking in disbelief.

"Hayley?" I say.

She's looking for the man who shouted at her, instead she sees me. When she does, she stands on her tiptoes, gives me a wide smile and then waves.

Gosh. She looks so cute and perky in her pink jersey, baseball hat and shorts, you would never know she's a foul-tempered heckler.

"She's coming up," Daniel says, laughter in his voice. "I thought she hated sports."

I nod. "Me too."

That's what she's always claimed. Clearly she's a fibbing fibber that fibs.

A chorus of "hey," "watch it" and "what's your problem?" follow as Hayley scrambles over the seats, elbowing her way up the row rather than taking the stairs. Finally she makes it to me, her cheeks pink and her eyes lit up with what I recognize as fervent fan sparkle.

The sunburned man glares at her, clearly expecting a

confrontation. Hayley ignores him, and gives me a blinding smile. "Hey! Enjoying the game?"

I nod, and then Hayley glances at the empty seat next to me.

"Where's your date?" she asks, the breeze catching her ponytail and tossing it about so that she looks like an innocent farmgirl out for a day of baseball.

Daniel sends Hayley a cheeky wave, shaking his head in amusement.

"He..." I look at Daniel, trying to think of what to say. I'm not great at fabricating untruths in the moment.

"Oh, he stood you up. Poor you," Hayley says sympathetically.

"Lady, sit down!" the sunburned man snaps at Hayley.

She wrinkles her nose at him, then drops into Daniel's seat. Daniel takes a step back, his legs passing through the man in the seat next to Hayley.

"Sorry," I say to Daniel, while pretending to say it to the sunburned man.

Daniel gives me a smile, "I'll go down, see if I can get a closer view." He points toward the outfield, and when I nod, he moves down the aisle, heading toward the stairs.

Hayley leans forward and takes a deep breath, and I get the feeling she's about to yell something inappropriate, so I say, "Why do you always pretend you hate sports?"

Her breath deflates and she leans back, casting me a side-eyed glance.

"Oh," she says, frowning, probably realizing that the crazed fan-girl look she has going today doesn't mesh with her manicured beauty queen persona from work.

She bites her lip and rubs her hands over her thighs, considering her answer.

The crack of the bat hitting the ball and the responding roar of the crowd rushes over us. My chair vibrates with the stomping of excited feet. I hold the popcorn bag over to Hayley and offer her some.

She smiles and takes a handful. The buttery smell drifts up to me, and I glance over the crowd, searching for Daniel. He's easy to spot. First, because he's shirtless and his tanned, muscled back glows in the afternoon sun. Second, because he's taller than almost everyone in the crowd. Third, because no matter where he is, my eyes are drawn to him, like a magnet, unable to resist.

"It's because..." Hayley begins, her voice hesitant, her hands squeezing her thighs nervously. "You want the truth?"

I nod. "Yeah."

She squints out over the outfield, not really seeing the game, and says, "The truth is, the night I first met Bernardo, he treated me like I was some snobbish former beauty queen *and* a space cadet. He didn't wait to get to know me, he assumed he knew everything about me from my looks. I was so angry that I decided to teach him a lesson and act *exactly* like the person he thought I was. And then when I first came to work, Ned treated me like Bernardo did, and so did Buck, and everybody else, and after a while it became easier to keep being a snobby space cadet then explain to everyone that I'm not really that way at all."

I stare at her, shocked, the sun beating down, the wind barely cooling my skin, and take in what she's admitting. "Did I..."

"No." She shakes her head. "No. You've always treated me like a person who is worth something. And you always buy my knock-offs, even if they're terrible."

I cover my mouth, hiding a smile. So she knows they're terrible, not "high-quality, luxury, genuine goods."

"I think," I tell her, giving her a reassuring smile, "after all these years, if anyone thinks you're snobby or a space-cadet, then they haven't been paying attention. Your articles are always on-point, you can haggle a nun out of her habit, and you're always nice, even to Buck."

She laughs, her cheeks pink. "Thanks." Then she looks down at the plastic chair she's sitting in and says, "Sorry about your date."

I smile down across the crowd and spot Daniel. He's turned back around. He lifts a hand in a wave, and I smile back at him. "There's no need to be sorry. Everything's perfect."

I fiddle with my beer cup, the beer's now warm from the sunshine, and Hayley watches the game for a minute. But she's shifting in her seat, her elbow bumping mine, her legs knocking against mine, and she finally says, "Since you're the relationship expert..."

I lift an eyebrow. "You've heard my stats right? I'm not *quite* the expert. And my job isn't exactly secure."

"I like your philosophy," she says loyally.

"Thanks," I say, smiling. Then I ask, "So you don't actually want to switch with me? You take dating, I take sports?"

She gives me an aghast look, like I just offered her a pair of dirty, sweaty socks.

"And give up this?" She gestures at the stadium, like it's her version of nirvana.

"Right," I say.

Then she drums her fingers on her thigh, ignoring the cheering of the crowd, and says, "I was going to ask, if I...let's say I like someone..." She flushes, and I immediately think about what Daniel said, that she likes Bernardo.

I nod. "Sure."

"But I'm nervous, because we have a completely platonic relationship, and I don't...I don't want to ruin it if he doesn't feel the same way." She grips her thigh, and looks at me intently, "What I'm saying is, I'm scared of ruining things. I know him, at least I think I do. But he doesn't *really* know me. I'm worried that if I show him me"—she gestures at her jersey, her torn jean shorts, and her sweat-lined, flushed face—"I'm worried he'll hate me."

"Why would he hate you?" I ask.

She shrugs helplessly, "Because I'm really good at being someone I'm not. And him hating me would be exactly what I deserve."

I shake my head in denial. "You want my advice?"

She nervously clenches her hands in her lap, "Yes."

"Start being yourself. From now on, always. People might think it's odd at first, but that's okay. Come in to work wearing a jersey if you want. Talk about sports if you want. Stop selling knock-offs—"

"No way, I love selling knock-offs."

I grin at her. "See, you're halfway there. Just be a hundred percent yourself. And then tell him."

"Tell him what?" she asks.

I let out a long sigh, thinking about how I feel about Daniel and how I'm about to give advice that I'm not following.

"Tell him the truth about how you feel."

She shakes her head emphatically, her blonde ponytail swinging. "I can't do that."

I hand her the popcorn, she takes the bag and sets it

in her lap, the salty, buttery scent rising. "Then ask him to a game, and wow him with your heckling, beer-swigging, cute self."

She flashes me a smile. "You think that would work?"

"Maybe not," I say, thinking about Bernardo, wondering if he likes sports, "but it's worth a try."

At that, Hayley flags down a vendor carrying a cooler strapped to his chest. She passes money down the aisle for beer. One for her, one for me, and one for the sunburned guy who looks like he could use a cold drink.

Hayley and I clink our beers together, the cold froth sloshing over to spill on my fingers.

"Cheers to being ourselves and taking risks for love," Hayley says.

"Cheers to that," I say, my eyes straying to Daniel.

When I swallow the velvety cold beer, toasting something I've always believed in, he turns to find me watching him. He smiles and I lift my beer in a toast.

He lifts his hand to his forehead, a man tipping his hat to a lady, and I warm from my toes to my lips at the heady look in his eyes.

25

When the elevator doors slide open, the bright flashing TV screens of The Wall greet me. It's Monday morning, and *The Daily Exposé* is hopping.

I hoist my purse over my shoulder and stride toward the back of the office. It's not quite nine, and the smell of brewing coffee and freshly fried cake donuts gives me a happy zing. I'm in a pencil skirt and a bright yellow cardigan because when I woke up this morning I had the feeling that today would be a *good* day.

I smile as I pass two interns copyediting a freelancer's article. I step over a mound of newsprint, and then dodge a ping pong ball tossed between two techies. The computer techs have been in an exuberant mood for weeks now, ever since they showed their supremacy by demolishing the dolphin sex link threat in less than three hours.

When the techies throw the ping pong ball again, Daniel reaches up and catches it, at least he would've if it didn't pass through his hand.

When he winks at me I flash a grin and keep moving quickly toward the back of the office, where everyone's gathered for the morning meeting.

At the wooden conference table, Buck gnaws on a cinnamon sugar donut like a rabid wolverine, the sugar and cinnamon flying about him like marrow from a bone.

There's a box of a dozen cake donuts on the table in front of him, and Ned stares at it wistfully. However, I'm fairly certain Buck will stab Ned's hand with a pencil if he tries to reach for one, which is why no one at the table is eating donuts except Buck.

I slide into my chair, dropping my leather purse on the table, and smile a greeting at everyone. Bernardo taps at his phone, completely engrossed in whatever he's reading. Hayley's busy applying a coat of rose-colored lipstick, glancing in her compact.

Buck grins at me, donut in his teeth, his thick eyebrows lowering, his bald head reflecting the fluorescent office lights.

Ned drums his fingers on the table, staring but pretending not to stare at the box of donuts. Poor Ned. His favorite morning snack is chocolate cake donuts with chocolate frosting, and right there in the box is a glistening chocolate frosted donut. He distractedly waves at me, his wispy brown hair messy from the windy day outside.

"Hi Jillian," he says, yanking his eyes from the donuts. "You survived the weekend."

I nod and give him a wave.

Ned is always surprised when we all show up to work on Mondays. He's convinced that one of these days we'll fall victim to alien abduction, organ harvesting, interdimensional vortexing, military testing, mindwiping, or one of the hundreds of crimes he's actually written about.

"Hey Ned, you want a donut?" Buck asks, grabbing another sugar covered one from the box and biting it with relish.

"This guy..." Daniel says, shaking his head. "He just can't give it up."

Ned jiggles his leg nervously and reaches for the box, "Wow! Thanks Buck, I missed breakfast—"

"It's too bad," Buck interrupts, "that we don't always get what we want."

He pushes the box out of Ned's reach.

Ned stops mid-reach. "Umm."

"Do you want a donut, Hayley?" Buck asks.

She rolls her eyes and sets down her tube of lipstick on top of her notebook. "Donuts are full of trans fat, Buck." She turns to Ned. "Don't sweat it, Ned. I have an apple." She reaches into her purse, grabs a bright red apple, and lobs it across the table like a star pitcher.

Ned fumbles the catch, dropping it to the table. It rolls a few inches then stops in front of him.

"Thanks," he mumbles, staring at the apple dismally. "You know. The same overlord companies own both big food and big pharma. They're in this...twisted symbiotic relationship. Big food adds trans fat, high fructose corn syrup, and franken-chemicals to the food to purposely make people sick. Then their...sister companies...in big pharma spawn the medications for the sicknesses they caused. And those cause...certain side effects...for which they have more magic medications. So eat...donuts, Buck. It's all a sadistic ploy engineered by the reptilians to weaken and control humankind." At that, Ned takes a satisfied bite of the apple.

Hayley gives him a smile.

Buck who had been devouring his donut, looks at the crumbling pastry, frowns, and then tosses it disgustedly back into the box.

Daniel stares at the donuts, their icing thick and glossy, the sugar sparkling in the office light. "I think Ned just ruined donuts for me," Daniel says mournfully. "I was looking forward to an éclair, with chocolate mousse and..." His eyes go all sad and puppy-dog like.

I restrain a laugh.

Daniel narrows his eyes on me, "Don't laugh. This is a serious crisis. I can't have you eat a donut for me in celebration of Bernardo telling you that your articles are crushing it if the donuts are a reptilian ploy to dominate humankind."

I choke back a snort and pretend to cough instead.

Daniel grins at me, clearly enjoying himself. "We'll get coffee instead," he decides.

Bernardo clears his throat and sets his phone down on the table. He glances around as if he's just now realizing we're all here.

He checks his watch, it's exactly nine.

"Let's begin," he says.

Ned waves his hand and squirms in his seat, "This weekend, during a public hearing, councilman Wagner displayed distinct AI behavior—"

"No," Bernardo says.

"The squirrels in Central Park are...tracking New Yorkers...sending data back to—"

"No."

"The city water is...contaminated with Viagra, resulting in—"

"No," Bernardo says, shaking his head.

"Hang on," Daniel says, "I want to hear more about that one."

I take my pen out and write in small letters for Daniel, "He mentioned it last year, it's the grays trying to make men horny so they'll donate sperm for more hybrids."

Daniel laughs, delighted.

Ned's reached the end of his spiel, so he says with a sigh, "Mugging on Roosevelt Island...electric apartment fire in Williamsburg...salmonella cover-up at an Upper West Side restaurant."

"Good. Go," Bernardo says, writing down Ned's stories, "Buck, what do you have?"

Buck nudges the box of donuts toward Bernardo, his usual goody-two-shoes offering, and then recites his latest story ideas and leads, finally making his bi-weekly push for why he should be in charge of the sports section.

While he talks I take in deep breaths of the chocolate sprinkle donuts, dreaming of swiping my fingers through the rich, chocolatey icing.

Across from me, Hayley twirls her blonde hair, her eyes distant, deep in thought. She doesn't look any different then she usually does, she's in tailored camel-colored pants and a rose-hued silk top. It makes me wonder if she's going to take my advice from yesterday or if she's decided against it.

"Hayley," Bernardo says once Buck's finished. "What do you have?"

She quickly glances at me, dropping her hand from her blonde hair. She looks almost panicked.

I nod and give her a confident smile. *You can do it.*

Across the office, past the elevators, someone in billing laughs shrilly, and the abrupt sound must kick Hayley out of her nervousness, because she squares her shoulders and then tilts her head in acknowledgment of my silent support.

She looks directly at Bernardo and says firmly, "I'm working on fielding interviews with a few of the Yankees players, I've got their hitting coach booked. The pitching coach is acting cagey. The Knicks are open to me coming by for a locker room interview, and I've got a few leads on the Rangers. I want the right wing, but I'll settle for the centerman. I also have a portfolio of player analyses in the works, and some season predictions I'm pulling together." She taps her pen against the pages of her notebook and then says offhandedly, "And there's a new Elizabethan jewelry exhibit for charity that I'm attending tomorrow night at The Morgan."

Hayley closes her notebook with a snap and then raises her eyes to the room, her expression calm. I give her a subtle thumbs up.

Buck rubs the side of his bald head, looking as if someone just kicked him in the skull with steel toed boots.

Bernardo, who never shows reactions to anything, stares at Hayley then ever so slowly, blinks.

On any other man, that blink is the equivalent of jumping on top of the table and shouting *what's happening*?!

Ned thrusts his chair back from the table and jumps to his feet. "I knew this would happen," he says, jabbing a shaking finger a Hayley. "Don't panic. You've jumped to another dimension. You aren't the Hayley we know. She's now in your dimension. Tell me, in your dimension is it Jiffy peanut butter or Jif peanut butter?"

Hayley sends me an amused glance, as if she's saying, *you said no one would make a big deal of this.*

"Jiffy," Daniel says confidently. "It's Jiffy peanut butter."

"Jiffy," Hayley says, lifting an eyebrow.

Ned throws his arms in the air and takes three quick steps away from the conference table and then three quick steps back, pacing. "This is bad. This is very bad. Hayley, there's no such thing as Jiffy peanut butter. That only exists in your former dimension. Tell me..." Ned leans forward and places his hands on the table as if this question is of utmost importance, "does Fruit of the Loom have a cornucopia in its logo?"

"Sure," Daniel says, "yeah."

"Yes," Hayley says confidently.

Ned shakes his head sadly. "No, Hayley. It does not. It never has. Not in this dimension."

I look at Bernardo, wondering when he's going to put a stop to this, but he's still staring at Hayley as if he's the one who's traveled to a new dimension. Either that or he's been mindwiped.

Overhead the heater clicks on, sending a stream of hot air over us, rustling the pages of my notebook.

Buck finally shakes himself out of his shock, most likely incurred from the fact that he now has even less chance of taking over the sports section than he did just five minutes ago.

"Bullcrap Ned. There aren't alternate dimensions. Hayley is as terrible at sports reporting as ever. Let me prove it," Buck lowers his bushy eyebrows and scowls at Hayley, "Who had the most runs in baseball history?"

"Rickie Henderson," Hayley shoots back, not even hesitating.

Buck's face bleeds to red. "What do you call an ump?"

Ha, you shouldn't ask a heckler that.

But Hayley keeps her heckler opinions to herself and answers, "Blue."

"Who set ninety MLB records in their career?"

"Ty Cobb," Hayley says, lifting an eyebrow.

The silence is deafening.

"Hayley," Ned says, dropping into his seat as if his bones have turned liquid, "When is the next dress sale at Bergdorf's?"

She frowns at Ned. "I don't know."

Ned gasps. "This is unbelievable."

Daniel laughs. "What I'm most concerned about," he says, "is apparently I'm also from another dimension. I swear I remember Jiffy peanut butter."

He stares out over the open concept office, the clacking of keyboards a constant rhythm, the flashing of The Wall brightening the space, the buzz and energy flowing around us.

"Who knew?" Daniel finally asks, sending me a wink.

I shake my head, restraining a smile.

At the head of the conference table, Bernardo shakes himself, like a man coming awake. Then he says, "Good. Sounds good, Hayley. Do that."

Hayley's cheeks pinken and she sits straighter, adjusting the cuffs of her silk shirt. "Great. Okay. I'll do that."

Buck's mouth is working, but no sound is coming out. Ned drums his fingers on the table, shaking his head. They're floundering.

"Hayley likes sports," I say, watching Hayley fidget with the gold bracelet on her wrist. When she looks up at me, I give her a wink. "She always has. Don't you remember her talent for Miss Ohio? It was making thirty free throws in ninety seconds. I thought you all knew that."

Hayley gives me a wide, grateful smile—which is also full of surprise because she's never shared that information. I looked up that tidbit last night.

And that is the extent of my ability to formulate a speech in support of Hayley, but it's enough.

"So she's not a dimension hopper," Ned says, sighing.

"I'd still do a better job at the sports section," Buck growls, rubbing his head.

Bernardo grabs his phone and quickly scrolls down, stopping to read his notes.

"Jillian," he says, scanning his phone.

Daniel strides to stand behind Bernardo, reading his phone over his shoulder. The glowing lights from The Wall flicker through Daniel as he scans my numbers. A nervous flutter rolls through my stomach so that the formerly enticing smell of chocolate donuts makes me slightly ill.

Maybe Bernardo will say my stats are still down, or that my unsubscribes have increased, or—

But then Daniel looks up from the phone, and there's a wide, celebratory smile on his face, and his blue eyes are lit with happiness.

"You did it," he says. "You did it, Jillian."

I look into Daniel's eyes, and for a second, I feel as if I'm floating, suspended in the sky, spinning in his arms. I'm smiling back at him when Bernardo glances up from his phone and says, "Negative comments are down, positive comments up. Your subscribe rate is the highest it's ever been." He glances at his phone again and says, "Traffic, shares, and inbound links are up."

"Jillian, we're celebrating tonight," Daniel says,

running a hand through his hair and smiling at me like we just climbed to the summit of Mt. Everest together and we're about to watch the sunrise.

"Keep it up," Bernardo says, glancing back at me, his expression neutral. "You have two more weeks to prove you can maintain this trajectory."

I nod, clasping my hands tightly in my lap.

"You've got this," Daniel says confidently, striding back to me with a grin. "And to celebrate we're getting coffee and freaky alien donuts while we brainstorm the next big idea."

I give a subtle nod, freaky alien donuts sound delicious, even if they have franken-chemicals.

Bernardo's still talking, confirming our assignments for the week and briefing us on housekeeping items like updating our passwords, new office money-saving schemes, and the departure and arrival of a new batch of interns.

While Bernardo's reciting his list of updates Daniel listens, absently running his fingers up and down my arm. A quiet, gentle warmth flows through my cardigan, all the way to my skin, like a warm spring breeze rushing over me.

I lean back in my chair, the plastic squeaking, and take notes on Bernardo's agenda items. But all the while there's a low panicky voice growing inside me, insistent that the better things get, the worse they'll become. The more I let go of the past, the more I succeed, the closer we are to moving on.

"I knew I was here to help you," Daniel says smiling down at me.

And what can I do but smile back?

26

ROASTING COFFEE BEANS, CHOCOLATE AND CARAMEL scented, wrap their inviting fragrance around me. The tiny coffee shop next to my office is a walk-in, wood-floored space, with ochre walls, the color of a monarch butterfly's wings, and soft music that sounds like a rainstorm in a tropical forest.

It's one of many cramped, walk-in coffee shops common in the city. It's unique though, in that it has a long reclaimed barn wood countertop, rehabbed industrial stainless steel espresso machines, and a towering glass cold brew system with twisting tubes and bulbous carafes that looks as if it belongs in a fifteenth century apothecary.

There's only room for three small square tables and five wooden chairs, all purchased at a farm auction in the Hudson Valley. I know this because sometimes I spend hours here, mainlining coffee while on deadline, and Lupita, the barista/owner, loves sharing origin stories. She'll tell you the history of every chair, table, light fixture, coffee bean, almond/rice/teff flour, and chocolate in her shop.

The three tables are already occupied, one with a couple holding hands gazing dreamily at each other, another with a mom and her toddler, and the last with a late-twenties man with dark brown curly hair and black-rimmed glasses, listening to music in his headphones and typing on his laptop.

I head straight to the reclaimed wood counter and the glass pastry case. There are slices of tres leches cake topped with vanilla-infused whipped cream and sprinkled with cocoa, crumbly carrot cake with cream cheese frosting, tiramisu with espresso-soaked ladyfingers and rich mascarpone, raspberry and chocolate macarons, palm-sized peanut butter chocolate chip cookies, and yes, on top, freshly made donuts—vanilla cake donuts dusted with powdered sugar, chocolate cinnamon donuts drizzled with ganache and rainbow sprinkles, and for Daniel...

"Éclairs," he says, smiling down at the glass case and the pretty 1940s pink milk glass platters displaying rows of dark chocolate éclairs, salted caramel éclairs, vanilla éclairs, lemon custard with raspberry éclairs, and passionfruit and mango éclairs. Lupita bakes the choux pastry, and then fills the eclairs with rich, creamy puddings, then tops them with glossy, sweet icings, a veritable rainbow of colors and tastes.

After a moment of appreciative silence, Daniel smiles at me, and says with utmost seriousness, "We should celebrate more often. Coffee and donuts, who knew—"

"Excuse me?"

I turn and find the twenty-something man with the

brown curly hair and black-rimmed glasses, holding up his hand in a wave.

Is he talking to me?

I look behind me, but no one's there but Daniel.

Lupita is at the sink behind the counter, washing out the stainless steel milk frothing pitcher. But the man's not looking at Lupita, he's looking at me.

When I glance back at him, his cheeks burn red, and he shifts, scuffing his feet on the wood floor. He has his laptop bag slung over his shoulder, and I'm guessing he's about to leave. Maybe I dropped something?

But no. He's not holding anything out for me.

I smile at him and he drops his hand and gives me a shy smile back.

"Hi," he says, "I...I'm not trying to be awkward...but, I come in here a lot, and I've seen you around and...I think I saw you at the last trekker convention in Jersey City. In January? You were in a comm officer's uniform, that was you right?"

Wait. What?

I nod. It was definitely me. I religiously attend every convention within two hundred miles and try my darnedest to make any other that I can. And I always wear the communications officer uniform (irony, you are my friend).

The man gives me a wide, excited smile. "I thought it was you!"

"He likes you," Daniel says, stepping closer to me.

He studies my fellow trekker with an intent scrutiny, taking in his earnest expression, his jeans and navy cashmere sweater, his nice-guy looks, and even the thousand-plus dollar watch on his wrist.

Daniel catalogues it all, and then something passes

over him, a hardening of his jaw, a tightness around his eyes, and he says, "He's going to ask you out. You should say yes."

An astonished, disbelieving alarm grips me, and I barely prevent myself from swinging around and snapping, *are you crazy? I'm with you!*

The man hefts his laptop bag, and his watch face reflects the overhead light. It's an Abry, and the only reason I know this is because Hayley had a slew of Abry knock-offs at Christmas, and she convinced me to buy one for my dad. According to Hayley, it's the epitome of Swiss watch luxury, has a sapphire-crystal case back, self-winding movement, gold and steel construction, diamonds, it's water resistant up to 60 meters and...I don't know, none of that was actually true for the knock-off, since the gold paint on my dad's watch scraped off after a day and then it died when he wore it while washing dishes. But this watch, I'm guessing, is the real deal, especially because apparently Daniel has decided that I should *date* the guy wearing it.

The man gives me an earnest look, "Ever since I saw you, I've been wanting to say hi. And today, I heard about this outdoor movie series, Sci-fi in the Park, it's a movie night and I thought..." He flushes then, even brighter red, and gosh, I know the signs, he's shy. "I thought you might want to go—"

He stops. Waits for me to say something.

"Jillian," Daniel says quietly, "you should say yes."

I look at him quickly, but his face is turned away, as if he doesn't actually want me to see his expression.

But I see the line of his shoulders, and they're tense, knotted.

I don't want to say yes, "I want to go with you," I tell

Daniel, forgetting that the curly-haired trekker is waiting for my answer.

The man lets out a sharp huff of air, a relieved exhale. "Great. That's...that's great."

The man opens the flap of his leather laptop bag and pulls out his wallet, while talking excitedly, "The first movie is *I'll Never Forget You* from 1951, it's about an atomic physicist, it's more romance than sci-fi, we could wait for the next one, that's *The Incredible Shrinking Man.*"

He pulls out a card. It's his business card, small, rectangular, and white. He takes a pen out and scrawls his phone number and email on the back.

He hands it to me, and the thin cardstock is heavy in my hands. "I'm Thomas, by the way," he says. "Sorry, I should've started with that."

I look down at his card. It says: Thomas Anand, Senior Software Engineer.

My throat is tight. Daniel watches me, waiting for me to respond. And I know, I *know* this is everything I've always claimed that I wanted. Here's a guy, a nice guy, a cute guy, a decent guy, who is asking me on a date. He loves sci-fi, he loves movies, he's friendly, he loves going to conventions. Serena would jump for joy if she knew this was happening to me.

Daniel must realize that I'm having trouble speaking, because he shifts into the stream of light shining through the front window, light dust motes floating through him, and gives me a steady, I'm-with-you look, and says gravely, "What's your name?"

I stare into his eyes, only for a second, but in that second I see what he's decided. He thinks that he has to step aside, to make room for a living, breathing man, because that's what I deserve. And right or wrong, that's what Daniel has decided he's going to do.

I watch Daniel's eyes flicker as he waits to see if I'll take what he's offering. His shoulders fall, as I say, "I'm Jillian Nejat. Nice to meet you."

Thomas takes my hand, shakes it happily, pumping it up and down with exuberance. "I'll call you, no wait. Do you have a card?"

I reach into my bag, and hand him my business card. When he reads it his eyebrows rise, "Wow. *The Daily Exposé*, huh? Didn't you guys have the dolphin..." He cuts off, his cheeks reddening again. "Right. I'll email you. We'll set it up." He hefts his bag on his shoulder again and then gives me another grin, a wave, and then stumbles over a chair as he backs toward the door.

With a flush, he says, "Bye. See you soon."

The noise of the city, the traffic, and a rush of wind blows into the tiny shop as he leaves, and then the door closes again, sealing in the aroma of coffee, chocolate éclairs, and the sound of espresso grinding.

Slowly I turn and level my gaze on Daniel.

Now that Thomas is gone, Daniel's crusading-knight-sacrificing-himself-for-the-ultimate-good expression has left him. Instead he looks weary and regretful. His outline flickers, and he's more faded than usual, his skin a pale, see-through gold.

When Daniel sees me staring at him, he straightens and wipes the weary regret from his face, and gives me a confident smile. "I think with your job saved, and the guy with the classic watch—"

"Thomas," I say.

Daniel nods, "Right, Thomas. I think..." He pauses and studies the tightness of my jaw, his eyes clouding.

"I'm helping you, aren't I? Isn't this what I'm meant to do?"

No, I want to shout. It's not. You're supposed to love me, stay with me, see me.

"Jillian," Lupita calls from behind the counter. She shoves a cardboard cup across the reclaimed wood. "I made your usual. You want anything else?"

I watch Daniel for a second longer, his hands clenching as he waits for my answer.

"A chocolate éclair please," I say, knowing it's what Daniel would want. "To go."

A smile flickers across his face as he fades in and out, his form like mist, transparent and hazy.

"Thank you," he says.

As I collect my coffee and the pastry, our *celebration*, I decide I'm going to take the advice I gave Hayley.

27

Yellow taxis swarm Grand Central, darting through the buzzing traffic that permanently surrounds the blocks around the train terminal and the subway below. I hurry through the thick pedestrian traffic, my hot coffee clutched in one hand, the éclair tucked safely in my bag.

Daniel strides next to me, unable to avoid elbows, shoulders, or passing through people as they hustle toward the sparkling beige stone and the towering, glistening arched windows of Grand Central Terminal.

Working on 44th Street near Sixth, I walk past Grand Central to and from work every day, and usually the energy surrounding the terminal invigorates me. Today, I'm glad for the roar of the traffic, the tat-a-tat of a jackhammer, and the thickness of the foot traffic because the roaring buzz matches exactly what I'm feeling.

"Daniel," I say, pulling his attention from the mirrored skyscrapers rising to the sky behind the stone statues topping the terminal.

He turns his gaze to me, his eyes crinkling, "Did you

ever notice, those buildings reflect the sky? You can see the clouds in them." He points at the drifting blue reflected in the building and the white clouds shifting in the glass.

I smile and shake my head. "No. I never noticed it." And then before I lose confidence, I say, "Why did you want me to say yes to him?"

Daniel stops at the crosswalk, and I stand next to him, my hand next to his, our fingers entwining. His expression is calm, stone-like, similar to the one he wore when he first learned he was dead and he was hiding his emotions from me.

Next to us, a food cart with a cherry red and sunshine yellow umbrella pumps out the scent of warm pretzels and broiling hot dogs. There's a row of colorful drinks propped on a plastic shelf, and a towering stack of pretzels coated in salt. Daniel ignores the cart and studies the crosswalk light as it counts down toward zero.

A gust of wind sweeps down the street, tugging at my skirt and flicking my hair across my mouth. I reach up and brush it away, and Daniel catches the motion, his eyes following as my fingers run over my lips.

"Because I'm not alive," he finally says, his gaze conflicted. "No matter how much I wish it, I'm not."

"It doesn't matter to me," I say, reaching out and pressing my hand to the outline of his chest.

Next to me, a middle-aged woman in a black trench coat gives me a side-eyed glare and takes three steps away, increasing the distance between us.

Daniel notices and nods at her. "It matters to everyone else. You can't—"

"I can," I say.

Daniel looks up at the sky, a beseeching expression on his face. "He was a trekker."

"So what?"

"He has good taste in watches. The one he had on, it was a classic '62—"

I scoff. "I couldn't care less. I like men who go shirtless and don't have watches."

A man in a navy suit next to me laughs in surprise and says, "Sweetheart, I'll go shirtless for you."

"No need, thanks," Daniel says to him, then the traffic light changes and the crosswalk light blinks in white *walk*.

We start forward and at the opposite sidewalk, I move away from the crowd of people, toward a less busy street. It's evening rush hour though, and with the warmth of the spring sun still lingering in the concrete and the brick of the buildings, more people are out than usual.

Daniel picks up where he left off. "He has a good job."

"Maybe," I say, noncommittally.

"He was friendly."

"Yeah?"

"You have similar hobbies."

I stop walking, and Daniel stops with me. We're at the entry of a pharmacy, the automatic doors sliding open and then shut and then open again, sensing my proximity.

I take a step away, closer to the long row of carnations, gerbera daisies, and roses positioned in tall red buckets along the glass wall of the building. We're surrounded by the perfume of flowers, hundreds of blooms, waiting to be wrapped in waxy floral paper and shared with a loved one.

"I want you," I say to Daniel, my voice breaking. "I don't want anyone else. I want *you*."

He closes his eyes, his form flickering in the early evening light, and when he opens his eyes the look he gives me is anguished and wanting. "Jillian, I'm not—"

"I don't care," I say.

Daniel reaches forward, his hand passing through the petals of a red rose. "I can't buy you flowers."

"I don't need flowers."

"I can't leave the city," he argues.

I shake my head. "I like New York. Everything I need is here. I don't need to leave either."

Daniel studies me, his expression grave. "I can't promise I'll always be here. I don't know why I go."

"I'll take what I can get," I tell him, my heart thumping against my rib cage, my hand shaking on my coffee cup.

Daniel paces down the length of the sidewalk, toward the daisies, and I hurry after him, keeping pace. We're only three blocks from home.

"I can't marry you," Daniel says. "What if you want to get married? You can marry someone like Thomas."

"I don't want to marry Thomas," I say.

"But someday, you'll want to marry someone, you'll want to—"

"I want you," I repeat, moving down the sidewalk, passing early spring blooms planted around a gingko tree unfurling its spring leaves.

"What about children?" he asks.

"If I want kids I'll adopt."

"They won't be able to see me," he says. "They'll grow up with me being like Santa Claus, they'll believe when they're kids, and then once they're old enough, they'll think you lied to them. They won't believe I'm real. And your family? Your friends? You'll be lucky if they don't have you committed."

We've made it to the apartment. I don't respond to Daniel. Instead I unlock the front door, climb the creaking wooden stairs up the four flights to my floor, then I open my front door, step inside my mirrored apartment, then slowly shut the door and lock it.

Daniel fades through the door and stands in front of me. I lean against the door, my back pressed into the warm wood, the mirrors on the walls reflecting my pale, resolute face.

Daniel presses his hands to the door, caging me in, "Do you still want me?" he asks. "No life. No marriage. No kids. No future. That's not what I'm here for. I'm here to help you move on, and then I'll move on."

His words are low, hard, and he leans over me, his gaze direct. And if I didn't know him as well as I do, and if I didn't understand him better than I understand myself, I'd believe him. And I wouldn't hear the shaking in his voice when he says, "I don't know what I was thinking these past weeks. I was selfish. I'm sorry. I forgot that I'm not here to love you, I'm here to help you."

My cup of coffee slips from my hands and clatters to the floor, the dark liquid spills over the wood, the rich sugary smell rising.

"Daniel?" I ask, ignoring the coffee at our feet.

He nods, holding my gaze, keeping me trapped between his arms, his chest pressed close to mine.

"Did you say that you love me?" I ask, the mirrors splaying golden light through the apartment, reflecting my hope.

He drops his head, his mouth inches from mine.

"Of course I love you," he says, his voice a low rumble that caresses me, warm like the breeze of his touch. "Me loving you is the only solid thing I have to hold onto in this half-life. It's the only thing I know is real."

He shakes his head, then reaches his hand out to brush his fingers down the side of my face. I lean toward the whisper of his touch.

"I love you too," I say, my voice quiet in the early evening hush.

Daniel gazes down at me, his expression full of yearning, but also denial, "You weren't supposed to," he says. "You're supposed to move on. I have nothing to give you."

I press my fingers to his lips. "You give me the kind of love that most people only dream of. What more could I want?"

His eyes glow, backlit by the setting sun, and his lips curve into a slow, exultant smile. "You don't want a living, breathing man? You don't want someone who can give you a life?"

I shake my head. "I just want you. I only want you."

At that, I watch all the doubt, and fear, and worry slip away, and the decision Daniel made in the coffee shop, to help me find someone who is alive, vanishes as he leans down and sets his mouth against mine.

28

A CONFLAGRATION LIGHTS INSIDE ME, AND I FINALLY KNOW what Daniel means when he says, there's darkness and then there's you.

Everything before him was the black ocean of space, a vacuum with no sound and no air. With his mouth on mine, his warmth flowing over me—now a blazing inferno—I feel, I see the color of his love, and I hear the song of his heart.

My knees buckle and I grip the door to stay upright. Before, Daniel's touch was a butterfly wing brushing over me, the lick of a warm breeze, now it's the rushing of a river, cascading over naked skin.

"Jillian," he says, his hands running over my face, the heat of his fingers sparking over me, an electric flame.

When he presses his mouth to my throat, and my pulse drums in response, I throw my head back and let him send starlight over me.

"I love you," he whispers, and the words are so quiet I can barely make them out over the wind rattling the window, the hum of evening traffic, and the murmur of the heater fanning dry, hot air over us.

I lift my cardigan over my head, tug off my camisole, and slip off my bra, freeing my breasts. Daniel closes his eyes, sends up a prayer of hope and thanks.

He runs his hands over my nipples and at the light, teasing breeze, they pucker and peak. A heaviness settles in my breast, and travels lower, growing into an aching heat as I unzip my skirt, and slip it free, kicking off my thong. Finally, I stand before Daniel in my black heels and nothing else.

His gaze sweeps over me, and everywhere his eyes light, my skin responds, glowing and humming. He smiles at me, his eyes bright and thankful.

I know he's thankful, because it's the exact way I feel right now. I'm so grateful he found me.

He flickers in the fading light, as insubstantial as mist. I reach out and run my hand over his chest his muscles tightening in response. When I touch him, he comes back into focus.

His blue eyes are the color of dark sea glass, shining in the sun, his sandy-brown hair curls over his forehead and brushes his jaw. His stubble is the same dark next-day dusting that I imagine feels rough and enticing as you run your lips over it. His wide shoulders tense as I stroke my hands over the lean muscles, tracing the surface of his skin, trailing my hands to the line of his abdomen, down to his hips, where his jeans dip.

He makes a noise in his throat, low and sweet.

"Lay down," he begs. "Lay down and I'll love you."

I give him a smile full of happiness and love, and then I saunter to the red-carpeted platform, my heels clicking on the wood floor. I climb onto my bed, the soft blankets rustling beneath me, brushing across my skin.

Daniel watches me, his eyes following my movements.

"You love me," he says.

I nod and kick a heel off. It clatters across the wood floor.

"You love me," he says again.

I nod and kick off my other heel, sending it skittering across the floor.

Then I lay back on my plush blankets, my curly black hair fanning around me, the light from the golden candelabra washing over me, painting my flushed skin in gold and rose.

I stare at the mirrors on the ceiling above, I'm spread out on the bed, my lush hips rolling, my legs opening, my breasts full, my nipples rosy and puckered. My green eyes are dark, the wet leaf color now a blazing emerald green. I look like a Rubenesque sex goddess.

Daniel stares down at me with an awe-filled gaze.

"You may love me," he says, his voice full of longing, "but no matter what happens, never forget how much I love you."

Then he reaches out and *touches* me. Not touch-touches. But touches me with his soul, which is the only way I can describe it, because suddenly my whole body lights up, and I'm vibrating with need. I tilt my hips, arch my back, dig my feet into the mattress, and ride the warm pulse building in me.

"If I were here," he says, his voice rough, "I would taste you. I'd taste how sweet you are."

I grip the sheets. "You always want to taste everything," I say, my cheeks flushing.

His eyes light at that, and then he says, "After I tasted you, I'd kiss the spot where your neck and shoulder meet, that delicate space where your skin looks so soft. And I'd run my hands through your hair. I'd finally learn whether it's as soft as it looks. Is it?" he asks, his eyes raking over my hair spilling across my pillow.

I swallow, my mouth dry, and nod. "Yes. It's soft."

He smiles. "I thought so."

I reach down and stroke a hand over my thigh, goosebumps rising at the scrape of my palm over my skin. Daniel's eyes catch on my fingers resting near the juncture of my hips.

"Then what?" I ask.

His eyes flick back to me, full of heat. "I'd breathe you in," he says. "I always imagined that you smell like violets opening in a spring rain"—he smiles—"with a dusting of sugar. So I'd breathe you in, and...do you smell like spring rain?"

I shake my head, mesmerized by his description. "I have no idea."

"You do," he says confidently. "Then I'd touch you, all the places I've longed to. The curve of your neck, the sensitive palm of your hand, the soft skin of your hip, the upward curl at the edge of your lip, the softness of your eyelashes, I'd touch every single inch of you."

"Do you know," I say, "you could do that now, you could do it vicariously through me."

Ever so slowly, Daniel smiles in response.

I touch all the places he wants to explore. I run my hands over myself, brush my hips, my lips, every sensitive inch, and as I do, his eyes fill with that hungry longing.

"Where else?" I ask, my body flaming from the heat in his eyes.

"You know where," he says.

I do.

I reach down, touch the warm heat of myself, and when I do, Daniel lets out a hungry noise.

"After I tasted you, and touched you, I would press myself over you, so we were touching everywhere, and then I would take your hands—"

"And?" I circle my fingers over myself, envision him spread over me, the weight of him pressing me into the soft mattress, the mirror above reflecting his naked back and his muscled legs, his mouth taking mine, our breath mingling.

"Then I would push inside you, slowly, because I already waited an eternity to be with you, and I want to savor every moment for as long as possible."

I slip a finger inside myself, imagine it's him.

"Then?" I say, my voice breathless.

"Then you'd hold me, your hands clutching mine, your legs wrapped around me, your heat gripping me, holding me inside. I'd slide in, until I'm so deep in you that I don't know where I end and you begin. And you'll say—"

"I love you," I say, slipping another finger in, rolling my hips to the rhythm of his words.

"I love you," he agrees. "And you feel so good, I feel you everywhere, then I start to move. I pull out—"

"And I don't like that," I say.

"So I thrust back in," he agrees. "And I want to stay in you forever."

I tilt my hips higher, as he says, "I kiss you, I hold you, I stroke you, and when you tighten around me and cry out, I can't keep going slow and easy."

"No," I agree.

"No," he says. His eyes light on my flushed chest, my hand working over myself, then he leans over the bed, reaches out to hold my hands, and sets his mouth over me.

And the warmth that was building at the base of my spine, the liquid heat pulsing and growing, as soon as Daniel's mouth hits my clitoris, every needing, aching ball of warmth explodes outward, rolls over me, carries me up, up, to receive his kiss, and when he gives it, I cry out, carried on the light rolling through me.

I float in his kiss, slowly descending to earth, a shooting star falling to the ocean, and when he looks up at me, his eyes the color of the vast sea, his smile tells me that he felt everything that I felt. More.

He brushes a hand over my naked hip, caresses me softly. "You're sure about this?" he asks solemnly, the evening shadows finally falling. "You're sure about this love?"

I smile up at him, my limbs heavy, my heart light, and say, "I've never been more sure about anything in my life."

He smiles at that. "I'll always love you," he promises. "Thank you for seeing me."

I brush my fingers over his hand, not sure if he means thank you for seeing his heart, or for seeing him as a ghost. I don't ask, instead I say, "Will you stay the night?"

He smiles down at me sprawled naked on my bed. "I'll stay every night."

Later, I fall asleep, the streetlights shining through the curtain, Daniel standing at the window, watching for the silvery glow of the crescent moon high over the towers of the city.

He's nearly translucent in the moonlight, like a dream

there on waking but soon forgotten. I try to keep my eyes open, keep him in my sight, but my eyelids sink heavily shut, drifting into sleep.

In my dreams I feel him brush a hand over my cheek, and I hear him—

"Jillian—"

"I can't—"

"Jillian, you have to—"

When the morning light wakes me, Daniel is gone.

29

The key here is not to panic. Don't panic, Jillian. Do *not* panic.

Daniel has disappeared before. He's popped in and out of existence plenty of times. In fact, the first time I met him and swung my aluminum bat at him, he disappeared for a full, hmmm, six hours? And some nights, he left for *at least* ten hours, maybe twelve.

He's even been gone for a solid twenty-four...I shake my head, no, he's never been gone that long.

I stare out my apartment window at the darkening evening sky, dreading the bluish yellow fading to a bruised indigo. Once it's dark, Daniel will have been gone for a full day.

My apartment has a tomblike stillness, an unsettling deep hush. The moan of traffic is absent, the pigeons that coo while perched on the window ledge are missing, and next door, Daisy is quiet.

And here? In this silent, mirrored room?

Usually Daniel would have a steady stream of

conversation, pointing out the little things to delight me, asking about sci-fi world building or fandom and conventions, or brainstorming with me about the next Big Idea. Now it's deathly quiet.

The only noise is the whisper of my breath and the creak of the wooden floor as I shift in a slow circle, trying to see through the lengthening shadows congregating around me.

I hurried to work this morning, a spring in my step, ready to tackle another article, certain that Daniel would meet me at my desk. I thought he'd tease me into finding a cup of coffee and something delicious for breakfast. I was only slightly worried that he wasn't there, my dreams haunting the edges of my mind. At lunch, when I picked nervously at my pastrami sandwich, I was moderately worried.

At dinner, when I ate a bowl of pho and watched a muted episode of *Star Trek: The Next Generation*, I was... okay, I threw out the pho after two bites and turned off the episode only three minutes in, because I was panicking.

Outside, a car engine backfires and I jump, my heart pounding in response. I press my palm to my chest and take a deep steadying breath, and then, suddenly a warm breeze blows across the back of my neck.

I swing around, my heart leaping, "Hello?"

I peer around my apartment, take in my couch, my bookshelves full of collectibles, my dishes drying on the counter next to the sink.

The floors creak as I slowly spin around. The light from my lamp barely keeps the shadows from the room. Down the hall, a door slams shut.

"Daniel?" I say, my voice shaking.

The apartment remains silent.

"Daniel? Are you there?"

I wait, expecting him to answer, expecting him to appear next to me, a smile on his face.

"Please," I say, clutching my hand next to my thigh. "I'm...worried. If you're there...Daniel? If you're there, please say something. Please."

He doesn't.

As the sky outside bleeds from bruised indigo to black, my chest tightens and tightens until it's painful to breathe.

I move through the apartment, searching behind my couch, under my bed, in the closet, in the bathroom, behind the shower curtain, and finally, stupidly, in the kitchen cupboards.

I search every inch of my mirrored sex maniac's love den, and finally come to the numbing conclusion, that I'm the only one here.

So I change into pajamas, climb into bed, yank the blankets up to my chin, and convince myself that Daniel will be here in the morning.

He isn't.

30

_____

ONE WEEK.

Seven days.

One hundred and sixty-eight hours.

Ten thousand eighty minutes.

With the resolute march of time, I plunge past panic to frantic.

I know. I know that Daniel's a ghost. I know that he's dead. But I didn't ever think that that meant I could *lose* him. That one day he wouldn't be here anymore.

Except, how can I know for sure? Maybe he is still here. Maybe time isn't the same for ghosts and he doesn't realize he's been gone this long? Or maybe he's here but I can't see him?

It's the not knowing that's the worst. There's a gnawing fear consuming me from the inside out, but there's also hope, fluttering like a wounded bird, trying to keep alight. To keep hope, even if each passing second that he's gone points in the opposite direction.

When Michael died, it was a bone-wrenching, soul-scorching devastation, but it was definite. He was gone and I knew it.

But Daniel?

He can't be gone, can he? He promised he would always love me. He promised to stay. He wouldn't leave me, not if he had any choice in the matter.

I haven't known what to do, so after work—where I've thrown myself into writing the articles that Daniel and I planned out—I scour the city. I go everywhere we went together, praying to catch a glimpse of him.

The Grange Tavern for an uneaten bacon burger and live music. A Broadway matinee, an empty seat reserved next to me, just in case. The Hayden Planetarium, to view the vast loneliness of space. The Bow Bridge in Central Park, its reflection mirrored in the cool blue waters below. The Empire State Building, cold and quiet at sunset. Chess in Union Square, the seat across from me empty. The symphony, alone. A dinner cruise, alone. A fragrantly steaming tagine in the East Village, alone.

The gray dusk wraps around me, a cold curtain, as I leave the warmth of the Moroccan restaurant where Daniel proved to me he was real.

The city is waking to spring, the nights are warmer now, tumbling toward the end of April and a sunnier May.

Evidence of spring hurtling toward summer is everywhere. Couples picnic in the parks, the dark soil fragrant from spring rains, yellow tulips unfolding around them. Adventurous kids wear shorts and t-shirts while joyously zipping down the sidewalk on scooters and bikes. Red-breasted robins hop in the emerald-green grass, their tsip-tsip call tutting a warning before they wheel into the pale blue sky.

Daniel would've noticed all of this. He would've pointed it out to me with a small smile, sharing the splendor of the ordinary. Now, I'm left to find it myself.

The gnawing teeth in my stomach grow sharper as I walk through the night shadows of the East Village, the subway three blocks down, past the quiet apartments and closed businesses. The Moroccan restaurant was the last place for me to visit, after this there's...nothing.

A chirrup sounds, the ringing of my phone. I pull it from my bag. It's Serena, and in Geneva it's after midnight.

"Why are you up?" I ask, answering the phone.

"I'm worried about you," she says by way of greeting. "It's been a week. You aren't sleeping, you aren't eating, you aren't trekking."

"Yeah," I say, pulling my yellow cardigan tighter around myself. There isn't any reason to deny what she's saying, it's all true. Besides, she knows what happened, I've told her everything.

At the intersection, the crosswalk light changes and I look both ways before crossing the street.

"I didn't want to mention this before," Serena says, in a tone that lets me know I won't like whatever it is she has to say. "You won't like it," she adds.

A taxi honks as I hop up onto the sidewalk into the dull light of a streetlamp.

"Tell me anyway," I say, desperate for any bit of wisdom, advice, or scientific insight she may have.

"Alright. Here goes. I think you need to explore all the options. You're under the impression that Daniel would never leave you. However, the evidence shows that Daniel was a sexy, shirtless player who owned a sex den apartment and died—probably—while having sex."

A flash of indignation rises in my chest. "That isn't who he was—"

"Those are the facts," Serena says firmly. "He may not have acted like that with you, however, in life he was the king of sexy times. Input those numbers into an equation. Two plus two equals four. Daniel, the king of sexy times, had wild sex with a different woman every night in his mirrored sex den apartment, and then he died...now he's a sexy, shirtless ghost and what does he do? He inputs the same numbers into his equation. He seduces the cute woman that moves into his apartment and has sexy times with her and then...look, Jilly, what if in death, he's the same as he was in life? I know you fell for him. You think you loved him. But you need to look at the facts too. This could've been the ghost version of a nail and bail."

"A nail and bail?" I say, my voice hoarse.

"Consider it," Serena says.

I halt at the end of the block, a brown townhouse with stone steps on my left, the street with a row of dark parked cars on my right and remember Daniel saying, *he's planning a smash and dash, a pump and dump, an ejaculate and evacuate.*

How do you know? I'd asked, disbelieving.

Because I'm a man, he'd said confidently.

I clutch the phone in my hand, my fingers cramping, and shake my head. "No. It wasn't like that. He wasn't like that. He *isn't* like that," I correct myself, "I know him and I know—" I pause, my desperation turning to elation as my eyes land on a blue fluorescent sign glowing brightly in the dark. "I know he loved me," I say with conviction.

"I don't know whether I hope you're right or hope you're wrong," Serena says, and over her I hear Purrk meowing for her attention.

"Jilly, I want you to eat, sleep, and go full out sci-fi geek. I don't want this to be as bad as it was last time. I'm worried about you."

She means how bad it was with Michael, because even though Serena lived in California, she knows how bad it got, and also that I've never quite recovered.

"It won't. It'll be okay," I tell her, as I hurry down the steps to the basement unit of the old yellow brick building. "I have to go."

We say a quick goodbye, and then I tug open the door of the place I should've come to right away. Incense and dry heat wash over me as I step past the threshold and smile at Zelda Vertruse, psychic.

31

THE TINY BASEMENT ROOM IS STILL INFUSED WITH A PINK glow from the Himalayan sea salt lamp and the gold lamp covered with a red silk shawl. Incense burns in the brass bowl by the front door, hitting me with a wall of sandalwood and ylang-ylang.

The bell on the door jangles, and then the door sweeps shut behind me, sealing out the cool night air of outside.

Everything is the same. There's the same threadbare blue and gold rug, the same folding card table with two metal folding chairs, and the same scowling glare on Zelda's wrinkled visage.

I smile widely at her, taking in her leather metal spike jacket, her obvious annoyance, and the to-go carton of white rice steaming on the table in front of her.

"I'm eating," she says, narrowing her eyes on me as she takes a forceful bite of her fire engine-red chicken skewer. The bright red, garlic-cumin sauce stains her lips, and she says, her mouth full, "You're one of kind, no manners. Always coming in the second I sit down for a meal."

I nod. Yes. For sure.

"You remember me?" I ask, stepping close and pulling out the chair across from her, the metal warm from the crackling heat of the room.

Zelda takes another bite of her chicken, the meat shredding off the wooden skewer, bits falling to the table.

I take that as a yes.

"What do you want?" she asks, eyeing me without interest.

I drop into the seat across from her, then lean forward and ask the question burning on the tip of my tongue. "When I was here last time, you could feel the ghost with me—"

"Yeah. The annoying horn dog." She bites the last piece of chicken from the skewer, looks at the wood with disappointment, then tosses it to the table. It hits with a dull thud.

"Well, he wasn't actually annoying—"

"What do you want?" she interrupts, looking down at her watch. "My TV show starts in three minutes."

"Is he here?" I ask, looking her in the eye, impressing her with the importance of my question. "Can you feel him here now? With me?"

Say yes.

Say yes.

Say yes.

"No," she says, not bothering to look around the room. "Congratulations, you got rid of that annoying ball of energy."

No?

No.

It's at that moment I realize how much I'd hoped that Daniel was still here, that for some reason I'd (temporarily) lost the ability to see him. Now that I know he's not with me, a cold numbness slides into me, like an iceberg slipping into the cold, dark sea.

My heart, previously pumping along with hope, flutters, seizes, and stutters. Then just as suddenly, it starts back up again, thudding to adjust to this new reality.

"He's not here," I say, just to be certain. "You can't sense him, at all?"

Zelda sighs, then looks up at the ceiling, cocking her head as if she's listening for something. After a silent minute, she snaps her gaze back to me and says, "No. Lucky you. He's gone."

"Bring him back," I say, gripping the edge of the table, filled with a desperate urgency. "You do that, right? Herbs, candles? Bring him back."

Zelda's face twists. "For crying out loud. Herbs? Candles? This isn't Christmas dinner! He's not a ham! How many times do I have to tell you that?"

My cheeks burn red, but still. "But can't you do some hokeypokey mojo thing? Can't you bring him back?"

She glares at me. The blue Christmas lights in the window spark off the metal spikes on her shoulders, and then she scoffs. "I see your career is no longer a trash fire. Your love life is improving. You're no longer all tight and loveless. He worked fast. He must've wanted to move on quite badly."

The heat in my cheeks vanishes, replaced with cold. This is what I've been refusing to face. What I didn't want to acknowledge. The possibility that Daniel moved on.

"What are you saying?" I ask, knowing very well what she's saying.

"He moved on," Zelda says slowly, enunciating each word. "You can't bring back someone who has moved on. He's gone. Dead. Not your problem anymore."

The backs of my eyes burn, my throat aches, I dig my fingernails into the palms of my hand. The cloying scent of the incense chokes me, smothering me like the suffocating incense burned at Michael's funeral.

Daniel said he was here to help me. He said he'd help me keep my job, he'd help me find love. Was that it? Once my job was safe, once a nice "decent-seeming" guy asked me out, then Daniel moved on? Or was it more? That I was supposed to help him? And once he loved me, he was pulled to the light?

"Are you certain he won't come back?" I ask, my throat raw, the incense overwhelming. "He's only been gone a week. He could—"

"What happened before he left?" she interrupts, looking at her watch impatiently.

When she looks back at me, she must see something in my expression because for once her expression softens and the pattern of wrinkles on her face irons out.

"He said he loved me," I admit in a whisper as quiet as the smoke rising from the incense.

She nods, then says, "I could've told you that from day one. It was obvious." She waves her hand, then scoots her chair back from the table, standing abruptly. "He's moved on."

I stand too, swallow down the urge to argue, to ask her to *try* to bring him back.

From experience, I know there are some things you can't change. You can't change the past. You can't bring someone into a future that isn't there. If someone is gone, they're gone.

Zelda is the only person other than me that met Daniel as a ghost, that truly knows that he existed and that he loved me, so even though she's never shown compassion or caring, I ask, like a child hoping for reassurance, "What do I do now?"

She considers my question, and as she studies me standing before her, the pink light falling over us, I look to the window where Daniel once stood. He stared through the glass, absent of his reflection, and bowed his head as Zelda told him he was dead. The picture of him is there, the ghost of him, vivid in my memory.

"What do I do?" I ask again, wanting him, wanting him desperately.

"You move on," Zelda says. "He moved on. Now you move on. That's the way these things work."

My chest squeezes as the ghost of Daniel residing in my memory fades from the room.

"I move on?"

Doesn't she know how hard it is to move on?

"You move on," she repeats firmly, then she holds her hand out, the leather of her jacket whooshing at the movement. "That'll be one seventy-five."

With that, I pay, and then I leave, moving on.

It's midnight. The flicker of the muted TV flashes over me, lighting the darkness, reflecting off the dozens of mirrors like shards of starlight. I clasp a pillow to my chest and huddle at the corner of my couch.

There's one thing that Daniel said to me that I can't

get out of my mind. It was the night I told him about Michael, and he said that all these years, I've been punishing myself.

I asked him if he'd thought I'd punished myself long enough, and he said, *only you can decide how long and in what way you'll punish yourself. Only you can decide when you're ready to be forgiven.*

I clutch the pillow, squeeze it against my chest, and wait for a breeze to ruffle my hair, or stroke the back of my neck. But the apartment is still, and the only noise is the hum of the heater overhead.

Daniel isn't here.

He's moved on.

I bite down on my lip, taste the tang of blood.

When I admitted my fear, that Michael never knew how much I cared for him, that he never knew that I was sorry, Daniel promised me—*he knows. Whatever happens after, he heard you, and he knows.*

I cling to Daniel's words, pray that what he told me is true, and then I whisper to the darkness, to the deep black night, "I love you, if you can come back, please come back to me, but if you can't, I'm grateful that you were here for as long as you were. Thank you for seeing me. Thank you for seeing my heart."

And then, with that, stars light on the screen, reflecting thousands of pinpricks of light around the apartment, and I finally let go, I let go of it all.

If Daniel can move on, then so can I.

32

A QUICK, HARD KNOCK RAPS AGAINST MY DOOR, JIGGLING the mirrors on the wall next to the door, distorting my reflection.

I grab my purse, straighten my skirt, my gray Starfleet t-shirt (for luck), and my blue cashmere cardigan. It's Monday morning, and today at the morning meeting I'll learn whether or not I still have a job.

I peer through the peep hole and smile at the sight that greets me. Then I unlatch the chain, slip free the bolt, and tug open the door.

"Morning," I say with surprise. "What are you doing here?"

Fran bustles in, bringing with her the warm scent of cinnamon and raisins, she embraces me in a tight hug and kisses my cheeks.

"It's a shopping day," she says happily, the plastic bag she's carrying crinkling between us.

When she steps back, I look at her with surprised

pleasure, even though I saw her yesterday when my parents hosted a game day brunch for friends and family. Fran was there, my grandpa, even my cousin Ari, who offered me a job at The Bargain Shopper's Mailer, just in case my current position "falls through." My mom clucked around me the entire afternoon, worriedly asking me if I was sleeping well, because I looked "gaunt."

It's the mirrors, she'd said. *No one can sleep well surrounded by mirrors. It gives a horrid haunted vibe. Haven't you covered them up yet?*

My dad on the other hand asked if I'd been having trouble with men, and if I still had my bat by the door. I assured him I wasn't having trouble, and my bat was readily available.

Fran, though, she's always been perceptive, and I knew she could see that I wasn't just tired, or having man trouble. Which I suppose is why she's here at eight o'clock on Monday morning.

"I made you cinnamon raisin bread," Fran says, pulling a large golden loaf out of her plastic bag and handing it to me with a flourish.

"You didn't have to—" I begin, but Fran's already dropping more plastic containers into my arms.

"Chana Masala. Mango chutney. Naan."

She loads my arms with container after container, and as she does my smile grows wider.

"Lentil potato soup. Lasagna, because you like my lasagna. Chocolate chip cookies, don't eat them all at once. And..." She frowns at me, her plastic bag empty now, my arms full. "Put it in the fridge, what are you waiting for?"

I laugh as she shoos me toward the kitchen, her pearl

necklace glinting and her leopard print sweater bright and happy.

"You didn't have to bring all this," I tell her as I set the containers in my (admittedly) barren fridge.

When I close the refrigerator and turn around, Fran's arms are crossed, and she's tapping her foot against the wood floor in an impatient, don't-B.S.- me kind of way. It's the same expression she wore when I was eleven and she knew that Michael and I had flushed his report card down the toilet and we were trying to pretend we hadn't.

"First you call and tell me that you don't want any more set-ups"—she holds up her hand when I'm about to protest—"which is fine. You tell me you're talking with a man, which is wonderful. But then, the next thing I know, you look..." Fran shakes her head, her dyed blonde hair shifting over her leopard print sweater. "Jilly, you look like you've lost someone you love."

I bite my lip and swallow down a denial. This is Fran after all.

I look around my apartment, at the small, rectangular space, whose qualities I listed in an effort to look on the bright side—wood floors, quiet, close to work, cheap. The best quality, though, was what I found here.

"I did," I admit.

Fran nods, like I'm only confirming what she already knew. "Have a cookie then. I put extra chocolate in them."

"Thank you, Fran," I say, my smile wobbling.

And when I unseal the container of cookies, their chocolate buttery smell wafting to me, I feel a surge of hopefulness.

The cookie crumbles in my hand, the chocolate melts right away against the warmth of my fingers, and when I bite into it, the caramelized sugar and chocolate flavor bring back the memories of all the years that Fran's cookies have brought me through.

She watches me with a smile, certain that the sugar and sweetness will help boost my spirits.

As I wipe my hands together, brushing of the crumbs, Fran folds the plastic bag and pops it into her purse.

"I'm off then, shopping calls," she says brightly, and then, "I'll stop by later this week, maybe we can have a girls' day?"

"I'd like that," I say, pulling my keys from my purse.

I'm determined to make it to work early today.

But as I step toward the front door, I realize I have another question.

"Fran?"

She zips her purse, patting the animal print bag, and then glances at me with a smile. "Hmm?"

I look down at the wood floor, at the cracks between the boards, the years of dust collected and sealed there, and I say, unable to look at Fran, "When Michael died, did you ever...did you ever think that if only you had done something differently, that you could've stopped it?"

I keep my eyes on the floor, my head down, the tips of Fran's bright red heels at the edge of my vision. After a moment, she steps forward, her heels clicking on the wood.

She reaches forward, takes my hand, grips my fingers in her own and gives a gentle squeeze. "My lovely Jillian. You have such a soft heart."

I look up then, meet her eyes, keep her hand in mine.

She smiles at me. "I give myself five minutes every day to think about the what ifs, and then I set them aside. There are a million could've beens and should've beens, and as a mom, we always accept all the blame and none of the absolution for whatever happens with our children. It's only natural."

"Do you think," I ask, "if I'd picked up his phone call then—"

"No," Fran says. "When I talked to him that day, he sounded happy, he told me to remember to make you cookies the next time you visited. If you picked up his call, he would've been saying goodbye and you wouldn't have even known it. Is that what you've been carrying all these years?"

I nod. "I'm sorry."

Fran reaches up and places her hand against my cheek. "There's no need to be sorry. You have always made me happy. There's no need to be sorry about that."

I reach out and pull Fran into a tight hug.

After that, she hurries me down the stairs, adamant that I get a coffee and get to work, so I can keep writing stellar articles about eff-you-see-kaying.

At the street cart, where the sad philosopher sells coffee, I order a black coffee for Fran and an iced coffee to go for me, and when I say yes to cream, and yes please to sugar, Fran gives me a surprised look that quickly turns to a radiantly happy smile. Because this is the first time in years that she's seen me speak in full sentences to a living, breathing man.

She tells me excitedly (as she hurries away to find a pair of new shoes) that this means her feeling was right all along—good things are coming my way.

33

I THINK THE NEWS OF MY TRIAL BY NUMBERS HAS SPREAD through the office, because when I step off the elevator there's a hushed, nervous quiet that I've never felt before at *The Exposé*.

The Wall still dances, flickers, and glows with the news of dozens of countries around the world, but The Wall seems to be the only thing immune to the nervous anticipation riding the office.

The interns, all fourteen of them, sit in small clusters of two or three, and dart nervous glances at me striding toward the back meeting table.

The computer techies watch me gravely, and from a computer speaker, one of them plays Taps, while they all give me a military salute. I smother a smile, tilt my chin up, and keep walking.

Billing, HR, every single person in the office watches me solemnly and silently as I wend my way past the mishmash of desks, the mounds of paper, and piles of old newsprint. A phone rings, its tone shrill in the strange quiet, and an intern picks it up and drops it without answering, cutting off the noise.

There isn't a single keyboard clacking, no shredding of paper, no shouted story ideas, no joking or heckling about dolphin sex, hackers, or subscription numbers. There's just watchful silence.

I wish suddenly that Daniel were here, walking next to me. He'd have something to say about all of this, and he'd say it with a laughing gleam in his eye.

And then he'd promise confidently, *you've got this*.

Which I do.

I think.

Probably.

At least, I purposely didn't wear red today, because I am not a redshirt, and I'm not going down.

At the back of the office, Bernardo, Buck, Ned and Hayley are already at the long wood conference table.

Buck's face is red, and he's gnawing on the end of a pencil. Ned drums his fingers on the table, his eyes darting nervously between Bernardo and me. Hayley, surprisingly, is wearing a Rangers jersey, tucked into jeans, and she's sitting stiffly as if she's readying herself for a brawl.

Bernardo is wearing a navy blue shirt with a dark gray tie today, his black hair slicked back, looking very aristocratic and cold, which makes my stomach give a nervous flip. Bernardo never wears ties, he hates them, which makes me think that today he's going to do something else he hates.

As I walk up, Hayley stares at Bernardo, her gaze as belligerent as a seasoned heckler's, and I get the feeling that she hasn't *quite* told Bernardo how she really feels.

Or maybe she has. Regardless, if Hayley calls umpires "Hey Blue!" then it's fitting that Bernardo's in blue today.

The only seat left is to the right of Buck, across from Ned and Hayley. Bernardo, of course, is at the head of the table. As I pull out the office chair, the tension at the table ratchets higher, so thick and viscous it feels like I can touch it.

There's a box of chocolate sprinkle donuts in the center of the table, the chocolatey smell wafting up, and at my place there's a mug of coffee, courtesy—I think—of Buck.

No one has touched the donuts, not even Ned.

Obviously I'm not going to drink the coffee.

My chair squeaks as I sit down and scoot into the table, then pull my notebook and an erasable pen from my purse.

I clear my throat as I uncap my pen, then scrawl the date at the top of the page.

I can sense everyone's eyes on me, Buck's, Ned's, Hayley's, and of course, the interns, HR, Billing, and computer techs spread around the open office.

My spine itches from all the attention.

Buck punches his fist to the table, and I jump, dropping my pen. The coffee mug in front of me bounces and the liquid splashes over the edge and spills onto the table.

"This is bull," Buck says, his face red, his ears redder.

I stare at him in stunned silence.

He shoves his chair back and stands, his brown suit wrinkled, his eyebrows lowering. He's more worked up than I've ever seen him. In my mind I picture him grabbing his chair and hurling it across the table.

"This is the biggest bull I've ever seen," he continues, thrusting his finger at Bernardo.

Most people in Bernardo's situation would react. They'd shout back, stand up too, or at least *blink*, Bernardo does none of that. He merely waits for Buck to continue.

Buck doesn't need any encouragement. He turns and gives me a wolverine-like snarl and then spins back to Bernardo.

"Jillian has been here since the beginning. She's loyal. She's smart. She worked for no pay and never complained. Yeah, her articles suck, but she never misses a deadline. When it looked like we'd fail, she stuck with us. When we didn't have enough money and had to push back payday, she stayed. When she was a mental case because of her personal problems, she still stuck with it. I have to tell you, Martin—"

Buck thrusts his finger at Bernardo, calling him by his last name, which is what he does.

"If you fire Jillian, you are the weakest, most disloyal, most cowardly son of a gun, because that's not what we're about here."

I raise my eyebrows and look around the table to see how everyone else is taking this. Buck—Jerk Bronson— taking charge, defending me like he's engaged in a deep space battle, determined to go out in a blaze of glory.

If I'd ever imagined someone standing up for me, I'd never in a million years have imagined it would be Buck.

Hayley's nodding her head vehemently, her ponytail swishing, agreement and appreciation written on her face.

Ned's jangling his leg, nervously watching Bernardo's reaction.

Bernardo just places his fingers together, the tips touching, his hands steepled, and calmly places his hands beneath his jaw.

Buck isn't quite finished yet though. He takes a deep breath and says with finality, "If Jillian goes, I go. You fire her, then this isn't the family I thought it was."

And with that bombshell, Buck drops into his chair with a loud thud. There's a stunned, charged silence.

Because did Buck just say that if I got fired, he was going to walk?

Buck?

Hayley kicks her chair back and stands, and oh no, she has her heckler face on. I do all I can to restrain the hysterical laugh rising in my chest.

"That goes for me too," she says, looking for all the world like a gorgeous beauty queen in a hockey jersey, about to deliver some ass-kicking. "If Jillian's out, then I'm out. We're a team, there aren't any trades. If Jillian's out, and Buck's out, then I'm out. We'll start our own news service. We'll be the Yankees to your Red Sox, the Rangers to your Flyers, the Knicks to your Nets, and Bernardo be forewarned, we will kick your a—"

Ned stands then, and Hayley stops mid-swear, "Me too," he says, his voice shaking. "Jillian is a trekkie, so she appreciates that...aliens are real." He glances at me for confirmation and I give him a quick nod.

He nods back, gaining confidence, "She attended two of my weddings and made me chicken noodle soup after every divorce, and I think her articles are decently written, even if I don't...agree with the premise...because my ex-wives...they never..." He trails off, looks around the table nervously because he's gone off topic, and when Buck waves his hand forcefully for Ned to continue, he clears his throat and says, "If Jillian goes, I go."

And with that, Ned sits down, Hayley sits down, and all three of them—Buck, Ned, and Hayley—stare at Bernardo with do-or-die expressions.

A great big welling of gratitude and fondness expands in my chest until I feel like I'm going to burst from it. Like I've said from the beginning, we might not have anything in common, we might not even get along half the time, but we all have a shared purpose.

I thought it was—come hell or high water—making *The Daily Exposé* a success. But maybe it's not that, so much as working together, accepting each other—quirks and all—and making a difference every day, for each other, and for people we'll never meet, but whose lives we touch.

I set my pen down, press my hand to the cool, smooth pages of my notebook, and give my work family the biggest smile I've ever worn.

Bernardo leans forward in his chair. It creaks beneath him, and he clears his throat, then says, "Did you have anything you wanted to say, Jillian?"

Everyone turns to me, not really expecting that I will. But things are different now. The tightness in my throat, the choke hold on my words, all that has loosened, washed away. Sure, I may always be self-conscious, possibly awkward, shy, but all that guilt that congregated like so many jagged rocks in my throat, the fear that pressed down on my lungs, that's gone.

So I turn to Buck and say, "Thank you, I didn't expect that. It means more to me than you can know."

Buck's large eyebrows rise high, and the tops of ears flush bright red.

"You talk now?" he asks, then says with a frown, "I didn't do it for you. I did it because I'm not an asshole."

Ned coughs into his hand, and Hayley smacks him on the back.

"I know," I tell Buck. "Thanks."

Ned's cough subsides, and when Hayley's stopped hitting his back, I say to him, "Thank you Ned. You're a good guy..." I look over his wispy brown hair, his wiry frame, and say, "And even if you don't believe my philosophy, I think someday, you'll meet the person who likes you for who you are."

If I did, then so can he.

I look at Bernardo then, to see how he's taking me thanking his staff for their mutiny. He stares back at me, then quirks an eyebrow as if he's waiting for me to go on, so I turn to Hayley and say, "Thanks, if you ever want a partner for a game, I'll be there."

"You're welcome," she says, a gleam in her eyes.

At that, we all turn to face Bernardo.

He glances at me, and I swear he's restraining a smile. Then he picks up his phone, scrolls through his notes, and says, placid as ever, "Jillian, your numbers from last week look good. Your article on finding love after heartache was the most shared of the week and had the most subscribes. I think it's safe to say"—he glances up at me from his phone, his brown eyes amused—"that I'm not a disloyal, weak..."

"Coward," Ned adds helpfully.

Bernardo nods. "Coward. However, if your numbers hadn't improved, then I'd been conducting market research on adding a science and technology readership and thought you may have wanted to pivot your expertise—"

"Are you kidding?" Hayley cries, "You let us all stand here and give dramatic ultimatums and all along you knew you weren't going to fire Jillian? Are you kidding me?"

Bernardo's mouth twitches when he says, "You were all having so much fun. I didn't want to interrupt."

He folds his hands in front of him and casually rests them on the table. I swear he's fighting a smile. But maybe not, you never know with Bernardo.

"Someday," Hayley says, leaning forward, a challenge in her eyes. "Someday, Bernardo, something is going to shock you right out of that imperturbable calm. And I hope I'm there to see it."

She leans back then, flicking her ponytail over her shoulder, and Bernardo gives a small, hidden smile, as if he's aware of some cosmic irony that's just waiting to hit him over the head.

"Moving on," he says. "Jillian you're still on dating and relationships, unless you want to transition and try your hand at science and technology?"

I shake my head. "No, I like what I do. I like what I'm writing. I like telling people the truth about love."

Bernardo's eyes light with approval. He hired me nine years ago, with only two conditions: that I do my best, and that I always tell the truth—in my articles and in my work relationships. He didn't need me to be outgoing, he didn't need me to talk at meetings, he didn't need me to win any prizes, all he ever asked was that I do my best and tell the truth.

These past months it didn't look good, all those negative comments and unsubscribes made it feel like I'd have to give up on my truth.

But I get the feeling that Bernardo's glad I didn't.

Be yourself, and the one who is meant to love you will see you and love you exactly as you are.

At my decision, Bernardo continues the meeting, Buck reaches for the donuts, Ned mentions a string of disappearances last year during Manhattanhenge, and Hayley keeps heckling Bernardo, probably because she's in uniform.

I lean back and enjoy the success that Daniel helped me find, wishing he could be here with me to see it.

Later, when an email comes through from Thomas inviting me to Sci-fi in the Park, I write back another excuse, just like last week when I told him I couldn't come to see *I'll Never Forget You*. But then, before I hit send, I remember what Daniel said—*you should say yes.*

And so, even though the only person I want to go to the movies with is Daniel, I decide to do what he asked me to.

I say yes.

34

ASTORIA PARK HUGS THE EAST RIVER, A LONG, GREEN STRIP of land, full of fanning trees, sweet-smelling grass, and tonight, at least two hundred people lounging in the grass, watching *The Incredible Shrinking Man* on a giant outdoor movie screen.

The sky has faded to a deep blue, with gray clouds that skitter past, obscuring the moonlight. The trees that line the river's edge are black in the night, their leaves gently rustling in the May breeze. Over the river, the RFK (once Triborough) Bridge stretches elegantly, reflecting its white lights in the deep blue water. And across the river, there's Manhattan, home, the buildings of Midtown bright in the night.

I press my hands into the cool spring grass and try to focus on the plot of the old sci-fi flickering on the screen. I brought a plaid picnic blanket and Thomas brought a take-out bag full of sushi and aloe juice to drink.

Which is nice. Really nice. Except, I don't like seaweed, or sea creatures, or sadly, aloe.

If Daniel had asked me to eat sushi I would've told him no. A hard no. Not even for his vicarious-I-love-what-you're-eating expression.

"Are you sure you're not hungry?" Thomas asks, gesturing at the spread laid out on the picnic blanket.

There are soft, fleshy strips of raw trumpet fish perched on pearls of white rice, golden brown brain-like blobs that he tells me are deliciously briny raw sea urchins, and tiny bright red congealed spheres that are dozens of cured salmon roe housed in their slimy egg sac.

Thomas takes a bite of the roe, and I can hear them bursting like juicy grapes as he crunches down on them.

"I'm good," I tell him, nodding as convincingly as I can.

The movie only started fifteen minutes ago, we're at the back of the grassy lawn, and couples and families fill the grass in front of us, sharing their own meals, bags of popcorn, or drinks.

The sweet tangy smell of ginger and the sting of wasabi tickle my nose as I smile at Thomas.

He's reaching for his bottle of aloe juice, but when he sees my smile, he jumps nervously and then knocks his aloe juice over.

"Sorry," he says, grabbing for it.

But instead of catching it, he knocks it again, spilling it over me.

The aloe globs and the sugary sticky juice is cold against my skin. It drenches my skirt. I grab the bottle and thrust it upright.

"Sorry," Thomas says again, as I hand the bottle to him.

"Don't worry," I say, reaching for a napkin. I blot the juice off my skirt and wipe it from my legs.

Even in the dark, I can tell he's flushing from embarrassment. He doesn't need to worry though. If anyone knows how it is to feel awkward or embarrassed in public, it's me.

"Aloe's good for the skin," I tell him. "You actually did me a favor. They charge two hundred dollars for this kind of treatment at a spa."

At that, Thomas smiles, and the nervous embarrassment that he'd been carrying since we met at the edge of the park, fades.

"Do you like the movie?" he asks, nodding at the screen showing *The Incredible Shrinking Man*.

I glance at the tall movie screen and the black and white couple on the screen, then back to him.

"I haven't really been paying attention," I admit.

"Me either," he says, grinning.

He's in dark jeans and a button-down shirt tonight, he's still wearing the classic watch Daniel admired, as well as the black thick-rimmed glasses. His curly brown hair is smoothed down, and I can tell he went to a lot of trouble for tonight, which makes it worse, because as soon as I saw Thomas I knew, no matter what Daniel asked, I can't feel something for anyone else.

He was it for me. Like Zelda said, we were opposite ends of a magnet, drawn together. Two halves of a whole.

Thomas watches me, then says, "I'm not getting a second date, am I?"

I give him a startled glance, and he says with a shrug, "It's kind of obvious you're hung up on someone else. At least, I hope you're hung up on someone. Otherwise, I'm a terrible date."

I shake my head. "No. You aren't terrible. You're a really nice guy."

He gives me an ironic smile, the one of a man being rejected and called nice.

"You're right," I say, taking a breath of ginger and the fresh cut grass. "I'm hung up on someone. I'm sorry. I shouldn't have come."

I was trying to move on.

Moving on from guilt and shame, that was necessary.

Moving on and succeeding at work, that was good.

But moving on from Daniel?

That's not something I can do.

He promised to love me forever, and I know he's still out there somewhere, loving me.

So I'll be right here, loving him. And the next time we meet, because we will, even if it's after I'm gone, I'll tell him—I missed you, I love you.

Beside me, Thomas flicks at the neon plastic grass sticking out of the sushi container and watches it vibrate. Then he looks back to me and says with renewed hope in his eyes, "Is there any chance this guy's a jerk and in a month you'll be over him? There's this convention in Connecticut in July, we could drive up together—"

"I'm sorry," I say. "He's not a jerk."

Thomas smiles good-naturedly and looks out over the lights reflecting off the East River. "Alright, but if you ever decide you need a 'really nice guy' who likes *Star Trek*, good food"—he gestures at the sushi spread—"and will spend weekends with you at conventions, then give me a call."

"I will," I say.

Then instead of watching the movie, we debate who the better captain was—Kirk or Picard—which Enterprise was the best, and whether alternate timelines really do exist.

At the end of the movie, we pack up and walk a half mile to the subway together, I take the N back to Manhattan and Thomas heads in the opposite direction.

As the subway rocks back and forth, the interior of the train flashing dark, then light, then dark as we speed through a tunnel, I watch the lights reflect off a train whooshing past on the opposite tracks. The rumble of the subway, the windy roar settles over me, and I lean back in the hard plastic seat and let the train carry me away.

"Sorry," I tell Daniel, remembering his promise that he can hear me, even if he isn't here. "I thought I could try moving on, since you told me to say yes to him, but I can't. I only want you."

Across the long train car, on the seat diagonal from me, a woman knits a scarf with orange yarn, a few rows down from her, a homeless man sleeps under a crumpled newspaper, spread over him like a bedsheet, and standing near the door, a construction worker listens to music on his headphones.

No one pays me any mind, not even when I'm talking to myself.

35

As I walk down my block, the picnic blanket tucked under my arm, I think about what I'm going to tell Fran. She's so convinced that good things are coming, that I'm going to find someone to love, that it'll be hard telling her that it's already come and gone.

The yellow of the streetlight spills over me in a warm glow as I pull my keys from my purse. The street is quiet, only a few taxis speed down Lexington, and down the block a bodega's lights are shining, but otherwise, the street is sleeping.

Which is why I'm surprised when my neighbor pushes open the door to the building and scowls at me. She's in a fuzzy baby blue bathrobe, and Daisy snuggles in the crook of her arm. He lifts his mouth in a half-hearted snarl and gives an irritated bark.

"There you are," she says, frowning at me from the top of the stone steps leading into our building.

I wave my hand, my keys jangling in my grip.

"Yes. Here I am," I say lamely.

I don't know what she could possibly want. I haven't made any noises in the last two weeks. In fact, the last time I was loud was when Daniel and I spent our last night together.

My neighbor jerks her head back at the building. "You were looking for Daniel."

At that tersely spoken sentence my body freezes, my heart spasms, and even though my mind doesn't articulate all the hope and expectation rising in me, it's still there.

She's talking about Daniel.

She wants to tell me about Daniel.

"Yes," I say, barely managing that one word over the pounding of my heart.

"He's here," she says, thrusting her hand back toward the door.

What?

He's...he's here?

Daniel?

"I told him you were looking for him. Not that I want any funny business. The walls are thin and Daniel is loud. All hours, all night, every night..." She glares at me as if that is my fault.

But I don't care. Because Daniel.

Daniel's here. He's back.

He's here and she can see him, and that means...

"He came back," I breathe.

He came back for me.

Somehow. Some way.

It feels as if I've stuck my finger in an electric socket, my veins buzz with electricity.

"Unfortunately," my neighbor says, then she points at the wooden stairs inside the building, "here he comes."

She stalks past me then, taking Daisy to sniff the nearby newspaper stand and trash can.

But I'm not watching Daisy or my neighbor, no, I'm watching the man coming down the stairs. I can see him through the glass front door, the hall light illuminating him like an angel descending from heaven. I can see Daniel.

Well, I can see his feet. He's wearing high gloss black dress shoes with dark denim jeans. He takes the steps slowly, and as he does I see the tight fit of his jeans, molding to his legs.

The wind drags across my face, cooling my flushed cheeks, bringing the scent of concrete and dirt. I clutch my still damp skirt, sticky from the spilled aloe juice.

I want to run to him, but I'm frozen in place, my breath burning my lungs, my body electrified.

Daniel steps further down the stairs, now his shirt is in view. It's a blue paisley-patterned shirt, buttoned, and tucked into his jeans, stretching over his chest.

There's his hands...

His arms...

His gold necklace...

Something's wrong.

Those aren't his hands. Those aren't his legs. That isn't his gold necklace. And that *definitely* isn't his face.

The man shoves open the door and gives me a wide, I'm-too-sexy-for-my-mirror smile. He's probably late-thirties. There's a cloud of pine-scented cologne around him, he has perfectly filed fingernails, a pencil thin mustache, thick eyebrows, and smooth short brown hair.

When he stops at the base of the steps, he sticks his pointer finger and thumb in his mouth, licks them, and then drags them over his eyebrows, smoothing them out.

I stare at him with mounting horror and confusion. This isn't Daniel.

My neighbor said that Daniel lived in my apartment before me. She said Daniel was a Lothario. She said...

My neighbor shoves past me, grunting at the man. Daisy lets out a growl and a menacing yip.

"Daniel," she says, then she sweeps around to glare at me. "You. Keep the noise down."

Then she stomps up the stairs and slams the glass door shut. I flinch at the bang.

When she's gone, it's just me, imposter Daniel, and a couple arguing outside the bodega.

"I heard you were looking for me," Daniel says, wagging his eyebrows.

I stare at him, all the electricity and anticipation in me fizzling, shorting out, and then dying.

"You lived in 4b?" I ask, clutching my dress.

He rolls his shoulders and puffs his chest out, "You like the mirrors?"

My body goes cold. He did. He lived there. His name is Daniel. He lived in my apartment, and he had lots of loud sex every single night.

And if that's the case, then my Daniel never lived here, and he was right when he told me that he'd never seen my apartment before finding me.

Unless... "Who lived there before you?" I ask, my voice scratchy.

The Daniel imposter gives me a strange look, "Some chick named Nicole. But I put in the mirrors if that's what you're asking."

It's not what I'm asking.

My Daniel never lived here. I don't know if that makes me happy or if it makes me terribly sad. I thought he lived in my apartment, and that made me feel as if I still had a part of him. But not anymore.

I shake my head and wrap my arms around myself. "No. I had a question about the hot water, but I figured it out. Thanks."

I wave my hand in a quick goodbye, then run up the steps, up the four flights of creaking, wooden stairs, and into my apartment.

When I close my door behind me, locking the bolt, I lean back against the wood, press my hands into the cool, hard surface, and stare into the dark room at the mirrors that never reflected Daniel. Not when he was alive and not when he was dead.

In the morning, I take my parents' advice and cover all the mirrors with large sheets of cream-colored paper.

36

It's Saturday, three weeks since Daniel disappeared, and the last of the spring chill is gone, replaced by the sweetly sunny warmth of May, with its candy-scented flowering trees, bright blue skies, and gently insistent sunshine.

The gray and beige stone of the old mansions and townhomes lining Fifth Avenue sparkle in the midday sun. The fountains in front of the Met splash and gurgle, and two little girls run alongside it, dragging their fingers through the water, laughing gleefully.

The cobblestone sidewalks around the museum are full of vendors selling brightly colored original art, vibrant museum posters, postcards, 3D cards of New York attractions, t-shirts—the list goes on. The folding tables crowd the sidewalk and tourists wander between them, as thick as the scent of hotdogs and pretzels pumping from the street carts parked in front of the museum steps.

"It's the perfect day for a girls' day out," Fran says,

cutting through a line of tables and pushing past a tour group.

She called this morning at eight and told me that she was on the train, and I better be ready in one hour for a trip to the Met and shopping. By shopping she meant visiting the Met's giftshop, which is one of her favorite places in the whole city.

"It is perfect," I agree, watching the sun glint on the tall stone steps, towering up to the sweeping columns and the glistening arched windows. I think the Met is one of the prettiest museums in the whole world.

Suddenly, I wish that Daniel and I had gone here. He would've pointed out all his favorite things and tried to make me laugh, and me, I would've laughed with him.

I stare up at the stone and glass above us and try not to let the heavy weight on my chest bury me.

Fran pauses at the base of the steps and turns to me. "Jilly?"

"What is it?" I ask, brushing back my curls as the breeze tugs at my ponytail.

I dressed casually today, a pair of jean shorts, my gray Starfleet t-shirt, and sneakers. I figured if we were going to be walking for hours, I should be comfortable.

Fran, on the other hand, wore a zebra-stripe tunic, black pants, and black flats.

She rests her hand on my arm, "I don't like seeing you like this. I think what you need to do is get back out there—"

I shake my head, a tour group moving around us, climbing toward the front doors. "No. I told you, I met the man I love. There isn't anyone else."

Fran drops her hand from my arm and lets out a long

sigh. "You're sure he isn't coming back?" she asks, ever hopeful.

I told her that the man I met was from another country, and that he was only here for a short stay. I told her that when he left it was with the understanding that he'd never be back, and we'd never see each other again, even though I loved him and he loved me.

"I'm sure," I say.

At that, Fran shakes her head, then grips the brass railing leading up the flights of stone steps. But after only three steps, she suddenly stops, tilts her head, and then looks over at me with a gleam in her eyes.

"Now Jilly, don't say no. Since he's here, it could be fate. You should just meet him, just say hello." She gives me her wide I've-just-matched-you-with-another-blind-date smile. "He may be everything you need to get over your heartache."

I shake my head. I can guarantee it's not fate, and whoever Fran found definitely won't cure my heartache.

"I'm sure of it, actually," she says, warming to her idea.

I look around, but the steps are crowded with tourists, families, and couples holding hands and I don't see anyone that meets her usual criteria for a blind date.

She grips my arm and says in a happy voice, "Remember the man I met at Bergdorf's?"

I shake my head. Fran is so outgoing and meets so many people, it's hard to keep track of everyone.

She nods her head meaningfully toward the entrance of the Met.

"He's here," she says, opening her eyes wide. "I told you, the ladies at the make-up counter said he's very wealthy, he has women hanging off him, which could be a problem, but he said he'd let you interview him for this article I made up about owning a yacht, and—"

I'm not listening anymore.

I don't know who Fran's talking about. I don't care.

Because as I scan the crowd of faces for the man she's describing, I see him.

Daniel.

We're fifty feet apart, three flights of stone steps and a crowd of people separate us. But all the same, I know it's him.

He stands at the top of the steps, the shining arched window behind him, the warm yellow sunlight bathing him in its glow.

And suddenly, he sees me too.

He looks right at me, his blue eyes as warm as the summer sky, and he smiles.

My heart bursts with joy.

He's back.

He's really, really back.

He heard me and he came back.

A half-sob, half-cry bursts from my throat. And then I'm sprinting up the steps, flying toward him. Tears blur my vision, and I blink them away so I can keep sight of him. He can't disappear again.

My chest burns as I run up the last of the steps, and then he's there. Right in front of me.

I fling myself at him. I don't care if there are dozens of people around. I don't care that I'll be hugging a ghost in front of tour groups and schoolkids. I don't care.

I'm laughing, I'm crying, I cling to him.

And I'm so overwhelmed that he feels as if he's really here. He feels solid. Warm.

I throw myself into his arms, and he catches me,

somehow, he catches me. I wrap my legs around him, hold my face in my hands, his stubble rough, his jaw firm, and I kiss him.

I kiss him with all the love I feel, all the pain of losing him, all the joy at seeing him again. I hold onto him and kiss him and kiss him. His lips are warm, his mouth is hot, his hands are steady on my hips, holding me up as I rub my lips over his, taste him—coffee, sugar, chocolate.

Wait...

His lips are warm?

He's holding me up?

He tastes like coffee and chocolate?

I leave my lips on his mouth, his warm, soft, *solid* mouth, and I open my eyes.

Daniel stares at me, his familiar cobalt eyes wide, surprised.

I stare into his eyes, my breath short, my heart pounding wildly, and fall into his stunned gaze.

His hands tighten on my hips, his fingers press into my bare skin, brushing just below the edge of my jean shorts. His hands are hot, his touch, his actual touch scalds me. My legs are wrapped around his hips, I'm pressed against him in the position most people would use for making sweaty, frantic love against a closed door.

A tear tracks down my cheek. A gust of wind tugs at my hair. I feel his heartbeat against my chest.

His *heartbeat.*

Finally, finally, he blinks.

I pull my lips away from his, the breeze rushing between us.

At that his eyes clear of the stunned surprise.

I want to bury my face against his shoulder, breathe in his soft scent of sun-warmed skin and spring breeze.

He smells like a day spent lying in the grass at the edge of the lake, watching the row boats pass under the Bow Bridge, the sun shining over us.

My hands feather over his warm cheeks, his rough stubble, through the ends of his wavy hair, as soft as I imagined.

His sandy-brown hair hits the collar of his shirt—a cornflower blue cashmere sweater, worn over a t-shirt.

That's right. He's wearing a shirt. Two shirts.

Daniel is wearing *two shirts*.

And that's when I can't deny it anymore.

If this is Daniel, if this is *really* Daniel, then he's alive.

My throat burns, my heart attempts to leap out of my chest, and I don't know whether I want to curl in Daniel's arms and sob, or lie in his arms and kiss him for forever and a day.

How can he be alive?

He looks down at me, as if he's not quite sure what he should do with me either.

He has that look, the one he wore in the shower, the one he called shocked stupid.

I imagine I look pretty shocked right now too.

"Daniel," a woman says in a light British accent, sounding like she's having trouble deciding between irritated and *slightly* amused. "Do women always have to throw themselves at you, wherever we go?"

I look over at the woman then. She's stunningly beautiful. Tall, long auburn hair, hazel eyes, a navy silk tunic dress and gold heels. She looks like a model, or a movie star.

"It seems your reputation proceeds you," she says dryly, running her eyes over me, wrapped around Daniel. "Unless you know her?"

Daniel gives the woman a sharp shake of his head, and when he does, she says, "Well then put her down! The last thing we need is a lawsuit from a crazed fan or a stalker."

I tune out the crazed fan stalker bit and focus on the fact that Daniel shook his head when she asked if he knew me.

He said *no*.

He turns back to me then, and slowly, carefully sets me on my feet, then he steps back, putting distance between us. The surprise in his eyes from the kiss is gone, the warmth is gone, his smile is gone. In its place is an impersonal, almost cold politeness.

I stare into Daniel's eyes and what I see there suffocates the warmth in my veins and replaces it with ice.

Because he truly doesn't know me.

There isn't a shred of recognition. Not a shred of love. Not a bit of shared memory. Not even the ghost of one.

Daniel doesn't know who I am.

I sway on my feet, suddenly dizzy.

Fran finally makes it to the top of the steps, huffing from hurrying after me. "What on earth? I didn't know that you've already met. If I'd known that you already knew each other—"

Daniel holds up his hand to stop her, giving Fran a quizzical look.

"I'm sorry. We've never met," he says, and his voice, it hits me in the chest, and squeezes.

It's *his* voice, that rich, warm rumble that I love, but it isn't filled with teasing laughter or familiar warmth. Instead it's the tone you'd use with a stranger.

Daniel looks down at me, his blue eyes distant, the

breeze blowing through his hair, the sun shining on him. "I think there's been some sort of mistake. I don't know you."

"It was a little more than a mistake," the woman says, giving me a disgusted look. "You can't accost people like that, you're lucky we don't report you—"

She tears into me, but the buzzing in my ears overrides her words, and all I can hear is Daniel saying, *I don't know you.*

Daniel says something to me, lifts his eyebrows as if he's waiting for a response. Then, he shakes his head and turns to leave, and I realize that the man I love, the one who promised to love me always, he's alive, he's here, but he doesn't know me, and he doesn't love me, he doesn't love me at all.

He doesn't see my heart. He doesn't see me. He's looking right through me.

As he moves to walk away, I throw my hand out to stop him, to tell him who I am, to remind him who he is, but when I try to speak, no words come out.

He's living.

He's breathing.

Thunder booms in my head, like the crash of the sound barrier breaking.

And then, I do what I should've done the *first* time I saw Daniel.

My knees buckle, my head spins, and the Met, the tourists, and Daniel are swallowed by roaring darkness, as I drop to the unyielding stone steps.

Right before I lose consciousness, I feel solid, warm arms catch me and pull me close.

37

I STAND IN THE CENTER OF TIMES SQUARE, THE SEA OF people crashing around me, the swirl of bright colors so vivid it's almost blinding.

I'm buried in the shouting, riotous jumble at the center of the city, overwhelmed by the roar of the subway rumbling in the tunnel beneath the street, the steam shooting up the metal grate, the street musicians busking, the living statues painted in silver and gold posing, the hawkers shouting, "show tonight, free show tonight," and the blinking, flashing, bright lights of the digital billboards.

Okay. Never mind.

I'm only overwhelmed by one billboard.

The billboard.

It's stories and stories high—fifty, a hundred feet tall? —towering over the thousands of people hurrying past, the honking taxis, and the nearby food carts pumping out the scent of charred kebabs, biryani, and spicy empanadas. The billboard reigns over it all.

How didn't I notice this before?

For one thing, even though Times Square is near my office, I don't make a habit of walking this way—first, because it's a zoo, second, because my office and my apartment are in the other direction, third, and again, because it's a zoo.

If I had walked through Times Square though, I would've seen him.

Daniel.

At least, I would've seen the giant flashing billboard of Daniel, shirtless, his six-pack on full display, a pair of low-slung jeans over his hips, and a sexy, knowing smile on his lips.

"Did I make it all up?" I ask.

Not one of the countless people passing answers as they jostle past pushing toward Madame Tussaud's, Ripley's, M&M World, or hurry for a photo with their favorite cartoon character.

No. I didn't make it up. I couldn't have.

But...Daniel didn't know me.

After I fainted, he swiftly carried me down the steps of the Met, with Fran hurrying after him, worriedly alternating between asking if I was alright and reassuring Daniel that I *never* kissed strangers and I must have confused him with someone else.

I stayed in a sort of stunned gray mist, my head resting against his solid chest, his steady heartbeat, until he set me down on a green bench at the edge of the park.

He kneeled down in front of me and asked with the polite concern of a good Samaritan, "Are you alright?"

When I nodded, my throat still refusing to open, he smiled, and the cool reserve he'd showed at the top of the steps disappeared as he said with his achingly familiar good humor, "I'm glad. I'd hate to think kissing me made you pass out. Even if the kiss was a mistake. If you thought it was so terrible that you had to faint, my ego would suffer a huge blow."

Then his eyes crinkled and his smile widened as he absolved me of all blame for the entirely awkward, completely inappropriate kiss that I'd given him—a stranger.

And when he stood to go, Fran assured him again that I wasn't a stalker, or a crazed fan, or anything of the sort, and he brushed it aside, said "Of course, don't worry about it," and then just as quickly as he was there, he was gone.

When he'd disappeared into the crowd, Fran swung around, her eyes wide, and said, "Jilly! Do you know who you just kissed?"

I'd kissed Daniel. But did I know who Daniel was? No. Apparently not.

I shook my head no.

"I've been trying to tell you about him! He's the one I thought would help you get over your broken heart! He's the one the ladies at the make-up counter said was an international playboy." Then she took my hand and said with gleeful delight, "He's Daniel Abry."

Daniel who?

Daniel...

And that's when it hit me.

I'd kissed Daniel Abry.

The Daniel Abry.

The Daniel Abry on the tallest, brightest, biggest billboard in Times Square.

I take my phone from my purse, pray that Serena's off

work, and when she picks up after the second ring, I say without preamble, "Daniel's back."

"Whoa, hi there," Serena says, the sounds of a restaurant in the background. "Hang on, I'm stepping outside. Did you say Daniel's back? And if so, why do you sound so unhappy? Was I right? Was he a nail and bail ghost prick? If you say yes, I'll figure out a way to kill him again."

I stare up at the billboard, my heart thudding hollowly in my chest. "No. You can't kill him, that would be murder."

"He's already dead," Serena says. "I'm allowed to kill ghosts. I bet I could figure out how. After all, I have one of the world's brightest minds."

"He's alive," I say quickly, blinking at his smile.

"What?" Serena says as the restaurant noise cuts off. "Did...what?"

I grip my phone and turn away from the billboard and stare at a cluster of pigeons fluttering around a man covered in gold paint, posing as a gentleman in a top hat.

"He's alive," I say again, my voice scratchy and thick. "I was outside the Met with Fran. I saw him at the top of the steps, so I ran to him and jumped in his arms and kissed him like I was about to make love with him, and... turns out, he's alive and not a ghost and..."

"But this is good!" Serena says, "Mind-blowing, but good. Except if he wasn't a ghost has he figured out how to project himself? Is he some techno wizard? I need to talk to him."

"No," I say, stepping back as a cluster of German tourists led by a loud tour guide, push past.

"No I can't talk to him?" Serena asks.

"No he isn't a techno wizard. No you can't talk to him, because he has no idea who I am. When I kissed him, he didn't kiss me back, he was stiff and distant and shocked, and he didn't recognize me. He didn't know me. He said we'd never met." My voice shakes as I say, "Serena, I looked in his eyes, and he truly didn't know me. It was him, I swear it was, but he didn't know me."

Serena makes a stunned noise, then says, "Your sexy shirtless ghost is alive and he doesn't know you?"

I look at the sexy shirtless Daniel on the billboard, his smile seeming more ironic now than come-hither.

"Yeah," I say, biting my lip, resisting the urge to run across town to jump back in his arms and beg him to remember me.

"Serena," I say, watching the waves of people pass by, none of them looking up toward Daniel. "What if I made it all up?"

"Please," she says, discarding my fear.

I shake my head, "I'm in Times Square—"

"Yeah, I can hear the hawkers."

"—and on the biggest billboard, it's Daniel. He's shirtless, and sexy, and he looks just like he did when he was with me, and...what if I saw this photo somewhere and my subconscious decided to—"

"First, what is Daniel doing shirtless on a billboard?" Serena asks, then she adds more firmly, "And second, you didn't make it all up and you know it."

I take a long, deep breath. I do know it.

"You're right," I say, rubbing my chest where the ache that's lived for the past three weeks is now throbbing with the urge to go to him. "I just don't understand. If I didn't make it up, then what? Because Daniel's alive and he's Daniel Abry."

"Who?" Serena asks.

"Daniel *Abry*," I repeat, emphasizing his last name.

Then when Serena stays silent, and there's only the high whine of the wind on her side of the conversation. I say, "You live in Geneva! How can you not know the name Daniel Abry?"

"Is he a physicist? Because if he's not a physicist, or a science nerd, or one of the many sexy men I've slept with, then I don't know him."

Okay. Fair enough.

"Have you heard of Abry watches? The oldest family-owned Swiss watch company in the world? Remember? I bought my dad that knock-off Abry from Hayley for Christmas. They rival Rolex and Patek Phillipe. Well, Daniel is an Abry. *The* Abry."

After Fran told me Daniel's last name, I went home and scoured the internet for any scrap of information out there. Instead of scraps I found a feast.

Daniel's family started making watches in Geneva in 1838, and each generation has improved and expanded the business. Daniel's father died of a heart attack nearly a decade ago, and since then, when Daniel took over as president and his older half-sister (the woman on the steps) became CEO, they've taken Abry watches from reliable, hand-crafted luxury to the must-have phenomenon it is today.

From what I can tell, Daniel and his half-sister, Fiona, accomplished that through brilliant marketing, calculated positioning, and a hard push into media, popular culture, and celebrity endorsements.

More than that, Daniel has become synonymous with the Abry brand. There are countless photos of him on his yacht in the Mediterranean the sun glinting off his watch, pictures of him gambling in Monaco wearing a tailored tux, looking at his watch, images of him backstage at concerts, at film festivals, attending royal weddings, always wearing an Abry watch, in full view of the cameras.

It's as if he's using himself as a walking advertisement for his company. I glance up at the billboard again and decide, it isn't *as if* he is, he actually is.

If I didn't know him like I do, if I hadn't known him without knowing who he is, then I'm not sure I would've given him a second look. No matter how much I talk about not judging people, no matter how much I wanted someone to see me for me, I'm not sure I would've seen Daniel for himself.

I would've seen the pictures of him dating French actresses, Italian supermodels, American reality TV stars, and I would've looked at the photos of him flashing his watch on the deck of his yacht and I would've thought... well, I would've thought he was a pompous jerk who had lots of money and entitlement and whose good looks covered up a personality with the depth of a rapidly evaporating puddle.

American heiress for a mom. European scion for a dad. Boarding school in Britain. Then on to Oxford. His whole life, from the pictures on the internet and the articles written about him, reads like a celebrity gossip magazine.

There's a reason I didn't recognize him as a ghost—it's because I don't read entertainment magazines. The only time I shop is when Fran drags me out, and if I ever did see a picture of him, I wouldn't have thought anything about it. We're from completely different worlds. Different planets. Maybe even different star systems.

The shy trekker from Long Island paired with the European mogul? It's so far-fetched it's almost laughable.

Serena's been silent for a good thirty seconds, it's just the rumble of the subway, the high-pitched honking, and the hustle of the tourists to fill the silence.

Finally she asks in a stunned voice, "Daniel Abry?" and then with more surprise, "Daniel Abry!"

"Yeah. Daniel Abry."

"That's..." She trails off, then says, "You're in love with Daniel Abry?"

"Yes."

"Daniel Abry haunted your apartment and now he's alive again?"

"That's right."

"And you love him but he doesn't know you or remember you?"

"Yes, that's what I've been saying."

"Oh," she says, which isn't the reaction I was hoping for.

I step back into the shade of a building, moving out of the heat of the sun and the flow of people hurrying past.

"I don't understand anything," I tell Serena, the hectic pace of Times Square swirling around me. "You said we can't conceive what we don't perceive, but I can't conceive what happened. I don't understand what's going on. I want to tell him, *I know you, I love you and you love me, we met when you were a ghost*...but you know what will happen if I tell him that? He'll think I'm insane. Except, if he was a ghost, doesn't that mean he died? Or...what?"

"Jilly!" I hear Serena snap her fingers, "Yes! I've got it. Physics, you are beautiful. It all makes sense!"

"What?" I look at Daniel's photo, and the fifty-foot tall

expanse of his golden skin, expecting the answer to appear miraculously in the air above me.

"Daniel *is* dead," Serena says, and honestly, she sounds entirely too happy about that prospect for my liking.

"He isn't," I say, pointing out the obvious. "I just made out with him on the steps of the Met."

"Shhh, I'm sciencing you," Serena says, putting on her lecture voice, the one she uses when she's explaining the science behind Star Trek, "Daniel isn't dead right now, he's dead in the future."

My heart trips over itself and misses a beat. I push off the wall I'm leaning against and wade back into the sea of people, walking swiftly east, toward my apartment.

"What do you mean?" I ask.

"When he was a ghost, did he look older? A few years maybe?"

I think back—strong jaw, golden stubble, wavy, sandy-brown hair, the tiniest lines around his eyes when he smiled, smooth, tan skin, he looked...he looked exactly like he did today.

"No, he looked the same."

"Hmmm," Serena says, "That doesn't matter really, we can't know exactly when he dies, because he didn't tell you, right?"

I cross the street, heading out of the bright flashing lights of Times Square, and move under the shade of a scaffolding. "He claimed he wasn't dead. He didn't accept it until the psychic said he was."

The last thing he remembered was leaning over a beautiful woman lying beneath him. And then pain.

"Alright, here's the deal. I think Daniel harnessed the Planck energy."

"He did what?"

"Listen," Serena says. "What we know, our rational, logical, scientific knowledge can only fit inside a very small box. The rest of the knowledge in the universe, that infinite universe, it can only be understood through our souls. It's a resonance outside of our logical mind. When we toss aside the resonance, that soft insistent voice of our souls, then we toss aside most of the knowledge of the universe *and* we lose our humanity. You can't think about this from a purely logical perspective. One of the greatest physicists to ever live said that when we describe the atom we can only use the language of poetry. He was in earnest, this wasn't hyperbole. When you follow science to its logical conclusion you find that the end of science is the beginning of the human soul. There are things we can't describe with logic. Things we don't understand. For instance, when we die, we don't scientifically know what happens. However, let's theorize that the human soul is composed of pure energy. It's like that psychic you went to said that she *felt* Daniel's *energy*. So once we die, we can theorize that we are pure energy. And this is where it gets interesting. Because once you go to the higher levels of energy, the laws of physics begin to break down."

Serena says the last with so much enthusiasm that I ask, "They break down?"

"Yes. The laws of physics break down. Now, at CERN our atom smasher—"

I smile as I walk past a halal cart, the spicy scent of roasting meat wafting to me, I love it when she calls the particle collider an atom smasher.

"—it does a good job of smashing atoms, but we haven't even come close to reaching the Planck energy.

That's ten to the nineteen billion electron volts, which is a quadrillion times more powerful than anything we've reached. And that level"—her voice rises to a gleeful note—"when you reach the Planck energy, both time and space become unstable."

"What does that mean?" I ask, dodging past a taxi and hopping up on the sidewalk.

"It means that space and time are your playground. At that level of energy you become the *master* of space and time."

I look at the intersection, the taxis and buses rolling past, at the blue sky peeking through the tall gray buildings, at the sidewalk trees, stuck in their tiny mulch beds, and I wait for...something.

Serena continues, "The human race in *Star Trek* could travel back in time, remember *The Voyage Home*?"

"Yes, obviously." Of course I remember *The Voyage Home*. It's my favorite, and Daniel and I just watched it together last month.

Across the intersection, my building casts a shadow over the coffee cart where the sad philosopher's reading, ignoring a couple standing nearby.

"Well, think of it like that. Daniel died, reached the Planck energy and then traveled through time and space to reach you. Why? How? We don't know. But if logic only takes you so far, then what your heart is telling you must take you the rest of the way."

I pause at the foot of the stone steps leading up to my apartment building.

"How sure are you about this?" I ask, thinking of what it means if it's true.

I can hear Serena's smile through the phone. "Point

zero zero zero zero zero one percent. Which is quite high, considering."

I smile. "Alright. But if it is true…"

"Then Daniel knew you before he died, and he came back to you after he was gone."

I think about the first day he appeared.

He knew my name.

He was certain I knew his.

He promised we were friends.

He called me his light.

"Do you know what this means?" I ask.

Serena makes a happy hum and says, "You're coming to Geneva's trekker con this summer?"

"No!" I say, then, "Maybe. No, what it means is, I'm supposed to know him, be his friend, fall in love, and then…save him."

"Is that what your heart is telling you?" she asks.

"Yes," I say. There's no doubt about it.

"Then sure. That too," Serena agrees.

I narrow my eyes, looking up at the fourth floor, toward the window of my apartment.

"If I save Daniel though, doesn't that mean he won't go back in time, because he's not a ghost, and he doesn't reach Planck energy, and if I save him, I'll change the future, so that I don't actually meet him in the past and then I don't save him, and then…it'll be this circle of saving and not saving and we won't be having this conversation and…time travel makes my head hurt. But seriously, if I save him, then I wouldn't have met him, because he doesn't die, and doesn't that mean that I already failed, because I met him, which means he died and…ugh."

"Yeah, it gets weird," Serena says, "which is why I never liked the alternate timelines in *Star Trek*. But I think him dying could be one timeline, and him not dying is another. Or not. There could be another explanation." She pauses then, the wind whistling past her on Geneva's streets and she says, "My date's getting antsy in there. I bet his steak's cold. I better go. But Jilly, what are you going to do?"

I think about it. About how Zelda said that Daniel loved me from the start. How he found me. How he said he'd love me always.

I think about how I couldn't save Michael, how I couldn't change the past, and I couldn't bring him into the future.

But if Daniel came back to me as a ghost, if I have the opportunity to love him, and save him, I can't do anything else but try.

Even if it means that he won't go back in time, or he won't be a ghost and I'll forget everything we had, or...if I save him, I could forget him? It's too much to think about. So I hang on to the one thing that I know is true. Not point zero zero zero zero zero one percent, but one hundred percent true. And that's that I love Daniel with all my heart.

That my soul calls to his, and his to mine.

And even if I forget him, or if he's forgotten me (which he has), it doesn't change the fact that we're two opposite ends of a magnet, drawn together, each other's light in the dark.

I love him, and that's the answer.

I think love is even more powerful than the Planck energy.

"What am I going to do?" I ask, coming to a decision.

"Yes," Serena says, "what are you going to do?"

I smile, the beginning of hope springing to life, and I say determinedly as the late spring sun shines over me and the warm breeze brushes past, "I'm going to interview Daniel Abry about his yacht."

38

DANIEL GIVES INTERVIEWS ON MONDAYS, IN HIS OFFICE
suites from six p.m. until seven p.m.

Apparently, it's something he's known for, his
accessibility to the press and his extreme affability.
Whether he's in Geneva, Paris, Singapore, or New York,
he's always available once a week for "polite inquiries."

Usually the interviews are booked out, far, far, far into
the future. However, a lucky star is shining down on me,
because the last interview of the day canceled and I was
offered the spot by the frazzled, harassed-sounding
public relations intern on the phone.

Obviously I grabbed that interview slot with the
aggressive tenacity of someone shoving onto the jam-
packed subway at rush hour, the doors banging shut with
only a hairsbreadth of breathing room.

I did it.

I'm seeing Daniel.

The shining brass doors of the elevator slide open,

revealing the New York headquarters of Abry Watch Co. Ltd.

Refinement, luxury, class, those are all words that could describe the sixteenth floor of the metal and glass skyscraper located near Bryant Park. Just like the offices of *The Daily Exposé*—located only blocks away—the space is wide open and expansive. That's where the resemblance ends though. While my office is frenetic, messy chaos, the Abry office is calm, clean, and cool.

The ceiling is high with tasteful gold chandeliers (not like my Liberace-inspired chandelier), the back walls are glass with a view of Bryant Park below, the leafy trees, green grass, and the spinning carousel painted bright. The colors of the evening blue sky, the green grass, and the carousel are the only vibrant colors—the interior of the office is all ivory and white and cream.

Even the air is scented with the cool, clean, crisp scent of an orchid in bloom. I step out of the elevator, onto the white marble floors, my heels loud on the stone.

I stand out, the blue of my dress bright against all the white, but all the same, I smile as I walk toward the reception desk facing the elevator.

A twenty-something woman wearing a white wool suit with hair slicked into a bun nods at me. The security guard called up to announce my arrival, and I assume she was the one who answered.

"He'll be with you in a moment," she says in a brisk, professional voice. "Please have a seat."

She gestures to her right, and I take in the rest of the space.

The open area is about one hundred feet by thirty feet, and there are multiple conversation areas where groups of low white couches and sleek white chairs form intimate seating. Since it's nearly seven o'clock, the front lobby is empty except for the receptionist and me. The only noise is the steady tick of the large, gold Abry wall clock hanging on the wall opposite the elevator, and of course, the quiet, soothing classical music playing over the sound system.

I imagine past the open area, down the hallway (discreetly hidden by a white wall) there are dozens of offices.

I give the receptionist a grateful smile. "Thank you."

Then I walk to the floor-to-ceiling windows, too nervous to sit and wait. At the window, I take a breath and tell myself it's going to be okay, that I have a plan, and I can't fail because Daniel's depending on me, even if he doesn't know it.

Five minutes later, an older male reporter leaves and the receptionist leads me down the hall, our steps echoing over the marble. We walk down the hallway, where framed photographs of Abry family history, the Geneva headquarters, and groundbreaking watches line the wall. And even though the lobby was empty and it's nearly seven, plenty of people are still at work in their offices, typing, chatting, or on the phone.

At the end of the hallway, the receptionist discreetly knocks on a tall dark wood door, and from inside I hear a short, "Yes."

She opens the door wide, gestures for me to go inside and then leaves.

My hands are sweaty, my legs shake, and my mouth goes dry.

Daniel's office is similar to the rest of the space, a calm, luxurious environment, with soothing white and cream, decorated with modern furniture. It's not at all what I would've expected. If I ever had to picture where Daniel worked, it wouldn't be this.

And I would never have expected him to dress in a crisply tailored gray suit, the jacket hugging his shoulders, stretching over his back, his sandy hair brushing the white collar of his shirt.

He looks like the president of an international watch company with a billion dollars in annual sales—which he is.

He's Daniel but he's not.

He isn't looking at me. Instead he sits at his desk—a large modern piece that belongs in an architectural magazine—and frowns down at a piece of paper, completely engrossed.

"Have a seat," he says distractedly, still not looking up. "I'll be just a moment."

He swiftly scratches out something on the paper, then scrawls a note in the margins.

My hands shake as I heft my purse over my shoulder and walk across his office, the air conditioning cool, the cream rug surrounding his desk soft under my heels.

I perch on the edge of a leather chair facing his desk and the fabric of my dress stretches tightly over my thighs. The leather is cold against my bare legs, and I resist the urge to squirm while Daniel continues to tap his pen against his desk and his eyes narrow on the paper in front of him.

I smile suddenly, remembering how appalled he was when the man in the coffee shop ignored me.

In the hallway outside Daniel's office, two men in suits walk past, joking about their latest squash match, their voices echoing down the hall.

I'm less than five feet from Daniel, I swear I can smell

his sunshine scent again, I swear I can feel his warmth, and I just want to say, *look at me, see me.*

Instead, I clear my throat, use his strategy, and say, "Do you have the time?"

I came prepared tonight. I wore the blue dress Daniel loved. I put on cherry red lipstick because Daniel loved my mouth. I wore mascara because he said he'd die happy if he could do it looking into my eyes.

But he has to look at me first before he sees any of that, doesn't he?

But without looking up, Daniel glances at his Abry watch and says in a business-like voice, "Six forty-eight. I'll be just a moment."

I stare at him in surprise.

Unbelievable.

"Do you know, when a lady asks you the time, you should look at her when you respond," I say, echoing Daniel's reprimand from weeks ago.

At that, he does look up, his eyebrows raised, the pen falling from his hand to clatter to the desk. "I apologize, I—"

He cuts off when he sees me, the apologetic expression vanishing into one of recognition. Not recognition of me, Jillian, but recognition of the woman who accosted him outside the Met and then fainted.

I can tell because he isn't smiling at me with love, no, he's giving me a hard, jaw-clenched, I-can't-believe-it-you-really-are-a-stalker-and-now-I-have-to-deal-with-you look.

His cobalt eyes freeze over into ice blue, and he says in an unyielding voice, "I gave you the benefit of the doubt on Saturday. However, I believe that benefit is gone."

He stands, thrusts his chair back and stalks around his desk. I look up at him, his suit molded to his muscular frame, his mouth in a firm line and his jaw hard. His steps are quiet on the carpet and I scoot back in the leather chair.

He narrows his eyes on my mutinous position, and it's then I realize that he's about to force me out. He's reached the (accurate but faulty) conclusion that I'm here for an ulterior motive beyond interviewing about yachts.

"Time to go," he says, jerking his head toward the door.

I blink up at him, stunned at his abrupt dismissal. Granted, the first time he appeared in my apartment I threw my Enterprise at him and then swung an aluminum bat at his head...but still.

"I...I...I'm not a stalker!" I say, outrage clogging my throat.

A tic starts in the side of his jaw and he crosses his arms over his chest. "You can discuss that with security."

Okay. This is bad.

Daniel isn't fun-loving, he isn't laughing, he thinks I'm some maniac with a fixation on the sexy European mogul.

He brushed it off the first time, but he isn't so forgiving now.

Wonderful.

He moves toward the phone on his desk, presumably to call security.

Unfortunately, that means I don't have time to pull out my bag of tricks all learned a la Daniel Abry. I can't flutter my lashes, hike up my skirt, twirl my hair, ask him to retrieve my pen, or delight him with witty conversation. Nope.

The only thing I can do is say, "I'm not! It's a coincidence! I'm a journalist at *The Daily Exposé*, and my boss"—oh gosh, lies do *not* come easily to me—"said if I don't get this interview then I'm fired. He wants the scoop on European yacht owners and he wants it yesterday. Our readership is demanding the inside story on luxury watches and super yachts."

Jeez.

Jeez.

I will fall over if Daniel actually believes me.

But instead of looking at him, I dig in my purse and pull out my business card. My cheeks flush as I hand him my card.

He takes it then, his tanned fingers dark against the white of my card. He rubs the edge of the cardstock, his eyes narrowed on my name and my credentials.

"Please," I say. "I really don't want to lose my job."

Or you.

He looks at me then, as if he heard the last, a slight frown on his face. Then he says, "You have fifteen minutes."

My shoulders sag with relief. "Thank you."

Fifteen minutes is plenty of time. I can do this.

Daniel steps back and perches on the edge of his desk, still skeptical, his arms crossed, his posture closed off, but at least he's willing to give me a go.

I tug my notebook from my purse, take out my voice recorder, ask permission to record, and when Daniel gives consent, I begin.

I start with the easy questions, what type of yacht does he own, where does he sail, how long has he been sailing, and then five minutes in, when he's started to relax and look at me with less reserve and skepticism, I ask, "If you could sail anywhere in the world, where would you go and who would you take with you?"

He looks at the white ceiling of his office, his eyes thoughtful, his hair brushing his collar, and the slightest smile forms on his lips.

He thinks for a long moment and then says in a quiet voice, almost as if he's forgotten I'm here, "When my sister and I were young, my father would take one week a year to sail with us to Santorini. It's a beautiful crescent-shaped cluster of Greek islands in the Mediterranean. We would watch the sunset from the hills of Oia, hike the Santorini volcano, swim in the crystal clear waters. If I could go anywhere, I would go to Santorini, and someday, I'd take my own kids."

He looks down at me then, his eyes as blue as I imagine the waters of the Greek islands are, and I lose my breath.

He's picturing a future with his children, taking them to his favorite place in the world.

I wish I could take you to sail the Mediterranean, he'd said.

I stare at him, yearning, and he must see something in my eyes, because the softness in his expression vanishes and he brushes the moment away with a shrug of his shoulders.

The intimacy of the moment disappears as he leans back and lifts an eyebrow in anticipation of my next question.

But I'm so flustered I say, "I have a place like that. Mine's Riverside, Iowa. I've always pictured sitting in the grass there, the person I love sitting next to me."

Daniel pushes off the desk then, stands and puts his hands in his pockets. "What's in Riverside, Iowa?"

I give him a surprised look. "Don't you know?"

He wrinkles his brow, thinks for a moment, then says, "No."

Could he have forgotten? He knew when he was with me before.

"It's the birthplace of Captain Kirk. You know, Riverside, Iowa."

The quiet rumble of voices echoing down the hallway is the only noise for a good ten seconds, while Daniel tries to figure out how to respond.

Finally, he says, "Ah. Is Kirk a military hero?"

What?

A military hero?

"No! He's the Captain of the USS Enterprise! Remember?"

Daniel gives me a blank look, then asks, "Is that a yacht?"

I'm stunned. So stunned that I forget my nerves and the worry that Daniel thinks I'm a stalker, and the fear that he'll never remember he loves me, and I say, "Of course it's not a yacht. It's a Federation Constitution-class starship operated by Starfleet. It's the Federation flagship, it's..."

I trail off at the amusement tugging at the corners of Daniel's mouth, "It's a big ship?"

A laugh escapes me, and I realize at the relaxed line of Daniel's shoulders that maybe, just maybe, he's starting to change his opinion about me.

I smile at him. "It's a very big ship. It's from *Star Trek*, and Riverside, Iowa is where my favorite character is born. In the future."

I'm at the edge of my seat, smiling up at Daniel, when he asks, "Is *Star Trek* the one with the Jedi?"

I cough, hit my chest, shake my head.

"I'll take that as a no." He gives me a self-deprecating smile.

There's a warmth growing in my chest. I've missed him. I've missed his humor. I've missed his conversation.

"As your friend," I say, leaning toward him, "I think it's my sacred duty to school you on the basics of the greatest sci-fi universe ever created."

The smile wipes from his face, as he reminds me, "We aren't friends."

Gosh. I wonder if Daniel found *me* this frustrating.

Before, he was the one telling me we were friends and I was the one rejecting him.

"We are," I say. "We're friends."

He glances at his watch then, apparently hoping our fifteen minutes is over.

For the first time, I notice the chill of the room. Outside, the sky has shifted to dark, dusty blue, the precursor to sunset.

When he doesn't answer, I ask, "Do you stay in New York often, or do you mostly live in Geneva?"

"Is this still part of the interview?" he asks.

I point at my recorder set on his desk and nod. "And how does that impact your sailing?"

He scoffs, runs a hand through his hair and then says, "I come to New York a few times a year. My home is in Geneva."

That surprises me. Before, with how comfortable Daniel was in New York, I thought he was from here.

"Was your mom a New Yorker?"

He gives me a surprised look, then nods.

"What do you actually write?" he asks me then,

shifting the questioning, weighing my response. "I know that you know nothing about yachts."

I flush. I didn't realize it was that obvious.

"It's called a master cabin, not a captain's quarters. The front is the bow not the stern. We use nautical miles and knots..." He trails off, although I'm sure there are countless more examples. Apparently, Hayley's impromptu yacht class wasn't as useful as I thought.

Daniel's patiently waiting for my response.

"I write an advice column and articles on relationships and dating," I admit.

Daniel nods, and when I bite my lip nervously, his eyes graze my mouth and snag on my lips.

I can feel the pressure and warmth of his mouth over mine, the memory of his lips brushing over me, consuming me. The air buzzes with electricity and my mouth tingles.

Suddenly Daniel breaks his gaze, turning away.

The air between us crackles, and his chest rises as he takes in a deep breath.

He feels it, I know he does.

"Have you eaten dinner yet?" I ask, knowing our fifteen minutes has come to an end.

Daniel turns back to me, studies me, then shakes his head. "I don't think that's a good idea."

Of course it's a good idea. It's a great idea.

"Look," I tell him, standing and smoothing out my dress.

He swallows as he tries not to glance at the fabric hugging my hips.

"I'm not some crazed luxury watch fan or celebrity stalker. Saturday truly was a mistake. I didn't realize who you really were"—which is the truth—"and I'm not interested in you"—which isn't the truth—"except for this article. However..." I cross my arms and say. "I'm hungry and I'm going to get a bacon burger for dinner and if you want to join me and learn more about Riverside, Iowa, then you are welcome to come along."

Please say you'll come along.

Please say you'll come along.

You *love* bacon burgers.

We stand two feet apart, Daniel's desk behind him, the darkening sky and the lights over Bryant Park beside us, as I attempt to telegraph to Daniel all of our history, and he attempts to figure out why he's being asked out to eat a bacon burger.

It's funny, when he was a ghost, Zelda complained about how loud his energy was. Now I understand what she meant. As a living, breathing person, he fills the room. His office is huge, open, with a city spread below, yet you aren't drawn to the view, you're drawn to him. He's magnetic, and if you look too long, you catch yourself leaning forward, your breath shallow, your heart racing. Or perhaps, that's just how I feel about him.

He's vacillating between saying yes and no, I know he is. He's drawn to me, I can tell. But he's also skeptical of my motives, more jaded than he was as a ghost, and more serious too. I think forgetting who he was and all of his responsibilities let him open up more.

He was open and I was closed.

Now it's the opposite.

Finally, Daniel comes to a decision. I can tell because the brisk, business-like expression is back on his face.

"No," he says, "thank you, but no. Goodbye."

He holds out his hand for me to shake, and without meaning to I say, "But...but you love bacon burgers!"

He gives me an amused look, "Do I? I wouldn't know. I haven't had one in years."

Oh my word.

He needs me.

Even if he doesn't die. Even if Serena's ghost theory is wrong. Daniel *needs* me. He needs a food orgasm, and a laughing walk through the city, and a weekend marathon of *Star Trek* with buttered popcorn.

"What have you been doing with yourself?" I ask in a stunned voice.

He quirks an eyebrow, "I've been working," he says, then he takes my hand, gives a firm shake as tingles skitter through me, and says, "Goodbye. And good luck."

He means with the article, but I take it another way.

I'm going to need a mountain of luck to help him.

"Thank you," I say, hanging onto his hand a second longer, feeling the solid strength of him, the callouses on his fingers, the warmth of him.

Don't die, I pray. Don't die before I can figure out how to save you.

And then, the efficient, brisk receptionist is at his office door, ready to escort me out of the luxurious, cold, elegant offices of Abry Watch Co. Ltd.

I leave then, and even though I don't turn around, I can feel the weight of Daniel's heated gaze as I walk away.

39

THE NEXT MORNING, I CORNER NED AT HIS DESK, AN offering of coffee and a box of chocolate sprinkle donuts in my hands.

"I need you," I say without preamble.

I laid awake most of the night, staring at my papered-over mirrors, trying to think of the best way to help Daniel, to save him. Zelda said that he came back to help me *or* for me to help him. But what if it's both? What if he helped me and now it's my turn?

From only fifteen minutes with him, I already know he needs more happiness, more laughter, and more to smile about. So we're going to start with that.

He opened up for a moment and surprised himself by letting me see the longing he has for a family of his own, but I wasn't surprised. I know how deeply he loves.

Anyway, before, when I wanted Daniel to go away, he just kept popping up. Everywhere I went, there he was. In my shower, on my dates, at my work. He was always there. As annoying as it was, it worked. In no time at all, I *wanted* him there.

So at six in the morning, when the golden light of dawn flickered through my curtains and fell over my wood floors, I decided that the best way to help Daniel was to follow his lead—and just keep showing up.

Be perkily annoying, doggedly persistent, and keep popping up, wherever he goes.

Okay, yes. Maybe he'll think I'm a stalker. Unless I'm very sneaky and very convincing that I'm not.

Hence, Ned.

I slide the box of chocolate donuts across his desk, an old wooden library desk Bernardo picked up for ten dollars at a thrift store, and open the lid with a flourish.

Ned's eyes widen as the delicious scent of rich chocolate cake donuts dipped in dark chocolate icing fills the air. Behind Ned's glasses, his eyes get a happy, dazed look in anticipation of the sugar high and he gives me a happy smile.

"My help with what?" he asks, his leg jangling nervously as he takes in the donut bounty.

I grin at him and set the large cup of black coffee in front of him. The cup makes a solid thunk noise on his wooden desk.

I glance around the office, trying to make sure that no one is listening in. Ned's desk is near the kitchen today, and relatively far from everyone else. Buck is near The Wall, and Hayley is closer to Bernardo's office. The interns are huddled around the ping pong table, and all the computer techs and the rest are across the office.

But still, I lower my voice when I say, "I've never asked you this, but am I right in assuming that you have the ability to track someone's movements? For instance..." I look around the office again, then say, leaning forward, "If I asked you to, could you find out where someone lives, their daily habits, where they eat, who they visit, that sort of thing? Am I right to assume that you can do that?"

Ned gives me a startled, nervous glance. He quickly looks behind him, then back to me, and when he does, a transformation comes over him. He's no longer fidgety, his leg isn't shaking, his fingers aren't tapping. He's completely still and completely serious. I feel like I've just watched a CIA agent in deep cover shed his persona.

"You wouldn't be wrong to assume it," he says, and then he gives me such a wickedly gleeful smirk that I almost laugh in surprise.

Then he reaches forward, grabs a chocolate donut and takes a bite.

Alright. That means we've sealed the deal.

I grab a chair from the conference table, drag it over, and sit down, leaning close.

"What are we looking at?" he asks. "Bugging, tapping, hacking, directional mics that can pick up conversations from—"

I hold up my hand. "I need to know everything you can tell me about Daniel Abry's daily routine. Where he lives, when he wakes up, his route to work, what he eats for breakfast, where he goes for lunch, dinner, what he does at night, when he goes to bed, everything."

"Daniel Abry, the watch guy? That Daniel Abry?"

Ha. At least I don't have to explain who he is to Ned.

"Yes. Exactly. Him. He's in New York, he comes a few times a year. What can you get me?"

Ned takes a long swallow of the coffee, then rubs his

hand across his mouth. "I can tell you everything from what he eats to who he sleeps with. But...before I take another donut, and enter a...potentially illegal breach of privacy, I need to know...why?"

Okay, I knew this question was coming, and the only answer I have is, "I can't tell you. It's top secret. The only thing I can say is that it's a matter of life and death."

Ned narrows his eyes on me. Around us, the buzz and chaos of *The Exposé* rises and falls, the lights of The Wall flash, and Buck yells a curse word into his phone. Ned's coffee smells sweet and delicious, and suddenly I wish I'd grabbed myself one, because I could really use the calming effect caffeine has on me right about now.

Finally Ned leans back in his desk chair. The springs creak and groan and then he says, "Daniel Abry. Is he an alien-human hybrid?"

I can't laugh, because that's exactly where I went the first time I met Daniel.

"No," I say.

Ned gives me a shrewd look. "A reptilian?"

"Absolutely not."

"Part of the military-industrial complex? Or one of their experiments gone wrong?"

"No. He's not. He's Swiss-American."

Ned's chair thumps forward and his eyebrows rise above the edge of his glasses. "Was he in the Swiss Guard, because they have archaic connections to the—"

"No," I interrupt. "He is not an alien-human hybrid, reptilian, military experiment, member of the Swiss guard, nor is he part of any other nefarious organization. He's just what he seems, the president of a watch company from Geneva, Switzerland."

Ned considers my answer, his mind whirring, his fingers tapping against his desk.

As he thinks, I smooth my pencil skirt and adjust my emerald-green silk top. I dressed with extra care this morning just in case Ned came through and I "accidentally" ran into Daniel during the day.

"Geneva," Ned finally says, and when I nod he takes another bite of his donut.

"Yes, he lives there."

"Have a donut," Ned says, pushing the box toward me.

"Thank you," I take the donut closest to me. The aroma of dark chocolate is so rich that my stomach growls.

"Is your friend at CERN in any way involved in this situation with Daniel Abry?" Ned asks, calculations taking place behind his eyes.

He means Serena. Ned loves thinking up conspiracy theories about the effect CERN has on our universe. Especially the theories that involve alternate timelines, mirror timelines, and alternate dimensions.

He's watching my reaction very carefully, and whatever he sees in my face makes him grin.

"I knew it," he crows. "I knew it."

"I didn't confirm anything," I say, trying to keep quiet so no one comes over questioning why Ned is practically dancing a jig on his desk.

"You didn't have to. He's a watch maker. From Geneva. How many more clues do I need?" He slaps his hand on his desk and says, "Holy shit, Jillian. We've got ourselves a dimension hopper."

I hold out my hands in the shhh shhh gesture, and then say, "He's not a dimension hopper. He's..."

"From another timeline?" Ned grins.

I stay silent.

Unfortunately, he grasps this and says, "Your silence is all the confirmation I need. You have no idea. I have been waiting for this day my entire life. I could kiss your best friend. Boom!" He thrusts his fist in the air. "In your face, Shareen!"

His ex-wife again. Honestly, he really needs to get over her.

"Will you help me?" I ask. "I'll bring you donuts every Monday for the next year."

He laughs, his wispy hair practically standing straight up from how excited he is. "Donuts? I'd do this for free! This is the best day of my life!"

"Why?"

I look up quickly, practically jumping out of my chair. It's Hayley.

Well, it's not *just* Hayley. It's also Buck, Bernardo, and a brand new, brown-haired intern rocking a burgundy pant suit.

I guess they were all drawn over by the uncharacteristic excitement emanating from Ned's desk. Or they were drawn by the delicious smell of chocolate donuts. The scavengers.

At Hayley's question and the curious gaze of four people, I send Ned a quick please-don't-say-anything look.

He ignores it. "Jillian wants me to track Daniel Abry for her. She has the story of a lifetime."

He grins then, enjoying his own joke.

"Daniel Abry?" Buck growls, his shoulders bunching in irritation. "Isn't he that jerk up in Times Square? Man, I hate that guy. He has a face just begging to be punched."

"Why?" asks Hayley. "Not that I don't agree with the

punching, I like a guy a little roughed up, like a hockey player, but..."

Buck scoffs. "Any guy who takes a submarine into the Hess Deep with his watch pinned to the outside of the sub, just to prove he's superior, is a classic jerk."

"Didn't he also send the Abry watch into space? It still worked when it came back from the Hess Deep and from space," the intern pipes up eagerly, her cheeks flaming. "He's amazing. I mean, his *watches* are amazing."

"Thank you," Ned says, then he gives me a meaningful look, "That was very helpful. He likes space, does he?"

Not really. He doesn't even know who Kirk is.

"He's not an alien," Hayley says, erroneously thinking she knows where Ned's mind is heading.

"I know," Ned says. "Jillian confirmed that."

Everyone turns to me.

I try to look as innocent as possible, even going so far as to twiddle my thumbs and smile blandly.

Finally, Bernardo who had been silently watching the exchange without a flicker of emotion, asks, "What is this "story of a lifetime" about?"

Oh gosh.

What?

What is it about?

Under Ned's desk, he gives my ankle a swift kick. I flinch and then blurt out, "Love."

When everyone stares at me blankly, I elaborate, making it up as I go along, nodding my head to emphasize my point. "I write articles about love and relationships, and Daniel Abry is a famous...European..."

"Jerk?" Buck says.

"Sex symbol," the intern says.

"Bachelor," I say, and when Hayley gives me a sort of confused where-are-you-going-with-this look, I continue. "He knows a lot about relationships, sort of...what wealthy, young, yacht-owning, watch moguls...want...and..." Oh gosh, I'm blanking, I'm rambling and no one is throwing me a line, even Bernardo looks confused. "Well, it's a sort of behind-the-scenes article on what international—" I grasp the intern's description—"sex symbols have as advice for people seeking relationships with spice and...love."

I stop nodding and stare at everyone with wide eyes.

Hayley seems slightly disturbed by my pitch.

Bernardo, for once, isn't straight-faced. Instead he's watching me with a sort of furrowed brow, older-brother concern.

Buck just looks angry, like he's considering punching Daniel's face.

It's the intern that comes to my rescue. "That is the *best* idea I have ever heard," she gushes, with so much enthusiasm that it yanks everyone else out of their appalled stupor.

"I thought so," says Ned, perking up, and joining in. "That's why I need to track him. So Jillian can get the scoop. Once she knows his schedule, she can guerrilla interview him."

Guerrilla interview? Is that like special ops journalism? Pop up and boo, you're interviewed!

I hide a smile while Ned holds up the box of donuts and says, "Donut anyone?"

Distraction is a great tactic.

"You know," the intern says, reaching for one of the chocolate sprinkle donuts, "I've seen Daniel Abry running around the Reservoir in Central Park. He's been there every morning at six for the past week. It's when I work out."

She says this as I'm taking a big bite of my chocolate donut, the thick icing sugary sweet and delicious. "Oh mmm," I say, mouth full.

"You could *run* into him while running," Hayley says. "Do you run, Jillian?"

I swallow my bite of donut and say, "I *could* run."

I could definitely run. If Daniel runs every morning, then I *will* run.

"I'll get you his lunch schedule," Ned says, taking another swig of coffee and turning on his computer. "It'll be a cinch."

Finally Bernardo clears his throat and says stiffly, "If you really want an opportunity with Abry, then you should go to the Leighton-Hughes Gala on Friday."

Everyone turns toward Bernardo and I give him a surprised look. The Leighton-Hughes Gala is one of the most exclusive events of the year. It takes place every May at The Tower. It's a fundraising gala to benefit youth music programs in New York City.

It's red-carpet, heavily photographed, and attended by some of the biggest names in fashion, Hollywood, politics, and business.

Apparently, Daniel's going to be there.

"Ohhhh right, Daniel Abry goes to that gala every year," the intern says, nodding sagely. "Last year he wore a Tom Ford tuxedo."

My word. Does she know *everything* about him?

And is that jealousy I'm feeling?

"Who even are you?" Buck snaps, giving the intern his feral wolverine look.

"Crissy Washington," the intern says. "Journalism major at Columbia."

Buck grunts. "Fine. You're not terrible. You can copyedit today."

Wow. That was one of the nicest compliments I've ever heard Buck give. He's becoming a softie. Crissy beams at him and he scowls back.

Then Bernardo says into the silence, "I have an extra ticket to the gala. You can join me. It's formal dress. Eight o'clock. I'll pick you up at seven-forty."

At that, he grabs a donut and walks back to his office, leaving everyone else staring after him.

"Did he just..." Hayley shakes her head. "What the..." Then she asks, "How does Bernardo have two tickets to the Leighton-Hughes Gala? Those tickets are twenty thousand dollars apiece, Bernardo won't even spend twenty dollars on a desk."

It really doesn't make any sense, but no one answers, because Ned smacks his hand on his old library desk again and says, "Gotcha, hopper! Look here, he eats lunch every day from twelve fifteen until twelve thirty in Bryant Park. Every single day he eats the same thing, barley vegetable soup—very boring—and bread, no butter—even more boring—and then he buys a black coffee and goes back to his office. I told you I'd get you his lunch schedule."

I grin at Ned and he happily lifts his cup of coffee in a toast.

"Give me a day," Ned says, "and I'll get you his whole life. From the day he got his first tooth to the hour he lost his virginity. At least, I'll get you his whole life in *this* dimension."

Buck's mouth falls open and his ears turn red. I bet

he's regretting all the times he pulled Ned's chair out from under him. "You are one scary mother—"

"Wow," Hayley interrupts. "Just wow."

"Can you do this on my boyfriend?" Crissy asks, peering at Ned's computer screen.

And with that, I grab my donut and hurry to my desk. I have three hours until lunch, and I need to strategize.

A SOFT BREEZE BLOWS ACROSS THE SPRING GREEN GRASS OF Bryant Park, carrying the sounds of lunch-time conversations and the laughter of children riding the carousel.

Tall metal and glass buildings surround the flat field of grass clashing with the stately gray stone edifice of the iconic New York Library. There's the boisterous noise of lunchtime traffic, the savory scent of burgers and French fries wafting from the park café, and plenty of metal café tables spread over the gray gravel at the edge of the grass.

The May sunshine is so warm that I want to lift my face to the cloudless blue sky and let it kiss my cheeks. The breeze tickles my bare arms and tugs at the silk of my shirt. I clutch the to-go bag in my hands, inside is a bacon burger and fries.

"There he is," Hayley says, walking next to me down the stone steps behind the library.

I asked her to tag along so that this meeting would

look purely accidental. Just two friends out for lunch, who accidentally run into another friend.

Daniel is just where Ned said he would be. He's at a small round metal café table, past the library steps, in the shade of a tall, graceful London plane tree, surrounded by flowering ivy, deep purple tulips, and the periwinkle blue hyacinth that bloom in late spring.

I stumble a bit on the stone steps, the to-go bag bangs against my leg, and Hayley grabs my arm, steadying me.

"He has a lot of sex appeal, doesn't he?" she asks, taking in Daniel. "Sheer sexual magnetism." Then she turns to me. "Are you sure you're up for this?"

Hayley has known me for many years, and for all of them, she's known me as someone who is tongue-tied around men. A shy, quiet, tongue-tied sort of person. And in all that time, in her own way, she's been protective of me, so I'm not surprised that she's asking whether I *really* want to talk to Daniel.

Because when you look at him, well, she's right, he's the type of man that I would never have been able to talk to in the past.

Today, Daniel is in a navy suit. In concession to the weather, he's taken off his suit jacket, thrown it over the back of his chair, and rolled up the sleeves of his white dress shirt. His forearms are tan and stark against the white of his shirt. He's leaning casually back in his chair, reading a book, his lunch set out on the table before him.

A white-throated sparrow hops near his feet and then in and out of the ivy nearby, piping a song as it searches for breadcrumbs.

I think about how Daniel would've pointed that sparrow out to me, popping in and out of the flowers, just to make me smile.

"I'm sure," I say, walking confidently down the steps.

There's an empty café table near Daniel with a single metal folding chair. I glance at my watch. It's twelve fifteen, which means I have exactly fifteen minutes.

Hayley and I casually walk toward the empty table, and I nudge her with my elbow, letting her know that the acting is about to begin.

"Oh my gosh," she says as we walk toward the table, her voice overloud. "I completely forgot!"

"What?" I ask as we stop at the table next to Daniel's, only three feet away from him.

He doesn't glance up.

Hayley says even more loudly. "I have a deadline. I can't eat with you! I have to go!"

She's so loud she's almost reached heckler volume. I restrain a snort and say, "Oh. Alright. That's okay, I'll just eat here alone."

Daniel heard us, I can tell, because he shifts away from us, turning his back toward me. I don't think he actually realizes that it's me.

Hayley gives me a big wink and then makes a show of flouncing away.

I count to five in my head, and then I say with as much surprise as I can muster, "Oh! It's you!"

Daniel doesn't lift his head, because apparently, he doesn't think I'm talking to him. So I step in front of him and wave, "Hi, Daniel. What are you doing here?"

He looks up then and blinks at me as if he's walked out of a dark room and been confronted with the full brightness of the sun.

I take advantage of his stunned silence, grab the chair from the other table and drag it across the stone. "My friend had to leave"—I point at Hayley's retreating figure —"who would've guessed I'd find you here!"

Daniel's still stuck in surprise at my sudden appearance. His gaze drifts over the wind tugging on my curly hair, the bright emerald green of my silk shirt, and the lipstick red of my lips.

He pauses on my lips and the pressure of his gaze on my mouth feels almost like a kiss. My heart picks up speed and I drop into the chair across from him.

He blinks as I plop the to-go bag on the small round café table.

"What're you eating?" I ask, pulling out the cardboard box with the bacon burger and bacon fries tucked inside.

I made the trip to Grange Tavern specifically for this meal.

Daniel's forehead wrinkles as he takes in me sitting across from him, taking over his table. "I find it hard to believe that in a city of millions of people, we keep 'accidentally' crossing paths."

"Me too," I agree. "I don't really believe in coincidences."

He considers this, then says, "I called your boss."

"Bernardo?" I ask in surprise, pausing with a bottle of water halfway pulled out of the to-go bag.

"He assured me that you're legitimate. That you are writing an article on *yachts*." He says "yachts" with a bit of skepticism.

"You checked up on me?" I ask, beaming at Daniel and mentally thanking Bernardo for corroborating my story.

"If I hadn't, I wouldn't still be sitting here," he says, tapping the tabletop, "because honestly, you come across—"

He lifts an eyebrow meaningfully.

I shrug. "I know. But...I'm a normal person. A normal, friendly person. What are you eating?" I ask again, sneaking a peek at his bowl of soup, steam curling above it.

"Lunch," he says.

I nearly roll my eyes. "Why don't you talk more? I know you can talk."

At that, he picks up his spoon, dips it in his soup, and silently takes a bite, watching me the whole time.

I nearly laugh out loud.

Instead I open my take-out box, the bacon and burger smell rising between us, "You're in luck. I'm going to share my lunch with you."

Daniel swallows the soup and sets his spoon back in the to-go container. "I don't want your lunch."

"Yes you do," I say, taking a plastic knife and fork and cutting through the golden brioche, the crisp bacon, and the juicy char-grilled burger. When the burger is cut in half I point my knife at his soup and say, "Because why would you eat soppy barley and mushy peas when you can have bacon?"

I pick up half of the burger and hold it out to him. "Mmmm bacon."

He eyes it like you'd eye a snake slithering through the grass.

"Take the delicious bacon," I say, waving it under his nose. "Repent from your barley ways."

A drop of the chipotle aioli drips over my finger and plops onto the ground with a squelching noise. The white-throated sparrow pounces on the aioli and pecks at it with abandon.

He laughs then. It's so spontaneous and delighted

that I think it catches him by surprise, because then he shakes his head and says, "You are oddly single-minded."

He has no idea.

"Take it," I say, holding the burger half out in offering. "You'd be surprised, someday you may regret not having a taste."

His eyes flick between the burger and my mouth, but he doesn't take the burger. Instead he looks down at his bowl of mushy vegetable barley soup and picks up his spoon.

Gosh, he's stubborn.

"Oh well. But I'll tell you something, this is probably the best burger you'll eat in your entire life," I say, taking a bite of the burger and then giving a small noise of appreciation at the savory, spicy, perfectly cooked burger.

Daniel's gaze flies to me at the noise, his eyes widening, then he quickly looks away. I swallow my bite and then realize, if he won't join me, then I'll just have to give him a vicarious food orgasm.

I take another bite, relishing the flavor then lick the sauce from my fingers. Daniel is trying very hard to *not* watch me eat.

"Why do you only date supermodels and actresses?" I ask, picking up a parmesan bacon fry.

Daniel frowns at me, "Because they don't ask personal questions."

I scoff and wave the French fry at him. "Uh huh. Don't you find it strange that in the whole slew of girlfriends you've had, you've never dated a..."

I pause and Daniel smirks when my French fry droops.

"I read some of your articles," he says abruptly,

pushing his bowl of soup aside and eyeing the French fries.

I sit straight and lean forward, closing the distance between us. "You did? What did you think?"

I'm filled with a warm pleasure. He called Bernardo about me. He read my articles. He's not immune to me.

He looks up at the leaves of the tree overhead, the green filtering light and shadow over him. "I think your advice column was..."

He pauses and I know what he's thinking because he said it the first day we met.

"Terrible," I finish for him.

He looks back at me and his mouth twitches, hiding a smile. "Your past pieces were average, the comments were brutal. But there was a series of articles you wrote about a month ago. That's when your column really got good. Those articles were—"

"Excellent," I finish for him.

"Yes," he agrees. "They were excellent. I thought the premise was quite good."

I grin at him. I can't believe he's sitting here, complimenting me on his own Big Idea articles, the articles that he helped me research and then read over my shoulder as I wrote them.

He is literally giving himself kudos.

He narrows his eyes on my wide smile, and I wave his look aside, taking another bite of my burger.

He watches me, and the look in his eyes makes me smile. I push the box of French fries toward him, but he ignores it.

"Why did you sit here?" he asks me then, and I feel a pinch in my chest at how skeptical Daniel is, how closed off.

"Because we're friends," I say.

He shakes his head, not buying it.

"Because you're easy to talk to," I admit, and when he lifts his eyebrows in question, I gesture to the crowds of people hurrying down Fifth Avenue, "There's millions of people in this city, but there are only a handful who I've ever been able to really talk to. It's not easy talking, but it's easy talking to you."

He gives me a cautious, skeptical look, "I'm easy to talk to?"

I smile at him, rest my hand on the table, near his, but not touching. "Have you ever met someone for the first time, but felt like you've known them forever?"

He studies me, the sun shining over him, the breeze rolling between us. On the street nearby a bus's brakes squeak and groan and a taxi honks, but between the two of us, there's only quiet.

Finally, Daniel nods. "Once," he says.

My heart thuds at that single word.

Then he looks down at his watch, and when he glances back up I know that he's going to leave.

I push the to-go box toward him, half of the burger still uneaten.

"Take this," I say. "Don't argue. If you don't want it, you can throw it away."

Daniel stands then, pushing his chair back and throwing his suit jacket over his arm. His blue eyes are still guarded, but less so than last night.

I wonder what happened to him in life to make him this distrustful?

I stand too and step close, holding the box out to him.

He's tall. Even when I'm in heels, he's still inches taller than me. I'm used to him in jeans and no shirt, but I have to admit, he looks natural in a suit. Especially with the serious expression he wears and the air of confidence that surrounds him.

I look up at him then and say, "I'll see you around."

He takes the box then, his fingers brushing over mine, my pulse leaping, and he says, "Do you think so? In a city this big, you really think we'll run into each other again?"

I let go of the box, my fingers tingling as we lose contact. "Why not?"

He smiles then and says, "Thanks."

Then he's gone and I'm left with the sparrow hopping on our table, pecking at the bits of bun, and a thrush perching on my chair, waiting for an opportunity to steal a lone French fry.

"That went okay," I tell them. Then I sigh, "Who am I kidding? He thinks I'm a maniac. It'd be easier to clobber him over the head and drag him to the mirrored love den for some sexy times than to keep this up."

I shrug. Head clobbering isn't an option.

But jogging in Central Park?

That should work.

41

SIX IN THE MORNING IS ENTIRELY TOO EARLY FOR EXERCISE. Especially because I had to wake up at four thirty, throw on a pair of running shorts, a blue Starfleet t-shirt, and my running shoes, and then ride the bus to 86th and Fifth.

I smother a yawn, and reach my hands over my head, stretching my arms in a swinging motion that looks vaguely athletic. I've decided to stretch near the stone gate house at the edge of the water, so that I'll be able to spy Daniel coming and then hop onto the path in front of him.

It's barely six, the morning light is a gentle, quiet gray, and the waters of the Reservoir are a smooth blue-green mirror. The birds are awake, goldfinches and thrushes sing from the tall grass and trees lining the water. A red-headed woodpecker hammers against a leafy maple, and a rusty brown grebe lands with a splash in the water.

It's actually really beautiful here in the morning, I can see why Daniel runs here when he's in the city.

Quite a few people are awake too, most of them jogging on the gravel path that surrounds the water, but some walk their dogs on the nearby bridle path.

I touch my toes, craning my neck so I can keep the running path in sight. It's a little more than a mile and half long and I'm expecting to see Daniel any minute. Crissy the intern confided that Daniel runs three loops every day.

Aaaand, there he is.

He rounds the curve of the path, running around the water's edge, the shade of the plane trees and cherry trees casting him in shadow. His stride is long, his movement fluid and athletic, and I stand still for a moment, shocked by how alive, how strong he looks.

Then I shake my head and run onto the path ahead of him, moving as fast as I can. Which honestly isn't fast at all, because in less than twenty seconds Daniel has already caught up with me, and is moving around me.

"Hey," I say, already a bit out of breath from my pseudo-sprint.

Daniel looks over as he passes and then when he recognizes me, he slows, *thank goodness*.

I guess he's already done a loop or two, because sweat drips down his forehead, and my gosh, I never knew that I found the sight of sweat sexy. But I do.

His sandy-brown hair is damp and for the first time since he was a ghost, he still has morning stubble lining his jaw. He's in running shorts, a faded blue Oxford Rowing t-shirt, and well-worn running shoes. He looks relaxed and happy.

"Good morning," he says with a hint of surprise.

He keeps his pace slow to match mine. The barely-there lines around his eyes crinkle as he smiles at me, and my word, my heart's pounding and I don't think it's from running.

"I guess you were right," he says, his voice morning soft. "We meet again."

"Morning," I say, my cheeks burning. "You're a runner?" I ask inanely, because obviously he's a runner.

He nods, then his eyes light with laughter as he takes in my flushed cheeks, and my heaving breaths, and asks, "You?"

"No," I laugh. "Gosh no. I felt bad about all the bacon and fries," I improvise.

And when he grins at me, I ask, "Did you try the burger?"

"That's for me to know, and you never to find out," he says.

I laugh and he smiles widely, the rising sun sparkling on the Reservoir behind him.

"You like running," I say, the soft gravel crunching under my shoes.

"Why do you say that?" Daniel asks, as a woman in spandex and a sports bra passes us on the narrow path.

"Because this is the best mood you've been in since"—since you were a ghost—"since I met you."

He nods and rolls his shoulders, his stride long and loose.

"What do you like about it?" I ask, ignoring the cramp that's pinching my side.

"Off the record?" he asks.

We round the north side of the Reservoir and I pray that I can make it the whole way around without falling over.

"Yes, off the record," I promise. "This is between friends."

He shakes his head at me, smiling at my insistence that we're friends, and then says, "When I run, I feel like myself."

He looks at me from the corner of his eyes, and at my silence he says, "Forget I said—"

"No," I say, "I know just what you mean. You can put everything aside and just be you."

He smiles. "Right."

Then we're quiet for a bit, mostly because I'm too out of breath to talk.

The sun rises higher in the sky, and sweat drips down my chest to pool between my breasts. My lungs burn and my legs feel like fire ants are crawling up them, but I push myself to keep on, because Daniel's next to me, and he's relaxed, happy, and he keeps checking on me, looking down, and giving me a reassuring smile. One that says *don't give up we're almost there.*

Then when we come around the northwest side of the Reservoir, he points at the graceful white metal bridge arching over the bridle path, the one with the curlicues and curving, elegant design, set against the deep shade of oak trees, dappled with spring flowers, and says, "Did you ever notice that bridge looks just like a Monet painting?"

I look at Daniel quickly, my heart skipping a beat and when I stumble, he catches me and pulls us to the side of the path.

"Are you alright?" he asks, looking down at me, his eyes concerned.

I swallow the sudden lump in my throat. He doesn't realize what he did, that he pointed out something just to make me smile, just like he used to.

"I'm okay," I say, wanting to hold him in a tight hug. "Just clumsy."

He accepts this and says, "I'm glad I didn't tell you to listen to the cello then. That would've been too much distraction."

I hear it then. The music. I hadn't noticed before. But in the shade of a cherry tree, there's a man playing a quiet song on his cello, so faint that it sounds almost like the singing of the birds.

I smile up at Daniel, about to tell him that I hear the cellist when he lifts his shirt and uses the material to wipe his forehead.

I stand less than a foot away from him and take in the expanse of his chest, the flat line of his abdomen, the solid strength of his biceps as he wipes his forehead. Then a second later, he drops his shirt and smiles at me, nodding down the track.

"I'm finishing up," he says. "Are you coming?"

"Yes," I say quickly, my voice high and breathless. I clear my throat and nod, then without looking at him I dart onto the path to start jogging again.

Unfortunately, I don't look where I'm going, and the running path has *runners* on it.

I bump into a man who is sprinting past. "Watch it!" he shouts, his elbow catching me in the eye.

A bright flashing star and a sharp crack sounds in my head. I stumble back, trip over a woman who swears at me, and then I slam into Daniel.

He tries to catch me, but he's too late. I hit the ground. My hands skid over the gravel and my knee cracks against a jagged rock.

"Ow," I say, reaching up to cup my hand over my right eye. "Ow, ow, ow."

My head gives a jarring throb and Daniel kneels down, reaching out to pull me up to him.

"You okay?" he asks.

"I think I've got a black eye," I say, pulling my hand away.

Daniel studies my eye and I can see the urge in him to run after the guy that elbowed me and either lecture him about good manners or take a swing at him. I'm not sure which, but the fact that he wants to and I know he wants to makes me grin at him.

"Is it hideous?" I ask.

He holds out his hand and I put mine in his.

"Not at all," he says. "It's just a little shiner. It adds to your appeal."

"My appeal?" I laugh and he pulls me up.

I wince as I try to stand and he scowls down at my knee, bruised and a little bloody from the rocks.

"Put your arm around me," he says. "I'll patch you up at my place."

He wraps my arm around his waist then and I lean into him for support. I think I'd take a black eye from a stranger every day of the week if it ended with this.

"Do you live close by?" I ask, knowing very well because of Ned's research that he lives only a few blocks away, on the top floor of a building on the west side of the park.

Daniel nods, taking us down one of the exits off the running path, heading toward the busy morning traffic of Central Park West.

"Thank you," I tell him. "You're a really good person."

If I weren't holding him for support, I wouldn't feel his muscles stiffen at my comment, but I do feel it.

"You are," I say. "All the articles about you say so. You're affable, courteous, always polite."

Daniel looks down at me, his eyes searching mine, the heat of his body scalding me.

He asks, "Is that what you think too? I'm affable and courteous?"

"No," I say.

He scoffs and shakes his head at me.

"What I mean," I say, "is that I'd like to think that I see you for you, that I don't need an article to tell me you're affable, because I don't think you actually always are, but...I'd like to think I can see the real you, and the real you is a really good person. Which is why we're friends."

"I don't understand you," he says, shaking his head.

We exit the green, grass-scented warmth of the park, and step onto the sidewalk, exhaust-tinged and noisy.

"I don't know why you're so..."

"Single-minded?" I ask.

He nods, starts to step into the street, then backs up at a taxi's honk, pulling me back on the sidewalk.

My heart aches, I want to hold him, kiss him, I want him to be okay, so I say, "What if I told you that we've already met, in the past—"

Daniel gives me an intent look, his hand tightening on my hip.

"—and you were a ghost who had time-traveled, and we became friends. And now I'm supposed to help you and make sure you survive, so that you don't become a time-traveling ghost. What would you think if I told you that's the reason we're friends?"

The sounds of traffic crescendos around us, horns, buses, and the rumble of engines. Daniel stares down at my earnest expression and I think for a minute he just might believe me, but then, he shakes his head and laughs, and says, "If you told me that, then I'd tell you to stop watching so much *Star Trek*."

The crosswalk light changes and Daniel holds me as I limp across the street.

"Wait. Did *you* watch *Star Trek*? Did you check out my articles *and* my favorite sci-fi universe?" I ask, smiling at him with ill-concealed glee.

"Maybe," he says, expression neutral.

I laugh, turning my face into his chest.

"You like me," I say, taking in the warmth of him, "You want to be my friend. You can't help yourself."

He sighs, like he's worried that I just might be right.

42

DANIEL'S NEW YORK HOME IS AN APARTMENT ON THE thirty-second floor of a stately brick building overlooking Central Park. I'm quiet as he leads me to the modern couch in his living room, taking everything in.

I didn't know what to expect, but now that I see his home-away-from-home, I decide that it fits him perfectly.

It's tidy and minimalist in that modern Scandinavian style. The front door opens to a large, open room, and the first thing I see are the tall windows overlooking the park and beyond that, the east side of Manhattan. French doors lead onto a large balcony full of potted plants, potted trees, and comfortable patio furniture. The entirety of the apartment is situated so that it feels expansive and open.

Inside the ceilings are high, the furniture is Scandinavian modern, there's lots of wood and curving lines, and everything is soft in color and unobtrusive. The floor plan is modern and the kitchen and the living room are one huge space. The floors are blonde wood, there are white rugs spaced about, and one of the windows is open, letting in a soft breeze scented with the herbs growing on the patio—thyme and rosemary.

The entire place would look too much like a decorating magazine, except for the fact that Daniel has a pile of books spread on the wood table by the couch, a stack of marked-up marketing proposals on his kitchen counter next to a half-finished cup of coffee, and on the side table, a hand-made frame with blue glitter painted macaroni holding a photo of him crouching next to a little girl with red hair, both of them grinning at the camera.

Daniel pauses at the couch, carefully helping me sit. He's back to his formal courteousness, because he gives me a polite smile as he lets me go.

"Alright?" he asks.

"Yes, thank you," I say.

I think I was enjoying my arm around him and the strength of him holding me up a little too much. It was making me imagine that he remembered me.

The cushions sink under me and when I'm settled, Daniel points toward the kitchen, "I'll be right back. We'll get you cleaned up."

He strides across the morning-bright space, giving me a reassuring smile. He opens his kitchen cupboards, pulling down a first-aid kit, and then finds a bag and fills it with crushed ice.

As he works, I study the picture on the side table. He and the little girl are at a sparkling blue lake with golden yellow sand, there's overhanging tree branches, a tree swing, and blue mountains in the background.

"Where's this?" I ask.

Daniel glances toward me and sees me pointing at the photo.

He smiles, his expression softening. "Baby-Plage in Geneva. That's my niece, Mila."

He has such a wistful expression I ask, "What's Baby-Plage?"

"It's a beach on Lake Geneva," he says. "My sister used to take me as a kid. When I was little I could never wait for summer for the water to warm up. I'd jump in when it was still ice cold and I'd swim until my lips turned blue. My sister would always stay on the tree swing, swearing I was crazy. Now Fiona says it's my cross to bear, taking Mila for freezing cold swims."

His eyes fill with laughter as he pulls out a white and blue striped kitchen towel and wraps the bag of ice in it.

"Is your sister older than you?" I ask, wondering about the woman on the Met steps—the CEO of Abry Watches.

"Four years," Daniel says, striding toward me, his hands full with the ice, the first-aid kit, and a bowl with soapy water and a washcloth.

"You liked growing up in Geneva?" I ask.

"I was only there until I was twelve. After that I was sent to boarding school, but yes, I liked it."

There's something in the way he says this that makes me wonder whether or not he wanted to leave home. I wonder if he missed his family. I imagine he did.

Daniel sets everything on the wooden coffee table, then kneels in front of me and slowly lifts the ice to the puffy, bruised spot beneath my right eye.

I flinch at the sharp sting, and Daniel murmurs, "Sorry."

"It's okay." I take the towel-wrapped ice from him, my

hand brushing his, and hold the towel gently against my eye.

"That should take the swelling down," he says, the side of his mouth lifting in a smile.

"Do you know from experience?" I ask teasingly.

"Of course," he says. "I've had my fair share of black eyes."

I grin at him. "Were you a hellion at school?"

He nods as he pulls the bowl of soapy water close. "I had to prove that I wasn't just another scrawny, coddled, spoiled-rotten twelve-year-old, didn't I?"

He grins at me, and while I'm distracted by the dimple in his cheek and the demanding urge to reach out and touch it, he takes the soapy washcloth from the bowl and gently rubs it over my bruised and bloodied knee.

I bite my tongue at the scratch of pain. Daniel tilts his head down as he concentrates on cleaning my scape. The light from the windows shines on his sandy hair, coloring it gold, and the muscles in his shoulders bunch as he drags the washcloth over me.

The bite of pain is almost sweet as he takes my knee and wraps his fingers around my calf, holding me in place.

His calloused fingers press gently into the sensitive skin at the back of my knee. His hands are warm and gentle. The hot water stings my broken skin, but his touch is gentle. He's so close that I can feel the warmth of his breath as he lets out a long, shuddering sigh, as if it's painful for him to breathe.

The tension between us is so thick, the desire for him to take his hand and move it past my knee, drag it up my thigh, part my legs, is so strong that I can barely breathe.

I don't want to move for fear of breaking the spell.

But finally he drops the washcloth back into the bowl, and the suds slide over the edge and splash onto the table.

"It looks better," he says, his voice rough.

The sandpaper sound of his voice rubs over me, rough against my skin.

He pulls ointment and a bandage from the first-aid kit.

"This may sting." He dabs the ointment over my knee and there's a line of concentration on his forehead as he works.

"I'll live," I tell him, then immediately regret it when he looks up at me and I remember that he might not.

The ointment is cold, and the sting only lasts a second.

"I've been wondering," he says, as he takes the bandage and peels the paper back.

I take the ice from my eye and set the bag and towel on the couch next to me. "Wondering what?"

Daniel glances at me, then back down as he smooths the band-aid over my knee. "I've been wondering who you thought I was on Saturday."

He looks back up at me then, still kneeling in front of me, his hand gently pressing the bandage in place.

My breath catches as I stare into his eyes.

You. I thought you were you.

"I thought you were someone I love," I tell him.

Someone I love who I was terrified I'd never see again.

He nods then and stands, taking a step back, cold air replacing his warmth.

"That explains it," he says, giving me a rueful smile, "You know, I think whatever I've been doing in the past, it hasn't been kissing. That..." He lifts a shoulder and my heart flips. "I hope he knows you love him."

I watch him, wait for him to realize it's him.

Then I shake my head no. "He did. But he doesn't anymore."

"Then he's a fool," Daniel says.

"No, he's not," I say, automatically defending him against himself.

It makes me remember how weeks ago he unknowingly called himself a douche who was compensating when Fran was trying to set me up with him. He wholeheartedly disapproved of me dating any guy who took models on a yacht and was known as an international playboy.

Speaking of...

"I've also been wondering something, and since we're friends and I can ask personal questions..." I trail off meaningfully.

Daniel scoffs, but the smile teasing the corner of his lips makes me go on.

"Why is there a giant billboard of you shirtless in Times Square?"

At that he laughs. And his laughter is so deep and rich that I feel it all the way to my core. It shivers through me, and I smile up at him.

"You like it?" he asks, and in his expression I see a hint of the warm, laughing, life-filled Daniel I love.

"No, I don't," I lie.

He grins. "I think you do."

"I don't," I say primly, sitting straight and lifting my chin.

His eyes dance with laughter. "I lost a bet."

"You...what?"

He shrugs. "Fiona and I made a bet last year. We were both overworked, stressed. We made a bet. Whoever found a partner first, someone that fit us, then they won. The loser would have to do something they hated. I said I'd do a shirtless advertisement, because I've been hounded to do that for years and always turned it down. Fiona was going to take a two-week vacation, something she's never done. Except then she took a two-week honeymoon, so there's that."

I raise an eyebrow as Daniel collects the bowl and the first-aid kit.

"I didn't think you liked it, but I did some research for my article and there were enough shots of you on your yacht, in Monaco, at concerts or premieres or festivals to span from here to the moon. So I wondered…"

He drops the bowl into the sink and sets the first-aid kit on the counter. "Yeah."

I don't think he's going to say anymore, so I stand and smooth out my shirt and running shorts. But then he surprises me by saying, "When my dad died I was still at university."

I nod. I read as much when I first found out who he was.

"Fiona and I were barely a week into grieving when we received the news that Abry Watches was financially stagnant at best and financially dead at worst. I'd spent twenty-two years leading up to that point resenting that my life had been already laid out for me. I was an Abry, therefore I was going to head Abry Watches. But with my dad dead, and thousands of people counting on me and Fiona"—he shakes his head—"I grew up fast. The week before my dad died I'd been out partying in Paris with friends. Some professional athletes, actors' kids, a few had titles, our pictures were all over the news, bad seeds, spoiled youth, etcetera. When the photos came out, Fiona slammed the paper on the breakfast table. I thought she was angry with me. Instead she said this was how we were going to save our heritage."

I walk to the kitchen, lean my elbows on the counter, transfixed by his story. "Through publicity?"

He nods. "Fiona went to Harvard Business. She was twenty-six when dad died. Even though she's brilliant, he said he'd never allowed her to advance beyond assistant director of sales. He said it had always been a son that ran Abry and that the company would continue to be run by a son. Luckily, since we're family run, Fiona and I made the decision after he died that our dad was wrong."

"So she became CEO and you president?"

"That's right. At the beginning the best strategy she saw was filling the media with images of me, always with an Abry watch. I became the de facto face of Abry. She claimed the media loved me."

"Are you telling me your sister pimped you out to the media?"

He raises his eyebrows. "I pimped myself out. I had six generations behind me, and countless generations in front of me, and the weight of all of them counting on me was enough to convince me to do anything. I don't want my grandchildren to say that I'm the reason their two-hundred-year-old family company was sold off and swallowed whole by some nameless, soulless corporation. I'll go to as many concerts, premieres, film festivals, and yacht races, and give as many interviews as it takes to make sure what my father and grandfather and great-grandfather built survives."

"I think you do a lot more than appear in photos.

From what I can see, you work incredibly hard." I gesture at the stack of papers on his counter. There are mock-ups of advertisements, a market analysis, a memo about supply chain issues, and a report on mechanical issues in a prototype.

Daniel glances at the clock on the wall, then lets out a huff of air, "I have to get going."

It's not quite seven. I don't know when he gets to the office, but he's still in his workout clothes and sweaty from the run.

"If you go get ready, I'll make you breakfast," I say, deciding that his kitchen is too stainless steel and white quartz beautiful not to offer to cook in it.

When he looks like he's about to refuse my offer I say, "It's the least I can do after you helped me."

He looks at the clock again, and I guess he doesn't have time to argue, because he nods, "Alright. There are eggs in the refrigerator."

I smile as he strides down the hallway off the kitchen.

I poke my head into the fridge, and while the cold air blows over me, I find a carton of eggs and a stick of salted butter. There isn't much else. There's a chicken breast still sealed in plastic. Oranges in the fruit compartment. A container of soup—probably barley with mushy peas.

I think he must be too busy to stock his refrigerator. He must be eating out instead of cooking at home. Fran would have a conniption if she saw the sad barren desert of his fridge.

I put the eggs and butter on the counter and find a golden loaf of Italian bread on the counter. After poking in the cupboards I find a pan and then I get busy. Five minutes later, I have a plate of scrambled eggs, two slices of gas-fire toasted bread, and a cup of fresh squeezed orange juice.

I set it on the counter and then wander to the living room. The room is heating from the rising sun shining through the east-facing windows and the thyme-rosemary scent from the herbs near the open window brings in a happy morning smell.

At the coffee table I take a closer look at the books. There are fiction books—thrillers and suspense—and non-fiction, mostly business and biographies. The more interesting thing is that the books are in French and German and Italian and English.

Daniel's a polyglot. I should've realized it.

Daniel's mom is American, but his dad is Swiss and he grew up in Switzerland, which means he probably grew up speaking many different languages.

Me, I only grew up speaking English and Klingon.

I hear his footsteps and ask without looking up, "How many languages do you speak?"

"This looks good," he says at the same time.

I turn toward him and then try hard to keep my expression under control, because the blue of his suit makes the blue of his eyes seem as deep as the ocean.

I feel conspicuous now though. He's in a tailored suit and I'm in a sweaty Starfleet t-shirt, sporting a black eye.

"Five," he says.

"What?"

He grabs the fork and says, "French, German, Italian, Spanish, Dutch."

"You forgot English," I say.

"Six then," he says, smiling at me.

"Do you speak them all equally well?"

He shakes his head and takes a quick bite of the eggs,

raising his eyebrows happily. He swallows. "What did you do to these?"

I smile. "Butter."

He grins. "No one makes good eggs in America, except apparently you. You're one of a kind."

Then he looks at me, realizes I'm not eating anything and says, "Did you eat?"

I shake my head no. He holds out one of the pieces of toast to me. "Here."

I take it, the butter dripping over my fingers.

"I'd offer some eggs, but I'm jealously guarding them."

I smile and take a bite of the bread, the char lines smoky, and the butter salty. It's delicious. "You should taste Fran's food. She's the most amazing cook."

"Who's Fran?" he asks, and when he does, my heart plummets a bit. I'd forgotten that Daniel doesn't remember Fran, or for that matter, me.

We've been talking like we used to, like we've known each other forever, and because of that I momentarily forgot.

"The woman that was with me at the Met. You fixed her watch at Bergdorf's about a month ago," I say, and to avoid any awkwardness I add, "Which languages do you speak the best?"

He scoops the last of the eggs up. "French and English are my primary languages."

"Which do you think in?" I ask, curious.

He pauses, considering this, then says, "It depends. If I'm in an English-speaking country or speaking with English speakers then I think in English. Or if I'm thinking about things I learned in school or at university, then it's in English because that's what I learned in. But if

I'm in a French-speaking country or speaking with French-speakers, then I think in French. And if I'm thinking about things from my childhood, my younger years, that's in French. Otherwise, sometimes I'll switch, some languages describe things better than others, some have words others don't, and sometimes one language fits a mood better than another. Does that answer your question?"

I nod, then ask, thinking about when he was a ghost, "What language do you dream in?"

He smiles at me, his eyes crinkling. "It depends on what language I speak that day. Or who's in the dream. If I dreamt about you, I'd dream in English."

I take another bite of my toast then, and when I do, Daniel follows the movement, his eyes catching on my mouth. I lick a crumb from my lips.

He blinks. Then shakes himself off, glancing down at his watch.

"I have to—"

"It's okay," I say, then joke, "I'll probably see you at lunch anyway. Please don't have the barley soup again. It's a food tragedy."

He lips twitch like he's fighting a smile.

We walk next to each other, back toward his door, but as we do, my eyes catch on something I missed before. In the corner of his apartment there's a TV and some comfy chairs. That's not unusual, what's unusual is that on the screen, he has pulled up the end credits for *The Voyage Home*. Which means...

I point at the TV as we near the door. "Did you watch *Star Trek* last night?"

His face goes carefully blank, like he's been caught with his hand in the cookie jar.

I grin at him. "Have you already watched one through four?"

I almost laugh out loud at the neutral expression on his face.

"I may have done some research," he admits, holding the door open for me.

I almost spin around in a circle, throw my arms wide, and sing a song of fan zealotry and glee.

"What did you think?" I ask, keeping my voice even.

This is why he knew trekker quotes when he was a ghost. It's because he watched the movies...because I like them, and he...likes me.

"I'm reserving judgment," he says, locking his front door.

"Well, when you decide, let me know," I tell him.

"I will," he says, and those two words lick over me and nearly set me on fire with the promise in them.

43

I DROP THE FRESH MOZZARELLA, TOMATO, BASIL AND prosciutto panini on the outdoor café table and pull a chair across the cobblestone, then sit down across from Daniel.

"That's for you," I say, nodding at the panini. "Where's your soup?"

Daniel closes his laptop and although his smile is restrained his eyes are filled with mirth. "What if I told you I already ate it?"

I scowl at him, the sunshine of Bryant Park filtering through the London plane tree, casting dappled shadows over us. At the edge of the table, a lone sparrow cocks his head and stares hopefully at the brown-paper-wrapped panini. That does not look like a bird that's had any crumbs.

"I wouldn't believe you."

Daniel's smile widens then. "I always tell the truth. Lying is too much trouble to bother with. Il faut bonne mémoire après qu'on a menti—I don't."

"What does that mean?" I ask.

"A liar should have a good memory. I'm too busy for that. Therefore, I ate the soup."

"In that case, you can save the panini for dinner." I nudge it toward him, then stand. "I have to go, I have an interview and my boss is on my case because I'm riding my deadline hard…"

I trail off because Daniel's giving me a bemused expression. His shirtsleeves are rolled up again, displaying his tanned forearms dusted with sandy hair, his cheeks are pink from the late spring sun and the cool breeze, and he's studying me with such bemused intensity that I reach up and touch my cheek.

Do I have food on my face? I did eat my panini really fast while I hurried from the sandwich shop down Fifth Avenue.

"What?" I ask.

He leans forward, the breeze running through his hair, pulling at his shirt. Around us, the park is busy, full of businesspeople taking a lunchtime break, moms with young kids playing in the grass, and tourists enjoying the library and the famed lion statues. But all that noise, shifting color, and distraction fades as he reaches across the sunlit table and slowly places his fingers on the brown-paper-wrapped panini.

"Did you come all the way here just to give me a panini?" he asks.

I lift a shoulder in a half-shrug and push back the tendrils from my bun that were freed by the wind. I'm wearing a conservative knee-length black dress, a classic, because I'm interviewing a research psychiatrist today. But by the heat in Daniel's gaze, I think he likes my dress.

"Well," I say, "it's been six hours since you last saw me.

I figured you were going through withdrawal and I better swing by."

He lets out a short laugh, picks up his laptop and the panini and stands.

"Maybe I was," he admits.

With that admission, my spirits are buoyed and I say on a whim, "There's a play in the park tonight. If you come down while I'm here, I'll walk you home."

He shakes his head, taking a step back toward his office. "You're determined to be my friend?"

I smile at him, telling him the truth. "I already am your friend."

And I'll do whatever I can to save you.

THE INTERVIEW WENT AMAZINGLY WELL.

The psychiatrist, Dr. Rishi, a woman in her sixties, is the seminal researcher on body language between couples. After analyzing a five minute video of a couple interacting she can determine with ninety-nine point nine seven percent accuracy whether that couple will remain together for the next five years.

Her data points to non-verbal indicators, for example whether the couple turns toward each other while speaking, how closely they sit, whether or not they touch, and most interestingly, the facial expressions of the partner when the other is speaking. Does the listener look interested, happy, respectful? Or do they look annoyed, derisive, closed-off?

I wish I'd interviewed Dr. Rishi years ago, this is going to make a stellar article. But even better, it makes me remember Daniel's expression when we're talking. He has a way of looking at me that makes me feel as if I'm the only person in his world, as if he can see straight into me, and he likes what he sees.

Well, he did look at me that way, and this morning when he was dragging the washcloth over my knee, he looked at me that way again.

I'm at my desk near The Wall, typing up my notes from the interview, when Buck stomps over and jabs his finger toward my eye. "What happened to you?"

I touch the bluish purple bruise under my eye. It's barely noticeable. At least I thought it was barely noticeable.

"Jogging accident," I say, giving a shrug.

"That son of a gun," Buck says, letting out a curse. His takes in a breath, like a bull about to charge, and his bald head, reflecting the lights of The Wall, turns bright red. "I will sucker punch the sex symbol, say the word and I will—"

"Whoa!" I hold up my hands.

Ned skids his rolling chair across the floor, avoids a pile of newsprint, and stops at my desk.

"Did you say the hopper...punched you..." Ned's leg jangles nervously and his eyes dart around the office. "Does he know you're on to him?" he whispers.

Oh my gosh. Why? Whhhhhy?

"Daniel did not punch me," I say firmly, making it very clear to the both of them. Buck snorts, and I glare at him, "He is a nice, good person. I got this"—I point to my barely-there shiner—"from some guy who elbowed me while he was running past."

Buck eyes my face, all the air puffing out, his chest slowly deflating, the red in his ears fading.

"Hmmph," he says, then just to make a point he jabs

his finger my way again and says, "I'll still sucker punch him if you want me to."

"Probably we can avoid sucker punching," I say, and when Buck looks put out I add, "thanks though."

"What are we talking about?" Hayley asks, wandering over from her desk. She's in jeans and her pink Yankees t-shirt today, her hair slicked in a high ponytail.

"Not punching Daniel Abry," I say.

Buck growls under his breath, then turns and stomps back toward his desk.

As we watch he knocks a folder full of paper off an intern's desk, sending the paper flying. After that, he unplugs a techies computer, to which the techie yells, "I got a battery back-up, buddy!" and then Buck disappears into the kitchen, presumably to gnaw on some coffee beans and swig some steaming water as a chaser.

"He's in a good mood," Hayley says. Then, "Why aren't we punching Daniel Abry?"

"Because he's a good guy," I say.

Ned taps his fingers on the plastic armrest of his chair, the drumming a nervous tattoo. "He doesn't realize, right?"

Ned's asking whether or not Daniel realizes I know he's a "dimension hopper."

"Right," I reassure him.

Hayley frowns between the two of us, then comes to her own conclusion. "Ohhh. Oh. You like him!"

I don't say anything, which apparently never works, because she says, "You do. You like him."

Then she frowns at my eye and says, "Why do you have a hickey on your cheek?"

I cover a laugh when she says, "Did Daniel gave you a

hickey when you interviewed him? Why would he suck your face?"

I shake my head no, unable to even come up with a response. If I ever needed an example of how people view the world through their own lens, then this is it—hopper, puncher, or hickey-giver.

"He didn't give me a hickey, it was a running accident."

Hayley doesn't believe me.

"Uh huh. Don't worry," she says patting my shoulder. "I have make-up."

"Thanks," I say, placing myself in her capable hands.

Which is well and good because by the time I leave work for the outdoor play in Bryant Park, I've been "professionally made-up," and I have to say, somehow Hayley made my eyes look bigger and greener, my cheeks look higher, and somehow, she made my lips look even more just-been-kissed than usual.

44

The play is a modern adaptation of *Richard III*, and I have to admit, I watch the door of Daniel's building way more than I watch the actors playing out the gory sequence of drama and death.

As the sun dips low in the sky, the light shifts from robin's egg blue to deep indigo. Around the park the windows in the buildings blaze bright yellow and white. During the day spring warmth settled in the concrete, the metal, and the stone paths, so even with the sun falling, the park stays warm and temperate.

My stomach growls, it's after eight and I haven't eaten since I hurriedly consumed my panini at noon. I know from Ned that when Daniel's in New York he typically stays at the office until nine, but even knowing that, I can't help but glance at the entrance to his building every other second.

I'm perched on a café chair, drumming my fingers on the cool metal of the table when I see him. The yellow light of the building entrance floods over him as he steps onto the sidewalk.

He looks tired. He rubs a hand over the back of his neck and lets out a sigh. He pauses at the entrance of the building and looks around, studying the shadows, the bicyclists and trucks driving by, the bus stop, the scaffolding, he even peers at the café umbrellas and chairs across the street near where I'm perched.

When he's done scanning the street, his shoulders drop and he shakes his head as if he's reprimanding himself. And that's when I realize he was looking for *me*.

I jump up and wave at him, hurrying down the steps out of the park toward the sidewalk. He doesn't see me so I call, "Daniel!"

But a woman walking through the door of his building catches his attention and he turns to her. That's alright. I hurry to the crosswalk, wait for the light to turn, and then jog across the street, the silk lining of my black dress swishing as I hop onto the curb.

I walk a bit slower, steadying my breath from my dash across the street. When I get closer to Daniel I realize it's his sister that stopped him.

"We'll leave Monday," she says, "it can't be helped, you know—"

She cuts off when Daniel's gaze flies to me and then stays there. When he sees me a flash a surprise lights his eyes, then pleasure, both quickly hidden.

His sister Fiona turns, and when she sees me walking toward them, her brow furrows. But then it clears and she takes two steps forward to stand protectively in front of her brother.

"May I help you?" she asks, her light British accent cold.

I hesitate, pausing on the sidewalk just outside the circle of light illuminating the building entrance. I wasn't expecting quite so much hostility.

Daniel touches his sister's arm. "Fiona, it's fine."

She turns to him and whisper-hisses, "Isn't she the one who accosted you on Saturday? Don't you remember Florence? Don't tell me it's fine."

Okay. Clearly something happened in Florence and whatever it was, it wasn't good.

Daniel and his sister are locked in a staring competition that not even a pink elephant waltzing down the street could break.

"I...can go," I say.

"Do that," Fiona says, not looking my way.

"Stay," Daniel says just as firmly.

"Fi, it's okay," he says, then he adds, "she's my friend."

He said it so quietly, and the traffic passing is so loud that I almost think I misheard. But no, I didn't because Fiona says in an incredulous voice, "Your friend?"

He nods, then says, "Fiona, this is Jillian. Jillian, this is my sister Fiona."

Fiona turns then, eyeing me like I'm waving a lit stick of dynamite and threatening to toss it in her purse.

I step forward and hold out my hand in greeting.

Daniel clearly loves his sister and she clearly loves him back, which means regardless of the fact that she thinks I'm unhinged and by the look in her eyes she wants to toss me off the Empire State Building, I still like her.

"I'm very happy to meet you," I say, my hand hanging between us.

She stares at me for a moment longer, her expression conveying a thousand warnings of pain and suffering if I hurt her brother. I can imagine why she's successfully run an international company. Her displeasure is like a storm crashing over me. But then she looks back at Daniel, who nods at her, so she pulls back in all that displeasure and takes my hand in a firm, almost painful handshake.

"A pleasure," she says, even though what I think she really means is, hurt my brother and I will maim you.

When Fiona lets go of my hand I take a step back.

"I was just walking home," I say, gesturing vaguely to the east.

"I'll walk with you," Daniel says, stepping forward.

Fiona sends him a warning glare which he doesn't seem to notice.

"I'll have them schedule the flight for Monday," she tells him, then with a final warning glance she turns and strides back into the building.

Daniel and I stand still for a moment, just looking at each other. The noise of the passing traffic and the actors clashing in the final battle across the street mixes with the hurrying people parting around us.

"Were you really just walking home?" he asks.

"Friends?" I say at the same time.

His eyes crinkle as he smiles at me, and suddenly he looks a lot less tired than he did a minute ago. "Aren't we?"

I grin at him as we start down the sidewalk, moving toward a food truck parked at the corner piping out the golden, melted cheese and fried maize smell of freshly prepared arepas.

"We are," I say. Then I ask, "What happened in Florence?"

Daniel's mouth hardens and he looks away from me for a moment. "You noticed Fiona was a bit wary?"

"Only a little," I say, nudging him with my elbow.

When I do, he looks down at me with a surprised, happy expression.

We're at the intersection, the light is red, and a crowd of people waits to cross.

"What happened?" I ask again, waiting for the light to count down.

"You can read about it online," he says, his voice wary. "It was written about enough."

I give him a quick look, take in the tightness of his jaw and the clouds in his eyes. I wonder if the memory of Florence is why he's so much more wary and skeptical than he was before.

"I'd rather hear it from you," I tell him.

The light changes and we cross the street. Daniel starts to turn east, to walk past the stately gray library, but I shake my head, "I'll walk you home, like I promised I would earlier today."

My apartment isn't far from here, but Daniel's is all the way up by the park, nearly two miles away.

"Are you sure?"

I nod. I'm sure.

At that, we settle into a rhythm. He walks on my right, near the traffic, blocking me from the whoosh of the cars and vans, and shielding me from the people jostling past.

Usually when I walk on busy sidewalks, I'm bumped and jostled by hurrying people and large groups that don't want to make room. But now Daniel's shielding me from that. It's surprisingly nice.

We head north up Fifth Avenue, toward all the jewelry shops lining the streets of the diamond district. The shops are closed for the night, all the diamonds and jewelry locked away in the store safes, metal grates lowered over the shop windows. The display cases are empty, the lights off. Here the crowds thin as we walk past the Saks Fifth Avenue window displays and the big name stores that draw people during the day. The sidewalks are wide and the traffic light. The delicious smell of arepas is long gone, replaced by the mineral scent of cooling concrete.

Even though the traffic on the sidewalk isn't as thick, I stay close to Daniel. The back of his hand brushes against mine, and a spark of heat travels through me. His fingers tangle with mine, and my breath catches at his accidental touch.

When he pulls his hand away I keep my gaze ahead, watching the wide sidewalk ahead bathed in evening shadow.

"Fiona is protective," he says looking down at me. "She's wary of you because of what happened in Florence."

I glance at him, but he's staring straight ahead again, his jaw hard.

"It was five years ago. I was there opening a flagship location. I met a woman—Elettra—at the opening. I shook her hand, took a picture with her, that's all." He shrugs, as if it was nothing, but the tension in his shoulders and the tightness at the corners of his mouth tell a different story.

"What happened?" I ask.

"She was unwell. I didn't know it, but she'd been fixated on me for months. The next day she came to the flagship location asking after me. She was not given my contact information, clearly. Then she came to the hotel I was at, and again she was turned away. The entire week I was in Florence, she kept trying to see me, at restaurants, at events. Finally, she came to the flagship store and threatened self-harm during a live interview I was giving, because I hadn't..." He shakes his head. "She had a knife and I stopped her in time, and she got help, she needed help, but...I wonder if I had seen the signs sooner, if it wouldn't have come to that."

I shake my head, touch his hand, and when I do, he looks at me. There's self-recrimination in his eyes, and wariness, and even if he doesn't know it, a month ago, he told me the exact thing he needs to hear.

He must've understood everything I'd told him, even though he didn't remember it, because he'd been through something similar himself.

"It wasn't your fault," I tell him. "You know it wasn't your fault, right?"

He stops walking then, stepping under the awning of a dimly lit bakery closed for the night. I step next to him, letting the city rush by as we pause in the light.

There's a hint of baking bread hanging in the air, a homey, comforting scent, and as cars speed down Fifth Avenue, their lights shine like candles flickering over us.

"I think," Daniel says, "I may know it here"—he rests a finger against his temple—"but it's hard to know it here." He touches his chest. "It happens sometimes still. Not so extreme, but when you're a public figure, people, they...focus on you and they don't want you, they want who they think you are. In the five years since, I've not...it worries me when someone is excited to meet me. I stopped dating anyone except women who were already in the spotlight and who only wanted...superficial. That's why Fiona's protective. That's why I'm"—he studies me —"why I'm wary."

Oh.

Oh no.

I step forward, close the distance between us, put my hand over his.

"I understand," I say, wanting to hold him, but I'm just as unable to hold him now as I was when he was a ghost.

So instead, I wrap my hand around his, pressing my warmth and understanding into him. "I know what it's like to be weighed down by something that we couldn't stop but wish we could have."

He studies me, his eyes scanning my face for the truth of my statement. Whatever he sees has him clasp my hand.

"What did you do?" he asks, his voice low.

I smile at him, a smile that shows all the gratitude I have in my heart. "I limped along, struggling under the weight of guilt, until someone came along and changed my life."

"What did they do?" he asks, his fingers brushing over mine.

"He loved me," I say simply, "and he told me something, he said, 'Only you can decide how long and in what way you'll punish yourself. Only you can decide when you're ready to be forgiven.' You didn't do anything wrong." I lean toward him, look up into his blue eyes bathed in shadow. "You can stop worrying, you can let go and move on. It's okay to move on."

My heart drops a bit when I say "move on," and I swallow down the old fear I had of Daniel moving on after he was gone.

Daniel watches me for a heartbeat longer, the air between us thick, and I see the wariness struggling against the yearning in his gaze.

His eyes catch on my mouth and I instinctively lick

my lips, the taste of cherry lip gloss strong. Daniel steps forward, his hand in mine, his legs pressed to mine, and my breath catches in my chest.

My legs shake and I start to lean into him, my body lighting like the Milky Way, as I remember the heat of his mouth on mine.

Then a siren sounds, loud and insistent, and an ambulance rushes past. And that loud wail yanks us apart as suddenly as a splash of ice water.

Daniel clears his throat and looks away, pulling his hand from mine.

I brush my hands over my dress, smoothing it down.

"Did you want to keep walking?" Daniel asks, nodding north, toward Central Park and his apartment.

"Yes," I say, "of course."

We continue on, side by side through the glowing city streets. As we walk, Daniel points out a macaron shop. There's a caramel macaron statue in the window shaped like the Eiffel Tower, with two bobble heads kissing under it. He grins when I give a delighted laugh.

He buys two Nutella crepes from a food truck for us to eat as we walk through Central Park, cutting across the bottom edge toward the west side. He nods to a squirrel, still awake, dragging a bagel back to his tree, and then he grabs my hand and pulls me to the top of one of the giant boulders spread around the park so that we can have the best view of the city lights shining over Midtown.

"It's beautiful, isn't it?" I ask, wishing this moment could last forever, terrified that it won't, knowing it can't.

Daniel turns from the bright lights and stares down at me, the cool evening breeze dragging over my cheeks, tugging my curls free.

He nods then, his gaze as firm as a touch, stroking

over me. "Is it strange that I feel like I've known you for longer than just five days?"

I shake my head. "No. It's not strange, it's just how I feel."

"Do you still love him?" he asks, watching me carefully.

And when I realize that he's asking whether or not I still love *him*, Daniel, the look on my face must tell him everything.

"You do," he says.

I shake my head. *I love you.*

"It's complicated."

I want to tell him. Standing on this boulder, the wind and the night tree scent blowing over us, the lights like stars, his gaze on me, I want to tell him.

But then I realize, it'll turn out even worse than I first thought. Because if I say, I've known you as a ghost, I loved you before you met me, I'm supposed to save you and you have to keep me close, I had my colleague track your daily activities so I could find you...oh gosh...he'd... he would never look at me like this again, and he would never speak to me again, and he would...die. Let's admit it. If I tell him that I loved him as a ghost, he'll die. He may anyway.

But regardless, if I tell him that I love him, because I knew him, then all of this will end.

Daniel watches me, then nods and starts back down the rocky, craggy boulder, heading toward the grass. We walk across the field, taking a path toward Central Park West.

"I'm leaving New York on Monday," he says finally as we step out of the park onto the brightly lit sidewalk.

At the implication of those words my insides go cold.

Not that he's leaving, but that he *won't* be leaving. At least...

"When will you come back?"

He shrugs. "Not until next year."

No.

No no no.

If Daniel really did die and get confined to the city as a ghost, it likely didn't happen next year, it happened...in the next four days?

My chest goes tight and my breath grows short. A delivery van speeds past, blaring its horn at a veering taxi. I flinch at the noise.

Daniel's watching me carefully, waiting for something, but I don't know what.

"Well," I begin, "you know you always have a friend in New York."

His eyes soften then, and the corner of his mouth turns up in a smile. "You're right. Thank you."

I wonder why he sounds so sad saying it.

His building is across the street, the sandstone beige bricks lit up and bright against the night sky. At the top of the building, the lights in his apartment are turned off. When he goes up, he'll be alone.

Suddenly, I have a picture of him in my mind, standing next to my window, watching the cars pass on Lexington as I fall asleep.

Stay tonight? I'd asked.

Every night, he'd promised.

I look up at his building, then back to him.

Ask me up for coffee, I think, trying to telegraph it to him. Remember how my date at the Moroccan place did it? *Ask me up for coffee.*

But he doesn't. Instead he flags a taxi, hands the

driver cash to pay my fare in advance, and wishes me goodnight.

The next morning, Thursday, I don't see him running in the park. I don't see him at lunch in Bryant Park. And I don't see him come out of his office at night.

He doesn't run around the Reservoir on Friday morning, and he doesn't eat in the park on Friday afternoon.

Which is why, Friday after lunch, I'm frantic with worry, searching the internet for any news, wondering if in between Wednesday night and now, he died.

45

Obituary? No.

Accident report? No.

Business section? No.

There's no news about Daniel. And as the old saying goes, no news is...no news.

It's after five o'clock and everyone at the office has either migrated out the door in their gleeful weekend flight or they're packing up. Not me though, I'm still hunched over my computer, playing out worst-case scenarios.

The one saving grace is that it's Friday.

Bernardo swung by my desk earlier, told me good job on my recent interview piece, and then reminded me that he'd pick me up at 7:45.

For the gala.

The annual Leighton-Hughes Gala that Daniel always attends.

Ever since the sun rose this morning, obscured by the

gray rain-soaked sky, I've been clinging to the hope of this gala.

If Daniel is there, like Crissy the intern says he'll be (in a black Tom Ford tux), then I'll know he's okay, at least for tonight.

I drum my fingers on my desk. The cold air from the overhead vent blows over me and I grab my cup of coffee and take a drink, hoping for calm.

"Are you ready?" Hayley asks. She steps behind me and peers at my computer screen. "What're you looking at?"

I frown at the obituary page of the Times and click the window shut. "Nothing. Just research."

Hayley brushes that aside and hefts the bulky beige garment bag in her arms.

"Never mind," she says, "We have to go if you're going to be ready in time."

She's in a fuchsia raincoat, belted at the waist, and a rain hat. She has on a subtle perfume that smells like roses and lavender, and her make-up is immaculate. I haven't seen her this dressed up since before the day she wore her Ranger's jersey to work.

Yesterday morning, when she asked whether or not I had a dress for the gala, I told her the only formal dress I had was a fruit-punch-stained prom dress from ten years ago. Instead of wearing that, I figured I'd pick something up from one of the upscale thrift stores on Madison.

Let's just say that Hayley didn't agree with my plan.

"You're going to the event of the year," she'd said. "You have to look stunning. Your dress has to be so ravishing that Daniel Abry won't be able to take his eyes off you."

I could've told her that Daniel couldn't take his eyes

off me when I wore t-shirts to bed, my red trekker dress, or plain old, conservative business dresses, but that was the Daniel that loved me. So I agreed to let her take charge.

"This is what I do," she'd said. "I have a lady in the garment district. If I give her twenty-four hours she'll create magic."

I'm guessing that the magic is inside the garment bag thrown over Hayley's arm. She also has the largest make-up case I've ever seen, a pink monstrosity that she opened earlier. It's full of brushes, blushes, eye shadows and a million other tubes and compacts. And then there's the case with curling irons, flat irons, and a blow dryer.

"Are you sure we have enough time?" I ask, eyeing her skeptically as I stand and zip up my raincoat.

She scoffs and puts on a watch-and-learn expression. "Do you think I spend all my time heckling from the bleachers? I'm a beauty queen, Jillian. Give me an hour and I'll have all the men falling at your feet." She nods at the elevator, as serious as a coach facing a championship game. "Let's do this."

I grab my purse from under my desk, popping my laptop inside. Hayley's already striding toward the elevator. I heft my purse on my shoulder, thinking, I don't want all the men falling at my feet. I don't even want one man falling at my feet. I just want Daniel, not at my feet, but standing by my side.

46

AT 7:45 WHEN BERNARDO RINGS THE BUZZER TO MY apartment, Hayley has delivered just what she promised.

I barely recognize myself. Scratch that, I don't recognize myself.

I took down a half-wall of paper on Hayley's request so she could have mirrors to work with. The apartment is strewn with make-up, accessories, high heels tried on and discarded, and still-hot curling irons and brushes. It looks like a whirlwind blew through my previously clean, sci-fi themed apartment, tossed me up like Dorothy in the tornado, and when I popped out, I looked...different.

If Ned saw me he'd say I was alternate timeline Jillian.

If Fran saw me she'd say she has a good feeling about tonight.

If Daniel sees me...hopefully he says hello.

When Hayley contacted her friend in the garment district, she gave specific instructions. She wanted a crimson red silk dress that caressed my curves like a lover, accentuated my breasts with a sweetheart neckline that made a man want to lay his head over my heart, a slit that flashed the white of my thigh, teasing and taunting, and an open back that left the curve of my spine naked and waiting for a man's hand to brush over my skin.

Those were her exact instructions. Then she sent over my measurements.

I'd say that the dress is exactly what Hayley envisioned.

The silk drapes over me, soft and luxurious, and when it ripples gently over my skin, it reminds me of the whisper of lips pressed softly to mine. The deep crimson silk is as rich and soft as a fallen rose petal. It gleams against the dark gold of my skin. The dress falls to the floor, pooling around my black, strappy heels. The slit lets cold air brush over my thigh. My breasts rise with every breath, their plump roundness lifted by the built-in bustier. Thin straps cover my shoulders and allow the back to fall open, leaving it completely naked, the silk pooling at the base of my spine.

I've never worn a dress like this before. I never knew I could wear a dress like this. It's not just the dress though. The last time Hayley did my make-up I was surprised by the transformation, this time I'm stunned.

She lined my lips and filled them with a deep red that matches my dress. They're pouty, inviting, not just-been-kissed-passionately but kiss-me-right-now-passionately. My cheeks are dusted with gold, bringing out the bronze of my skin, my eyelashes are thick, sooty, and long, and my eyes are a wide, alluring, sparkling green. It took thirty minutes for Hayley to spin my curls into a twist with braids and pearls woven through. My neck is exposed, a long column, with curling tendrils brushing against my skin.

To top it all, I wear a gold necklace that hits below my collarbone, drawing attention to the curve of my breasts. I smile at the necklace, it's the only thing about myself that I recognize.

Hayley asked if I had any expensive jewelry. The only expensive necklace I have is the gold and diamond Starfleet insignia necklace that Fran bought me for Christmas years ago. It's funny, even when I look like I could be walking down a red carpet (which I will be in a few minutes), I'm still a sci-fi geek at heart.

The buzzer rings again, Bernardo letting me know he's here.

I take a breath and nod at myself.

"I look good," I say, then I turn to Hayley and give her a quick hug. "Thank you."

She rolls her eyes. "Don't insult me. You look better than good. You're stunning. When Daniel Abry sees you..." She thinks for a moment then says, "You'll either get your article or you'll get another hickey. Either way, win-win."

The buzzer rings again, a grating mechanical buzz. Hayley rolls her eyes then stalks to my window, flings it open, and shouts in her stadium voice, "She's coming! Hang on, will ya?!"

Then she slams the window shut, closing out the noise of the city street, and turns back to me, shaking her head.

"He's in a tux. I never thought I'd see him in a tux. And he has a black Rolls Royce with a driver. I don't know what he's playing at, but the next time he tries to cheapskate me on office supplies, I'm going to put the hammer down." She frowns at me, picks up a bottle of perfume and gives me one last quick spray. The subtle jasmine scent floats over me. "You're ready. I'll see you there."

I raise my eyebrows. "You will?"

Hayley's in work clothes, gray dress pants and a coral top, not anything you'd wear to a gala. Plus, like she said, the tickets are twenty grand a piece.

She smirks at me. "I found a scalped ticket. I had to trade a case of imitation Abrys, their new watch that went up to space, but it was so worth it." She gets a happy, little bit wicked smile on her face. "I'm wearing this dress that practically floats around me. Bernardo..."

She stops then and turns aside, gathering up her make-up case and cooling curling irons.

"I hope it's everything you imagine," I say.

"It will be," she says, slipping on her raincoat.

Thankfully, the rain slowed to a drizzle and then stopped a half hour ago. Now we just have to be careful of puddles.

When we walk down the stairs, my neighbor pokes her head out of her door at the sound of our heels on the wood stairs. But when she sees that it's just me and Hayley she slams the door without saying anything. There's only a tiny yip from Daisy as a farewell.

At the stoop Hayley waves a quick goodbye, ignoring Bernardo stationed by his black Rolls Royce, double parked at the curb.

I lift the hem of my dress to avoid dragging the silk through the puddles. The air is warm and humid, licking at my skin. It's dusk and the gray of the day seeps into the falling night, blending with the gray of the buildings surrounding us. The street is quiet, even the sad philosopher has closed his coffee cart early.

The breeze lifts the silk around my legs, catching it

like a parachute. I hold on to the fabric as I stride toward Bernardo. He pushes off the side of the car, his face inscrutable, and gives me a curt nod.

"Ready?" he asks, opening the back door.

"Thanks," I say, sliding onto the buttery soft brown leather.

The interior of the car is spacious, comfortable, and full of leather, shiny wood panels, and polished chrome. There are flat screens turned to news stations and even a chilled bottle of champagne and two fluted glasses.

I give them a wary glance as I scoot over the warm plush leather to the far end of the backseat.

The air is warm and dry, and there's classical piano music tinkling over the speakers. There's a driver in the front, a man with gray hair and a thick neck.

He turns and gives me a brisk nod, "Evening."

"Good evening," I say, smoothing the silk of my dress over my legs.

Bernardo slides in after me, shutting the door with a firm click. The sounds of Lexington Avenue, the distant sirens and cars splashing through puddles cut off.

The driver smoothly pulls forward, heading south. He'll have to take a cross street over to Madison and head north toward The Tower and the gala.

Bernardo clears his throat and glances over at me, ignoring the champagne.

I point at it and lift a questioning eyebrow.

He grimaces.

"It isn't my car," he says stiffly, as if that explains it all.

I nod and watch the buildings pass, their lights hazy in the still humid air. I've never ridden in the back of a car like this before. I have to say, it feels a bit like floating on a cloud. The bumps in the road that I know are there (at least when you ride the bus they're there) are conspicuously absent. We stop at a light and I watch a woman holding a red umbrella let her dog sniff a mailbox.

The piano music is as light and soothing as rain drumming on a rooftop, but all the same, the closer we get to The Tower, the more nervous I am.

Please let Daniel be there. Please let him be okay.

"Are you nervous?" Bernardo asks.

I glance at him quickly. The trouble with Bernardo is that he's way too perceptive. Granted, that's the nice thing about him as well. He's perceptive and sensitive, which is why he hired a bunch of misfits who most people would pass over. He sees potential and gives chances where others don't.

"A little," I admit.

A lot.

Bernardo nods. He's in a black tuxedo tonight, with a crisp white shirt and jet black cufflinks. His dark hair is smoothed down and he's clean shaven. I've never seen him in a tuxedo, but now that I have, it seems to me that he's entirely too comfortable in it to never wear one. He's also very comfortable in this car.

He sees me watching him and shrugs. "You expect to get your interview tonight?" he asks.

I glance away from him, out at the store window displays of Madison all lit up in the dark. When I look back, I say, "I'll do my best."

That was one of only two of Bernardo's conditions for working for him. Do your best and tell the truth.

Bernardo studies my expression. Then he decides something. There's a flicker of emotion on his face. He settles back in the leather seat and says, "I went to boarding school with Abry."

Okay, so that is not at all what I was expecting. "You did?"

He gives a curt nod. "He called me after your yacht interview," he says, his face still inscrutable, but the way he says "yacht interview" lets me know that Bernardo knew it was bull and for some reason he covered for me.

"Right, he mentioned that," I say, wondering what exactly Bernardo is getting at.

"I like Daniel," he says. "He's decent, he's straightforward, hardworking. He had a rough go of it for a bit."

I nod. I know all of this.

"My point is," Bernardo says, "if this is a gotcha piece where you're planning on exposing some peccadillo, or an exposé"—he gives me a stern glance (darn well knowing we *are* the exposé)—"on bad behavior or a voyeuristic dive into his personal life, I want you to know up front, it won't run. I won't publish it."

I stare at Bernardo's stern countenance, stunned that first, he knew Daniel as a boy, and second, that he's telling me to walk the line.

"I thought you told me to always tell the truth?" I ask, watching Bernardo's reaction.

He finally gives an incredibly rare half-smile. "Jillian, I know you aren't telling the truth where Abry's concerned. What I don't know is whether or not it's in his best interest. If it isn't, we aren't running it."

I wonder if Bernardo thinks this is only about a story, or if he realizes that it's more. Like I said, he's one of the most perceptive people I've ever met, so I expect it's the latter.

"You'd give up a story as a favor for a friend from boarding school? That sounds a bit like the old boys network," I say, glancing around the luxurious interior of the Rolls Royce.

I'm verbally prodding him, because I'm curious about what exactly all this means, and Bernardo is always so calm that you have to prod to get any reaction at all.

Bernardo's face is impassive, and I wonder what kind of life he had to make it so that he barely shows emotion, even when being provoked. I always thought that since he was drawn to people who needed a second chance, that he must've needed one once too. Although, it seems to me, he probably never got his.

"Daniel helped me once and he didn't expect anything in return," Bernardo says. "If that's an old boys network, so be it. I expect you to get a story, but if it is inflammatory then it's not seeing the light of day. Clear?"

I nod. Then, because we're pulling up to a long line of limousines and town cars, and the gold of The Tower gleams and there's the red of the carpet leading to the front doors, I ask, "By the way, how did you get tickets to this?"

Bernardo narrows his eyes on the tuxedo-clad men and the glamorous women walking down the sidewalk, the press lined up for photographs.

"I come every year," he says with a frown. "Typically I go alone. It's a game my family and I play. They send tickets and a car to remind me of everything I'm missing, and I arrive in a tux and the same car and remind them of everything they're missing. It's a lot of fun."

"It doesn't sound like fun," I say, frowning at him.

He flashes me a rare grin, his brown eyes filled with suppressed laughter.

The car rolls to a stop at the red carpet and a tall man in a black suit opens the door. The car's classical music and the intimate leather and luxury scent fades replaced by traffic noise, loud conversations, and photographers yelling "Over here! Look here!"

A rumble of thunder breaks overhead from the heavy-bellied gray clouds hanging over The Tower.

Bernardo unfolds his long frame, stepping from the car, then holds out his hand for me. I take it, sliding from the leather seat onto the curb. The air has cooled since we left my apartment and the leaves on the trees rattle, as if they're warning of a storm.

Bernardo holds out his arm, and I rest my hand on the wool of his suit, as we walk toward the red carpet. No one takes our picture. Neither of us is famous in any way. Up ahead, The Tower glows gold and burgundy, with giant marble columns and mirrors lining the lobby. I've always heard The Tower is an ode to one man's ego. I guess the rumors are true.

I wonder what Daniel thinks of it. I wonder if it makes him laugh.

As we enter the cold marble and gold-plated lobby, Bernardo hands over our tickets, and then we're in the elevator, riding up dozens of stories, to a party at the top of the city.

"I hope he's here," I say, voicing my worries out loud.

"He will be," Bernardo says, not a trace of doubt in his voice.

Then the gold doors slide open, revealing a ballroom made from dreams full of glittering, laughing people, sweeping orchestra music, and sparkling revelry.

But it isn't the magic of the gala that clasps my heart and squeezes, it's Daniel.

47

THE ELEVATOR DOORS SWEEP ASIDE AND REVEAL A decadence that would make Cinderella swoon. I've never seen anything like this, not in movies, not in real life, not in my imagination. I doubt even the holodeck could create something as extravagantly sumptuous.

The ballroom is massive. It takes up the entire fortieth floor of The Tower (home of the famous, or infamous, Leighton-Hughes family).

There's so much marble—all creamy rose-colored columns and floors—that I think they must've emptied an entire quarry in Italy. Gold—it has to be real gold—coats the walls and the ceiling, and yes...that's a Lamborghini on a pedestal and it's coated in gold too.

There are chandeliers which are even more gold, gaudy and gem-studded than my Liberace-inspired chandelier, and light sparkles from the crystals, falling in prisms over the ballroom.

Soft orchestral music sweeps over the room, echoing

off the marble and bouncing from column to column. The cellos, violins, and violas sing a quiet song. It isn't unusual for a small orchestra to play at a gala. What is unusual is for the orchestra to play from a suspended platform, raised ten feet off the ground, and shaped like a flower petal.

They're high in the air, surrounded by an aerial display of tropical flowers, full of vibrant magentas, bright yellows, wild purples and coy oranges. The entire ceiling and back wall are blanketed in tropical flowers and their perfume—loamy rainforest, vanilla, and seduction—teases through the ballroom.

There are at least one hundred people here, the men are dressed in formal black tuxedos, setting the leafy backdrop for the brightly dressed, glittering women, as vivid as the flowers arching over them. The rumble of their conversation and tinkling laughter vibrates over me and nearly overwhelms the music.

On the far wall, across the wide ballroom, there's a bubbling waterfall, spanning from the ceiling to the floor, and next to it a bartender in a white tuxedo dips a champagne flute into the frothing golden liquid. Yes, there's a champagne waterfall next to the mirrored bar.

There are round white-cloth-covered tables set with tropical flower arrangements and gold and burgundy china and crystal glasses. White-tux-clad waiters weave through the crowd, precariously balancing silver platters full of savory-scented hors d'oeuvres or sparkling champagne.

Finally, and most stunningly, hanging from the fifty-foot-high ceilings, aerial gymnasts costumed in tight gold and burgundy bodysuits twist in slow flips and controlled spins. They weave between the tropical flowers and the waxy green monstera leaves like butterflies flitting overhead.

Below them, the musicians pour music across the room, and the guests are as bright and vivid as the flowers surrounding them.

I take all of this in in the three seconds it takes for Bernardo and me to step from the elevator into the noise and swirl of the ballroom. It's overwhelming. I feel like someone who has lived in an orderly, metal, concrete city all my life and I've suddenly been thrust into a neon-colored, flashing, color-saturated world teeming with the unexpected.

If I'd attended this gala two months ago, I would've faded against a wall, avoided eye contact, and prayed that no one would try to have a conversation with me. The fact that I'm not doing that is because of Daniel.

I step forward, scan the room, and it's like Daniel said when we first met.

You're like a flame. I'm drawn to you. Everyone else is muted, but you burn bright.

Even in a room full of men in tuxedos and women in turquoise, fuchsia, lavender, all the colors of the rainbow, when I see Daniel, they all become muted, while he glows bright.

He's here.

Thank goodness he's here.

He stands near the champagne waterfall, a champagne flute held carelessly in his hands. He has a half-smile on his face, and he's standing casually, his eyes drifting over the ballroom as if he's been to a thousand of these events and nothing can surprise or impress him anymore.

But then his gaze falls on me. At first, he doesn't

realize it's me. I know because he looks past me, his stance still loose and casual.

But then he stiffens, pulls in a noticeable breath, and looks back to me.

He's across the ballroom, hundreds of feet across an expanse of marble and laughing, mingling couples. We're separated by a tropical rainforest of people, but when his gaze captures me, it's as if I'm standing right in front of him.

All the fear and worry of the past two days rushes out of me and I smile at him. It's a wide, happy, joy-filled smile that radiates from my heart.

When Daniel sees it, he straightens, the half-smile falls from his face, and he watches me as if he's making a promise. Then he drops his champagne flute on the tray of a passing waiter and stalks toward me, his gaze intent.

The lines of his black tuxedo flow with his stride, making him look as if he was born to wear it. The black material stretches over his shoulders, and the white shirt outlines the flat expanse of his chest. The bowtie is crisply tied around his neck and his sandy-brown hair hits his collar and glows gold under the chandeliers. He doesn't look like my laughing, light-hearted Daniel anymore, he looks driven and intent.

The orchestra music swells, and the strings crescendo in a climbing arpeggio.

"It appears that you'll be getting your interview," Bernardo says, drawing his arm from mine.

He tugs on his tuxedo jacket sleeves and then casually flicks non-existent lint from the black fabric as he watches Daniel stalk toward us.

I pull back on my joyful smile, reducing the radiance to one that is merely happy-to-see-you. When Daniel's only a few feet away, gliding around a round table, and two women in pink dresses, I resist the urge to run to him and jump into his arms.

My insides thrum at his nearness, my skin tingles as his gaze runs over me, and I take an unconscious step forward.

"Abry," Bernardo says, holding out his hand.

The heat in Daniel's eyes winks out as he turns from me and looks to Bernardo. He takes his hand and then a grin breaks out on Daniel's face. "Good to see you, Bern."

Bernardo nods, his face placid, not even a smile for Daniel, but I guess Daniel is used to Bernardo, because his eyes fill with mirth and when Daniel lets go of Bernardo's hand, he clasps his arm in a show of friendship.

I look between the two of them, clearly old friends. It stuns me that when Daniel was a ghost he didn't remember Bernardo. Except he didn't remember his sister, or his niece, or that he lived in Geneva, or even *who* he was. The only thing he remembered was that he knew me and that we were friends.

Daniel steps back and says, "It's been a while."

"Since this event last year," Bernardo says, eyeing the decadence swirling around us.

"I never understood why you keep coming," Daniel says, watching Bernardo with a friendly smile. "How's business been?"

My skin prickles at Daniel's nearness. He isn't looking at me. If you were watching this conversation from afar, you'd believe that Daniel hadn't even noticed me standing here. He appears to be completely engrossed in Bernardo's answer and their conversation about The Exposé.

But he isn't. He may be talking to Bernardo, looking at Bernardo, but I can feel the heavy, pressing weight of all of Daniel's attention focused on me. I can feel all that heated focus as if he's pressed his warm hand to my cheek, stroked his fingers over my skin, and finally settled on my mouth.

I swallow, my mouth dry, my lips tingling. I reach up and press two fingers to my lips. At my movement Daniel finally turns to me. I drop my hand from my mouth.

Bernardo looks between the two of us, calculation taking place in his perceptive gaze. "Abry, you remember Jillian Nejat? She's with me at *The Daily Exposé*."

Daniel smiles at me, reaches forward, and takes my hand. He squeezes my fingers and a jolt travels all the way from my hand to my core.

Suddenly, the room is very, very hot.

"Hello Jillian," he says, keeping my hand in his for a moment longer.

Oh gosh. My brain just short-circuited. The words in my mind aren't traveling to my mouth. I should say *hello Daniel*, but the only thing in my mind is, *yes, let's do what your eyes are telegraphing, let's have steamy sex all night long.*

Bernardo clears his throat then and Daniel lets go of my hand.

Then Bernardo looks down at me, back to Daniel and then after coming to a decision, he says, "I have a family matter to attend to. If you'll excuse me?"

He doesn't wait for confirmation, he just leaves me standing there, in the middle of a shockingly opulent gala, Daniel Abry by my side.

"I have a question," Daniel says, taking my arm, guiding me through the crowd.

His arm is rigid, his posture stiff, and I wonder, where has he been the last two days?

"Yes?"

He moves past the champagne waterfall, below the suspended orchestra, and heads toward a hallway hidden by a wide marble column.

"Why did you smile at me like that?" he asks, looking down at me, his jaw hard.

The music from the orchestra, the riot of conversation, it all fades as we walk down the long hall. It's a service hall, I think. We pass the catering kitchen, full of brown butter and thyme smells, shouted orders, and the clatter of dishes. Long past the kitchen and the catering staff, the hallway turns a corner and ends in a darkened alcove with a floor-to-ceiling window overlooking the city.

Daniel pulls us to a stop in front of the window and faces me. The city lights are bright and the alcove is dark and intimate. Daniel's face is shadowed and his eyes are unreadable.

We're only inches apart. I can smell the clean spice of his shaving soap and the lingering sunshine scent on his skin. I can feel the warm heat of him.

A hum of expectant quiet surrounds us.

"I was happy to see you," I whisper into the dark. "I was very, very happy to see you."

He lets out a sharp exhale and takes another step forward, closing the distance between us.

"I wish you could forget about him," he says, his voice low and insistent. "I stayed away because you said you love another man, but when you smile at me like that, it's like you're reaching inside me"—he points to his chest —"right here. The first day I saw you at the Met, down at the bottom of the steps, it felt like you were it for me. Then you kissed me and..." He shakes his head, looks down at me with dark, searching eyes. "It felt as if I'd finally ended up where I'm supposed to be. It felt like fate. Jillian, when you smile at me like that, it makes me forget my promise to leave you for the man you love, and it makes me want to..."

He stares down at my mouth, his gaze hot. The way his eyes linger, stroke over my lips, feels like a kiss.

The alcove is dark, intimate, filled with the sparks floating between us, as bright as the city lights glittering outside.

"I want you to..." I whisper. "I want you."

I need you.

I love you.

I'll always love you.

I smile up at him, a smile with all of those unsaid words said.

At my smile, Daniel's mouth crashes down over mine. And this time, when he kisses me, it isn't the whisper of a breeze, it isn't a gentle warmth, it's a hard, insistent claiming.

His mouth is hot, firm, and when I let out a noise and blindly reach up to wrap my arms around his shoulders, he swears against my mouth, grabs my hips and lifts me. The silk of my dress opens, spreads over my thighs as I wrap my legs around him.

He makes a sharp noise of satisfaction as I settle over him, and a jolt of lightning strikes through me when I realize that he's hard and ready. I tilt my hips against him and whimper at the blaze of fire kindling deep inside.

I want him. I need him. I love him.

I grip his shoulders, kiss him with all the love I've

been holding in. Daniel's hands travel over me, the silk running under his fingers like water, my skin burning under his touch. I want to touch him everywhere.

My hands fly over him, seeking the heat of his skin. I tug at his jacket, pull at his shirt, send my hands to the line of his abdomen.

When I do, he bites my mouth, nibbles at my lip and then thrusts his tongue into my mouth. He tastes like champagne and love, and I suck on him, and each time I do, there's an answering echo, aching for him to yank up my dress and make love to me against the window, forty stories above Manhattan.

As if he hears me, Daniel pushes my back against the floor-to-ceiling window. He presses me between the cold, unyielding glass surface and the heat of his body.

I'm consumed by him, need flows between us, and everywhere he touches burns. His mouth is still on mine, his kiss still insistent, still demanding. And so I wrap my arms around him, settle against his hardness, and open to him.

He strokes my thigh, runs his hand over my leg. He pushes my breasts free of the silk and whispers his hand over my nipples. All the while, he keeps his mouth on mine, as if he wants us to be touching in every way possible.

I rock against him, only the fabric of his tuxedo and thin silk separating us. There's a mounting pressure, a delicious, sumptuous, welcome need growing with each movement of his hips and each thrust of his tongue and each caress of his calloused hand over my breast.

Nothing in my life has ever felt so right as being in Daniel's arms.

I love you.

Then, the loud clatter of dishes hitting the floor, and a shout down the hall, yanks me out of the tight need that Daniel has wrapped me in.

Another shout sounds and I open my eyes.

It feels as if I'm swimming up from the bottom of the ocean, as if I've been drinking him and I can't possibly catch my breath.

Daniel's watching me, his eyes are open, his lips still whispering over mine. He gives me a gentle kiss and then pulls away, studying my expression.

I'm wrapped in him, tied up in him, and I don't know what he's looking for but whatever it is, I think he finds it.

His expression softens, his firm lips tilt into a smile, and his blue eyes burn with something that looks a lot like the love I remember.

He leans forward, his breathing fast, his heart racing against mine, and then he presses a kiss to the corner of my mouth.

"You're beautiful," he whispers. "Stay with me tonight."

My heart drums at his words, kicking against my chest. "You want me to come home with you?"

He nods, pulling my dress back over my breasts, smoothing the silk back over my thighs.

I let the warm silk pool around my legs, breathe in the cool dry air, and sink into Daniel's gaze. I remember what he said on my first date, *he's planning a smash and dash, a nail and bail, he doesn't care about you, Jillian.*

I smile at him, stand on my tiptoes, my heels pinching my feet and press a quick kiss to his mouth.

"Just for tonight?" I ask. "Or for more?"

"For as many nights as you'd like," he says, his expression open and unguarded.

"Did you know," I smile at him, "my best friend lives in Geneva and I've been meaning to visit."

He flashes me a surprised smile, "Really?"

"Mhmm. I imagine we'd probably run into each other."

"I imagine we would," he says, his honeyed voice running over me.

He tucks in his shirt, tugs down his shirtsleeves, and smooths out the wrinkles I made. Then he steps forward, gently smooths my straps over my shoulders, brushes his hands over my hips, and makes sure I'm put to rights.

"Do you mind if we go straight to your place?" I ask, thinking about the torture of spending four hours at a gala without being able to touch him again. "You didn't have business here, did you?"

Daniel shakes his head, "No. I come because I'm friends with Jace Morgan," he says, casually mentioning the famous musician from the Bronx. "He did an endorsement for us years back, his mom was Swiss, and we hit it off. But I already said hello, so I think...we could go. As long as Bernardo..."

I wave that away. "He'll be fine. Hayley's coming and it's better if I'm out of the way."

"Hayley?" he asks, an eyebrow raised.

I keep forgetting he doesn't remember.

"She works with us. She's coming." I look around at the darkness of the alcove and listen for the sounds of platters and dishes being cleaned up down the hall. Then I grab Daniel's hand and give it a quick squeeze.

At that, he tugs me down the hall, past the white-apron-clad caterers cleaning up spilled prosciutto and fig tartlets, through the ballroom, flower scented and tropical colored, under the orchestra playing long singing notes, and toward the bank of shiny, gold elevators.

Out of the corner of my eye I see Hayley in a stunning white dress that floats around her like a cloud. She looks like an angel and I think Bernardo imagines she does too, because they're dancing and he has a look on his face that I've never seen before. I wonder if she finally told him how she feels.

But I don't have time to figure it out because the elevator doors whoosh open and Daniel pulls me inside, determined to take me home.

48

DANIEL'S APARTMENT IS THE SAME SERENE OASIS ON THE west side of Central Park as the last time I was here.

The lights are on, casting a soft yellow glow over the blonde wood floors and the Scandinavian furniture. There's a gentle breeze blowing in from the open window, carrying from the patio garden the scent of the rosemary and thyme.

Daniel shuts the front door and the lock clicks in place.

I smile then reach forward and turn down the lights.

During the ride across town, I placed my hand palm up on the leather seat between us. Daniel laced his hand over mine and traced his thumb over the center of my palm, sending needy pulses through me with each whispered touch.

After fifteen minutes of silent stroking in the backseat of Daniel's Maybach, the driver ignoring us, my heart was pounding and my body was electrified.

Daniel's eyes fill with heat as the lights click off, and

the dark of the apartment is offset by the lights of the city. The glow from the city catches the diamonds on my necklace.

Daniel reaches up and touches the Starfleet insignia, a flash of light in his eyes. He recognizes it.

"I like it," he says, running his finger along my collarbone.

I take in a sharp breath at the heat of his touch, and the sound is loud in the quiet of the apartment. After the clash and noise of the gala, the still quiet of Daniel's apartment makes the beating of my heart and my nervous breath more noticeable.

It's not that I'm nervous to be with Daniel, it's that I'm nervous not to be with him. What happens if I fail? What happens if I lose him? What happens if I can't save him?

He reaches out and tucks a loose curl behind my ear, his hand lingering on the smooth line of my jaw.

"Are you sure about this?" he asks, studying my expression.

He stands before me, the lines of his tuxedo stark against the white walls of his apartment.

"If you want, I can take you home." He watches me carefully. "Because I have to be honest, if you stay with me tonight, I'm going to try my best to make you forget any man that came before me."

He's talking about himself, he wants me to forget him. He's the only one that came before.

"What if I told you that I've never felt about anyone the way I feel about you?" I ask.

I reach up and touch the soft black fabric of his tuxedo and set my hand over his heart. "What if I said that whatever you feel here, I feel too?"

He smiles then and puts his hand over mine. "Then

I'd say let's make love until the morning light falls over us."

"And then what?" I ask.

"And then it's the weekend, and I have two days before I fly to Geneva. I think we could do a lot in two days. Watch your favorite movies" the corner of his mouth lifts in a smile—"eat delicious food"—his eyes crinkle—"pretend we're tourists and explore museums. Or..."

"Or?"

"Stay here. In bed."

The last one. The last one is very, very tempting.

I reach forward, touch the line of his skin under the sleeve of his tuxedo jacket, where his watch shackles his wrist.

"Before we do," I say, breathing in the sunshine warm scent of him, "I have to tell you..."

"What?" he asks, standing still beneath my hand running over his wrist and the back of his hand.

I met you as a ghost.

I'm terrified you're going to die.

"I've never done this before," I say.

"Done what?" he asks, then when I open my eyes wide, he tilts his head and asks, "You've never made love?"

I shake my head.

I haven't. At least, I haven't with anyone but him.

"Not even with him?" he asks, frowning when he says *him*.

"It's just you," I say. "Only you."

The gravity of my words falls over him. He reaches out, cups my face in his hands, and presses a kiss to my mouth.

49

Daniel's mouth plays over mine, and I drown in the champagne tastes of him and the sunshine warmth. His fingers light on my skin like stars in the deep night and my body glows everywhere he touches.

The warm silk slides over my skin, rustling as Daniel spreads his hands across me, pulling me into the circle of his arms. I grab the lapels of his jacket and hang on as his mouth works over mine, and his hands move to the naked skin of my back.

His fingers tease over the base of my spine, sending sparks down my legs, circling and spinning through me. I reach up, drag my hand over the stubble lining his jaw. It's soft and rough, his jaw firm, and I spread my hand over him, reveling in the feel of him.

I spent so long wondering what the shadow of his stubble would feel like, and now I know, it teases my fingers and tempts me to lean in for a deeper kiss.

Daniel drags his mouth over my lips and says, "You taste sweet, like heaven." Then he gently bites my bottom lip and says, "And you smell like violets opening in a spring rain. Did you know that?"

His hands play at the base of my spine, spreading over the flare of my hips. He pulls me closer, nestling me between his legs. I feel the hardness of him, the heat.

I look up at him, smile. He once asked me if I smelled like spring rain, and now, I know.

"You think so?" I ask.

"I do," he says, his hands dragging over my hips, rubbing the silk over my skin.

Then Daniel presses his mouth to the curve of my neck, his stubble rubbing over me, his hot lips settling as I tilt my neck to let him suck on the sensitive space where my neck and shoulder meet. His lips trace up my throat, and he presses a kiss against my throbbing pulse. He drags his hands through my hair, brushing back the curling tendrils that have fallen loose.

"I want to touch you everywhere," he says, his hands feathering over my lips, my cheeks, my mouth.

I wrap my arms around his shoulders and then brush my mouth over his.

"Then you should," I whisper. "Right now."

He looks down at me, his eyes bright blue even in the shadows, his forehead resting against mine.

"Jillian, I'm trying very, very hard to not terrify you with how desperately I want you," he says in a rough, strained voice.

"You...are?" I stare up at him.

He nods. "Right now, I want tear this dress off you, strip you naked, and set my mouth on every inch of you. Your lips, your breasts, your hands, your hips. I want to taste you and make you come. I want to hold you. I want to take it slow. I want to take it fast. I want you over me. I want you under me. I want to press you against that window"—he points to the floor-to-ceiling window lit up by the city—"so that all of Manhattan can see me make you come. And then I want to lay you down in my bed, make love to you, and keep you there until you agree to never leave."

Oh my word.

I sway toward him, my body thrumming at his words, at the raw insistence in his eyes.

He loves me.

"You do," I say, my throat tight, my hands shaking as I clasp his shoulders.

Daniel studies my expression, the heat and energy of him rolling over me like a wave. I'm carried away by it. I lean into him, clasp myself to him as tightly as possible.

"I do," he says, pressing a kiss to the corner of my mouth. "But I very much want you to know I'm a decent man."

"I already know that," I say.

He smiles down at me and brushes a curl back, his fingers lingering on my cheek.

"So instead of doing what I want, we're going to change into something comfortable."

"What?"

"And I'm going to cook you dinner."

"You're what?"

"And put on your favorite movie—"

"Why?"

"And we're going to take it slow—"

"I don't want—"

"Because you deserve dinner and conversation, and a movie, and flowers if you want. So when we make love tonight, you won't think this is a one-night deal. It's not."

"You want to feed me before you make love to me?" I ask, smiling up at Daniel, reaching up to brush my hands through the ends of his hair, tangling my fingers over his wide shoulders.

I press my lips together, trying not to laugh. He's the same. He's my same Daniel.

He sees the laughter in my eyes and pulls me closer, pressing my thighs to his. "Don't tempt me," he says. "I'm holding on by a thread."

I grin at him. "What if I told you I'm not hungry?"

But then my stomach lets out a low rumble and Daniel laughs.

"I'll make dinner," he says, "and while I do, you can tell me all about your life before I met you."

Daniel takes a determined step back then and leaves me for a moment to change into comfortable clothes. He says he'll find me a button-down Oxford to wear as a dress.

I wait in the living room, browsing through the episodes and movies he has saved, wondering which he'll want to see, and wondering if we'll even make it through the opening credits, much less dinner.

Outside, a flash of lightning streaks diagonally across the sky, lighting up black, heavy clouds shrouding the skyscrapers. A crack of thunder roars and the windows shake. A gust of wind swoops past, dragging through the herbs on the patio, and then far below, the wail of a siren shrieks past, a loud cry that quickly dies.

I shiver as another lightning strike knifes the sky, the answering thunder rumbles, and the drum of rain begins, beating against the stone of the patio and the cold glass windows. I hurry across the living room, my heels beating against the floor. Rain drives against the window, and mist and drops fly onto the wood floor. The rain smells like wind, wet concrete, and thyme. I slam the window shut.

When I do, lightning lights the sky and illuminates the window, casting my ghostly reflection back to me, and behind me, Daniel.

I turn, grip my silk dress in my hand and take him in.

He's holding a white Oxford shirt out to me, a slight smile on his face. But that smile fades when he sees my expression.

"What is it?" he asks.

My hands twist the silk as I take him in. His hair is wavy, sandy brown, nearly touching his shoulders. He has a light dusting of stubble. He's wearing a comfortable navy blue t-shirt that molds to his biceps and chest. He isn't wearing his watch. But he is wearing a pair of jeans. A pair of jeans that fit him perfectly. A pair of jeans I recognize.

My heart jars in my chest as another crack of thunder splits through the room. The lights are still off, and the apartment is only lit by the streaks of lightning and the city lights around us. The shadows cast a foreboding dark and I start to shake.

When Daniel described the day he died, he'd said there was a woman in a dress, she was lying under him, and his heart was pounding, and then...pain.

I shake my head, my skin running cold.

"Jillian?" he asks, stepping forward, concern clouding his features.

"It's nothing," I say, jumping at a loud rumble of thunder. "Nothing."

The rain drums against the window, a relentless beating.

Daniel studies me and I give him a bright smile. It's okay, if we don't lie down and start to make love, then he won't die. It's as simple as that.

We've been forewarned, it's okay.

"I just realized I haven't eaten since noon," I say, glancing at the blue numbers of Daniel's oven clock. "And it's almost nine. I felt light-headed for a second."

Daniel searches my face, then nods and holds out the shirt, "Change into this and I'll start..." He pauses, then gives me a comical grin. "Eggs. I forgot. I never shop here. When you come to Geneva, I'll make you—"

He cuts off at the ring of my cell coming from the silk clutch I brought to the gala. It's the tone I save for work, an insistent alarm ring.

"It's work," I say. "We can ignore it."

I take a step closer to him, my heart drumming in time with the beating rain, the darkness closing around us.

Daniel nods, brushes his hand across mine. "When you come to Geneva, I'll make you rösti, the best potato dish in the world. Longeole with fennel, raclette, a whole meal—"

My phone rings again, insistent and loud. It's the office ringtone again.

"I'm sorry," I say, pulling my phone from my purse and checking the display. It's the main number at *The Daily Exposé*. The ringing cuts off and then a second later starts again.

"You should take it," Daniel says, taking a step back, giving me space.

I glance at him worriedly then back to my phone.

It's nine o'clock on a Friday night. No one ever calls from the office this late unless there's a big story and

Bernardo needs all hands on deck. Except...thinking about Bernardo makes me realize that he might have left the gala early, he might be at the office, calling to make sure I'm okay. I didn't exactly let him know I was leaving with Daniel.

Whatever it is, I should answer.

On the fifth ring, I say hello.

"Jillian, it's Ned. We've got a problem."

"Ned? What?"

I look to Daniel. He sets the white Oxford on the arm of the low slung Scandinavian couch nearby and gives me a smile. He nods toward the kitchen, motioning that he'll start making us dinner.

Ned's voice is ridiculously loud over the phone, almost up to Fran volume.

"Bad news. I just learned Daniel Abry is leaving for Geneva this Monday at noon," Ned says, his voice as loud as the rolling thunder.

When he says those words my eyes fly to Daniel and I stiffen, gripping my phone tightly.

At the mention of his name, Daniel stops mid-step, his back stiffens, and then he turns and looks at me, his blue eyes piercing. My stomach drops and my heart tumbles down, skittering through my chest.

"Ned—"

"I have his schedule. He's running a 5K for charity in Prospect Park at nine tomorrow morning. He has dinner reservations at seven with his sister at Per Se. Sunday, we're looking at—"

With each word Daniel's expression turns from confusion, to disbelief, to shock, to anger, and then, finally, and worst of all, every emotion flashes out of existence into a stone cold, expressionless hardness.

My breath comes in sharp, jagged spikes, my throat is tight, and I can barely say the words, "Ned, I have to go."

"But Abry will be difficult to track in Geneva and the hopper—"

I hang up.

My hands shake as I drop my phone back into my purse.

There's a chill emanating off Daniel, one I've never felt before. The entire room is filled with the icy coldness of his stance and his expression. All the warmth that surrounded us before, the heat of him, the sunshine warmth of his gaze, it's all gone. That warm breeze, that electricity that sparked between us, that viscous warmth, Daniel has pulled it back, snuffed it out, frozen it.

His jaw clenches, his eyes are as cold as a glacier, and he looks at me with the same contempt and derision you would give a rat scuttling in the trash and slime of the dank dark depths of the subway gutter.

But then even that contempt and derision vanishes, and it's left with cold nothingness, and that coldness chills me to the bone.

"I can't think of any explanation..." He pauses and I wait for him to shake his head, smile, see me. There's a flash of lightning then, and a flicker of pain lights in his eyes. "I think you ought to leave now."

I step toward him, "Don't," I say. "Please. I can explain. I know it sounded bad, but I can..."

I trail off. Can I? Can I explain?

He sets his hands in his pockets, his stance deceptively uncaring. But I know how this looked. It looks like I'm as bad as the last time. It looks like a repeat of Florence. Except this time, Daniel fell for me, opened himself to me, and told me he wanted all the nights with me. Which for him, would make this cut a thousand times deeper than the last.

He thinks I've betrayed him. Or he thinks I'm a stalker, a fan gone mad, or at best, a deceitful reporter using him.

Can I explain? I have to. There isn't any other choice.

"All right," he says, his face expressionless. "Tell me." His eyes narrow then and he says, "Why you knew where and when I eat lunch, where and when I run, what…gala I'll be at."

Oh. It sounds bad. It is bad.

My throat feels as if there's a fist around it, squeezing and choking off my words. I know this feeling. It's one of guilt and shame and desperation. It's one of heartbreak. Where one moment you have everything and the next you have nothing.

I touch my throat, press my hand against it and remember that this is Daniel, and I've always been able to talk to Daniel. He's always believed in me. He sees me.

"Remember," I begin, my voice scratchy. I clear my throat, push aside the fear, and say, "Remember the day at the Met?"

He gives a short, curt nod. "You planned that too?"

"No," I say, shaking my head, wishing the lights were on so that I could read his expression better. "No. But I knew it was you."

He scoffs. "Yes. I see. Let's go." He nods at the door, and when I don't move he steps forward and clasps his hand around my wrist.

"Daniel," I say, my throat burning, the rain beating loudly against the windows. "I met you before then. I know this will sound unbelievable, but please listen. I met you as a ghost. You were dead. You appeared in my apartment and I…"

I trail off. Daniel's grip has loosened, his hand falls away, and he's staring at me as if I've lost my mind.

"Please," I say, "I know how this sounds, but you were a ghost. You traveled back in time to me after you died. I promise, I only asked Ned to track you so I could be close. I'm terrified you're going to die and I won't be able to stop it. I'm so scared because I love you. I've loved you since before I met you when you were alive, I—"

"Stop," Daniel says, cutting me off. "Stop."

His mouth forms a hard line and he looks at me like he's saying goodbye to a dream he had that he should've realized would never come true.

"I know how it sounds," I tell him. "But we can go see the psychic that we went to when you were dead—"

"Psychics aren't real."

"That's just what you said last time! But if you talk to her, and my friend, she's a particle physicist—"

"Jillian. Stop." He steps back, puts more distance between us, and shadows fall across his face. "I don't know what game you're playing, but I'm not interested."

He moves toward the door then, clutching my hand in an iron grip, pulling me with him.

A roll of thunder echoes through apartment as I stumble after him, and all the hope that the night started with tumbles to the ground, like rain dashing against concrete.

He doesn't care. He's not listening.

He thrusts open the door and tugs me down the hall toward the elevators. The harsh lights of the hallway hurts my eyes, and I blink at the glare. Daniel's grip is tight, his back rigid. Our footsteps are quiet on the thick carpet of the hallway, and the only noise is my tight breathing, and the slamming of my heart against my ribs.

Daniel hits the elevator down button, and the taste of panic rides the air.

He doesn't believe me. But if he doesn't believe me then that means that I can't be around to save him and he's going to die.

"Listen to me," I tell him, scared that this is my last opportunity to warn him. "If you are going have sex before Monday, don't. That's how you die."

He gives me a derisive look, then the elevator doors slide open and he drags me on behind him.

"Listen," I say, "when you were a ghost you told me—"

"Right. I was a ghost."

I nod. "Yes."

"We met. Fell in love."

"Yes," I say, my stomach rolling as the elevator plunges toward the lobby.

He looks down at me, his eyes grazing my lips, heat in their depths, then it all snaps away and he says, "If you are going to lie, lie better."

"I'm not—"

"You could've told me you were after an exposé, at least that would've been believable. Or maybe that you wanted me, and because you're gorgeous and I'm a fool then—"

"No," I say, and the elevator jerks to a halt and the doors whoosh open.

Daniel pulls me through the marble lobby, over the black runner laid out for the rain, past the porter and the doorman in their camel-colored uniforms, and out the tall glass doors.

The night is thick with darkness, the clouds are heavy

black shrouds curtaining the lights, and the rain that sleets over the city swells at the curbs, speeding toward the sewers.

The cold wet air hits me as Daniel pulls me to the sidewalk. The noise of the rain drums against my ears, and the light of the cars speeding through the wet street spears us.

Even under the long awning, covering the entrance, the sideways tilting rain hits me like bullets. Within seconds the crimson of my dress is a darker, deeper red, dripping over me. Goosebumps rise on my arms and cold wet rain slides down me.

I fight the panic at the cold, unmoved expression on Daniel's face.

"Daniel," I say, my voice breaking, my throat clenching.

He shakes his head. "I thought it was fate. Turns out I was wrong."

Another crack of thunder sounds, ricocheting off the buildings, and the wrenching crack echoes in my chest as my heart breaks. He hates me. He's going to die, and he's going to die hating me.

The rain lessens then, the downpour cutting off, like it's been sliced by a knife. The air skitters with mist and electricity.

Daniel clutches my hand, pulls me into the dark outside the light of the awning. The cold wet air slices against my skin. I drop my chin, water dripping over my face and in my eyes, my hair falling from the pins. Daniel's hand is slick in mine, but he still hangs on.

Water floods against the curb, and even though it's impossible to see anything in the dark, and in the gray mist rising off the concrete, Daniel thrusts his hand in the air, flagging for a taxi.

Their lights slice through the dark, lighting the wraithlike mist, and I shake my head.

"Please," I say. "Daniel, please."

Daniel shakes his head, his expression unmoved. There's a taxi angling toward the curb, here to take me away.

I can't. I can't let it end this way.

I jerk my hand from Daniel's, wrench from his grip. My movement is so unexpected that he lets go of me, and as our slick hands tangle, I teeter on the curb, my heels slip over the wet rounded edge, and I trip on the wet silk of my dress.

Daniel's eyes widen. He lunges toward me as I fall.

The taxi veers toward the curb. In a fraction of a second, Daniel takes in my falling backwards, the taxi charging toward me, and the impact about to happen.

"Jillian," he says.

The taxi's brakes screech, a wet shriek on the flooded pavement. A flash of water floods over me as the taxi hits the puddle in front of me, and then Daniel dives forward, grabs my wrist, and throws me to the side, out of the path of the taxi.

My arm is slick, my wrist wet, and I slip from his grip. I fly through the air, tumble over the curb, and slam into the sidewalk. My head hits the pavement. There's a loud crack as my head smacks the sidewalk, my teeth snap together, and I taste blood. Stars spark, and red then black coats my vision. Pain snaps my skull, its teeth sharp. I lay against the cold, wet sidewalk, my face pressed to the concrete, and drag in a breath.

Then, two seconds after Daniel threw me, I hear the

hard metallic crunch of the taxi hitting the sidewalk. I press my hands to the wet concrete, lift my head. The world spins, and I feel like I'm going to be sick, but I have to know if Daniel's okay.

I peer through the gray mist and the dark, past the lights of the awning. The taxi is stopped at a sharp angle, its front end against the curb, its back end stuck out into the lane. The driver is climbing out, yelling, "What're you doing? What's wrong with—" but I tune him out, because Daniel's okay.

He's okay.

He drops to his knees, crouches next to me, his eyes scanning my body, searching my face.

"You're bleeding," he says. "Jillian, are you okay? You're bleeding."

I reach up, touch the wet, sticky numbness on my head and flinch at the pain. When my hand comes free, it's covered in crimson red blood.

Head wounds bleed a lot, I know. I blink back the wetness in my eyes, I have to say something, there's something niggling at me, sharp and painful.

"Daniel...I..."

There was a woman.

She was in a dress.

"You're bleeding too much," he says again.

Then he looks around, his face white, his mouth tight, and when he doesn't see anyone, he tugs off his t-shirt. He pulls it off, quick and efficient, wads it into a tight ball and presses it to the gash on my head.

"No," I say desperately, trying to sit up.

"It's okay. I've got you. You're okay. I'm here."

"No," I say.

He's leaning over me. I'm on the ground, dizzy, bloody, wearing a dress. He's shirtless, he's...

"Daniel, no, you have to—"

There's the screeching of tires, the sudden, explosive noise of metal crushing metal. Over Daniel's shoulder I see a flatbed truck slam into the taxi. The mist was too thick, the roads too slick. The taxi folds like an accordion. The driver—thank goodness—was out of the way, down the sidewalk on his phone. The flatbed truck screeches, jackknifes, and then the load on the back—one of those industrial-sized generators, a metal rectangle fifteen feet long and at least six feet wide—snaps free of its bindings and flies through the air.

I scream. Daniel's eyes widen. The generator slams through the air like a flaming rock thrown from a catapult. It rushes toward us, and the metal edge of the generator clips Daniel's back as it careens past.

His eyes widen. He clutches his chest. The generator slams into the brick wall of the building and crashes to the sidewalk with a roar as loud as thunder.

"Daniel?" I say.

He blinks at me, opens his mouth to say something and then collapses to the concrete.

No.

No, no, no, no, no.

I struggle across the wet pavement, grab his shoulders, his skin wet and cold, and flip him over. His eyes are closed, his chest isn't moving. My hands shake as I struggle to find his pulse. My hands slip over the wet of his skin.

I can't...

I can't find a pulse.

I can't...

I drop my head to his chest. There's no heartbeat.

There's no...he doesn't...there's no...

"Daniel," I say.

I can't breathe. I can't...

"Daniel," I grab his hand, clutch his fingers, "Please. Daniel. Don't leave me. Please. I'm sorry. I'm sorry. You came back and I couldn't...please don't leave. Don't."

Thunder sounds again, there's the flash of lightning above. The doorman and porter run out of the building. The taxi driver and truck driver are yelling. Everyone is yelling. The rain starts again, cutting over us, drowning everything.

I press my hand to Daniel's chest, and beg, pray, plead.

"Why are you crying?"

I turn quickly, my hand still on Daniel's cold chest, his heart silent beneath my fingers.

And what I see does make me cry. I let out a sob, a harsh, sobbing breath.

"No," I say, "go back." I point down. "Don't die."

Daniel stands in the rain, the water drops falling through him, hitting the concrete. The light doesn't touch him. The shadow doesn't touch him. He's shirtless, his jeans buttoned, slung low over his hips.

He looks just like he did the first day I met him. Then, I thought he was a shirtless sex maniac who died while having an orgy. Later I thought he died while making love to me. Now I know, the reason he wasn't wearing a shirt was because he was saving me. He saved me and because of that he died.

"I'm so sorry," I tell him.

He flickers out, disappears for a second then reappears again.

"Why?" he asks, giving me that smile that he used to, the carefree, happy smile I always loved.

"Because," I say, "I couldn't save you. I tried, and even knowing you died I still failed. I failed with Michael and I failed with you. I can't ever stop people I love from leaving. I can't stop them from dying."

"Jillian," he says, then he flickers out, he's gone.

The cold rain drives against me, wetting my face, washing away the tears and the blood. The copper salty tang drips over my lips, and I wipe it away.

The truck driver is at my side, feeling for Daniel's pulse.

A black puddle of cold water forms around him.

Then Daniel's back again, and he asks, humor in his voice, "Why do you have a bat in your apartment?"

I look up at him. "Please don't die. Please come back. Even if you hate me. Come back."

"He's gone," the truck driver says. "I'm sorry."

Daniel flickers in, then out, as if he's hopping between times, and I suppose he is. He's back with me right now, at my apartment, helping me, opening me up to love, helping me heal. And now he's here again.

When he flicks back again, he looks at me, and there's something in his eyes, something that tells me we just made love in my apartment.

"Save me," he demands.

I look up at him, the light and the rain falling through him.

"Jillian. I'm asking you. Save me."

I shake my head. "I don't know how."

"You do. Jillian, you do." He steps forward, presses his fingers against my mouth, "I love you," he says.

And then he's gone. And I know that this time, he isn't coming back.

But he told me, he told me to save him.

It's been less than a minute since Daniel collapsed, less than thirty seconds since the truck driver ran to my side. And I realize, Daniel's right, there is one thing I know how to do.

After I nearly drowned, my parents put me through a CPR class, and every year after I've taken the class again, recertifying, always in the event that someone needed me. I always thought, if I'd been with Michael, I could've done CPR, given him a chance when his heart stopped.

And now?

I do what Daniel asked. And with each breath forced into his open mouth and each compression against his chest, I pray.

Come back to me.

Come back to me.

Come back to me.

The ambulance arrives seven minutes later, my arms are weak and shaking, my lungs are aching, and I pray that every breath I took for Daniel, every heartbeat I gave him, is enough.

50

THE HOSPITAL PERCHES ON THE WEST SIDE OF CENTRAL Park. It's a mammoth red brick building with towering panes of glass letting light inside. At least that's the idea.

I was stitched up—five stitches to close the gash in my head—and evaluated in a dim, beige-tiled, gray-blue walled room with claustrophobic drop ceilings. The air was heavy with the smell of alcohol swabs and sanitizer, there were moans and coughs echoing through the halls, and the oppressive curtained rooms and the *not knowing* nearly brought me to my knees.

Literally, I almost dropped to my knees on that sanitized hospital beige linoleum, just to hear a whisper of whether or not Daniel was alive.

But I wasn't family. I wasn't a friend. I wasn't anything but the woman in the accident with him. I was brought in by a separate ambulance and I haven't seen or heard anything since his ambulance sped away.

That was five days ago.

I tried to call his New York office, but I was fobbed off

and put in a circular phone purgatory that never ended and only resulted in me being passed from one assistant to another to a voicemail to an assistant to...everyone saying Mr. Abry was not available and would I like to leave a message?

So I told Bernardo I was working from home. When he saw the gory bruised stitches on my forehead over video chat, he told me to take as long as I needed.

I lean against the red brick of the hospital, the warm air teasing through my hair. There are metal grates in the sidewalk and warm steam floating up. The afternoon sun bounces off the building's glass, making this section of the sidewalk as hot as mid-July.

I brush the hair back from my forehead and wince at the sting of the stitches pulling at my skin. I've been here, either in the main lobby or at the front entrance since last Friday. I sleep sitting up in the beige cushioned vinyl chairs. I eat to-go food in the lobby, the containers perched on my knees. I drink buckets of coffee.

I need to know that he's okay. There hasn't been any news of his death. If he'd died they would've announced it on the Abry website, right? They would've written a press release. They would've posted it online. Surely.

And since they didn't, I cling to the hope that he's alive.

And if he's alive, I cling to the hope that he remembers me. Before, he hadn't gone back yet, he hadn't been a ghost. Now he has.

If he's alive, he'll remember me. I'm sure he will.

Serena thought he would too, she said science was on my side. So there's that.

I let out a breath, squint up at the sun and the pale blue sky, and peer out at the ambulances lined along the curb, the taxis rushing past, and the leafy trees rustling in the wind. There are two pigeons on the sidewalk pecking at a chunk of sesame bagel, and I smile, wondering if Daniel would point them out.

I stretch, take in the warm concrete, leafy air smell of late spring and think about going back into the quiet, antiseptic, sterile hospital lobby.

If I go inside, I can pull out my laptop, set it on my knees, and write my next article.

I push off the building and walk back toward the entrance. I heft my bag over my shoulder. I have my laptop, water, granola bars. I'm in jean shorts and my gray Starfleet t-shirt, because I wanted to be comfortable. Sitting and especially sleeping in a hospital lobby chair in a dress and heels is horribly uncomfortable, I know because I tried it.

At the entrance, the automatic glass doors open, sending the smell of hand sanitizer and the chill of air conditioning over me. The calming, classical music on repeat pipes through the speakers at the entrance.

The lobby is massive, the ceilings are at least fifty feet tall, the walls are dark beige, and the floors are light beige. There are fake plants, beige vinyl chairs and curved vinyl-cushioned benches, and a fake wood half-circle visitors desk. The rest of the lobby is a wide-open tiled space with hallways branching like octopuses' arms to the bowels of the hospital.

The lobby is huge and hundreds, maybe thousands of people walk through it every day. I've seen them.

I pause in front of the open door. Half in and half out of the hospital.

Daniel's there.

He's alive.

I know because he's walking across the lobby and he's wearing a clean pair of jeans, a black t-shirt, and he's moving as if each step is painful. There are blue smudges under his eyes, and he looks like he hasn't shaven in days.

His sister is with him. She's hovering, watching him like she expects him to fall over any second. He sends her an exasperated, affectionate smile.

At that smile all the fear, all the worry, it flies away like birds migrating south, and I'm only left with joy, and hope, and... "Thank you," I whisper. "Thank you."

Then there's a whimper, a short cry, and I realize it's me. And all that relief and gratitude is welling inside of me, fighting to get out.

I want to run to him. I want to sprint across the linoleum tile, through the wide lobby, and throw myself in his arms.

Instead, I take a step back, let the doors close and send up a prayer.

Let him remember me. Let him remember.

I move out of the flow of the doors, letting a stooped elderly man holding his wife's arm walk through. I clench my fingers, feel the breeze over my bare arms, and pray.

Finally, the doors slide open, and Daniel is there, his sister tugging on his arm.

"I told you, Fiona, I'm fine. I'm—"

He cuts off, his gaze falling on me.

My heart lurches in my chest and I take a step forward, smiling hesitantly.

Remember me. Please remember.

"You're alive," I say.

Fiona drops Daniel's arm and steps forward, her stance angry, her eyes narrowed. "You have a lot of nerve—"

"Fiona," Daniel says, holding out his hand.

She turns to him, "What?" she says, jerking her head at me.

"Let me take care of it," Daniel says.

Take care of it? My stomach sinks at his words.

But Fiona gives a sharp nod and stalks down the sidewalk, giving Daniel space.

To take care of it.

He steps forward, wincing a bit, then stops a few feet in front of me, leaving an ocean of space between us. If I held out my hand as far as I could reach, I still wouldn't be able to touch him.

I swallow, my throat aching, the back of my eyes burning. For a moment, Daniel just watches me, the traffic noise loud, the breeze tugging my hair, silence between us.

"I wanted to thank you," he says.

His voice is even and polite. His expression cordial.

It's then I know.

He doesn't remember. He doesn't remember any of it.

I nod, unable to form any words.

"The paramedics told the doctor that if you hadn't done CPR until they arrived, I wouldn't be here."

He watches me, his blue eyes grave.

"Right," I say, the word choking past my lips. "Right."

He nods, glances at his sister watching us from down the block and then turns back to me. "I had a while to think about what happened," he says.

I stare at him, wishing I could reach out, take his hand, tell him again how much I love him.

"I called Bernardo, he confirmed you were writing an article on me for your relationship column. He was aware your colleague was tracking me for your article. A piece about what an international sex symbol wants." A bus's hydraulic brakes hiss as it passes and Daniel flinches, pressing his hand into his side. "I could've told you," he says, "I only wanted you."

I feel as if I've just been crushed by that generator slamming through the night air.

I nod and hold my breath, telling myself not to cry.

Don't cry, Jillian. Don't cry.

He's alive and that's really all that matters.

"Thank you," I whisper, "for wanting me."

He lets out a harsh breath, his expression solemn.

"Thank you for saving me," he says.

I suck in a breath, my gaze flies to his, expecting to see recognition in his eyes. A remembrance of the words "save me," but there's nothing there. Nothing but goodbye.

"I think," he says, "since I didn't die while having sex like you claimed, and I never became a ghost like you said, we can agree that your story was...just that. I know about your article, and while I'm impressed by your creativity in offering an alternate explanation, I...I think it's best we part ways."

He holds out his hand, a cordial parting.

I stare at his long tan fingers, his strong hand that held me and caressed me and loved me.

He's alive.

And even if I can't be with him, at least I know that he's somewhere in the world. That he's living, and breathing, and laughing, and loving. That he's out there, somewhere. And when I look up at the stars, somewhere in this world, I'll know, he's looking up at them too.

I take his hand, hold it in mine. Memorize the

warmth of him, and the feeling in my heart when we touch.

"I'm very glad to have known you," I say, my voice thick, my throat tight, but this is important to say, maybe it's the most important thing I've ever said. "I'm grateful to you for everything you've done. Thank you for coming back. Thank you for saving me. Thank you for seeing me and letting me see you. If you ever doubt it, know that I'm here." I reach up, let my hand hover over his chest, touching the air above his heart. "I'm here if you need me."

He watches me, his blue eyes opaque, his emotions hidden under reflective waters.

"Goodbye, Jillian," he says, his voice quiet and barely heard above the rumble of passing buses and trucks. "Thank you again."

And then he pulls his hand from mine, the whisper of his warmth fades, and then he turns and walks away.

He moves on.

51

Time moves on.

Even if you wish it wouldn't, it moves on. It's like the universe. You can't tell it to stop expanding, it just does, taking us farther and farther away from any other hope of life. Every second of every day we spin farther out into the dark reaches of space, carried away from other stars, other galaxies, other life. And after enough time passes, we'll be all alone.

Thursday passes. Friday comes and goes. Saturday is forgotten. On Sunday my parents and Fran come to the city, alarmed after my mom video called and saw my stitches and the hollows under my eyes. My mom brought a rosemary-scented candle, Fran brought chicken noodle soup, and my dad brought another bat—just in case the first one wasn't cutting it.

After my parents assured themselves I was still alive and didn't need to come home to Long Island to work at The Bargain Shopper's Mailer for my cousin Ari, they decided to catch a show in the theater district.

On their way out, Fran gripped my hand and said, "Jilly, don't worry. I'm sure something wonderful is about to happen."

I squeezed her hand and said, "You're wrong. It won't happen. It already did."

Monday dawns.

My stitches are less gruesome, and I'm less sore, less bruised.

I know from experience that the ache in my chest will remain, a heavy, bruised pain, but the strength of it will ebb and flow. It's better than before though, because Daniel's alive.

Right now, he's a world away, in Geneva.

I can imagine him there. The lake will be ice cold, even though it's nearing June. I can picture the dark blue waters from the photograph in his apartment. The hunter green trees, the yellow sand, the overhanging leaves of the reaching plane trees. He'd dive into the water, the cold flashing over him, and then he'd float on his back and stare at the bright blue sky.

The same sky I have here.

I don't know why Daniel found me, but I'm so grateful he did. Over the weekend I remember that Zelda had said that the reason Daniel hadn't moved on was because of unfinished business. He had to help me or I had to help him.

Well, we both helped each other. He saved me and then I saved him.

And if I feel like there's still unfinished business?

Is love unfinished business?

Or can you just keep loving someone, even if you're not together and they don't know that you do? Is that the end of it? Is that finished business?

I find myself wishing that I could harness Planck energy, and like Serena says, make time and space my playground. I'd travel back in time and find a way to convince Daniel, make him remember, tell him...

Anyway, I can't. I can't go back in time. I can't ask time to wait. I can't ask time to stop. I can't change the future from a past that's already happened.

The only thing I can do is change this moment. Live in this moment right here.

What can I do right now, in this moment?

It's Monday.

The pale blue morning sky streaks through the tall buildings outside my apartment window. A pigeon perches on my window ledge and calls a coo-coo, barely heard through the glass.

My eyes are gritty and dry from too many sleepless nights and I rub them as I look four stories down at Lexington Avenue.

The woman who runs the laundromat pulls open the metal gate over her shop. A bicycle delivery man in a neon vest cycles past. A city bus lumbers slowly southward, heaving uncaringly in front of a honking van. My neighbor paces the sidewalk in a blue bathrobe, an unlit cigarette hanging from her lips, Daisy sniffing the concrete. The sad philosopher hands a cup of coffee to a construction worker.

It's Monday.

Which means right now, I can take a shower, put on a dress, get a cup of coffee and make it on time to the morning meeting. After all, Bernardo hates it when people are late.

∽

IT DOESN'T TAKE LONG TO GET READY, AND IN FIFTEEN minutes I'm at the coffee cart in front of my building, breathing in the smells of sugar and milk and freshly brewed coffee.

"Sugar and cream?"

"Yes please," I say, giving the barista a smile. I nod at his book, Plato's *Republic*. "Still working through it?"

He grunts, dumping about twelve teaspoons of sugar into my cup. "Everything we see is a reflection of a reflection of a reflection. Even this cup of coffee. Is it even real?"

He stares at me, waiting for an answer.

"Yes."

At least I hope it is, because I'm thirsty, and I could use the sugar.

"No," he says, leaning over the metal counter of his cart and giving me a sad-eyed, disappointed look. "It's not. You only think it's real. Everything we sense, we think it's real, but it's not. It's only reflections of reflections of what's real. Reality? We can't see it. It exists outside of space and time."

He shakes his head and pours a load of cream into my cup. But I'm stunned. "What did you say?"

He sounds just like Serena.

"Reality." He pulls the cream jug up and mixes it into the coffee, turning it from black to caramelly brown. "Plato said it exists outside of space and time." He taps the book. "For instance, love exists beyond time."

"You think so?" I ask, my expression softening. Maybe he isn't such a sad philosopher, maybe he's a hopeless romantic.

"Don't know." He shrugs and hands me the cup of coffee.

I take it, and the hot cup stings my hands.

Plato also said that every heart sings a song that is incomplete until another heart whispers back.

"Maybe he was on to something," I say, dropping money into the tip jar.

The sad philosopher shrugs and picks up his book.

I hurry to work.

52

I'M AT THE OFFICE TWENTY MINUTES EARLY AND WHEN I stride from the elevator, the early morning chatter cuts off.

My hair's in a high ponytail and I guess since no one has seen the black stitches and bruise on my forehead it's a bit of a shock.

A group of laughing interns stop short when Crissy nudges them and nods my way.

One of the techies was about to drink from his coffee mug, but when he sees me, he misses his mouth and spills the coffee down his white dress shirt.

Ned turns from his computer at the sudden silence and sees me in front of the closing elevator. He halfway stands from his rolling chair, his mouth falling open. "Did...did...hop..."

I'm not sure what he's going to ask, but I can imagine.

Buck's stomping across the office, kicking newsprint piles out of his way, arguing with Hayley about hockey penalties. When he darts an angry glance my way, he stops mid-sentence.

Hayley looks my way, and her eyes widen. "Jillian, what happened?"

Everyone in the office waits for my response. The computer techs, billing, the interns, Ned, Hayley, Buck, they're all quiet waiting for my response.

I smile at them all, the sort of smile you give when nothing's okay and you want to convince someone everything is.

"I fell."

"Into another dimension?" Ned asks, and to be honest, he sounds hopeful that I did.

"No," Buck growls. "She fell into someone's fist. Did you get mugged?" Buck's shoulders bunch together. "This is why you wear brass knuckles when you walk home. Jeez."

"Who wears brass knuckles?" Crissy asks, piping up from the intern circle. "And where can I get some?"

"Or...she literally just fell," Hayley says. "Was it the heels? I once fell during a pageant and had to get three stitches on my knee, it was..." Hayley trails off when Bernardo strides toward us.

His eyes flicker over me, ignoring everyone else. His expression doesn't give anything away. You'd think, by his placid demeanor, that I look the same as ever and the gala and Daniel calling him to ask about me never happened.

Hayley's back stiffens, her chin goes up, and she very pointedly doesn't look at Bernardo.

He very noticeably doesn't look at her.

Bernardo nods toward his office. "Jillian, do you have a few minutes?"

Oh.

Aha.

I blink.

Suddenly, the stitches pinch and burn, and that nice, calm feeling I had from my coffee vanishes. I'm left with an acidic gnawing in my stomach.

I wonder, has Bernardo been waiting since last week to fire me?

I nod slowly and follow Bernardo, and as I weave through the desks and the clutter of *The Exposé*, I can feel everyone's eyes on my back.

I step after Bernardo into his office. It's the only private office in the entire space. It's near the kitchen and doesn't have any windows. It's the size of a large walk-in closet and is dominated by Bernardo's metal desk and a wall lined with filing cabinets.

The beige paint on the walls is faded and chipped, and there are large white boards hung from nearly every surface with layouts, story ideas, subscription numbers, to-do lists, and more—basically it's an accurate representation of the chaos of Bernardo's mind.

Except, I've always felt that Bernardo is like that kid with the room that looks as if everything's been tossed up in a tornado, yet they know precisely where everything is. And if you dare clean the room then they can't find anything, because their system has been disturbed.

So, there's order in the chaos.

He closes the door after me and the click of the door shutting sounds final, like the click of an executioner's gun.

"Have a seat," he says, walking around his desk to sit in his old leather office chair—the one he found on the curb the night we went out for drinks for *The Exposé's* five-year anniversary.

I step to the brown vinyl chair in front of his desk, move the foot-high pile of manila folders from the seat to the floor, and sit down, setting my bag on the floor next to me.

Bernardo has piles of papers on his desk, a broken whiteboard, a stack of the day's leading newspapers and magazines, and a tall cup of black tea, with the steam curling between us.

I clench my hands, pressing my nails into my palms and wait.

Bernardo studies me for a moment, his expression unreadable, and then he says, "I lost a friend last week because of your article."

I nod, a sharp ache crawling up my throat.

Here it comes, the in-person firing.

"I need to know," Bernardo says, giving me a direct stare, "if I'm going to lose a writer as well."

Wait.

What?

"You aren't...I'm not...what?"

Bernardo leans back in his leather chair, the old springs squeaking. He gives a long sigh.

"Can you still do your job?" he asks, "Can you still write articles that tell the truth? Will you still do your best?"

My hands shake.

I look at Bernardo, at his black hair, his dark brown eyes and straight nose, at that implacable expression he always wears. He looks like he should be in a suit, or a tux. Instead he's in a white t-shirt and dark jeans.

He weighs my expression, waits for my answer.

I take a breath, breathing in the smell of old newsprint, black tea, and whiteboard markers.

"Yes," I say. "I can. I will."

"Good." He nods, the hardness in his eyes softening. "I'm glad you're okay," he says, and then, "I'm glad you saved Daniel's life."

"Did he..." I pause and clasp the hem of my navy dress. "When you spoke to him, what did he say?"

Bernardo steeples his hands in front of his chin and says, "He told me you'd done CPR and saved his life. He calmly asked whether I knew my staff was tracking him for the purpose of writing a story. Then he casually asked what the story was about. I told him. That was the end of it."

Something in Bernardo's eyes makes me believe the conversation wasn't as clean and dry as he claims. Especially because he admitted he'd lost Daniel as a friend.

"I'm sorry," I say, and then because Bernardo has always only ever requested that I tell the truth, I take a deep breath and say, "It was more than a story for me."

He nods, his gaze perceptive.

"Can I scrap it?" I ask. "I don't have an article. Not even about yachts."

His mouth twitches in an almost smile. "Surely you could write something about yachts."

I shake my head. "I really couldn't."

His eyes fill with suppressed laughter. "Fine."

Then he looks at his watch—one of Hayley's Abry knock-offs—and sees it's a minute until nine.

So he pushes back his chair and stands.

I grab my bag, stand too, and smooth down my dress.

As he opens his office door, he glances at Hayley

sitting at the conference table and his face goes stone cold. He pauses and says without looking at me, his jaw hard, "By the way, word of advice. Daniel wouldn't have been so hurt if he didn't care."

Then he strides toward the conference table and I stare after him, wondering how after nine years of working here, everyone still manages to surprise me.

53

It's June.

Another Monday is here. Weeks have passed since Daniel left. My stitches were taken out, the bruises faded, and there's only the sliver of a pink scar, barely noticeable on my forehead.

When I look in the mirror, that's the only evidence I can find to show that Daniel came and went. The rest of my life has changed though. I'm open, I talk, I laugh—even if it hurts—I live. I stopped punishing myself for a past I couldn't change, I stopped wishing for a future that couldn't happen, and I thanked God for giving me people to love—for however short or long of a time.

I drop my purse on my desk and take a sip of sugary coffee. It's seven thirty. I walked to work early today, wanting to enjoy the soft morning sunshine, the pigeons cooing from window ledges, and the summer breeze licking through the tall city buildings, making sidewalk tree leaves dance, blue hydrangeas nod their heads, and dogs sniff the air.

I love the sound of traffic rushing by, horns and sirens, and the metallic squeak of shop owners opening the metal fencing pulled over their storefronts, welcoming a new day. I especially love saying good morning, and hello, and have a nice day, and how are you, and thank you very much.

I smile at the office, the quiet before the chaos of the day. And if that smile feels a little bit forced, and a little bit sad, that's okay.

"Ugh, your cheerful insistence that you're okay is killing me," Hayley says, slapping a sheet of paper on my desk. It looks like a letter.

I set my cup down. "Good morning."

"If you say so," Hayley says, frowning at me, a pucker between her eyebrows.

She's in tight black pants that mold to her long legs, high black heels, and a Rangers jersey that she's cut off above the belly button. Her hair is in a high bun, her make-up is perfect, and she's wearing a half-dozen knock-off Cartier bangles and a faux Abry diamond watch.

Basically, she looks adorable except for the expression on her face, which reminds me of a hockey player about to throw off their gloves and body slam someone.

"You alright?" I ask, wondering if I should've brought donuts.

Ever since the gala Hayley and Bernardo have been excruciatingly polite to each other, painfully proper, and so stiff it's almost unbearable.

Sometimes when Bernardo says flatly, "Hayley, would you be so kind as to relay your article line up," and Hayley says in a stilted voice, "Of course, Bernardo. I would be delighted to," I just want to shake them both and yell, "Just make up already! Obviously you care about each other!"

Which I guess is what Hayley's thinking about me and Daniel because she says, "You should call him. You haven't been the same since he left."

I glance around the office. No one is really here yet. Just Bernardo, but his office door is closed. So it's just me, Hayley, and The Wall, flashing the news at us.

"No," I say, and when she starts to argue I add, "I called and left a dozen messages when he was in the hospital."

He didn't respond to any of them. Obviously.

"Email?" she asks, and when I shake my head, she says vehemently, "It's just not right. For years you were so quiet—here but not. And then, Daniel's here, and suddenly you're talking and smiling—and to be honest, I've never seen you smile the way you did when you were with him—and I'm thinking, wow, she's finally living again, and I figured he was the one who helped you do it."

She studies me, looks over the blue fatigue lines under my eyes, the way I press my lips together, the bright cheerfulness of my summer yellow sundress.

She sighs. "Jillian, I deal in fakes. I know one when I see one." She shrugs, her midriff jersey lifting higher. "You're hurt and you're pretending you're not."

"It'll pass," I say.

It won't pass.

She shakes her head. "I think you should write an article about him. Make it a big one where you talk about what happened." She clasps her hands, holds them to her chest, and says dramatically, "'It started as a story assignment, but it became so much more. I thought he was just an international sex symbol with a big yacht, but it turns out'"—she blinks, pauses, then says—"'it turns out he changed my life and I love him.' Write that article and he'll fly here in a second and sweep you off your feet."

Right.

"That only works in the movies," I say, shaking my head. "In real life if you write an article like that, the person it's about thinks you're a stalker who can't let go and they file a restraining order. Because let's face it, it's weird writing an article for thousands of people to read about a man you love who doesn't want anything to do with you, begging him to love you back."

Hayley frowns, tugs down her jersey, then says, "Are you telling me the article writing scheme to get the guy back is like boiling a bunny?"

"That's exactly what I'm telling you."

"Huh," she says. Then she flicks the thin silver watch on her wrist and says, "If you want, I'll stop wearing my faux Abry watches. Out of loyalty to you."

"No," I say, smiling at her. "That's okay. It's a nice watch."

"It isn't actually," she admits. "I got a box of them off the back of a truck and they all stopped keeping time after a week. The box was completely waterlogged, the battery is dead, and the logo says Obry instead of Abry. So..."

I fight a smile, then give in. "You should definitely keep wearing it."

She grins back at me, her cheeks pink and her eyes sparking with humor. Then she nods at the sheet of paper she put on my desk.

"I wanted to let you know before I hand this in," she says.

I look at her a second longer, then slide the paper off the desk and flip it over to read the stark black print. The letter is short, to the point, impersonal.

The paper rustles in my hands and I hold it tightly as the cool air from the air conditioning kicks on and blows over us.

"Well?" Hayley asks, her voice quiet.

I scan the last line. She's given her two weeks' notice.

"Why?" I ask, setting the paper on my desk.

Hayley glances at Bernardo's closed door then back to me.

"I took your advice," she says.

And I know that when she says she took my advice, she means she told Bernardo how she feels.

"The night of the gala?" I ask.

She nods. "I told him I had feelings for him and that I had for a long time. I said I liked that he was messy and chaotic, and that he accepted everyone for who they were, and he never lost his temper and that he was driven to succeed, but even if he never became a huge success or made a lot of money, that I didn't care, because I liked him for him. Then I admitted that I'd been angry when he first met me and he treated me like a dimwitted airhead beauty queen and so I pretended to be one to pay him back."

"What did he say?"

"He said he knew," she says, her mouth tightening into a firm line.

"He knew what?"

"He knew I was pretending. He knew I had feelings. He already knew."

Gosh. I knew Bernardo was perceptive, but I never realized he was that perceptive.

Hayley takes a steadying breath and then slowly tilts her chin in the air, regaining her composure.

So, he rejected her.

"Is that why you're quitting?"

She gives a short laugh. "No. I'm quitting because after I told him, his mother, his *mom*, strolled over, and she's dripping with diamonds, wearing a custom Versace gown, and she asked him who his pretty little *friend* was, but by her tone it was clear "friend" meant bimbo side-piece, to which he replied, 'Hello mother, she's no one of consequence,' to which his mother said, 'Clearly,' and then she looked at my dress, which, let me tell you, was the highest-caliber knock-off I've ever worn, and—"

Hayley cuts off, her face is red, and she's shaking she's so angry. She clenches her hands and then says quietly, "And it turns out, he's not Bernardo Martin, he's Bernardo *Martin*, the eldest son of the Martin family. You know, the media proprietor family that owns most of the major news stations in the US and a daily paper in nearly every freaking country in the world. *That* family."

She heaves another breath, grabs the resignation letter off my desk, and says, "I was an idiot, telling him I didn't care if he never succeeded, or never made any money. I actually told him that if he ever needed, I'd take a salary cut, because I make enough to scrape by with my side job. And while I was dumping all the contents of my heart at his feet, he was stomping on it." She shakes her head, glancing at Bernardo's closed door. "I love it here. I love *The Daily Exposé* and I love my job. But I can't stay." She smiles at me then and reaches out and squeezes my arm. "I'll miss you. It's been a good nine years. But I think...I think it's time to find something new." She nods. "It's time for me to go."

"Are you sure? You could—" I start to say, but Hayley shakes her head, her expression resolved and her mind made up.

So instead of arguing, I grab her and pull her into a swift hug.

She's one of the original five, she's been here through thick and thin with the rest of us. We're family. I know her favorite lipstick brand, the rose perfume she always wears, what salad dressing she likes best. I know her ironic sense of humor, all the tricks she uses to haggle and sell knock-offs at outrageous prices, and I know what articles she likes to write best and the hooks she uses.

She's a part of *The Exposé* as much as the Empire State Building is a part of New York. It seems unfathomable that she's moving on. But she is. And I suppose that's what we do as humans, isn't it?

"I'll miss you," I say, letting her go and stepping back.

"We'll go to games together, the Rangers, the Yankees, the Knicks," she says. She shrugs nonchalantly, then smiles cheerfully. "You all will barely notice that I'm gone."

I match her smile and nod.

"Right, we'll barely notice," I agree.

But we both know that isn't true.

54

THE MORNING MEETING IS COMING TO A CLOSE. THE BOX OF chocolate donuts at the center of the conference table is still full. The atmosphere is too strained to eat, even if they do smell like chocolate ganache and sugar.

Hayley's nervous. She tapped her nails against the table for the whole meeting, and everyone noticed.

Even Ned, who usually fidgets, shakes his legs, and squirms has sat still and watched Hayley with a worried frown.

Buck's scowling at her, and deep frown lines crease his bald head.

I keep giving her reassuring smiles, but even so, she's still drumming her fingers on the table, trying to hold in her nerves.

The only person who seems completely unaffected by her uncharacteristic bout of nerves is Bernardo. He's as unflappable as ever. His black hair is smoothed down, his jaw is clean shaven, his expression is distant and he's still being meticulously polite to Hayley, even with her hour-long finger tapping session.

"That's everything," he says, glancing around the table. "If there isn't any more business, then—"

"I have something," Hayley says.

She stops tapping her fingers on the table and sits straight, leveling her gaze on everyone at the table, finally turning to Bernardo.

He nods, clearly not expecting the bomb she's about to drop, because he seems as calm as ever.

Hayley lifts her blue faux leather Chanel purse and pulls out her two weeks' notice. She hands it to Bernardo.

When he takes it, her chin is in the air, and she no longer looks nervous. She looks like a queen.

Bernardo holds the paper in front of him, scanning the words. As he does, his shoulders stiffen, his face goes —if possible—even more blank, and the knuckles on his hands turn white.

Suddenly it feels as if all the air has been sucked from the room.

Ever so slowly Bernardo lowers the letter to the conference table. He spears Hayley with intense focus.

"What is this?" he asks, his voice even and controlled.

"It's my two weeks' notice," Hayley says, as if she's speaking to a child. "It says it right there."

"Hold on," Ned says, looking between Hayley and Bernardo. "You can't...you...you're leaving?"

Hayley nods.

"No, not happening," Buck says, the tips of his ears turning red.

"Why?" Hayley asks, turning to him.

"Because." Buck jabs a finger at her from across the table. "We have a thing. I gun after writing sports, you hang on to it like a priest holding in a fart in church. I say I'm better, you say I'm not. I prove I'm better, you still say I'm not. One day, I'll write sports because I fought a worthy opponent and won. It doesn't work if you walk away. The victory is worthless then."

Hayley wrinkles her nose. "Is that what we've been doing? What if I told you that you still can't write sports because you don't know the difference between slashing, spearing, hooking and holding, *and* Crissy volunteered to take over for me?"

"Like hell," Buck says.

"Is it the reptilians?" Ned asks, his eyebrows lowering in concern. "Are they offering you a job at the *Times*? It's owned by the reptilians, you know. Everything they publish is psy-op propaganda to incite fear...divide the population, and...make us weak so we're easier to control—"

"Hayley," Bernardo interrupts.

She turns to him, swiveling her office chair toward him. She's poised, and if she's going for untouchable and beautiful then she's nailed it.

"Yes, Bernardo?"

"Why?"

She stiffens and I see a flash of temper in her eyes, a bit of her heckler side rising to the surface. "Why does it matter? I figure you won't miss me. After all, I'm not of any consequence. Two weeks from now you won't ever have to see me again."

Bernardo flinches as if Hayley's taken off her gloves and punched him in the gut. His face is wiped of the imperturbable mask, leaving pure shock.

Hayley stands then, thrusting her chair back, about to make a grand exit.

The shock on Bernardo's face shifts to incredulity.

"It was a compliment," he says forcefully.

Hayley scoffs, "I'm not stupid."

Bernardo's eyes blaze as he takes her in.

He stands. "It was a compliment," he says more firmly. "You don't want to be a person of consequence in that world. I wouldn't want you to be."

"Thanks," Hayley says, waving her hand, discarding Bernardo's words. "Now that that's cleared up, I'm going to get to work."

"It's not cleared up," Bernardo says.

Hayley pauses mid-step.

Buck, Ned and I watch Bernardo like we've never seen him before. He's shown more emotion in the past thirty seconds than he has in the last nine years.

"You can quit," he says.

"Good," Hayley says, "because I am."

"You can quit as Hayley Bancroft."

"Yeah. Okay."

"But then I'm hiring you again as Hayley Martin."

Hayley blinks, and then blinks again.

Bernardo takes a step toward her, his gaze intent, his face full of turbulent emotion, "You told me something at the gala and you didn't give me a chance to respond. You found out who I was and you ran. Well now you can listen. From the second you tried to sell me the worst knock-off Rolex I've ever seen, I've wanted you by my side. I want you when you're pretending to like opera and gallery openings, and I like you when you're heckling an umpire. I want you when you're in a bad mood and need to eat the chocolate you keep hidden in your desk and I want you when you're in a good mood and hum 'There she is, Miss America.' You think I won't miss you if you leave? I've been missing you for nine years, because you aren't mine. But I'm not a lecher, I'm not that employer who goes after his employees. I stayed away. But if you're quitting, if you're telling me that you don't care who I am, that you want me—"

He cuts off and Hayley nods, her eyes wide, her expression stunned.

Bernardo smiles and when he does he looks boyishly handsome—like he's about to propose one of his whirlwind visionary ideas.

"Good," he says, taking another step toward Hayley. "Then you and I, we're finishing what we started nine years ago."

"Great," Buck mutters. "If they get married, I'll never get the sports section."

I restrain a smile.

"What do you say?" Bernardo asks, his brown eyes searching Hayley's. He holds out his hand. "You and me?"

Hayley's expression softens, her mouth trembles, and then she slowly reaches out and puts her hand in Bernardo's.

When she does, he tugs her forward, gives her a look that probably curls her toes, and then he drags her toward the elevator.

"Jillian, you're in charge. We'll be back in two weeks," he calls over his shoulder.

"What?" I say.

Hayley gives me a wide-eyed stare as Bernardo hits the elevator button.

"But...but...what about the sports section?" I shout across the office.

Everyone in the room, the computer techs, the

interns, billing, and Ned and Buck all look between me and Bernardo.

"Buck can do it until I'm back," Hayley calls.

Then the elevator opens, Bernardo tugs Hayley through the doors, and she waves at us like she's a princess in a pageant.

The elevator dings, the doors shut, and then the office descends into stunned silence.

"They're getting married," I say, and then, "and I'm in charge."

"Just great," Buck says. "I'll be living the dream for two weeks and then bam it'll disappear. Isn't that just life?"

"Do you think," Ned asks, still staring at the elevator, "that Bernardo and Hayley get married in other dimensions too?"

I consider his question, then nod. "Yes, I think so. I think they do."

At that Buck grunts in disgust, Ned grabs a chocolate donut, and I wonder how in the world I'm going to take over for Bernardo for two weeks.

I guess I'll just have to channel my inner Kirk.

55

It turns out that keeping *The Daily Exposé* running is even harder than it looks, especially because I'm not nearly as good as Bernardo at turning down Ned's story pitches, keeping Buck in his own lane, or finding zen in the middle of chaos.

Bernardo didn't completely throw me to the wolves, he checked in every day while honeymooning with Hayley, and really it was fine, it worked, but let's just say I'm ecstatic they're back.

I lie in the middle of my bed, the comforter pooled around me, my arms and legs spread wide, wearing an old t-shirt and sweatpants. Outside, morning traffic noises are climbing in volume, sunshine spears through the window, and I can smell frying bacon and brewing coffee from my neighbor's apartment.

It's Saturday and I'm considering staying in bed all day. I can watch a marathon of *Star Trek: The Next Generation* season two, maybe defrost some of Fran's chana masala, or maybe her lasagna, or even better, I'll have a dozen of her chocolate chip cookies and just—

My phone rings.

I smack my hand on the nightstand, reach around and grab it, "Hello?"

"Oh my gosh, you are not staying in bed all day."

I sit up and rub my eyes. "What are you, psychic?" I ask Serena.

She laughs, "Hardly. You sound like you just woke up and I can practically hear the sweatpants in your voice."

I scoff. "I'm not wearing sweatpants," I say, kicking them off.

The bed sheets rustle and rumple around me, and the cool air hits my naked legs. My toes curl in the red carpet around my bed as I stand. Then I stretch my back, roll my shoulders, and say, "And I'm not in bed."

Serena chuckles, "Uh huh. I'm glad, because you have a flight to catch."

I stop halfway down the stairs from my platform bed. "Excuse me?"

Serena hums an ascent. Then I hear Purrk's distinctive purr. "You're flying to Geneva today—"

"No," I say. "Serena. I'm not going to harass him. I'm not going to hang around outside his office or wander his stores. That's the opposite of what he'd want. He doesn't want to see me—"

"For the Geneva trekker convention," Serena finishes.

"Oh," I say, remembering that Serena's been asking me to come out to this convention for months now. "You want me to come to Switzerland for the convention?"

"Of course I do," she says, her voice matter of fact. "It's the best way I know to yank you out of this...well, let's just say, live long and prosper, baby. You'll love it here. First, you'll get to see me, which is amazing in and of itself. Then you'll get to see Worf, son of Mogh, your first true love. I know you don't speak French, but you speak Klingon like a champ—"

"yIDoghQo'" I say, stepping down the stairs onto my creaky wood floor.

"I'm not. I'm serious," she says, "I bought you a ticket for today, you'll be in Geneva in less than twelve hours— qoSlIj DatIvjaj."

It's not my birthday, it's not even close to my birthday. "If I didn't love you so much," I say, "I'd kill you."

"Heghlu'meH QaQ jajvam."

Today is a good day to die.

Her saying that reminds me of Daniel, *I'd die happy if I could die looking into your eyes.*

My smile vanishes.

"I'm sorry," I say. "This is really, really wonderful of you but—"

"No buts, you're coming."

"—but I can't. If I see him there…"

It would break my heart.

And he'll think I flew all the way around the world because of some bunny boiling obsession. My stomach rolls and I feel sick at the thought.

"You won't see him," Serena says. "The probability of that happening is one in twenty million. I'm a physicist on a budget, living in a three-hundred-year-old apartment building with leaky pipes and an ancient death trap elevator. I hang out with researchers and grad students at cheap coffee shops and ride the bus everywhere. We'll be at the convention with other trekkers, and in the unfashionable part of town with the other working schlubs."

Purrk meows and Serena continues, "Meanwhile, people like Daniel Abry are in a different part of Geneva. They're living in their castles perched in the mountains overlooking the lake. They're eating at five-star restaurants, driving their Rolls Royces—trust me, it's like we're solidly on the ground, and he's flying in the stratosphere. Your paths won't cross. Not even if you wanted them to."

"Which I don't," I lie.

"Right," Serena says, knowing it's a lie, but letting me have it. "Look. Jilly. It's been more than a month and I know in the grand scheme of things that isn't a long time, but...I miss you. I miss your easy laugh, I miss your determination. Where is that determination? I mean, for crying out loud, you're the girl who chased down Wil Wheaton with me, and you're the woman who went on a hundred terrible dates because you believed someone would see you for you. Well, someone did. And now he's gone. Okay. Fine. But are you going to let that stop you from living? And are you going to let that stop you—most importantly—from trekking? Because in the grand scheme of things, life may let you down, but *Star Trek* never will."

I smile at Serena's impassioned speech.

Outside the window a bus chugs by, and the flow of morning traffic rolls steadily onward. On my kitchen counter, the coffee maker calls to me. I flip it on. Almost immediately the drip begins, spreading the smell of roasted beans and the anticipation of caffeine.

"Well?" Serena asks, "Are we doing this, or not?"

"HIjah'" I say, giving Serena the answer she wants. "We're doing it."

I can practically hear her grin over the phone.

"Thank you," I say, already mentally packing my suitcase. I'll have to send Bernardo an email and let him know I'll be working remotely next week.

"Come on," Serena says. "You know you'd do the same for me. If I was knocked to the ground and kicked in the head by life, you'd be right there to pick me up. So, pack your bag and get to the airport."

"I'll pay you back," I say, thinking of the cost of the flight.

"I know. And you can also buy all my food and drinks and all the collectibles and memorabilia I want, and you can keep me company while I stand in hours-long autograph lines," she says, a smile in her voice. "Go on. Get to the airport. I'll see you soon."

As I pack my suitcase, folding my communication officer's uniform, and my red (stitched and fixed) Uhura dress, a frisson of electricity passes through me. It feels like the current in the air right before lightning strikes.

And no matter how much I tell myself it's because I'm going to a convention with Serena, I can't make myself believe it.

56

THE SUN SETS, A GOLDEN YELLOW ORB, SLOWLY DESCENDING over the lush summer greens and the deep, icy blues of Lake Geneva. As the sun falls, the air fills with a quiet, breath-held sort of expectation.

The only sound is the last evening song—a throaty whistled melody—of a tiny fuzzy-breasted blackcap. He's perched overhead, in the gnarled, reaching limbs of the plane tree planted in the sand at the edge of Lake Geneva's shore.

I drag my feet through the still warm sand, the coarse grains tickling my toes as I push the tree swing back and forth, catching the long streams of sun running over the beach. The green leaves whisper overhead, rattling with the swaying of the thick limb as I swing back and forth, kicking my heels in the sand.

My stomach flips and falls as I breathe in the summer-green and cool water smells of Baby-Plage.

My feet are bare, my legs too. I'm in my red Uhura dress—the one I wore to the conference today—and my sleeves are rolled up. I hang onto the rope and let the cool breeze drifting off the lake wash over me.

It's my last day in Geneva.

Serena was right. I love it here.

The city is full of classic gray and beige stone buildings with elegant architecture and history lining the streets. She lives by a park with a meadow and a stream gurgling through the grass, there's a playground always full of laughing children, and a coffee shop that sells the most delicious pastries in the world.

The city has a different feel than New York. It's older, less chaotic flash and more elegant timelessness. There are gardens to stroll, statues to admire, and hidden cobblestone streets to explore. And of course, there's hours and hours of trekker convention heaven to indulge in.

I did it all.

And tomorrow morning I'm flying home.

Serena was also right about not running into Daniel. Like she said, we're on the ground, and he's Kirk, all the way up in the stars.

Since I'm leaving in the morning, I told Serena I wanted to catch one last sight, on my own. I'm sure she guessed it was about Daniel, but she didn't question me.

I take one last long look at the mountains turning deep indigo blue in the fading light, and the rippling water of the lake, shining like the setting sun is tossing gold coins into the water.

I breathe in the cool water smells and smile at how when I dipped my toes into the shallows, the water was bracingly cold. I can picture Daniel here, diving into the cold blue lake, the setting sun glinting off him as he comes up for air.

I hope he's been here since he came home. I hope he's been happy.

I dig my feet into the sand and pull the swing to a stop.

It's time to go.

The wind tugs at my hair, the curls brushing over my face. The blackcap's song comes to an end, and in the distance, the quiet sounds of traffic reach through the trees.

And that's when I see him.

It's like I've conjured him by picturing him here. Or the song into my heart called to his and his own whispered back. Because there he is, striding across the sand.

He looks better. He isn't clutching his ribs, or stepping with pain, his stride is loose and long. His hair is a little longer, it's brushing against his t-shirt collar. The hollows under his eyes are still there though and he's looking at the lake as if he doesn't actually see it. As if his mind is a million miles away.

There's a grim loneliness about the way he's moving that makes me want to spring off the swing, sprint across the sand, and fling myself into his arms.

My chest clenches and I grip the rope of the swing, digging my fingers into the scratchy material.

I hold as still as the blackcap above, perched silently in the branches of the plane tree.

I'm frozen, watching as Daniel kicks off his shoes and pulls off his black t-shirt, dropping it to the sand. He's only in a navy swimsuit, and the sloping sun drifts over his skin. But even though he's bathed in the sun's golden light and although he looks so physical, so alive, so much a part of this world, I can't help but notice that he's not smiling, he's not...happy.

I hold still. Hold my breath, waiting for him to dive under the cold water.

When he does, I'll go. I'll walk away and he won't have to know I was here.

But then he stops mid-stride, he pauses as if he heard something, and then he slowly turns my way.

I clutch the rope and the swing teeters beneath me, suddenly unstable.

I'm buried in the dappled shadows of the tall tree, and Daniel's twenty feet away, but even so, he recognizes me right away.

My hands shake and there's a whooshing drumming noise in my ears that I know has to be my heart, trying to claw its way out of my chest and run to him.

He searches the shadows, studies my expression, his forehead wrinkling, and I see the second that he comes to the conclusion that I followed him here.

I stand, thrust the swing back, and grab my sandals.

My shoulders hunch and I hurry across the sand, kicking up the grains as I walk quickly toward the road.

I have to pass him to get by. I pause a few feet away from him, my breath short.

I'm trying very hard to not let my heart split in two and shatter at his feet. I'd rather wait until I'm home for it to do that.

His expression is hard, but his gaze searches me, taking in my red dress—the one he once loved—my bare feet, and the heat in my cheeks.

It's not as if I expected it, but it still makes my heart plummet when I realize—again—that he doesn't remember. That he thinks I broke his trust, used him, and lied.

The lines on his forehead deepen as he frowns at my dress.

I clear my throat, forcing out the words, keeping my voice even, "I'm here visiting my best friend for a convention. I didn't know I'd see you. I—"

I love you.

I miss you.

"—I'm sorry." I push down the other words and turn to go.

Daniel's still studying my dress, his eyes intent, his gaze searching. He looks confused. Uncertain.

My heart pounds, and I let out a shuddering breath, but when he doesn't say anything, I nod.

"Sorry again. I'll go—"

I cut off, step past him, the sand shifting as I pass. I won't look back. I won't hurt him by making more of this than he knows it is.

Only thirty feet more, fifty at most, and then I can let free the tears pressing at the back of my eyes.

I can feel him behind me, the heat of him, the warmth, the feel of him.

Then I hear him turn and he says, "Jillian?"

I stop, my breath cuts off, and I slowly turn around.

He's facing me, and when I turn and look at him, his eyes go wide, his chest expands in a shuddering breath, and he looks as if he's about to fall to his knees.

The falling sunlight spears the sand between us.

"Jillian?" he says again, uncertainly.

The sky holds it breath.

I take a step closer. "Yes?"

There's something in his eyes, something in his

expression. He looks down at his bare chest, then back to my dress, and then he looks into my eyes, and I'm watching him with all the love I've ever felt, all the want, all the need, a whole expanding universe of love.

He stares into my eyes, then his own open wide, and it's as if sunlight has pierced the dark blue depths of the ocean. His hand flies to his chest, presses against his heart, and I see the exact moment he remembers.

It's all there in his eyes. My apartment, the mirrors, the bat, the dates, Zelda, bacon burgers and coffee, finding a decent man, the mugger, Michael, my job, baseball, movie marathons, walks in the park, and then, when his eyes flare and his shoulders tense, I know he remembers kissing. He remembers making love.

"Jillian," he says, his voice breaking. He looks at me with all the tenderness and love that he did the night we made love. "Jillian, my love."

I take a step forward, and then he can't wait any longer, because he pulls me into his arms, wraps me up in him, and holds me tightly against his warmth.

57

Daniel lives above the city, up a twisting, narrow country road, past stone fences and deep alpine woods. The country is full of pine scents, lush grass, and crickets singing to the night.

Daniel's home is sprawling, tall windowed, and open. It's situated on the edge of a hilly, mountainous expanse, with a view of the lake, the night-blue mountains, and the glowing city.

I had only a moment to take it all in—cool white walls, entire stretches of windows framing the lake reflecting the city lights and the night dark sky shining with stars, modern furniture, bookshelves, thick rugs, a kitchen worth lingering in—and then we were past it, heading down a long wood-floored hallway.

At the front of his home, Daniel had unlocked the door, smiled at me, then picked me up, kicked the door shut behind us, and carried me to his bed.

Now, I lie on his king-size bed, the mattress plush, the white down comforter sinking beneath me. My hair spreads over the pillow, a cloudy mess, and my red dress rides up my thighs. Daniel leans over me, brushing a heated kiss across my jaw.

My hand trembles as I reach up and trace my fingers along the stubble at his jaw. "I missed you so much."

His eyes heat and he cups his hand over mine.

"We almost didn't have this," he says, his voice raw with emotion. "I never forgot I loved you. I just forgot everything else. I'm sorry I didn't believe you. I'm sorry I left. Forgive me."

I shake my head. "There's nothing to forgive. I'm the one who—"

"No," he says, brushing his hand over my cheek. "You saved me." And then he presses his lips to my mouth, a feather-light kiss, "You saved me."

He feathers his lips across mine and presses the heat of his body over me. I taste him, sunshine and fresh air, desire and love.

"You saved me too," I tell him, threading my hands over his shoulders, pulling him close. And then, because I'm still scared this is all going to disappear come morning, I ask, "You remember everything?"

He smiles at me then, cups my face, and teases my mouth.

"Everything," he says, his hands moving over me, touching all the places he dreamed of—the curve of my neck, my eyelashes, my cheeks, my hair, down my arms to the pulse beating at my wrist and the softness of my palms. "I came back to you when I was gone. You're my light. My fate."

He rocks against me and the warmth that's been blossoming inside me grows even more.

"I don't know if I believe in fate," I say.

"After all this?"

"I think," I say, "I just believe in love."

A wide smile grows on his face then and I brush my fingers through his hair and pull his mouth down to mine.

"I love you," he says, trailing his hands over me, pressing kisses into my skin with the heat of his hands.

"I love you," he says again, working his lips over me, tasting me with the heat of his mouth.

I pull my dress over my head and drop it to the wood floor of his bedroom. He lets out a harsh breath, taking in the curve of my hips and the fullness of my breasts.

The light on the nightstand spills over me, a golden hue, and Daniel stares enraptured as I unstrap my bra and then pull my thong down my legs. I'm naked beneath him.

If I didn't know him, if I didn't love him, the intent look on his face and the yearning depth in his eyes might frighten me—but I know exactly what it means—it means forever.

You're my light and even in the dark I'll recognize you.

You're my forever and even when I'm gone, I'll love you.

I'll love you, forever.

"I love you," I say, and at that, his intent expression fades, replaced by the smile I love.

He pulls off his shirt, drops it next to my dress. He's leaning over me then, shirtless, but in no danger of leaving.

"Remember when I kissed you at the Met?" I ask.

He nods, tossing the rest of his clothes to the ground. He's naked, warm, and all I want to do is reach out and touch him everywhere, pull him to me.

"You said you thought I was someone you loved," he

says, kissing down my ribs, placing his mouth over my hip.

"You are someone I love."

"I was very jealous of myself," he says, spreading his hands over my thighs, the callouses on his palms sending electric pulses through me.

"It's only ever been you," I tell him. "Even if you never remembered, if you never wanted me, it's only ever been you."

I rock my hips toward him, and he looks up at me, his eyes blazing, and sets his mouth on me, kissing me.

"Tell me more," he says, strumming his mouth over me, making me dig my heels into the bed, and grab his shoulders at the mounting pressure building beneath his mouth and his hands.

"I want to laugh with you again," I gasp, and he kisses me in approval. "I want to see the beauty of the world with you," he strokes his hand over me, sending his fingers questing, and I cry out.

"Tell me more," he says.

I lift my hips, and he presses his mouth to me.

"I want to go to Riverside, Iowa with you and lie in the grass," I say.

His fingers roll over me, sending sparks through me, and when he hums against me, I see stars.

"More," he says.

Yes, more.

He lifts his mouth from me then and smiles up at me, his eyes as blue as the sea, and I say, "I want a life with you. I want to be your refuge, and your confidant, and your friend, I want to be your family, and your love—"

Daniel rises up then, takes my mouth with his, as if he wants to seal my words into both our hearts.

"You are," he says. "Let me be yours."

"Always," I say, then I take his hands and thread his fingers with mine.

He rests over me, presses his chest to mine. I can feel the beating of his heart. I can feel how much he wants me.

I take in the feel of him. He presses his mouth over mine. Then I wrap my legs around him, pull him close, and he settles over me.

He rests there for a moment, his breath short, his heart pounding against mine. I rock my hips up.

"I love you," I whisper.

He smiles, gripping my hands tight, and then he rocks forward, slowly thrusting into me. I clench around him, hold on tight as he fills me.

He watches me with all the love in the world.

And when he's buried in me, his mouth over mine, his hands clasping me, he says, "I love you. Even when this life is done, I'll always love you."

Then he pulls out, and I rock toward him, trying to keep him with me, and so he thrusts back in. And we start a dance, a hand-holding, love-making dance that we began the minute we met.

It starts slow and then when it can't be slow anymore, Daniel kisses me, whispers his love to me, strokes me, and strums me, so that I'm spiraling up, clenching around him, crying out, and when I tighten around him, and the whole world lights up, Daniel grips my hands and thrusts into me, carrying me higher and higher until we're both reaching up and touching the stars.

And when I fall down, back to earth, I land in his arms. Daniel rolls onto his back, pulls me over him, strokes my hips and kisses my lips. Outside, the stars shine bright.

I lay my head against his chest and press my hand to his heart.

"Thank you," I tell him, curling into his warmth. "Until you, I didn't know what love could be like, I only imagined it. But you are more than anything I ever imagined, you're more—"

I cut off, unable to continue because my heart's too full.

Daniel pulls me closer, lays a kiss to my mouth. "I know," he says. "I know because I feel the same way."

Then there aren't any more words, there's only lips, and hands, and hips, and beating hearts and love.

We love in the bed, in the comforters piled on the floor, against the floor-to-ceiling window so all the stars can see how much Daniel wants me, and then on the kitchen counters after Daniel makes me a midnight snack, and finally, back in bed where Daniel whispers, "Marry me. Marry me and I'll give you the stars."

And when I say yes, he loves me again.

58

DAWN LIGHT STREAKS ACROSS THE RUMPLED WHITE SHEETS gathered around us. I lie engulfed in the warmth of Daniel's arms, my cheek pressed against the steady thudding of his heart.

His fingers drift over my naked hips, a gentle, steady kiss that makes me want to stay curled up in his arms for the rest of forever.

On the wooden nightstand next to us, he's brought two ceramic mugs of steaming, creamy, sugary coffee that fills the room with a lovely dark, roasted coffee scent. I'd appreciate the smell more if it didn't mean that my flight leaves in a few hours.

"Stay," Daniel says, brushing a kiss across my forehead. "Don't leave today. Stay and when you fly back to New York, I'll come with you."

He sits up in bed, resting against the wooden headboard, and pulls me up against his chest, wrapping his arms around me.

Last night there was kissing, there was talking, there

was making love, but there are still some things that I have to say.

Daniel's watching me, a hopeful expression on his face. It's Saturday morning. If I stay we have the weekend, and if I stay longer...

I nod. "I'll have to let my family know, and work—"

I cut off with a laugh as he grins down at me, flips me over onto my back, and starts nibbling at my neck, sending his hands over me.

"Stop," I laugh, pushing at him.

He rolls over and lands on his back, puts his hands behind his head and grins up at the ceiling, satisfaction radiating off of him.

"You'll stay," he says happily.

Outside the bedroom window, the leafy green expanse of the mountainous forest shines emerald green and is filled with the melodious trilling of song thrushes hopping between the branches of the spruce trees.

The window takes up almost the entire wall, with a view of the sloping mountain and Geneva below. It fills the bedroom with soft morning light and a warm glow that lights across my naked skin. I blush to think I was pressed against that window last night, Daniel thrusting inside of me, with the city below us.

"I'll stay," I agree, "and when we're married"—he flashes a grin at me at those words—"then we'll stay here and we'll stay in New York, we'll stay wherever, as long as we're together."

He sits up then, takes the mugs of coffee from the nightstand and hands me one.

"Thank you," I wrap my hands around the warm mug, breathe in the nut-scented steam, and take a sip. It's hot and creamy and sugary and delicious.

"You know how I like it," I say, smiling at the pound of sugar he clearly added to the cup.

He nods, smiling over the rim of his mug, "Of course."

Which reminds me...I set my cup down on the nightstand and smooth the sheets over my legs, the soft, silky cotton crinkling under my fingers.

"Daniel?" I look down at the white sheet, feel the cool air of the bedroom on my bare skin.

He reaches out and places his hand over mine, rubs his thumb gently over the back of my hand, and when he does, I look up at him.

"What is it?"

"I'm sorry," I say again, "I started to tell you last night, but I wanted to say it again. I'm sorry that I had Ned look into your schedule. I didn't know about Florence and I didn't think about how it would look or how it would feel. And by the time I realized, I was desperate to save you and it was too late, I'd already—"

Daniel grips my hand and shakes his head. "Jillian. If I'd been in your shoes, there isn't anything I wouldn't have done. It's entirely possible that I would've grabbed you, hauled you to my apartment, tied you to my bed and made love to you until you admitted you loved me, and then I would've kept you there forever, tied to my bed, until I knew you were safe."

"You wouldn't have," I say, and when I do, he sets down his mug of coffee and pulls me close.

"How do you know?" he asks, pressing a kiss to my neck.

"Because you're a decent guy, it's not in your personality—"

He laughs, "Fine. Let's just say, I understand. I understand and I would've done the same."

"Ned thinks you're a dimension hopper," I tell him, looking at him from under my lashes, waiting to see his response.

He grins. "I bet he does. I can see why he wanted to track me. What about Buck?"

"He just wants to punch you," I say, shrugging.

Daniel laughs.

"Is that how your sister will feel?" I ask, and Daniel shakes his head.

"No, she'll love you. She's the most loyal person on the planet. If you're mine, then she'll claim you too."

I smile. "She's like Fran then. You know, she'll think she set us up," I say, thinking about how happy Fran will be to know that her feeling that something wonderful was coming was right after all.

"She can think that," Daniel says, giving me a smile.

Then I ask. "What about Bernardo? He said he lost you as a friend."

Daniel looks over the morning-bright bedroom, staring at the nightstand, the wooden dresser, and the vibrant modern abstract painting hanging on the wall, mirroring the colors of outside.

He's quiet for a time, absently running his hand over mine.

"I was so confused," he finally says, looking down at me. "In the hospital I was a mess. I loved you with an intensity that was frightening, yet I didn't know why. It was more than anything I'd ever felt before. I wanted to forgive you anything, I wanted to believe anything, I wanted...I just wanted you. You saved my life but I thought you were a liar and a fake and I didn't understand why I still desperately wanted you with every breath I took, even knowing that you planned all our accidental meetings."

"I was using your strategy," I say, "popping in everywhere, all the time. I thought if I showed up enough you'd know you loved me, and you'd believe me if I told you that we'd met before, and you'd see that I was trying to save you."

"Except I didn't believe you and I didn't remember."

I nod then thread my fingers with his.

He tilts his head and a ribbon of sunlight falls over him. "I called Bernardo, ready to hear terrible things about you so that I could stop wanting you so desperately. Bernardo admitted you were writing an article on what a sex symbol wants—"

He cuts off when my cheeks burn.

Then he shakes his head, his eyes bright with humor. "I can just imagine your pitch for that piece—" he starts, laughing.

"I'm not good at improvising!" I say. "Ned thought you were a dimension hopper and agreed to find your schedule, and then Buck found out and he was going on about punching you because you sent a watch up to the moon—"

Daniel laughs. "To the International Space Station, not the moon."

"—and Crissy the intern said you were a sex symbol, and then Bernardo wanted to know why I was researching you, and I had to come up with something."

"You did good," he says, pressing a kiss to the edge of my mouth. "And Bernardo and I had words because he defended you. He said you had integrity and courage and if you told me something unbelievable"—I lift an eyebrow and he adds—"I didn't tell him what. But he said if you told me something unbelievable then I should believe it regardless, because you had more integrity in one second of the day than most people have in their whole lives. Then I told him he was an idiot and he said I was a damned fool." He shrugs. "Which I was."

"You weren't," I say.

"I was. But I'm not anymore."

"If you hadn't remembered?" I ask, running my hands over the soft sheets, "if you never believed me—"

"Then after another miserable month where I felt hollow and was aching for you, I would've flown back to New York and found you. Then you would've brought me back to your apartment, and I would've seen your kinky sex mirrors and..." He smiles, his eyes filling with mirth. "It would've been all over for me."

"I covered them up with paper," I admit, and the stunned, horrified look he gives me is enough to make me laugh. "I'll take it down. For one time. *One* time."

He grins at me. "One time," he agrees.

Then he says, his eyes grave, "When I couldn't touch you...when I couldn't keep you safe...or...I wanted you so much. I wanted to give you the world, but I didn't have anything to give."

"I've only ever wanted your love."

He stares into my eyes, his expression serious. "You have it. But I hope it's okay, if now I give you the rest of my life, and someday, perhaps I'll help you give me a little girl with your green eyes, and a little boy with your smile, and—"

He pauses, searches my expression.

Slowly, I lean forward, press him down to the rumpled bed and lay over him, press my mouth to his.

His arms come around me and he holds me close.

"And?" I ask.

"And I'll love you when we're young, and I'll love you when we're old, and I'll love you when we're gone." His hands smooth over me, pulling me close.

"And today?" I ask, the rising sun spilling over the purple mountains, climbing higher in the bright blue sky.

"And I'll love you today," he says.

And he does.

EPILOGUE

ONE YEAR LATER...

THE WARM JUNE BREEZE DRIFTS ACROSS THE LUSH GRASS, carrying with it the inviting scent of blossoming honeysuckle.

The limbs of a maple tree stretch overhead, shading the soft grass I'm lying in. The sun flashes and winks through the unfurled leaves, and the happy sounds of a robin chirruping blends with the quiet of the slow weekend traffic on West First Street drifting by.

A fuzzy honeybee buzzes past, weaving toward the purple flowers of the hostas planted at the base of the stone marker.

I tilt my head back, let the lacy flashes of sun lick over me, and then smile over at Daniel as he slowly drags a blade of grass over my bare leg, up my thigh, to the edge of my shorts. His eyes crinkle as he smiles at me, lazily lounging in the grass, enjoying the summer breeze.

"Is it everything you dreamed?" he asks, dropping the blade of grass and moving closer, wrapping his arm around me.

I cuddle into the shelter of his arms and take in the stone plaque. I remember how I dreamed of coming here someday, and eventually, how I dreamed of coming here with him.

"Future Birthplace of Captain James T. Kirk," he says, staring at the sandstone stacked almost as high as an adult, and then the solid granite with the words etched for all to read.

Then Daniel turns to look at me, his eyes catch mine, and then he smiles and spreads his palm over the round bump of my belly, where our son is growing, waiting to meet us.

My heart fills with joy, with love, with gratitude, and all this love feels so big that I think it's enough to fill the universe.

"It's more," I say, placing my hand in Daniel's. "It's more than I ever dreamed."

His gaze softens, and I know he understands, because he pulls me against him, wraps his arms around me, and holds my hands as we watch the breeze blow in the leaves, listen to the robins sing, and let the sunshine stream over us.

Soon our baby will be born. And when he is, we'll tell him all about time, and love, and life, but until then, we'll just dream of him, knowing that our dreams will never be as wonderful as the love that lies ahead.

"My love," Daniel says, brushing a kiss over my lips.

Then he stands, helps me up, and holds my hand as we walk out of an old dream and into a present that is more beautiful than the stars, more wonderful than dreams, more than either of us ever imagined.

THE SECOND EPILOGUE

MAY
New York, NY
(aka The Alternate Timeline)
(aka The First Meeting)

DANIEL

THERE'S A WOMAN CROUCHED ON THE GLISTENING WET
pavement near a storm drain. Rain trickles over the
concrete, little rivulets streaming by and disappearing
into the gutter. The water flows around her, as quickly
and uncaringly as the morning commuters outside
Grand Central hurrying past.

No one notices her scouring the pavement, searching
for...something.

Maybe they don't notice because the traffic lurches
past in a distracting blur. Maybe they don't notice because

the noises rise high from the rain and the wind gusting through the buildings, or maybe it's that they *do* notice but no one helps strangers in a city full of strangers.

But looking at her—her long inky curls wet in the misty rain, her red raincoat belted tight, her head down scouring the concrete—it doesn't feel as if she's a stranger.

I haven't even seen her face, but it feels like we've met before.

I step closer to the curb, outside the stream of people passing, and crouch down.

"Do you need help?" I ask.

She shakes her head no, not bothering to look up at me, instead she peers into the storm drain.

"The clasp on my Starfleet necklace broke. It fell and I can *see* it, I just can't *reach* it."

I move closer, decide that I can sacrifice my dry clothes in the name of a good deed, and kneel in the cold, dirty puddle at the edge of the drain. I peer past the concrete lip, down the wide storm drain.

There. Hanging precariously from a metal bar, a gold necklace with a few diamonds on a pendant winks in the dull light.

"I see it," I say, leaning closer, catching the spring scent of her.

It reminds me of home. In the spring, after the snow thaws and runs in streams down the mountains, the grass grows wild and violets bloom in the meadow, opening to the spring rain.

When I was young, I used to lie in the meadow and breathe it all in. I haven't done that in more than twenty years, but suddenly, I ache to again.

I give her a stunned look, wondering how she can elicit that kind of response in me without even trying.

"Can you reach it?" she asks, and when she does, she finally looks up and turns her face to mine.

And if I weren't already on the ground, I'd fall to my knees.

She's...

She's...

I can't say she's the most beautiful woman I've ever seen. That's like saying Mont Blanc is just a hill, or Lake Geneva is merely blue, or New York is a small town.

Her eyes are the color of a spring meadow bowing under the sun. They widen when she sees me and her hand flies to her chest. But she doesn't look away and neither do I. Instead we kneel on the ground, in the misting rain, with the blur and noise of New York rushing past, and stay silent for a second, two, ten. Finally, she lowers her hand from her chest and smiles.

That smile? It's like she just reached into my chest and took my heart in her hands.

"I can reach it," I say.

Then I balance myself over the wet pavement, reach into the drain, and stretch, until my hands graze over the cold metal chain.

I grasp it, then pull it free.

When I drop the necklace into her outstretched hands, her cheeks flush red.

"Thank you."

"I'm Daniel," I say, helping her stand. Her hand is warm and I don't want to let it go.

"Jillian," she says, giving me a surprised look.

"Why do you look so surprised?" I ask, hoping

desperately that she's never heard of me, doesn't recognize me, and that she can get to know me as me.

"I'm not..." She trails off, a wrinkle forms between her brow. "You're easy to talk to," she says, watching me with wonder, as if I'm some sort of rare breed. "Not many people are easy to talk to. In fact, I've never met anyone who...is so easy to talk to. Who I can talk to."

She keeps the expression on her face, like she's never met anyone like me before. Someone she can talk to.

Then she looks west, past the rain-slicked stone of Grand Central, and I can tell she's considering saying goodbye. It's Friday morning, after all, and she's clearly headed to the office.

Just like me.

On Monday Fiona and I fly back to Geneva and today's schedule is full. Today is busy, tonight I'm supposed to go to the gala.

But the thought of losing Jillian to the city, letting her walk away to become another faceless stranger in New York, has me clenching my hand, fighting the urge to reach out and take hers.

She hesitates, looking west and then back to me.

I can feel it, this is one of those moments you are supposed to grasp with both hands and say yes to.

So instead of saying goodbye, I say, "Spend the day with me."

She blinks. Gives me a stunned look.

I realize that it came out abrupt. That I should've phrased it better. But I don't want to play games.

"I..." She hesitates, "I have to go to work."

I nod. Of course she does. "Okay. I only thought, it feels like I've met you before. I'm not in New York often, I'm leaving Monday and—"

"Do you like *Star Trek*?" she asks suddenly.

Star Trek? "Is that the one with the Jedi?"

She laughs, her eyes lighting up, and she shakes her head. "No. Not even close."

I grin at her. Her laugh is the best music I've ever heard. I think I'd like to make her laugh again. Or smile. Her smile is like the warm sun rising over the Alps in winter.

"We could get a cup of coffee," I say, nodding at a coffee shop nearby, its soft lights glowing welcomingly through the mist. "As my friend, you could tell me all about *Star Trek*."

She studies me for a moment, the rain pattering against the pavement, the traffic and morning commuters streaming past, and then her eyes lighten and she smiles at me, her decision made.

"I'd like that."

At her words, the tightness around my heart unknots.

We have a day together.

Twelve hours later, I swear I'm in love.

Jillian recounted all the best *Star Trek* history and plied me with coffee and éclairs while we sat on a couch in a coffee shop and she scrolled through episode highlights on her phone.

Then she held my hand and tugged me through the Met on a whirlwind tour. I pointed out my favorite art and grinned when I made her laugh. Then we sat huddled together under plastic raincoats on the top of a double decker tour bus, while she described everywhere we should go together next time I was in New York.

She pointed out the Chrysler Building, and the Empire State Building and the Statue of Liberty, but I've seen them all plenty of times before—what I haven't seen is her next smile. So instead of looking at the sights, I watched her.

For dinner, we went back to my apartment and ordered in. And now, it's late, and instead of asking her to stay the night, I'm sending her home. I'll see her tomorrow, and the next day, and Monday I'll ask her if we can keep on seeing each other.

It's dark, the night is black and starless, and the rain whips through the street. We stand under my building's awning and the yellow lights shine over us.

Her face is turned up to mine, she takes my hands, and I want to kiss her. I want to kiss her so badly it hurts.

"Do you think it's strange that I feel like I've known you forever?" she asks.

I shake my head, grip her hands. "No. I think it'd be strange if you didn't feel that way."

"Why?"

"Because I feel the same as you."

She smiles then, unclasps her hands from mine. When she does, I decide, I'm going to spend the rest of my life with her.

"Tomorrow," she says then. "I'll see you tomorrow. I'll show you my apartment. Let you see my Enterprise."

I grin at her, then she's walking toward the curb, out into the dark night. Thunder booms, and lightning cracks through the sky. I hold out my arm, flagging a taxi through the mist.

Then...Jillian falls, the taxi skids, I grab her, yank her out of its path.

She hits her head on the concrete. She's hurt. She's bleeding.

My heart pounds. I drop to my knees. There's too

much blood. There's so much blood. I don't have anything to stop it with.

"Daniel," she says, lying beneath me on the pavement.

I tug off my shirt, roll it up to stop the bleeding.

"It's okay," I tell her, "You're okay. I'm here."

I lean over her, look into her green eyes, and then—

Black.

Dark.

Pain.

Nothing.

Then…I can't remember…I can't remember…I can't remember…

Light.

There's Jillian.

I know Jillian.

I remember Jillian.

It's okay. I'm okay.

Jillian's here.

She holds a model in her hands and she's happy.

Everything's okay.

Everything will be okay.

I'm with Jillian.

So I smile at her and say, "Now that is one big spaceship."

ACKNOWLEDGMENTS

I would like to thank my husband for the inspiration behind this book. As a little kid, he and his family went to Star Trek conventions, dressed in matching Starfleet uniforms. His favorite character was Wesley Crusher, and as a kid he stood in a long line for his chance at an autograph.

When my husband and I first met, his mom made me complete a quiz to identify which Star Trek character I was to determine whether or not I was compatible with her son. Let's just say, I passed the test.

I was more like Daniel though, not quite sure what all the fuss was about. Luckily, my husband-to-be stuck with me.

So, this book is for my favorite trekker. Thank you for all the adventures we've had.

Thank you as well, to all the wonderful, passionate, and kind bookstagrammers, bloggers, and reviewers. You are an incredible community just as amazing as any interplanetary organization.

Thank you for reading, for trusting me when I say, "wow do I have a story for you!" And for believing in love, and most of all, happily ever afters.

JOIN SARAH READY'S NEWSLETTER

Want more Ghosted? Get an exclusive bonus epilogue!

When you join the Sarah Ready Newsletter you get access to sneak peaks, insider updates, exclusive bonus scenes and more.

Join today for an exclusive epilogue:

www.sarahready.com/newsletter

ABOUT THE AUTHOR

Award-winning author Sarah Ready writes women's fiction, contemporary romance and romantic comedy. Her books have been described as "euphoric", "heartwarming" and "laugh out loud".

Sarah writes stand-alone romances, including *Josh and Gemma Make a Baby*, *Josh and Gemma the Second Time Around*, *French Holiday*, *The Space Between*, and romcoms in the Soul Mates in Romeo series, all of which can be found at her website: www.sarahready.com.

She lives in a house by the beach on a small Caribbean island with her family and her water-loving pup.

You can learn more and find upcoming titles at: www.sarahready.com.

Stay up to date, get exclusive epilogues and bonus content. Join Sarah's newsletter at www.sarahready.com/newsletter.

ALSO BY SARAH READY

Stand Alone Romances:

The Fall in Love Checklist

Hero Ever After

Once Upon an Island

French Holiday

The Space Between

Josh and Gemma:

Josh and Gemma Make a Baby

Josh and Gemma the Second Time Around

Soul Mates in Romeo Romance Series:

Chasing Romeo

Love Not at First Sight

Romance by the Book

Love, Artifacts, and You

Married by Sunday

My Better Life

Scrooging Christmas

Stand Alone Novella:

Love Letters

Find these books and more by Sarah Ready at:

www.sarahready.com/romance-books